Sleeping Above Chaos

Ann Hite's novel, *Sleeping Above Chaos*, leads her readers and follows her characters from Black Mountain and Swannanoa Gap into deep and perilous consequences from wasting love and cherishing hate. The chaos in the title is human. The sleeping are not as far above it as they think; they are about to wake.

Hite's characters do not choose hate instead of love. Sometimes they are born into it. Sometimes they grow into it. Sometimes they are driven to it, and sometimes they walk. There's no map. It is easy to get lost along the way, courting comfort or oblivion or revenge. "Love is for fools," one character testifies, in favor of friendship. But the tangled loyalties, bloodlines, secrets, and silences in *Sleeping Above Chaos* are deeper than friendship, more vital than blood. Hate is part of "the beautiful wreck" Hite's fictional people create, are created by, and witness. Hite's fiction mirrors and reflects today's dreams and realities and what we make of our prejudices and heritage. We dare not look away.

—Mary Hood, author of
A Clear View of the Southern Sky,
How Far She Went,
and other fiction

BLACK MOUNTAIN NOVELS BY ANN HITE

Arlene,
Hope you enjoy this story!

SLEEPING
ABOVE CHAOS

A Black Mountain Novel

Ann Hite

Ann Hite

MERCER UNIVERSITY PRESS | MACON, GEORGIA

2016

MUP P535

© 2016 by Mercer University Press
Published by Mercer University Press
1501 Mercer University Drive
Macon, Georgia 31207
All rights reserved

9 8 7 6 5 4 3 2 1

Books published by Mercer University Press are printed on acid-free
paper that meets the requirements of the American National Standard
for Information Sciences—Permanence of Paper for Printed Library
Materials.

ISBN   978-0-88146-584-6
Cataloging-in-Publication Data is available from the Library of
Congress

Ella Ruth Hite, I miss you something terrible. You told the stories about Buster and you. I listened.
I didn't do you justice but I had fun writing this novel. I know you would like that.

IN LOVING MEMORY
1925- 2011

Swannanoa Gap

Rock
Quarry

ALLEN

BLACK

ELLA CREEK

DRAGONFLY RIVER

N E
W S

SJ

MOUNTAIN

Jerry C. Hite.

Acknowledgments

Thank you to the Hite Family Members for putting up with my writing habit. You'll recognize some of the stories your mama shared. This isn't an account of her life. It is a story peppered with her truths. She was an amazing woman who walked through a lot of pain and challenging times, along with tons of happy years. It is a privilege to be part of this family. If my daddy were alive, I'd thank him for all his stories about World War II and for taking me to visit the places where he fought. I don't think he knew he was raising a writer at the time, but maybe he did. Thanks to my loving husband, Jack, for all his hard work on the maps for my books and for being my best fan. Thank you to my Ella—the namesake of her grandmother, Ella Ruth—for putting up with a mom who isn't always present and accounted for because she is creating another time and place. Many thanks to Marc Jolley for believing in my work and publishing my books. Love to Miss Marsha, who always makes me happy I'm with Mercer. To Mercer's outstanding marketing director, Mary Beth, who gives the authors 110%, and she is a lot of fun at events. To Jenny, who keeps everyone at Mercer straight and loves to talk grandchildren with me. Thanks to my buddy, Myra Crawford, who is my side-kick in research travel and one of my best friends. We always have fun. But most of all thank you to all my faithful readers, who never fail to raise my spirits and help me believe I can write another book.

Sleeping Above Chaos

Part One

Gabriel's Horn

1939–1940

Chapter 1

Buster Wright

The sound coming from the belly of Christ Deliverance Church was so loud, Buster was sure the congregation wouldn't hear nothing. The pure determination of those people floated on the hot stale air. The preacher stood in the pulpit shaking his Bible, telling the crowd where sin would take them if they continued on their present path. Part of Buster had to respect those folks. It was half past three and none of them had eaten a bite since breakfast. That was called living off the word of God.

The small window in the attic of the church was the best way to get to the rafters without anyone noticing. He opened the flour sack and removed his great-grandpa's Civil War bugle, tucking it into his overalls. Larry—Buster's best friend since he could remember—pointed to the back of the church. Buster tossed the flour sack behind a bush. The two boys had caused plenty of trouble during their friendship: hiding a snake in old Mrs. Barker's desk, putting sugar in Mr. Plank's gas tank, howling like a ghost at Mrs. Tidwell as she walked home at dusk, and driving Daddy's truck across the railroad trestle before the oncoming train reached them. But this time was the worst. They were messing with bona fide Bible-thumping Christians.

Buster pulled himself into the old oak tree at the far end of the church. He and Larry were both acting like a couple of ten-year-olds, pulling that kind of crap when they were half-grown men. Mama was always telling him to act more like Lee, his older brother, who was seventeen going on forty. And that very comment probably caused Buster to make the bad decisions he made. Shoot. He was fifteen and half; why act like he was Daddy?

Larry followed him close on the limb that hung across the roof like a tightrope. Buster edged one foot in front of the other, arms spread like an eagle's wings. He could just make out the top of his house, sun glinting off the tin. They tried not to make too much noise when they dropped to the roof, but in all reality they probably sounded like a couple of horses. Buster hurried across, Larry breathing down his neck. He took one more look in the direction he came from, as if he might run. Heat waves rippled into the air. He jumped onto the porch roof just below and scooted through the open window, where he settled in the V of two rafters directly over the congregation while Larry perched near the window.

The preacher, sweat pouring down his face, eyes bulging like a bullfrog, arms like beanpoles waving above his head, paced back and forth, shouting his message of repentance. Buster touched the brass bugle inside his overall bib. Mama would kill him for taking the thing. She had given it special to Lee. Mama would see what Buster did as stealing and would tell Daddy, that could be counted on. Sweat ran down Buster's face, too, dripping off his nose, running into his eyes. The Bible-toting souls wound themselves into the preacher's words like a spinning top. It was amazing just to watch them.

The preacher went on for another thirty minutes before he drew a deep breath and began his altar call, placing himself close to the tall open window for a little air. "Now, good Christians, God has told me that there are souls out there who need to be saved, to be washed in the blood of the Lamb." He bowed his head while folks stirred in their places like restless cattle. "Oh Lord, I know you are speaking to the souls of these sinners. They are right here with us. I won't leave this place until they come before you heart in hand."

A man, straw hat held to his chest, and a woman holding onto the hand of a small boy, pushed out of a pew into the aisle. Larry moved beside Buster as if he might fling himself on the mercy of the altar.

The preacher raised his Bible in the air. Buster pulled out his bugle.

"Lord, don't let these souls go to hell. I've told them your plan for salvation. I've warned them of your coming in a twinkle of an eye."

More people pushed out from their pews. Buster saw the Allen girl from his class. She was left behind in her spot while folks moved around her.

"God, I'm waiting with no fear in my heart. I'm ready for your

4

return."

Neighbors he knew—folks from his very own church, where Larry's daddy preached—began to pray with a rhythm like notes in a bad piece of music. Here it came, the best part. Buster placed the bugle to his lips.

"Lord, send your angel Gabriel with his horn to take us home."

The bugle blasted, blaring sour at first but gaining strength. Buster gave two more blows for good measure. The earth stood still for a minute, and the God-fearing preacher pitched himself right out the open window like a man in a burning building. Later folks would claim he landed right on the back of Widow Harper's old bull. Buster drank in the chaos, people running in all directions, crying, praying, and raising their faces to meet the Lord.

The Allen girl looked him directly in the eyes. That's why he didn't leave when he had the chance to get out before he was seen by anyone else. Then, another good soul—maybe a practical soul pulled to the service by a wife bent on saving him from hell—looked right at Buster. He raised a finger to Heaven.

"Up there. You fools, up there."

No one paid the man a bit of attention. Buster struggled to move his stiff legs. The man punched another man, pointing at Buster and Larry. Larry pulled Buster's arm in an attempt to get him to move faster, and the bugle slid from Buster's sweaty fingers, twirling, slow—a glittering decoration—clanging to the church floor, bouncing once before resting at the feet of their accuser. "It's some fool boys. See them."

Larry pushed through the window before Buster and was halfway across the beam.

God's breath turned Buster's neck hot. Both boys crossed the limb with a carelessness that would have made their mothers faint. Buster hit the ground running, headed for home. Daddy would protect him. Yes, Daddy would save the pleasure of killing Buster for himself, but that was okay. He'd admit how stupid he was. He'd even explain the whole reason behind the stunt. Daddy would listen.

Buster wasn't sure who decided to split up, or if both boys just did what came natural to sneaks and cowards. But he was alone, cutting through the thickest part of the woods, branches pulling at his face, thorns tearing at his bare skin, running, running into a deafening noise, the sound of his own breathing. He jumped off an embankment right smack in the middle of a road. A car flew by, almost running into a ditch. Then it gunned backwards.

Damn! Caught!

"Buster." Donald, Daddy's deputy, struggled for breath. "Get in."

Buster jumped in, thinking Donald had been sent to save him from the approaching mob.

Donald pressed the gas pedal to the floor, spraying gravel and turned the patrol car onto the quarry road. "Some fool boy tried to climb the quarry wall again. He's got himself stuck. Your daddy figured it was you 'cause of last time."

Buster had been known to play the game, but he never got stuck. Surely Daddy gave him that much credit.

"He'll be glad to know where you are."

A cold thought slid up Buster's neck as they pulled up to the quarry, and he jumped out of the car before it came to a complete stop. Damn, the boy was clinging on the sheer wall of rock. Way too high.

"Son, hold on. I'm on the way."

Stupid Jake Markem hung by his fingers for dear life. How had he gotten so high? A crowd of kids gathered at the foot of the wall on the edge of the lake. All the boys were friends of Buster's. He ran past them, determined to talk some sense into Daddy before he made a big mistake. He was too old for a boy's foolish game. To climb that wall, a person had to be young, strong. Shoot, Buster had spent too much time studying that wall, testing each foothold for strength, feeling for grooves to hook his fingers on, finding a point to stare at, taking a few inches at a time until he found a stopping place, that place where his heart beat in his ears like a brass drum, his foot knocking pebbles to the ground, his fingers searching for one more hold, looking down for the first time to find his challenger far below, long ago stopped.

Daddy teetered on what seemed to be thin air high above the lake. His fingers gripped a rock above his head like he would a rung on a ladder. One small, careful step at a time.

Jake Markem whimpered. Daddy inched within reach.

"I'm going to give you my hand." Daddy took a step sideways. Pebbles clattered, bouncing off the wall.

Buster saw his brother Lee standing next to the lake closer to Daddy's spot on the wall. The stupid asshole always came out smelling like a rose. He was Daddy's favorite. Buster just wished Daddy could know who Lee was, that he was sweet on a colored girl, slipping around all over town to see her. Everybody else knew. If the church business came up, Buster might just have to tell what he knew. At least he wouldn't be the only person in trouble.

More pebbles fell from the wall into the lake. "We're going to have to be real careful. Okay, buddy?" Daddy yelled but in a kind voice, patient and caring. He touched Jake's hand. In turn Jake latched on like a leech. "Whoa, now. One step at a time. You go first. Find a foothold."

Jake felt with his foot until he found a comfortable place, which moved him about three inches down.

At that rate Daddy would never get off the wall. "Okay, I'm going to take a step down." Daddy's foot knocked another shower of rocks into the lake. "See, now it's your turn, son."

Buster let a breath out of his lungs he didn't know he had been holding. He looked over at Lee, who ran his fingers through his hair.

"Wait." The word escaped Buster in a whisper. He looked back at Daddy. Jake seemed to be standing in midair. "Just let him go, Daddy." He wasn't sure if he yelled this out loud or not.

Daddy didn't have it in him to loosen his grip. He wasn't made of that kind of stuff. His fingers pulled away from the wall, and both fell head over heels.

Lee dove into the water before the splash and towed the thrashing body to the side. Buster grasped Lee's free hand. It wasn't Daddy. Lee had saved Jake.

"Where's Daddy?" Buster yelled at Lee, who sprawled out on the dirt, leaving Jake to climb out on his own. "Where's Daddy?" Buster looked at the water, waiting for Daddy to surface.

"He landed over there." A man said as he rushed by.

Buster left Lee and tore into the group of men now huddled together. Donald held out his hands, trying to stop Buster. This didn't do a bit of good because Buster punched him in the gut and kept going. A body, twisted in an odd position, blood puddling around the head, was only inches from the lake. Daddy. Buster knelt down and took his hand, the hand that whipped him when he needed it, ruffled his hair to say good job. A lifeless hand. A shadow passed over Buster. Lee was towering over him.

"He's going to be okay. Ain't he, Lee?"

Lee gave Buster a funny look and walked away. Buster held on to his lifeline until the men forced him to move.

⊂⊃

Daddy was buried three days later in the churchyard not far from the house he grew up in, the house where Buster lived. Folks lined the road leading out of Swannanoa Gap so they could watch him pass for the last time. They bowed their heads, hats in hand, rain dripping from their hair. It was as if God was crying over the terrible mistake he had made. The rain filled the grave with water. As the men lowered the casket into the gaping hole, Granny screamed into the air with a long, mournful wail. Mama and Buster's little sister, Billie, threw roses on the shiny casket as it bumped the walls of the grave. Lee was gone. Never even came home after he left the rock quarry. His leaving worked as a second death. Granny kept saying he would be back when his grieving ended, but Buster knew better. His brother was gone for good, a shadow passing over a full moon.

8

Chapter 2

Ella Ruth

1940 was the year Ella Ruth Allen turned fifteen and busted at her seams, the year she couldn't hide her figure with baggy blouses, the year she hated everything, especially the darn old mountain she lived on. The year she finally started to understand who she was and what was important, but didn't pay attention to important stuff until it slapped her upside the head.

She lived on a farm near the bottom of Black Mountain with her grandparents who seemed a million years old. A sin was committed on the day she came to live under the same roof as Grandmother Allen, who rode her high horse about Ella Ruth's mama each and every day, refusing to tell anything but Paul Allen's side of the story. To hear Grandmother Allen talk, that poor mama of Ella Ruth's only did one decent thing while living on Black Mountain, and that was to leave Ella Ruth behind when she hightailed it off the mountain in search of better things. Grandmother Allen always assured Ella Ruth that her mama left with some fellow who worked in Asheville. Ella Ruth knew for sure that her mama was gone and had never come back, but she also knew she was out there somewhere, wishing she could snatch her away but too afraid of Paul Allen. Ella Ruth's own daddy.

Everyone was. Folks had always whispered that he was the meanest man around, the only exception being Hobbs Pritchard. But Ella Ruth never knew him except in Grandmother Allen's stories that told of Mama being a selfish wife, one who spent all of Paul Allen's hard-earned money on store-bought clothes, instead of the home-made ones folks wore on the farms.

Ella Ruth couldn't much blame her. If she had known how to get into Swannanoa Gap by herself, she would have bought her own nice dresses too.

Mama was book-learned at some fancy college, and Ella Ruth figured that hurt her worse than anything she could have done. On the mountain, women couldn't be too smart. That worked against them. Look at Maude Tuggle, the granny woman. She was so smart, and no man would have her, not one. Grandmother said uppity was as uppity do, whatever that meant.

In the old barn out behind her grandparents' house, Ella Ruth found a big trunk tucked in a corner full of spider webs. Inside was a bunch of books. It took her entirely too long to snitch one out of there. It was all about painting, not house painting but picture painting. Art. She dearly loved art. So she figured Mama had to be a whole lot like her, and that would explain why Grandmother Allen didn't much care for her only grandchild. Ella Ruth hid under her bed to read the book because Grandmother believed there was only one book to be read: the Bible. That was it.

Grandmother Allen's stories about Mama didn't even touch the white, scalding-hot truth. She never told what life had been like for Ella Ruth before her mama left. But that didn't keep Ella Ruth from trying to picture it. Mama sitting her only child on her lap with colors and paper, teaching her to draw. Of course she was just guessing, because the last time she saw Mama she was two, and at that age memories were just flashes of pictures fading in and out. What she remembered about Paul Allen was a beet-red face and mean, dark eyes. It was plain as a stubborn mule pulling a plow that she had been abandoned, orphaned. And that was not fair. Not that she hated her grandparents. She didn't. Grandpa Allen was quiet, mild-mannered, and never bothered to bicker back with his wife. He just listened like Ella Ruth had learned to do. And Grandmother Allen meant well. At least, Ella Ruth was sure she did.

In June 1940, when the silly so-called preacher came roaming up Black Mountain and talked Grandmother Allen into visiting his makeshift congregation at the deserted church building in Swannanoa Gap, Ella Ruth decided she wanted nothing more than to go to college and become a real painter, one like her idol, Georgia O'Keefe. Her high school teacher had told her about the famous artist and her pictures of flowers. She even brought a magazine with photos to show Ella Ruth, who loved the red poppy best. How could oil paint be mixed to such a brilliant reddish-orange like the maple leaves in the fall? The college she longed to attend was right there in the valley, an art college. But Grandmother Allen only huffed. She couldn't imagine a school that taught grown people how to play.

Mostly folks on Black Mountain didn't even go down to the Gap. They said folks there thought they were better, smarter. But thank goodness Grandmother Allen insisted on going to the Gap for coffee and sugar. That woman loved her coffee every morning. So her going down the mountain, dragging Ella Ruth along to attend church services wasn't a bit surprising. The old building was right next to the sanatorium grounds where people with consumption went to recover. Ella Ruth had heard folks saying more of them died than lived.

On each and every morning the whole month of June, Ella Ruth woke up early with the gray light that spread over the woods and headed out the back door, tiptoey like. That was the time of day a girl could see a spook if she looked hard enough. That summer she planned to meet a haint face to face and get something settled. For a while, things were not going her way. Then one morning she took the main path that snaked near Dragonfly River and came up on the witch house without even thinking of where her feet had led her. Everyone knew that no one but the most desperate of souls went there. The witch could throw a hex that could cripple or kill.

The house was gray from all the paint wearing off, but Ella Ruth thought a coat of yellow would suit it. Folks claimed the witch had died a horrible death, that she was an outsider and wanted to pay them all back for not helping her, for letting her die. Ella Ruth didn't want to believe such nonsense at fifteen, but she'd had problems of her own that made her believe in ghost stories.

That morning a cloud had settled on top of the mountain, and wisps of fog trailed here and there. Nothing was strange about that until Ella Ruth saw a shadowy figure on the porch of the witch house. A thrill worked up her neck as a streak of sun broke through the thick cloud and gave her a good look at the shadow.

"You're the Allen girl." The witch's voice was the sound of music rustling the tops of the trees.

Ella Ruth nodded.

"You're looking for the haint that is bothering you. Why?"

"I don't know."

"Look at me. Do I remind you of anyone?" The witch had gray eyes that seemed to sparkle. "I know you and your story."

"Then you know a lot more than me, ma'am." Ella Ruth found her voice and tried to sound strong.

The witch smiled. "The haint you look for is a whisper in the night. She cries out for you. That's why you're searching. You don't hear but your soul does. She cries for you. It's your mama."

A cold sweat broke out on my forehead.

"That can't be, 'cause my mama is alive. She ran off with a man from Asheville and left me behind." She wanted to turn and run, but the witch was pretty in a soft way.

"Lies, lies, lies." The witch shook her head.

"What do you mean?"

The witch moved to the first step of the porch. "I know your story, Ella. I know all about your father. If you sit down and listen to me, I will tell you a lot. Help you sort through the problems all around you."

"Are you the witch the folks around here talk about?" Ella Ruth studied the woman's face. The smooth clearness. The youth in spite of her age. Nothing about her was scary, but what she had to say might turn Ella Ruth's blood cold.

Her dark red hair fell down her back. "They don't know me, never did."

Again, Ella Ruth wanted to run, wanted to leave so she never had to go one step further in the hunt for her story.

But the woman's voice stopped her. "Do you want to know the truth, Ella?"

"I'm not sure," Ella Ruth managed.

The witch came to stand right in front of her. "Child, do you really believe your mama would leave her baby with someone like Paul Allen? Think about it. If she were alive, even living with another husband, would she leave her child all that time with that family?" She searched Ella Ruth with her gray stare. "Your heart already knows the truth."

Ella Ruth didn't dare take a breath. She didn't want to be there, and she didn't want to leave. "No, I guess she wouldn't have."

"Now there's something to think about." The witch turned and walked back up the steps. "Find her."

"Who? My mother?"

The witch looked suddenly exhausted and sad. "No. Find your aunt. She knows you." And she went into the house.

Confused, Ella Ruth stood outside for a while before she gave up and left.

CR

Grandmother Allen stirred grits on the stove. "Where you been, girl? You scared me plum silly being gone. Your grandpa went out to the river to look for you. What are you doing wandering around at the crack of dawn? That's what I want to know."

A smart girl would have kept her mouth closed, but Ella Ruth was too desperate for the truth. "Do you know the witch house? There was a woman there. She says I've been told a lot of lies."

Grandmother Allen's shoulders became straight as a board. Her knuckles turned white as she gripped her wooden spoon. "You know not to go to that house. You're grown and you still don't listen. It's evil, and any person you saw there is evil or the devil himself."

"But what about the lies. Have I been told lies?" Ella Ruth pushed for the answer she already knew.

Grandmother Allen spun around and slapped the wooden spoon across Ella Ruth's cheek. The grits flung across the room and burned her skin where some of them stuck.

"You ungrateful child. You reap what you sow. Stay away from that house, or I'll give you a reason to think you've been lied to. That woman you speak of ruined Paul's life. We lost him because of her. We have no son. You have no father. Stay away from her, or I'll lock you away in the shed. Don't tempt me."

Ella Ruth had no doubt that Grandmother Allen would lock her away. Several crows cried as they swooped past the kitchen window.

CR

That afternoon Ella Ruth followed the path right back to the witch house, but it seemed empty. Ella Ruth scanned the yard and looked back at the house. The witch suddenly stood behind the old screen door.

"Ready for the truth?" She smiled like she had won some battle. For the longest time, the two stood there looking at each other, not speaking, only staring. The woman's skin was smooth and perfect. What looked like a smudge of paint streaked one of her fingers. "You were greatly loved and wanted by your mama, but you were stolen, lied to, and tucked away like Rapunzel in the tall tower. You know nothing about your family, your past, or your mama. This was calculated by him. Even if he is not here, he is among that family." She looked at Ella Ruth with the saddest expression.

This was no witch after all. It seemed that Ella Ruth had found her haint.

Grandmother Allen hadn't figured out that Ella Ruth had changed, gone silent, held a secret. A few mornings after she spoke with the haint, she woke to Grandmother Allen giving Grandpa the dickens.

"She's plenty old enough, Charley."

"But them are real sick folks, Agnes." Grandpa Allen's voice was quiet but steady.

"Well, it ain't like she's going to be kissing them or eating out of their plates." Grandmother Allen slammed down a pan on the stove.

"No need to sling things. I just don't want her around consumption patients."

"I'm not slinging a thing. The money would help us, and she ain't going to be in a bit of danger. She has to do something with herself all summer. There's not a boy in these parts that wants to marry her. She has to have something. Joyce wouldn't put our granddaughter in a bit of problems."

"I don't know the woman."

"Well, I do. And maybe if you had cared this much after Paul, he would have stayed around."

Grandpa Allen huffed. "Seems to me someone was giving him plenty of caring. So much he thought he could do whatever he wanted. Like there wasn't a bit of law on this mountain."

"Hush up, Charley. I won't have you running our boy in the ground."

"He wasn't a boy the last time I seen him, Agnes." There was a touch of a smile in his tone.

"You know what I mean, Mister. Ella Ruth is going to work. You take her down and meet Joyce at the church this morning. This experience will teach her a thing or two. They're going to pay her two dollars a day."

Ella Ruth's stomach turned stone cold. Part of her wanted nothing more than to leave her prison on the mountain. The other part was scared to death of catching consumption and dying.

"I don't like it," Grandpa Allen said.

"Ain't a whole lot you can do, Charley." And that sealed the deal. Both Ella Ruth and Grandpa Allen knew who was the boss at that house.

ʘ

Joyce Clay was a crotchety woman who grumbled under her breath about sinners all the time. She wore a navy work dress and tied a pink scarf over her steel-gray hair. On her feet were clunky men's work shoes. The old truck they rode in seemed to barely hold together. Ella Ruth watched the sanatorium looming in front of them. Six huge columns and a wide front porch would have suggested a fine hotel to any visitors. Maybe that was the feeling they were looking to give patients who were forced to come stay there. She had heard from many folks on the mountain that people had to go once they were diagnosed with the terrible sickness. A soul was much better off if he had money and could stay in a private cabin near the lake.

The air smelled sweet from all the flowers in the beds that scattered the huge front yard. Joyce Clay led Ella Ruth around the back, through a large kitchen door. Four colored women and two men worked at cooking in the huge kitchen. Their uniforms were a crisp light blue and their heads were covered by hairnets.

"We're supposed to begin working the rooms and the sleep

porches," Joyce Clay snapped.

One of the women gave her a stern look and nodded toward double doors. "Go through the dining room and follow the hall until you come to a left. That will take you to Miss Diver's office. She takes care of all the new workers."

"Obliged." Joyce Clay even walked as if those shoes weighed her down. But one of Ella Ruth's biggest sins was judging people. What if poor Joyce Clay didn't have nothing but those big shoes to wear? This was exactly what Grandmother Allen meant when she said Ella Ruth was self-centered.

The place smelled clean, like somebody waited behind one of the many doors to scrub as soon as folks walked by. The tables in the dining hall were long with lots of chairs lined on each side.

"Catch up, girl. You got to walk the line here. Agnes done filled me in on you. What blood you come from."

A lump formed in Ella Ruth's throat. She sped up her steps. Part of her wanted to scream ugly things at Joyce Clay, especially about her shoes.

Miss Diver, a young blond, sat at her desk. Anybody could tell by the dark-rimmed glasses perched on her head that she was smart. She gave both Ella Ruth and Joyce Clay a look that made Ella Ruth think the woman could see straight into her.

"You're here to attend the rooms and the sleeping porches on the second floor."

"Yes ma'am." Joyce Clay sounded downright humble.

Miss Diver rubbed the bridge of her nose. "There is a strict schedule. You must follow it or the patients become agitated and grow sicker. Do you understand?"

"Yes ma'am, we'll follow the rules just like you say." Joyce Clay actually gave a half smile that revealed some bad top teeth.

"They are on so much more than rules. We don't call anything a rule here. This is a schedule for 'the cure.' These patients have tuberculous."

A chill walked right through Ella Ruth.

"Do you know what tuberculous is?"

"Yes ma'am." Joyce Clay looked at her ugly shoes.

Miss Diver placed her complete attention on Ella Ruth. "Does your friend here know how to speak, Mrs. Clay? She looks awful young."

"She's plenty old enough. Finishes high school this next school year. Works real hard."

"I do have a voice, Miss Diver. How do we keep from getting tuberculous?"

Miss Diver picked up papers from her desk. "Read over these pamphlets. They'll explain all the precautions you have to take. Also you must read the booklet the patients received when they entered this sanatorium. What you must understand is some of those here don't want to be here. Well, none of them truly want to be here, but some were forced to come. This is a public sanatorium. They would rather be with their families.

"You have to be leaders. Encourage them without becoming attached. You're on the woman's ward, of course. There will be all ages." Miss Diver smiled and handed them little books.

Joyce Clay's frowned grew deeper. "Thank you ma'am."

"Go to the office down the hall and give Mrs. Tucker your sizes. Always remove your uniforms before you leave the building. Never wear them home. They could be contaminated."

"Yes ma'am," Ella Ruth replied.

"Check back with me after you've read the material. I want to make sure you understand what you read."

Joyce Clay shot Ella Ruth a black look.

Ella Ruth understood. When they were out in the hall, she spoke. "Do you mind if I read these out loud? It helps me concentrate better."

"Go ahead. Don't they teach you kids anything in school these days? Read nice and slow." Joyce Clay looked relieved.

"Coughing is undesirable and unnecessary. Think of coughing as a bad habit." Ella Ruth looked up at Joyce Clay.

"Never heard of such. It comes natural. How you going to hold it in?"

"The schedule even tells when they go to the bathroom." Ella Ruth pointed to the place on the page.

Joyce Clay never looked. "Sounds like we're jail deputies to me."

Nine o'clock in the morning was sunshine hour, so Ella Ruth had to stand on the sleeping porch and make sure the women didn't get up and move around. Sixteen beds, made up with crisp white linens, lined the walls, facing the screen. All but one was taken. All were supposed to be full. One of the girls looked to be Ella Ruth's age. Big black circles ringed her blue eyes. When Ella Ruth smiled, she only frowned.

"We're missing someone." Ella Ruth stated.

"Gertrude's still in her room," said a woman. "She thinks she's a lot better than the rest of us." So much for the requirement to be polite all the time.

"What is her room number?" Ella Ruth asked.

The woman gave a sly smile. "She won't be nice to you."

"I'm not here to make friends," Ella Ruth snapped.

"203 at the end of the hall. Don't you tell her who snitched."

The door stood open slightly. A woman sat on the edge of the bed with her back to Ella Ruth, humming a beautiful melody. Ella Ruth tapped on the door.

The woman swung around, glared, and opened her mouth to speak, but nothing came out.

"You're supposed to be on the sun porch for the hour."

"Hell." The woman spit the word, followed by a rough cough.

"See, you're aggravating your condition. I need you to come out to the porch. I've only just started this job. I plan on saving to go to Black Mountain College, but I won't get to go if I am fired."

The woman had dark red, curly hair that was way too thin. Her skin was pale. At some point she had been very pretty. "Who are you?"

"I'm the new attendant."

"I figured that out. What's your name? And don't give me that crap about not sharing names. I will not listen to that stuff today."

"Ella Ruth. Could you come outside now?"

She stared at Ella Ruth. "Where do you live, Ella Ruth?"

"I live on Black Mountain."

For a minute she looked like she might protest, call Ella Ruth a liar, but another cough came on.

Ella Ruth crossed the room out of reflex.

"Don't," the woman managed to say. "You should never come near when one of us is coughing." She hacked a little more.

"I wasn't thinking."

"Exactly." The woman closed her eyes for a few minutes, and when it seemed the spell was finished, she stood. "Let's go. I don't want to ruin your first day. But you owe me, Ella Ruth from Black Mountain."

"What do I owe?"

"A story of course. It has to be about you. I collect them. They keep me going in this place. Learning stories."

Ella Ruth laughed.

"I'm not kidding. Come here this afternoon in 'time up' hours."

"Okay."

The woman nodded and the two of them walked, one tall and regal, the other keeping pace behind.

"Well, by God, the girl got you out here, Gertie," the snitch said when they reached the porch. She cackled and broke into a cough that shook her body.

"You told on me, Shirley?" Gertie frowned.

Shirley shrugged. "I had too. The poor thing can't afford to lose her job." She nodded at Ella Ruth. "Look at her. She's so skinny she'd fit right in with us."

"My uniform is too big. They didn't have a small one." Ella Ruth looked down at her dress.

"That's because you're a child playing like a woman," Gertie said.

"Good Lord, she's not a baby. Just young." Shirley squinted, studying Ella Ruth. "I bet you're my Harold's age. He's going to college next fall. You should meet him."

"The last thing she needs is a boy," Gertie fussed.

Ella Ruth's cheeks heated. "This is sunshine hour, not jabbering hour."

"Oh, she has a backbone." Shirley smiled. "Tell her where you're from, Gertie. She's not from here. She was born somewhere else. That's for sure."

Gertie waited a minute. "I came here looking for my missing sister. I got sick, and they forced me here in this place. Don't you ever believe you have freedom, young lady, because you don't. I've demanded to go home, but the authorities wouldn't allow it. I could have stayed in my own house. It's not far from here. But they said I was too much of a risk. There were no openings at the local rest houses."

"I haven't heard of anyone missing," Ella Ruth said.

"It's been years ago. You would have been a little child." Shirley coughed again.

"You wonderful ladies are supposed to be resting." Ella Ruth tried to get them quiet.

Gertie frowned. "Another jailer. Good Lord."

Shirley had turned a shade paler after her latest coughing fit. "They're all jailers, Gert."

"Lay down before you die. Look at all these other well-behaved patients." Gertie said with a laugh.

"It's hot as hell out here," Shirley fussed.

The rest of the women nodded but didn't open their mouths. Ella Ruth realized that Gertie would never stick to some schedule, and she loved her for it.

CR

Ella Ruth went to room 203 and tapped on the door.

"Come in. I've been waiting." Gertie watched her from a small chair near the window. "You owe me a story." Another chair was pulled close to Gertie.

"What do you want to know?" Ella Ruth asked.

"I can smell a story a mile off. You've got one, Ella Ruth."

"I live with my grandparents on their little farm at the bottom of

Black Mountain. My grandmother takes care of me because she is a good Christian woman. She does not like me."

"Why?" Gertie's stare made Ella Ruth uncomfortable.

"My mother ran off with another man, and my father left me with them on his way off the mountain."

"Both of your parents are gone?" She looked concerned.

Ella Ruth ignored the question. "What about your sister? When did she go missing?"

"Oh no, you don't." Gertie smiled. "You're not going to wiggle out of your story. How do you know your mother ran away?"

Ella Ruth studied the green lawn out the window. "I guess because my grandmother told me." She thought of the haint and what she said about lies.

"Not everything that comes out of an adult is true. What is your last name?"

"Allen."

The room turned quiet and took up all the air between the two of them. "As in Paul Allen?" Gertie whispered.

"Yes. Do you know him?" Ella Ruth's heart skipped a beat.

Gertie coughed and struggled to stand. She went into her closet and brought out a frame, placing it in front of Ella Ruth.

The woman was even prettier in the photo than the first time Ella Ruth had seen her. There was a softness around her eyes, as if she were happier than she had ever been.

"That was taken right after you were born."

Ella Ruth held the picture in her hands, staring at the haint she had seen at the witch house. "I don't understand." But she did. She didn't want to but she did.

"That's your mother, my sister. I suspected the first time I saw you this morning. You look just like her. No wonder your grandmother doesn't like you." She touched Ella Ruth's hand. Touching was not allowed in the sanatorium. Ella Ruth didn't move her hand. "Your mother died, Ella Ruth. That's why you live with your grandmother. She didn't leave you. She died in childbirth. At least, that's what they told me. I don't believe any of it. I've been searching for the truth a long time."

"Did I have a little brother or a sister?" Ella Ruth asked.

"I don't know."

◌

The sun balanced on the treetops as Ella Ruth stood in front of the witch house. She prayed that the witch, her mother, the haint, would come again.

All was still.

She looked out at the woods and saw a white figure darting through the trees.

"They're all liars," she screamed.

No answer.

Ella Ruth ran as hard as she could through the woods. Her mother had been dead all this time and no one told her. Her grandparents allowed her to believe she might find her one day. They didn't tell her about the baby. Ella Ruth had to talk to Gertie more. What in the world would she do with this new story? How could she stay in the house with her grandparents without spilling her guts?

What Ella Ruth didn't know as she ran through the woods in an overdue mourning is that back at the farm, word had arrived on the mountain. Paul Allen was coming home.

Chapter 3

Ella Ruth

Grandpa Allen's voice cut through the sound of rushing water and the tangle of trees surrounding Ella Ruth's thinking place, her rock that jutted out of Dragon Fly River. She could only reach it by wading out to the middle where most sane folks wouldn't risk going. The warmth that collected in the stone healed her when she couldn't take anymore. She remained stretched out with her eyes closed, even though she knew Grandpa Allen was close. His mama, a full Cherokee, had taught him many of her people's ways. He had learned to use the rocks as guides.

Aunt Gert would have listened to her problems, but Grandmother Allen had forced Ella Ruth to quit her job. That's when Ella Ruth knew even more problems were headed her way.

"I thought I'd find you out here."

Ella Ruth remained in place, flat on the rock. "I don't want to leave with him. I liked my job." The words came out in a sob.

"Now child, we been through this. It's out of my hands. Your daddy's come home. That's that. Never thought he would but he did." Grandpa Allen knocked his pipe ashes on the ground and mashed out the fire with his shoe.

"I don't care. He ain't never been a father to me and he can't start when I'm fifteen. I'm grown. It's too late."

"Don't let him hear you talking like that. He's set on bringing you to that little house he bought in town. And what Paul Allen wants, he gets. That's partly your grandmother's fault. She babied him, made him too special. You might as well face what you got to do. He may give up on the idea after a few months if you keep low. And sweetie, me and your grandmother are getting old. We ain't going to be around forever. You need someone to live with besides us."

"I'm just his trophy."

A wrinkle of feeling crossed Grandpa Allen's face. "Maybe. But don't go against him. Trust me on this. You can't reason with him."

"What happened to my mama? You never told me. I don't think she ran off. I think she died. I know she did 'cause I seen her haint."

"I know you been talking to your mama's sister," Grandpa Allen said. "If you're smart, you won't never mention her. Your daddy would love to make her life worthless. You don't want that on your shoulders."

"If it wasn't for the haint, I wouldn't have found Gert."

"Ain't no such things as spirits. Your grandmother found you the job. I guess you could say she helped you find the truth. And that would purely kill her." He laughed. "You done grown up."

"I'm fifteen, Grandpa Allen. And I hate Paul Allen." Ella Ruth spat the words at the river.

"Get on over here. If you say anything else like that again, I'll spank you myself. Somebody's got to try and save your life. Paul Allen is liable to do anything. Your mouth is only going to cause you trouble. Don't you understand?"

œ

Paul Allen's truck sat next to the house with Ella Ruth's mirror and dresser in the back. She was glad she had hidden her sketchbook and pencils the night before.

Inside the house was Paul Allen's new wife. Ella Ruth wished she could just die.

Grandpa stopped at the corner of Grandmother's flowerbed. He fiddled with a vine of morning glories with purple blooms so big he could almost fit his fist in them. Grandmother Allen hated morning glory vines, so that was probably the reason they sprang up and grew so well in her garden. She swore that Grandpa planted them there every year on purpose. Who knew? Maybe he did.

"Running away won't help you none," Grandpa said as he worked on the vine. "Where would you go? He'd see it as a sport and hunt you down. That aunt, even if she could get out of the sanatorium, couldn't hide you good enough. She's no match for him. There would be a terrible price to pay. Don't be stupid." The vine, tender in his old gnarled fingers, gave with one last soft tug, torn up by the roots. "Stay on his good side and find a boy to marry. Get out of there as soon as you can." He tossed the vine to the side. The blooms would wither and shrink in on themselves.

℃

The new wife, a look on her face that could curdle fresh milk, sat in Grandmother Allen's favorite rocker near the potbelly stove. She wore her gray-streaked hair long, pulled back in a knot at her neck. She reminded Ella Ruth of an old maid teacher sour on life.

Paul Allen walked through the room with the frame of Ella Ruth's iron bed.

"That sure looks too big for her room," the new wife said in a high-pitched voice.

Paul Allen stopped, a vein popping out on his forehead like a ridge of mountains. "Woman, if I need your talk, I'll ask for it."

As much as Ella Ruth disliked the new wife, she had to look away. His words made her hurt for the woman. She went to the kitchen.

Grandmother Allen hobbled to the stove, leaning heavy on her cane that Grandpa Allen had made her one winter after she slipped on the icy steps. "Sit yourself down. Your daddy's done a big thing coming back home to make you a family. You make me proud. You got it?"

Ella Ruth took a seat at the table. What use was it to fight Grandmother Allen?

She'd never listen to reason.

The wrinkles around Grandmother Allen's narrow eyes softened and smoothed. "I'll tell you one thing. You can try the patience of Job. If that old mule in yonder thinks she can do better by you, than let her have at it. But if she lays one hand on you, I'll give her a taste of my stick here." She shook the cane. "She's not messing with white trash. We're Allens, and we come from a long line of God-fearing Christians. She's not fit to wipe your daddy's boots. She's got Jew blood. That's what I heard." Grandmother Allen slammed a plate of eggs and grits in front of Ella Ruth. "Paul really knows how to pick women. Don't you get uppity like the rest of them, you hear?"

Ella Ruth picked at her food.

☙

Less than two hours later, Ella Ruth sat in the truck, sandwiched between Paul Allen and his new bride. Grandmother and Grandpa Allen stood on the porch. The weathered gray house stood like a fading flower in the heat of a summer day. The flower boxes were barren of any color, and the swing swayed as if a haint sat there.

Paul Allen started the engine.

Grandpa Allen took out his pipe; he was bent like a gnarled tree. A deep black shadow moved over Ella Ruth's heart.

Paul Allen began to whistle while the new wife croaked little snatches of "I'll Fly Away."

Ella Ruth turned to take one more looked at her grandparents, watching them fade away into the distance.

Paul Allen took a sharp curve too fast. "I got to learn this mountain road again." He looked over at Ella Ruth. "Bell, here, is your new mama. You are to call her that."

"I have a mama, but thank you."

Bell sucked in air. Or maybe that was the sound of the crisp clear moment of revenge. The air split like lightning hitting a tree, splintering as Paul Allen's hand crashed across Ella Ruth's mouth.

"There'll be no more sass from you."

Ella Ruth's ears rang.

"Do I make myself clear?"

Ella Ruth looked straight ahead.

"Answer me, girl."

Bell pinched the inside of Ella Ruth's arm. "Yes."

"Yes what?"

She refused to look at him. "Yes sir." A spot on the horizon blurred as a big part of her soul broke away and soaked the air with a silent scream. She had to see Aunt Gert, but how would she ever find a way?

Paul Allen picked up his whistling again. Bell looked out the window as if he had hit her instead. Ella Ruth's lip tightened and the metal taste of blood filled her mouth.

☙

Two weeks later Grandpa Allen fell over dead in his garden. Grandmother Allen found him when he didn't show up for dinner. Before two months were out, Grandmother Allen would be gone. She would die in her sleep one night just as Ella Ruth's life began to heat up.

Part Two

Tangled

1940–1941

Chapter 4

Buster

The weeks and months following Daddy's death should have settled Buster, but instead he grew a wild streak as wide as a two-lane highway. Maybe it was the weight of all his secrets that helped him make bad choices. There was the secret of stealing the bugle, promised to Lee when he was grown. There was the secret of him climbing the quarry walls that probably caused Daddy to be there on that day. Sure, Daddy was sheriff of Swannanoa Gap, but on Sundays he always sent Donald to calls so he had time with his family. There was the secret of Lacy and Lee. How Buster had seen them just two afternoons before Daddy died. At seventeen, Buster was now the man of the Wright family, and he was a sad example.

Most Saturday nights Buster hung out with Larry at the pool hall, Jeb's Dart Bar. Jeb ran a clean business out front with dartboards, pool tables, music, and plenty of sodas, but the back room housed the real business, a profitable one for any quick-thinking young man with a fast truck and guilt for brains. He couldn't remember who had the idea first, Larry or him, to run shine. They were good, better than most of the seasoned runners twice their age. It was a thriving business, seeing how most of the counties in Western North Carolina were dry as a bone. Buster was cashing in on his piece of the fortune.

Jeb's shine was so pure that adding a little water to double the batch meant a little extra money, actually a lot. How could it be stealing when shine was illegal anyway?

Buster and Larry were cocks of the walk—smart, handsome, and smooth as a sheet of glass until the day they sold a watered-down batch of shine to the wrong overpaid town official.

⋈

Buster made it around the house before anyone saw him. He'd laid out of church again and was trying to sneak home before Mama returned. He was pretty hungry and looking forward to a sandwich before hiding out the rest of the afternoon. But there was Sheriff Cooper's patrol car, sitting in the driveway in plain view of God and all their Christian neighbors. Jeb had been arrested the night before by Cooper's deputy. Now he was in that rotten jail cell, stone sober, bawling like a big baby and spilling his guts to save his own hide. Yep, he had figured out that Buster was stealing shine.

Old Widow Porter, known throughout town for her bad sinuses and her dislike of organized religion, was out sweeping her front yard. Clouds of dirt exploded around her with every stroke. The good sheriff must have been waiting on Mama to get home, but he wasn't in the car. Buster wondered how late it was. Maybe church was over already.

Carefully, Buster peeked around the corner of the house. Then he took two steps back into the big lilac bush. The sheriff stood on the porch and Mama was by the door.

"Miz Wright, you know this ain't a trip I wanted to make, especially on the Lord's day, but we can't sweep this under the rug, even if the late Mr. Wright was a fine sheriff. This ain't some childish prank, and I got a feeling your husband would agree with me on this. I'd like to believe Old Miz Wright, but you and I both know Buster ain't spent no Saturday night reading a Bible with her. I wasn't born yesterday. Of course his granny would lie for him. If them federal boys get wind of this, Buster is looking at real time in the federal pen. Is that what you want for your son? 'Cause to them, moonshine is moonshine. We ain't some hick town anymore."

The sheriff spit tobacco juice off the porch and it landed only a few inches from the lilac bush. "I got the Mitchell boy red-handed. My undercover deputy bought the shine from him. It's going to be a sad time letting Preacher Mitchell know. Them two boys ain't got one lick of sense, and when you put them together, they get even worse."

"Sheriff Cooper, now, you're going to listen to me. My husband was proud of both his sons. Buster took his daddy's death hard, harder than most. That's no excuse to break the law, but you haven't shown me he committed the crime. Just because Larry was selling it doesn't mean Buster was in on this. I don't abide by the messes Buster always seems to be getting himself into. And I'll not shut my eyes to your faults either just because this town was dumb enough to give you a badge. I would imagine if the rumor is correct, that moonshine was purchased not to catch Larry but for your personal use, which makes you a lawbreaker." She was quiet for a minute. "Buster will regret the day he got tied up with the likes of Jeb Foster. If he did. But before you come to my house again on your mighty high horse, you had better think about who you replaced. You don't hold a candle to him. You're nothing but a joke in Swannanoa Gap."

Sheriff Cooper gave a snort. "You have a real good day, Miz Wright. We'll be seeing each other sooner than later." He stomped down the steps. "I'm not going to take Buster in this time out of respect of his daddy. Me and Frank go way back. But the next time, I'm sending him to the federal boys." The door to the patrol car slammed, the engine gunned, and the good sheriff peeled out of the driveway throwing gravel.

"Buster Wright." Mama barely spoke above a whisper. "You've been hiding in the same place since you were old enough to get your first spanking. I'll meet you at the woodshed." There was silence and then she spoke again. "Hello, Mrs. Porter. So nice to see your sinuses have gotten better." The windows shook as Mama slammed the door.

Did Mama still think she could whip him? He was a full-grown man, or almost. He walked back to the woodshed.

∞

"Buster," Mama said, the strap swinging by her side. "I've let this mess of yours go on too long. I've done wrong by you. I let the loss of your daddy blind me to the trouble you're making. It's time to quit acting like a horse's ass and grow up." She pointed the strap at the woodpile. "Put your hands up there."

Billie was peeking off the back porch, enjoying every minute. Buster was sure Mama had gone around the bend.

"Mama—"

"I don't want to hear a bit of it, James Franklin Wright." Oh

Lord, she was using his real name.

The strap fell harder than Buster imagined. He had to fight the urge to pull it from her hands. When she'd hit him about ten times, she dropped the strap to the ground.

Buster's whole backside stung like a million ants were biting him.

"You're finished with roaming this town causing trouble. I mean it. Things are going to change."

And change they did.

Chapter 5

Buster worked calluses on his hands that whole summer of 1941. He planted bushes so big you couldn't see the house from the road. Mama decided this would be only part of a fitting, back-breaking punishment, but it seemed to Buster it caused poor old Widow Porter more grief than it did him. She couldn't see a thing over those bushes.

Granny's job was to watch him. Her eyesight was terrible, but that didn't stop her from being a prison guard on a one-man chain gang. Shoot, the whole summer had been spent breaking his back, weeding the garden, picking the vegetables, fixing the roof, and cutting grass, and now he dug his last hole for the last bush. He needed to get away from the houseful of women. Billie nearly drove him crazy with all her friends flitting in and out like tiny blue butterflies around a rain puddle. They would collect on the back porch just to watch Buster work. They had grown into something besides silly girls, and that meant nothing but trouble. Not for him because he had better things to do, but Mama was about to have her hands full.

Granny came out on the front porch, yelling as if Buster was in the next county. "That nice Mr. Sounders from the sawmill called. He said you can start on Monday. Have you told your mama about this new job?"

"Not yet but I will."

"Well, I got another job for you."

He leaned his shovel against one of the large oak trees in the yard. "Yes, ma'am."

Granny held out a basket covered with a dishtowel. "Take these apple turnovers to Mrs. Mitchell for the ice cream supper tonight."

"I'll take care of it right now." He tried not to grab the basket too quick.

"Now don't dilly-daddle. I don't want to be sorry for letting you go to the Mitchell place."

"Yes, ma'am." He hiked across the yard two steps at a time.

"And don't forget you have to escort Billie to the ice cream supper."

"How could I forget that?" Buster shouted over his shoulder. He was honestly looking forward to something besides working, eating, and sleeping.

CR

Buster walked the railroad tracks so no one would see him with a prissy basket swinging at his side. Heat bugs sang in waves, mosquitoes zapped his neck, and sweat ran down his back. The sky was the hazy blue of August heat. Maybe he'd see Larry. He had an idea and wanted to see what his friend thought about it.

The once well-worn path through the gathering of skinny pines was now overgrown. And there among the trees, with his back to Buster, an ax in one hand, and a lit cigarette in the other, stood Larry. A perfect ring of smoke formed above his head, a halo.

"Don't you think running whiskey is enough? Now you're smoking." Buster sounded just like Cooper at his worst.

Larry went into a coughing fit. "You asshole!" he managed when he turned and saw Buster.

Buster laughed. "You missed me?"

Larry frowned. "Like a damn toothache."

"And I missed you." He clapped Larry on the back. "I got a plan."

"Shit no! I'm passing on this one."

"Come on. The last plan made money. You're going to chicken out on your best friend?"

"What's the damn plan?" Larry grumbled like some old man half the time.

"What do you have to lose?" Buster grinned and looked around at the busted wood.

Larry fished a flat-shaped bottled out of the stacked wood. "I got me some hooch."

"And you talk about me?" Buster shook his head. "Granny has a nose like a bloodhound."

"So tell me your plan." Larry stuck the bottle back inside the woodpile without taking a sip.

"How the hell did you get that bottle tethered so close to home?"

He shrugged. "Had it left over from before. Tell me the plan."

"No worrying over that. It's all up here." Buster tapped his temple. "Let's just say we're going out in style like Al Capone." He grinned once more. "I got some apple turnovers to deliver to your mama. I'll see you at the ice cream supper."

"Oh hell." Larry slammed the ax into a log as Buster walked in the direction of the house.

"Hey," Larry called.

Buster just laughed and kept walking.

"Damn Capone did eight years in the federal pen."

଼

Later that evening, Buster walked three steps ahead of Billie. In her hands, she held a box, a dinner she had cooked herself.

"That stupid creepy Bobby better not bid on my supper."

"Ain't no one going to bid on your old supper. You probably poisoned it." To Buster, the ice cream social was stupid.

"Shut up. I'm going to sell my box supper to the cutest boy in town."

At fifteen, she had shed her tomboy ways and looked almost like a woman. The whole thing didn't make sense. Sisters weren't supposed to look good.

"Don't laugh at me, asshole, or I'll punch you in the mouth." Billie glared at him.

"Ah, that language will get you a lot of favor."

"You're the one that taught me how." She picked up a rock and lobbed it at Buster.

"Damn. You're really acting your age." He rubbed his shoulder. "I'm planning on having a good time tonight."

"I know there ain't no church girl that will go out with you."

The very thought of some goody-goody girl made him smile. "Ain't no girls at church I care about, but if I did, I wouldn't have a hard time getting them to like me."

"Is your dumb friend Larry going to be there?"

"What's it to you?" Buster cut a look at her. "I can tell you he won't have time to bid on no suppers tonight. He's there because his daddy's making him go."

"You're really an idiot, Buster."

℞

The crowd gathered in Mrs. Weehunt's back yard. Folks nodded at Buster, but no one relished the chance to talk to him.

"Hey sis, there's your man." Buster pointed his head in Larry's direction, where he leaned against a big oak tree.

"Leave me alone." Billie pushed past him and headed toward Larry.

The people mingling in the yard looked at him like he was some freak from the circus. He tipped his cap at a giggly bunch of girls, who quickly looked the other way. Adults sat here and there on blankets.

Buster strolled over to Larry, where Billie stood awkwardly beside him. "Get lost, Billie."

"Who says?" Billie looked like she could do some damage if she ran through him.

"I do."

"I'll see you in a little while," Larry told her. Buster and me got to talk." He smiled and Billie nearly fell over her own feet leaving.

"If you promise." She giggled.

"I promise."

Billie headed toward the bunch of girls.

"Are you kidding? That's my sister. There's something wrong with that. It's not natural." Buster punched Larry's arm.

"Damn." He rubbed the place. "She's fifteen, Buster."

"Just barely." Buster stared at this person who was supposed to be his best friend. "It's weird. You're not helping matters here. What if she starts hanging around, and we can't slip off?"

"I didn't know we were going to leave." They stood by the tree watching everyone having fun. "Still, I reckon any plan you've got has to be better than standing around here with this bunch of losers."

"Now, you're seeing things my way." Buster turned toward the

38

house just in time to see an angel with dark red curls framing her beautiful eyes walk into the backyard. His throat went scratchy. The Allen girl. They had gone to school together. She had seen him with the bugle in the rafters of the church.

"So, what's your plan?"

Buster watched the angel shake hands with Preacher Mitchell.

"Are you listening?"

Still, Buster stared. What was wrong with him?

"Naw, you don't want nothing to do with her. Her daddy is Paul Allen. He's the biggest asshole in Swannanoa Gap. Even my daddy says stay clear of him, and you know he never talks bad about anyone."

She carried herself like a queen or something.

"Buster, are you listening to me?"

Buster turned away and gave himself a shake. "Yes. When I give you the signal, meet me on the road. Don't make a spectacle of yourself. Just blend in. Let's split up. We got to look like we're having fun." The angel moved closer to him. "We'll have to bust our asses to get back here before the party is over."

"I'll be watching." Larry moved off toward the group of girls.

The angel laughed at something Sam White said. Sam had joined the Navy right after school was finished and ended up stationed in Hawaii. What a stroke of luck for him. Buster wandered over to say hi to Sam, who had never liked him anyway.

"We got to go to war," Sam was saying. "The allies are grasping at straws. Hitler is crazier than a bedbug and he's winning. What are the American people doing? Putting their heads in the sand. We're the strongest country in the world, and we're just standing on the sidelines."

Buster laughed.

"Do you think something is funny, Wright?" Sam wore his navy fatigues, and something about him wasn't so boyish anymore. He was bulkier.

"I think some people get a uniform, and it goes to their head."

Sam turned to the angel. "I've got to speak with the doc for a minute. I'll be back."

She nodded.

Buster scraped his shoe back and forth across a rock half-buried in the ground. "He sure has war on the brain."

"Actually, I think a lot of people do."

"Did you fix a supper tonight?" His words fumbled around like a football player trying to recover a ball.

She looked him up and down. "Yes."

"Do you like to dance?" Buster knew the question was stupid.

"I have never danced. My father and stepmother don't approve of such things." Her words sliced the air.

Buster plowed deeper into his mess. "You don't know what you're missing, then. Certain songs get you right in the gut. You know what I mean? Makes you want to hold someone close." He moved to imaginary music.

Her look washed over him like ice water. "Well, if you're trying to shock me, you can't. I'm not surprised you know all about holding girls. Running moonshine makes you the bad boy, the outlaw. Some girls like that stuff." Her eyes, a cool gray, turned cold. "But I'm not interested in boys that hang out in the rafters of churches, scaring folks to death. Go on back to your kind of girl."

"I could teach you how to dance," he pressed.

"I just bet you could." She laughed. "Take me off your list."

"Hell, nobody said anything about a list." He wondered how the conversation had gotten away from him.

"Don't use that language with me." She made a sideways movement.

Buster moved too. "Wait. I'm sorry. Shoot. All this is turning out wrong."

"I'm not like all those girls that chase after you." She twirled to go, stopping. "And you've never met a girl like me. I'm not one bit impressed with you." She floated away to stand near the very group of girls he had made fun of when he arrived at the social.

Buster turned his back to her. What the hell was he thinking? The girl was a witch, not an angel. He stood under the big oak tree alone, waiting for the right time to leave.

Larry hovered on the edge of the yard, half-heartedly fighting off

Billie when she came near.

Buster had intended to walk off when Preacher Mitchell began taking bids on the box suppers, but the first box held up stopped him in his tracks.

"Ella Ruth Allen has made a fine supper. What do I hear? Remember, the money goes for the purchase of new choir robes." The angel stood beside Preacher Mitchell, her cheeks crimson.

"A dollar," yelled Sam White.

"Three dollars and fifty-four cents." Every penny in Buster's pocket. Ella Ruth Allen looked at Buster in surprise.

"Five dollars," Sam countered.

The crowd groaned and turned to see what Buster would do.

He shrugged. "You got me." He tipped his cap, looked at Larry, and walked away.

"We got a winner. Sam White, the choir thanks you for your donation."

 С

The sun pushed down into the pines when Buster crawled under the loading platform at the train station. So much for not making a spectacle of himself. Larry waited up the hill, out of sight, near the sheriff's office and jail. The building was as old as the town of Swannanoa Gap and was built right next to the polished white train depot, making it even more of an eyesore. Everyone complained about its shabbiness. The jail cell stood just outside the back of the office alone. Some kid had painted the word "outhouse" above the door in white. Whenever Sheriff Cooper had one of his deputies to paint over it, somehow it always came back. Mostly the place was used for storage, seeing how there was no crime in town. Until that summer anyway.

The light began to seep away. The ground under the loading platform smelled of dampness and mold. Buster was stretched out on his stomach, watching the tracks through the white latticework. If he pulled this off, then he wouldn't do another bad stunt. He promised. A rumble shook the ground. Here came the train right on time. The blast of the whistle made him jump, and he whacked his head on a

41

beam. The train came to a rolling stop, and Buster crawled out of his cramped hiding place. Larry's bird call came from the hill. Buster raised his hand, and Larry walked lazily in the direction of G.B.'s Grill.

Buster kicked at rocks, eying the chain stretched down the hill like a snake sunning itself in the middle of the road. The conductor leapt from the train. A few passengers milled around on the platform. Swannanoa Gap was mostly a stop-off place for those headed to Montreat, a church retreat a short ways up the track.

The conductor moved to the end of the train, leaning against the caboose. Buster tugged the end of the chain in one graceful motion, crossed the open area, and fastened the heavy hook to the coupling between the cars. He took a deep breath and leaned out. The conductor was gone, so Buster stepped out and walked without hurrying, hoping he didn't draw any attention.

"Son, what are you doing?"

Buster thought of high-tailing it as fast as he could up the hill, but everyone in town knew him. Where would he hide for long? Instead, he turned around and walked back to meet the conductor, who had suddenly reappeared.

"I was looking at your train, sir. One day I'm going to make me a trip." The chain stuck out like a sore thumb. Twilight settled across the sky. The moon balanced on the treetops, a big, late August moon.

"You weren't thinking about jumping the train, were you?" The conductor pushed his hat back on his head.

"Sure, I think about it all the time, but Mama would tan my hide. And there ain't much worse than a mama that thinks she can whip her grown son." He laughed.

The conductor cracked a grin. "Do I know you?"

"Naw, I doubt it."

"Are you Sheriff Wright's boy?" The conductor clapped Buster on the back. "Lord, I haven't seen you since you were knee high. You and your brother used to come up here running like wild Indians and your daddy laughing."

"I guess that would have been us." Buster did not want to think about Lee.

"I sure hated to hear about your daddy. He was the best. Nothing like that damn idiot now. Hell, he'd put one of us in jail if he could find a good reason." He chuckled. "You the good son or the wild son?"

"Good. Mama keeps the wild one under lock and key."

The conductor laughed again. "You'll find you never outgrow your mama. She'll be there the rest of your life telling you how to mind."

"That's what I'm worried about. Well, I got to go. Mama will send someone looking for me."

"Tell you what. Come on back one day, and I'll let you ride to Montreat and back."

"Great. I will, sir." Buster threw his hand in the air and broke into a trot.

Larry stood in the dark behind G.B.'s.

"Hey," Buster shouted.

"What the hell took you so long?"

"I was talking to the conductor." Buster started to run to the water tower sitting in the center of town.

"Are you crazy?" Larry tried to keep up.

"Here comes the best part." The train gave three short whistles. "Shit, come on."

"Slow down." Larry puffed behind.

Buster reached the ladder as the whistled blasted again. "We're going to miss the whole damn show." He scrambled up, taking two rungs at a time. Larry was right behind.

The stars in the sky moved like a spinning top. Train wheels turned, singing a warning, "Here we go."

Buster leaned out over the water tower's rail just in time to see the train give a lurch forward, heading to Montreat in the last of the daylight. "Get your ass up here."

Larry climbed onto the platform. "Wow." He looked at the sky. "Look at the train."

The chain tightened around its prey, springing the snare.

"Anytime now," Buster whispered.

The jail cell seemed to take a breath as the train moved down the track, gathering all the slack, finally tipping the building on its side. There sat poor old Jeb on the cot. The train wheels turned, never missing a beat. In the dead silence that followed, before folks started yelling and running, before Jeb made a run for it, Buster was sure he heard Daddy laugh. His heart was full of joy.

"Look at Jeb run," Larry exclaimed.

"They'll never find him now." Buster laughed so hard he fell backward onto the platform. Tears ran down his cheeks as the folks below ran around like chickens with their heads cut off.

Chapter 6

Lee Wright

Montana—land of cattle and horses, mountains and fast-flowing rivers, cowboys and hard work—spoke to Lee in a soft whisper that tickled his ear with an ease he hadn't felt before jumping the train that took him away from the Gap. He'd spent the last two years doing odd jobs where he could find them, but he just might stay there in Montana. He got a job as a ranch hand, where he settled into a bunkhouse with a bunch of cowboys. He was a quick learner. Before he knew it, he was riding horses as good as he could jump trains. At nineteen, he was set for a while. There was even a girl.

Wasn't there always a girl? This one lived on the ranch, where she broke the new horses. The guys laughed at her because she came at the job just like a girl would, all soft and easy. Most had bets on how long she would last. Every cowboy knew a horse had to be broken with a two-by-four up the side of the head. It was the only way. Their spirits were too strong. Even Lee, who didn't know nothing about horses, had to wonder how else one could tame such a beast. But he liked to watch the girl move around the skittish horses with soft, dainty steps. One or two times she caught him watching and frowned. He wanted to love something the way she loved her horses, except the thought hadn't formed solid in his mind. Instead, it was a fuzzy yearning that startled him on most days.

He had no intention of knowing the girl, or anyone for that matter, on the ranch. His mind stayed cluttered with Lacy, unsettling thoughts tangled with blame and guilt. Part of him could still hear her sweet, soft voice…until Daddy's angry words about the foolishness of loving a colored girl broke through and reminded him of all he had lost, of the price he was paying. He had promised Lacy he'd stand up to his daddy, that he would make a life with her no matter what. But Daddy died, and Lee ran as hard as he could from the place he called home.

One day about a week after he came to the ranch, he saw the girl walking a horse from the barn, her blond hair tucked under a hat and her face so dirty that he thought she was just another cowboy. She even jumped on the back of the pinto like a man. But, when she bent over the horse's neck, her hat fell off and her hair tumbled free. She stroked the pinto, speaking too soft to be heard.

"Silliest shit I've ever seen," muttered Carl, who was old enough to be Lee's daddy. He had been on the ranch since he was thirteen, and liked to brag he was part of the dark dirt, the river, and the sky. A guy had to trust someone with Carl's kind of history. "That one is right pretty when she's cleaned up. That's how she got the job. The boss's son thought with his dick instead of his head." They watched her together, and Carl added, "Can't say I've seen anything like this here girl and what she calls horse-breaking."

The pinto pushed back and danced around on his hind legs, only to settle again as the girl talked and rubbed his neck. One lone blond curl fell across her sweaty forehead.

"It's the damnedest thing I've ever seen. Girls in Georgia don't act like this. That's for sure." Lee watched the dance between girl and horse.

Carl patted his shoulder. "Don't get no ideas. Other cowboys did, and they lost their jobs. She's going to marry the boss's son."

Lee hooted. "That fancy-pants college boy?"

"Yep. I'd hate to see you leave over some tumble with that gal."

"Why do you think she would even give me a look? It's plain she loves one thing, horses."

Carl shrugged. "She sure ain't going to be satisfied with Mr. Clean Cut."

"I don't need no girls. One reason I'm here is to be free of those kinds of obligations." Lee laughed.

The pinto settled and trotted with the girl on his back.

"We don't always go after what we need, son."

"You ain't got to warn me. I'm careful."

Two days later, the girl was working a jet-black stallion, and the damn thing bucked her right off. Out of reflex, Lee jumped the fence when the stallion rared back again to stomp her. He would have done it for any cowboy. He grabbed a board and went after the horse to stop him.

"No!" The girl got to her feet and flew into Lee like a funnel cloud. "You're going to ruin all my work with him. Don't you do it." She grabbed the board raised above Lee's head.

He let her take it and jumped out of the way.

"Leave." Her hat was gone and her hair spilled around her face in a mess of curls.

"You're welcome." He left the way he came.

The next afternoon he was fly-fishing at the river and saw her out riding the same damn horse. The thing was just as sweet and tame. Lee was deep into casting when he caught her watching from the bank. The ice water churned around his knees.

The mountains sat in the distance, waves on an ocean, nothing but the music of the water playing on the air. He raised the rod and pulled back, performing the dance movements of fly-casting. The line floated through the air, landing on the water, alive, a fly pausing to rest. The line jerked. He worked the fish, giving it play, reeling it back, until it came close. A large trout. Lee held the fish with one hand and released the hook with the other. Then he stood watching as the trout swam away.

"You'll let a fish go, but you insist on beating a horse with a board?" The girl and the horse were now on the bank nearby. She gave him an interested look. "You may just be worth getting to know. What's your name?"

"Wright."

She nodded. "Cooper is mine."

And that started the whole crazy situation. Lee was drawn to impossible challenges. Had been since he was a kid. Cooper would show up when he was fishing and watch him from afar, never attempting to talk to him. Once she ambled over to the mess table and sat down by Carl, across from Lee. Carl turned clumsy and spilled his coffee.

She always left before she finished what she started. Lee took to watching her in the horse ring when he thought no one could see him.

One such afternoon, Carl clapped him on the back. "I told you, son. Don't be messing with her."

"Not me. I'm just watching."

"You're watching her like some love-sick puppy. Don't do it. The guys are talking."

"Cowboys are worse than old women."

"Somebody seen her following you to the river to watch that fancy fishing of yours."

"I can't keep her from doing what she wants. Fishing is what I do with my free time. She won't ruin it."

"Hell, free time should be spent on drinking some whiskey, Wright. Not fishing. I don't want to lose you. You're a good hand with the cows. We're going on a drive. Get that damn girl out of your head."

"She ain't in my head. I'm looking forward to the drive."

And Lee told the truth.

No girl was going to get in his head again, not like Lacy. He reckoned he had a lot in common with the horses this Cooper girl broke. He was wild and free for the first time. He wouldn't let himself be broken. It wasn't going to happen. Nope.

"Keep your nose clean," Carl said as he walked away.

Lee had every intention to do just that.

Cooper waited by the barn the next evening, wearing her cowboy hat and gloves. "I talked to the boss, Wright," she began, loudly enough for every cowboy to hear. "He wants you to work with me. I told him at the rate he brings new horses in, I needed a helper."

Lee thought about ignoring her but knew he wouldn't get away with it. "Oh hell no," he replied just as loudly. "The boys would never let me live it down. I do things like a man, not some sissy ways."

She pushed her hat back. "Damn, you mean how you let those fish go?" She turned to leave.

"Wait."

"Meet me tomorrow evening right here. I can't take you away from your other duties until you prove yourself. Boss's orders." She took a couple of steps. "I have an Appaloosa. He's a beauty." Cooper left him standing there with his mouth open. God help him.

He showed up the next evening just for fun. A couple of the guys hooted when they saw him cross over the fence into the horse ring.

"You two act like a couple high school kids," Cooper shouted.

"Oh, Wright," Billy yelled in a high squeaky girl voice. "Come here and let me teach you how to break a horse."

"We can break horses, gal." Darrel, the other cowboy, laughed as he nudged Billy. "You need to take someone like me on, honey, not Wright."

Cooper laughed. "You wish, Darrel." She walked into the barn, and Lee stood there like some kind of idiot.

"She's got you, boy. Better be careful," Billy warned.

Cooper led the Appaloosa out of the corral, and he shook his mane and looked straight at Lee, snorting and pawing the ground. It had to be the prettiest horse Lee had ever seen.

"He's letting you know to keep your distance." Cooper laughed.

The tension building in the air was familiar to Lee. "That's not a problem."

Cooper moved closer to the Appaloosa, which blew through his nostrils. "Listen." Her voice was sweet and low. "I know. I want the same kind of freedom. We all do, honey, but I'm going to be working you, like it or not."

The horse blew into the air noisily again. And this time shook his head. "Accept it. You got to learn to like me."

The animal's hide rippled.

"We're going to be great friends, and you're going to be a fine horse."

Amazed, Lee watched as the appaloosa relaxed.

Cooper rubbed her hand over the horse's neck and motioned Lee closer. He did as she asked.

"Now this is my friend, and he's going to be your friend too."

She reached out and took Lee's hand, pulling him into her scent of sweat and flowers. "Come close. I won't bite," she whispered. The horse shuffled his feet and became tense.

"Here, here." She took Lee's hand in hers and rubbed the horse's neck. Lee relaxed and the horse took his lead.

"There you go. See, we're all friends." Cooper's breath tickled Lee's ear.

"What are you doing with that cowboy?" The words shut off whatever magic had begun.

The Appaloosa's hide tensed, and Lee stepped back as the horse reared on his hind legs, knocking Cooper to the ground.

Mr. Fancy Pants College Man jumped into the pen, grabbing Cooper and glaring at Lee.

Cooper jerked her arm back. "Get out of here, Walter. I've told you not to interfere in my work."

Walter looked like he was good and pissed, but he smiled at Cooper. "I'm sorry. The thing was trying to kill you."

She laughed sarcastically in his face as the horse wandered to the far end of the pen. "You ruined all the work I did with this horse. You can't just come in here acting like Tarzan saving his Jane."

"You have that cowboy in here." Walter stood his ground. Lee kept quiet.

"He's training, Walter. Must I always defend myself? I'm not interested in another man."

Walter hung his head. "Well, it didn't look right."

"Do you want me to be able to have more time with you?" Walter didn't say a word. "You know I won't allow just anyone to touch my horses. I've been watching Wright. He's good. If you'll leave us alone, I can work."

"I'm sorry."

"You should be." Cooper looked at Lee and smiled, then turned back to Fancy Pants. "Now go up to the house. I'm glad you're home for a visit. I'll put the horse up and be there soon."

"I'll expect you'll act like a gentlemen," Walter said, pointing his stare at Lee.

"My mama taught me how to treat a lady." Lee stared Walter down. They were close in age but a whole country apart.

Finally, Walter left, and Lee joined Cooper with the horse.

"He's a silly, silly man, Wright. Don't worry. He won't bother us again. Now come close." She never turned to look at him. "Good, you're not afraid anymore." She took the rein and led the horse into the barn. Lee walked on the other side with his hand on the Appaloosa. An unnamed desire passed between him and the horse. The sky turned orange and pink as the sun sank behind the mountains, all the colors that made him think of Cooper.

"We want to give him some room in here. He's not crazy about that stall." She spoke barely above a whisper.

"He loves the open land."

The horse swished his tail as if he was affirming Lee's comment.

Cooper looked over the horse's back at Lee. "He has to get used to the stall." Her fingers brushed Lee's hand. "You did well for your first try."

Lee stepped out of the way so she could lead the horse in. She brushed the horse's mane, whispering a conversation. He had to check on the cows, but he felt unable to leave.

When she stepped out of the stall, she touched his arm. "Thanks."

And suddenly she fit right into his body, better than Lacy ever did. He kissed her. Cooper didn't pull away.

He stepped back, and she gave him a hard look.

"That's not part of the job, Wright." She walked away, leaving him there to wonder what he was supposed to do next.

☙

Soon his work became as smooth as Cooper's. He caught her watching him when she thought he wasn't looking. Her ways turned softer with Lee, as if she liked him in spite of herself. The Appaloosa was not having any part of a saddle and came to Lee before Cooper. Part of him took pride in this.

"He's the toughest I've had in a long time," Cooper admitted a few nights later as they led the horse to the barn. "If I didn't know better, I'd think he likes you more. It's like you two have some way of talking without words."

"Nothing special about me and that horse. I'm a cowboy. I'm going on the trail ride next week. It'll be a shame if he doesn't like the saddle by then."

"What do you mean?" She gave Lee a stubborn look.

"I was thinking since he's wild—you know, since it's in his blood and all—I'd take him as my horse. I got my own wild streak. He'd like being on the trail, back out on the land. And I got a name for him."

She laughed a little. "What?"

"Cove."

"You can't take my horse from me, Wright. I have to break him. He's going to belong to Walter. I do like that name, though. It's a calming name." She came close to Lee. "You've gotten better at this than I ever expected."

She touched his face and kissed him, pushing her little body against his, running her hand up his shirt. Then, she led him to the fresh hay in the loft. There he released all his pent up sadness over all that had happened back home. But he knew he'd crossed a line, and there was no going back. Nothing good could come from falling for a two-timing woman with a mind of her own.

"You know I'm marrying Walter, but we can have some fun for a while. I'll break *you*." She gave a teasing laugh.

Lee promised himself he would only enjoy Cooper, not become serious, but she stood in his mind all the time, whispering her thoughts. Daddy would have said that once again Lee had chosen the wrong girl. He was nothing but a fun time to her. Cooper would marry Walter so she could have the life she wanted. Lee couldn't give her anything like that.

One day just before the trail ride, Cooper took him to the river for a picnic. She actually wore a pretty yellow dress and spread a fancy blanket on the soft grass. Her eyes were a vivid violet and watched his every movement with total interest. They ate thick ham sandwiches and talked. A flower-scented cloud surrounded her.

"I love this place. I could sleep right here on the ground by the river every night." He watched the water churning, white and foamy, rocks appearing and disappearing in the movement. The rhythm rocked him, loosened his tongue the same as drinking whiskey.

Cooper touched his hand from across the blanket from where

she sat, legs tucked under her, the dress fanned around her. "It is a beautiful place. You are changing me, Wright."

"You changed me." He moved his hand, thinking that would stop the burning from her touch.

"Yes, I know."

"I'm leaving on the trail ride day after tomorrow. I'll be gone for weeks." He never looked at her, couldn't.

"I know. I'll miss you." Her voice caught in the wind. "I don't think Cove will be ready for a trail ride. These things have to move slow. If something happened to Walter's horse, he would be very angry. He can't be your horse, Wright."

The pain caused by her words was worse than a hornet sting.

Lee stood. "Yes, well, I guess I should have known that."

"Now, don't get mad. You can't get attached to the horses."

He looked at her for the first time since the conversation began. "You don't get close to the horses?"

She shrugged. "Of course, but I know they can never be mine. I have to be happy with our time together. That's it."

As he opened his mouth to tell her how he felt about her, a horse charged out of the woods nearby. Walter sat straight in the saddle. Cooper jumped to her feet.

"Well, isn't this cozy," Walter said as he neared them, slowing the horse. "And you, Kathleen, look like a picture."

Lee had never known Cooper's first name, and she didn't know his. "Now don't get all excited," he said.

Walter gave him an expression that Lee knew he also wore at that moment. Both of them fighting for this girl, this ray of sunshine in all the loneliness. What crap was running through his mind.

"I ought to kill you."

"Walter, stop this right now. Wright works with me. Nothing more. And yes, I am dressed like a woman today but that doesn't mean anything. We're having a picnic to celebrate your horse. I named him Cove. What do you think?" She had moved next to Walter, who still sat tall on his horse.

He looked down into her face. "Does this idiot know we're getting married next week?"

Cooper never looked at Lee. "Yes, why wouldn't he?"

Lee took two steps back. His mind twisted and turned. "I'm heading back to the ranch. I've got a trail ride to get ready for."

"Wright, I'll see you at the barn in a little while," Cooper said casually.

Lee gave her a hard look as he swallowed the words he really wanted to say. "Sorry Cooper, boss says no more playing with horses. I've got to work. Take care of Cove. That's a damn clever name."

"Wait," Cooper said.

"I don't know if I believe this shit," Walter said. "You better not be lying to me, Kathleen."

Yes, Lee should have waited. He should have told their whole story. Instead, he walked away.

☙

The next afternoon, Lee approached the Appaloosa out in the pasture. The horse snorted and moved with a side step; the soft gray tail reminded him of a rope. As his wide-brim hat flew off his head, he slung his leg across the Appaloosa's bare back in one smooth movement. For a moment, a sweet time, the horse stood completely still. Maybe it was that simple. Some sweet words, some stroking. The mountains in the distance seemed to move. The long grass rustled in the constant wind. The smell of fresh manure filled the air. Then, the Appaloosa threw back his head, pushed up on his hind legs, and leaped forward in a smooth motion, bucking and jumping, spinning in a circle. Cooper's image passed through Lee's mind as his whole body tossed like a puppet on a string. Hoots and whistles came from a distance. The Appaloosa's front legs kicked out like he was boxing some unseen enemy. Then the horse ducked his head low, and Lee flew forward like a man shot out of a cannon. The ground ran to meet him. He rolled as the horse preformed his dance of freedom and shot out of the fence, heading across the pasture at full speed.

Lee's head pounded.

The Appaloosa cleared the second fence with a fluid jump. Lee stood and brushed at his dirt-coated pants.

Cooper ran from the barn. A group of cowboys gathered and cheered him as he walked up to the fence.

"You'll never work a ranch again!" she screamed.

The cowboys laughed.

"So much for breaking this cowboy." Lee looked at her, took off his hat, and shrugged.

Several of his buddies clapped him on the back as if he'd been gone a long time.

But he just climbed over the fence and walked past them to the bunkhouse to grab his stuff.

ଔ

When Lee slipped off the train in Dayton, Ohio, he had a plan. He found the nearest recruiting office and joined the Navy. America couldn't stay out of the war raging in Europe. After basic training, he got a beautiful deal. He was shipped to Pearl Harbor, Hawaii, where he would be a gunner on the *USS Oklahoma*. He was a little past his nineteenth year and felt like the luckiest man alive.

Chapter 7

Ella Ruth

"Ella Ruth met a nice young man at the ice cream supper the other night," Bell said to Lacy, the colored maid. "He's a sailor too. Wore his uniform. Bid five dollars on her supper. The most Pastor Mitchell could remember a supper bringing."

Ella Ruth grabbed a fresh sugar cookie from the plate on the table. "I'm going for a walk." She tried not to talk to Bell or that crazy Lacy.

Bell sat in a wicker chair by the big window in the kitchen. "Don't be gone long."

"I'll be back when I'm back." Ella Ruth flipped her hair and walked out the door to the sound of Lacy whispering. The colored girl acted like she knew so much. She wasn't but two years older than Ella Ruth and had a child and a husband already. The girl sure wasn't no wise woman as far as Ella Ruth could tell.

CR

Ella Ruth was allowed in for the strict visiting time at the sanatorium. Gert sat on the porch in a straight back wooden chair.

Her face lit up when she saw Ella Ruth approach. "I thought you died or something."

"No ma'am. Worse."

"What happened?" She nodded at the chair beside her. "We don't have but a few minutes. Visiting is short."

"Paul Allen came back for me. He's married again. We're living in the Gap, not far from here. They made me quit my job."

Gert closed her eyes and barely breathed.

"Are you okay?" Ella Ruth whispered.

"I would be a lot better if I could just leave this damn place. I have a nice little house close to the river. You could go ahead and stay there if you want."

Ella Ruth shook her head. "No. That is too dangerous. I don't want Paul Allen to know you're here. No telling what he'd do. He's capable of a lot."

"How do you know that?"

"I just do. He married this woman, Bell, and told me I had to call her mama. She's not my mother."

"Well, of course she's not."

"I met a boy at the ice cream supper the other night. Actually I met two boys, but one of them is a sailor and has money. I told him he could write me. He's stationed in Hawaii. His daddy is the doctor here."

"Dr. White." Gert spat the name. "He's the reason I'm here."

"I hope I can convince Sam to marry me. That way I can get out of Paul Allen's house."

Gert gave her a hard look. "So that's your answer. Get married at what, seventeen?"

"I don't have a lot of choices. I can't live with that man. No telling what he did to my mama."

"I agree with you, but marrying someone isn't the answer. It's more trouble. Look what happened to your mother. You have to find the right person or no one at all." She smiled. "You mentioned another boy."

Ella Ruth looked away. "Buster Wright. He's a troublemaker. His daddy died."

"Yes, Sheriff Wright. I know him or knew him. He was the sheriff when your mama died. He was just starting out and tried his best, but when it came to facing Paul Allen, he didn't have it in him. I didn't fault him for that. Paul Allen scared me too. He scares most people. What's so special about this Buster?"

"He tried to outbid Sam White for my supper."

Gert laughed. "So they are fighting over you. You're more like your mama than you know. Stay away from both of them. You hear me? I'm getting better and they have to let me go soon. When they do, you can come live at my house with me. Maybe we will leave this place for good."

Ella Ruth loved the thought but knew it wasn't something she could count on.

"Don't give me that look. Let me tell you, men are all the same, child. You can line them up across the earth and you'd see different hair, eyes, and body builds, but they're all the same inside. Don't be fooled. Paul Allen and Buster Wright is one and the same. Paul Allen is more honest than most. Everyone has a front row seat to his meanness. He doesn't hide behind a kind look. He worked on your mama, broke her down, made her question herself, accused her of being disloyal, of causing trouble. That's how they are. All of them."

Ella Ruth stayed quiet.

"Anyway, don't keep me wasting our time on that. What do you want to do when you finish school, Ella Ruth?"

"I draw. I love to draw."

Gert's eyes grew watery. "You must keep at it."

"Grandmother Allen said Mama left Paul Allen for another man. But she died. Did she leave me or not? The stories don't go together."

Gert took a deep breath that rattled in her chest. "I hate your father because he preyed on your mother. I hate him because he gave that newborn baby away. He killed your mother and gave away her baby. Could anyone blame her for a choice outside of other people's morals?"

A hum as loud as a thousand bumblebees filled Ella Ruth's head. "I thought the baby died when Mama died. I thought mama died because of childbirth."

"She did, but I never said the baby died. Did I?"

"You mean my brother or sister is still alive?"

"Yes, I think a brother. He would be one year younger than you."

"Where is he?"

"I don't know."

"You said you didn't know anything about it the first time. Now you say this."

"No one could find the baby." Gert frowned. "Paul Allen said he gave the boy away. Who knows? He might have killed the child and hid the body. But he claimed the baby belonged to another man. A man your mother was seeing. I know women make desperate choices when backed into a corner. He had your mother in a corner. This I know."

Ella Ruth stood. "I have to go."

Gert looked sad. "I've hurt you by telling the truth. I'm sorry. I should have kept it to myself. But you deserve to know what happened."

"No, yes, maybe. It's just too much. I don't know what to believe." Ella Ruth left the hospital. She didn't know when or if she'd go back.

CR

Bell sat at the old square table rolling biscuits with thick, tough hands. Lacy glared at Ella Ruth as she walked in the door. The three women seemed stuck in this small kitchen together while the evening sun washed across the room.

"Why are you out of breath?" A ball of dough was between Bell's fingers. "Your walk didn't go well."

Ella Ruth took an apron from the hook by the door. Perfect balls of dough were lined on the baking pan.

"Work is good for the soul, Ella Ruth. Ask Lacy here because she knows. It takes a woman to a better place. We all have our secrets. Don't we Lacy?

"Yes ma'am, I reckon we do."

"You have to work through them or push them down deep inside. Pushing them down kills a person. Stops them from living."

Ella Ruth plunged her hands into the bowl, dough oozing between her fingers, goo sticking to her like glue.

"Flour your hands first, Ella Ruth." Bell laughed.

Lacy shook her head, but her face was softer around her eyes that looked guarded, painful.

Ella Ruth rubbed the soft powder on her hands, dough peeling off like old paint. She formed a ball and then another and another and another.

CR

Ella Ruth stood on the back porch watching Lacy walk down the drive. She looked so big with her second baby. Bell had tried to get her to wait and ride with Paul Allen when he came home. Fear had flashed across the girl's face for half a second. Without thinking much about her actions, Ella Ruth followed Lacy. Maybe she was curious about where she lived, what her husband looked like, but she kept far enough behind and in the shadows to hide like a criminal.

She was about to turn around and go the other way when a truck came whizzing past her. Paul Allen's truck. She stepped over the ditch behind some brush. His voice was loud, full of hatred.

"What you out here doing, Lacy?"

A fluttering took off in Ella Ruth's belly.

"I'm going home to feed my husband and boy. I'm surprised they haven't come looking for me yet. I'm so late." Lacy never slowed her pace.

"You're one of them good coloreds, ain't you, Lacy?" He put the truck in gear and jumped out.

Lacy walked faster.

Ella Ruth walked in the ditch and jumped behind another bush when Paul Allen grabbed Lacy's shoulder.

"I got to tell you that things ain't looking a bit good for Tyler Kurt, Lacy."

Ella Ruth's heart did flips in her chest.

"Let's just talk about this."

Lacy turned to face him and spoke with an even voice. "I don't know what you're talking about, Mr. Allen."

He gripped both of her shoulders. "Well, I'm trying to tell you. I think you know just what I'm speaking of. You ain't a stupid girl. I wouldn't have you working in my house if you were stupid."

The wind picked up and smelled of rain. The road ran straight for another mile and cut a path through the Settlement, the colored part of the Gap. Not one soul would come along this time of day.

Ella Ruth was sure his stare was as cold as a January night, and Lacy had better take heed to the warning it gave.

"I got you a deal."

Lacy never moved. She didn't try to run. She just stared back at

Paul Allen.

"See, my colleagues want to do something about your husband, Tyler, taking all their car business. Everything was fine and dandy until he decided to start fixing engines for himself instead of Bob. That wasn't a bit of a good idea, little girl."

She needed to step out in the road and yell. Something.

"Let's say me and you take care of the problem." His hand brushed Lacy's breast. Ella Ruth thought she might throw up.

"See, they do what I tell them to do. If you go along with me, don't fight none, and just give this away free, I'll keep them boys off your man for now." He cupped his hand around her chin. "But I ain't promising you a whole lot, Lacy. He's got to stop taking white customers. You got to tell him so. If you fight me, I'm going to get what I want anyway, and I'll kill Tyler myself tonight. You know I will." He was close to Lacy's face.

Ella Ruth opened her mouth but closed it. Her knees shook.

"Come on, I knew you'd see things my way." He took Lacy's arm and led her to the truck.

Ella Ruth stood behind the bush long after Paul Allen's truck had turned on the road that led to the quarry. What kind of girl was she? She didn't even help Lacy. Why didn't the girl fight? But Ella Ruth knew that answer already. It was the same reason she never stepped out of the bushes.

Chapter 8

A large bowl of string beans sat on the small wooden table. Each time Ella Ruth broke one, peeling the string to the very end, a fresh garden smell filled the kitchen. She wished she could say she enjoyed the chore, but that would have been a lie. It was one of those rare days when Paul Allen was home, out in the barn, chopping wood for the winter. Fear and nerves hung in the air of the house. Lacy—whom Ella Ruth had a hard time looking at ever since she spied on her— had broken two cups. Bell decided to make a cake and stirred the batter as if she was beating someone to death. Ella Ruth broke each bean into pieces. There was no faster way. One at a time. Lacy moved to a chicken to be carved up for supper. The three women had a couple of things in common, fear and maybe, if the truth was told, a lot of hate for Paul Allen.

"Who is he out there talking to?" Bell titled her head to the side like a barn owl perched on a rafter.

Lacy went to the window to look out. Ella Ruth wondered if she had told her husband what Paul Allen said or did. How could someone keep that kind of secret?

"Who's he carrying on with?" Bell asked.

"Looks like some boy he got to stack the wood he be cutting out there," Lacy said.

Bell slapped the bowl on the table and waddled to the window. "He ain't never used no boy's help here."

Ella Ruth looked over their shoulders as they crowded around the window. "It's Buster Wright."

"Yes it is." Lacy cut Ella Ruth a look.

Ella Ruth shrugged and went back to her beans. "Why would he be here?"

"I don't know. But we need to pour some tea in glasses 'cause here they come." Under her breath Bell added, "That no-good hoodlum has no business here."

Lacy smoothed her hair and took two jelly jars from the cupboard. "You want some lemon with those, Miz Allen?"

Bell frowned. "Don't overdo it."

Ella Ruth's hair hung in wet ringlets around her face; sweat stains marked the old pink blouse she wore. The screen door creaked open. Paul Allen tracked mud on Lacy's clean floor, laughing at something Buster had said. Lacy wrinkled her face and left the jars on the table.

"Buster here has come to take you to some cookout tonight." Paul Allen rarely spoke to Ella Ruth, so she was caught off guard.

"Pour the tea, Ella Ruth," Bell snapped.

Lacy handed her a pitcher, and Ella Ruth poured a good amount in each jar. She handed one to Buster and their fingers touched.

Bell's knuckles were white as she gripped the table's edge.

"You got to give the boy credit for respecting me enough to come ask." Paul Allen chuckled and grabbed a jar of tea, turning it up, splashing it down his chin, wiping it with the back of his hand. "Get me some more tea, girl." He shoved the jar at Lacy, who took the glass, looking at Buster a tad too long.

"I sure would like you to go to the cookout with me tonight. If you don't have nothing else to do." Buster's stare landed on Ella Ruth.

"I got a lot to do here in the kitchen. We're putting up vegetables."

"You mean to tell me you're going to turn this boy down to can green beans?" Paul Allen frowned.

"There's a lot of them." Ella Ruth fought hard to keep the sassy tone out of her words.

"You're going. I give you the night off." Paul Allen grinned at Buster.

Buster frowned.

That is exactly what he got for showing up at her house without a warning. He got Paul Allen.

"Well, I guess that settles it. He says I'm going with you." Ella Ruth released her feelings in her words.

Bell took a breath. Lacy actually gave Ella Ruth a smile.

"You're damn right. You're going," Paul Allen said, a bit too loudly.

Buster gave Paul Allen a long look, and Ella Ruth feared he might start a fight.

"What time are you going to pick me up?" Ella Ruth touched Buster's arm.

He folded his cap in his hand. "I'll be here around six."

"Okay."

"She'll be here waiting, all prettied up." Paul Allen gave his ugly laugh.

Buster nodded. "I'll see you then, Ella Ruth. Thanks for going." He gave a goofy smile and left.

Bell wiped her forehead with the old dishtowel. "Do you have any idea the name that boy has made for himself, Paul?"

Paul Allen looked at his wife for the first time since he entered the kitchen. "Tell me, Bell. I don't know the town gossip." Deep creases formed on his forehead.

Red washed over Bell's face. "Decent folks won't let their girls near him. He's the one who pulled the jailhouse over."

"Lord, woman. It sounds like he has some gumption. His family owns the town. They can't talk against him too loud. Anyway, whoever said we were the decent sort? I don't remember anyone ever talking about me that way." Paul Allen huffed and went to the sink, turning on the faucet.

"There should be rules." Bell began to stir her cake batter, slow, as if she had cement in the bowl.

Paul Allen came over and stuck his finger in the creamy batter, scooping some out and plopping it in his mouth. "I'll leave the rules to you. That's why I married you." He strolled to the door. "I'll be back in time to make sure Ella Ruth goes with Buster." He looked at Ella Ruth. "I want you to dress real nice now." He gave Lacy a harsh look. "Come out to the barn. I got something for you to do." He left.

"What does he want with you, Lacy?" Bell had fear in her voice.

Ella Ruth looked away but not before Lacy caught her look. "He's upset with Tyler and his mechanic business."

Bell's face turned stormy. "I wonder why I mess with Paul. Be careful."

Lacy nodded, wiped her hands on a dishtowel. "There ain't much being careful with men like Paul Allen, ma'am." When Bell turned the other way, she pushed the butcher knife into her deep apron pocket.

God, Ella Ruth prayed she'd kill him. While Lacy was gone, she worked on the beans as long as she could. But she couldn't stop thinking that no girl deserved to fight off a man old enough to be her daddy. "I'll be right back." Ella Ruth left the kitchen without Bell paying her a lot of mind. She couldn't let it happen to Lacy again. This time she'd step up and help her against Paul Allen.

ↂ

"You want me to take that girl off somewhere and dump her?" Lacy said this loud. Ella Ruth stood just outside the barn door to listen.

"Don't take that tone with me, girl." Paul Allen kept his voice quiet but mean all the same. "You can kill this girl for all I care; just don't let her stay in the barn. I won't have her bastard child born here."

Ella Ruth moved to the barn wall and looked through the cracks of the boards.

Some young colored girl was tied to a post. Stripes of blood colored her dirty white blouse.

"I'm taking her, and if you come near her again, I'm telling Miz Allen what you done. I'm telling her that she's having your baby." Lacy's hand was inside her apron pocket. She was so much braver than Ella Ruth could ever dream of being.

Paul Allen slammed a bucket into the wall close to where Ella Ruth stood. "Don't threaten me, girl!" he roared, loud enough for folks all over to hear. "You'll pay for your mouth, Lacy. You take that girl out from here or I'll kill her. And you get off my property and don't come back. You ain't go no job here no more. But it ain't over. You ain't going to get away that easy. You better look behind you all the time."

Ella Ruth slid behind the barn door as Paul Allen stomped toward his truck. When he was safely out of the yard, she stepped into the barn. "I came to help you, but you did fine without me."

Lacy looked up from the girl, now crumpled on the barn floor. "Get on out of here," she hissed. "This ain't some game."

"Didn't say it was. Nobody knows that better than me, seeing how he killed my mama and gave away my baby brother. I won't leave." Ella Ruth knelt beside her. "We have to get this girl out of here before he comes back."

"She's having a baby, fool. How you think we're going to get her out of here. She can't walk."

Ella Ruth turned sick. "I don't know, but I won't let him do this again."

Lacy gave her a funny look. "You talking crazy. Go on back to the house. He'd kill you for sport."

"I won't leave." Ella Ruth stood. They heard a vehicle come to a stop in the yard. "Oh God."

"He's back. He'll kill her, you, and me too." Lacy tried to sit the girl up, but she just flopped back and cried out in pain.

"He's not doing it without a fight." Ella Ruth walked to the door, ready to do battle with the man who was her father. Instead, she saw Buster. "Why are you here again?"

He looked away from the house. "Ella Ruth, I just wanted to say I don't want you to go with me tonight if you really don't want to go. I didn't come here to cause you trouble. Everybody talks about how mean your daddy is. I'm sorry. I know you're only going because he's making you."

Ella Ruth stood straight and pushed out her chest like she just might have to fight him. "I need your help now. We need your truck."

A look of confusion crossed his face, but he came to the barn door. "What's wrong?"

"We have to take this girl somewhere safe now before Paul Allen comes back."

To her surprise, Buster never missed a beat with a question. He pushed past Ella Ruth into the barn. "Move over, Lacy. I'm going to get her."

Lacy stood. Her face was softer. "We can take her to me and Tyler's house. Paul Allen will kill her, Buster. He's said as much. He told me to get her out of here. To dump her somewhere. She's just a girl."

"Who is she?"

"I don't know. She doesn't live in the settlement."

Buster scooped the child against him as if she were weightless and started to the truck.

Ella Ruth followed.

"You stay here, fool," Lacy hissed.

"No. You can't tell me what to do. I won't leave this girl until I know she is okay."

Buster put her in the bed of his truck. She moaned louder.

"God, hurry. Miz Allen is going to hear," Lacy fussed.

"Miz Allen has already heard." Bell stood at the back door. "What is going on?"

Ella Ruth stepped into the back of the truck. "My father, your husband, ordered Lacy to dump this girl somewhere. She's going to have a baby, and he doesn't care if she lives or dies. Said so. He also fired Lacy, threatened her. I'm going with them and you can't stop me."

Bell pulled the door closed behind her. "I'm going to too. Let me in the truck." Bell got in and scooted across the front seat.

"All these white folks on Settle Street is going to cause a stir," Lacy said.

"Get in this truck, Lacy," Bell ordered.

"I can't do that, ma'am. You know it ain't right." Lacy climbed in the back of the truck with Ella Ruth and the girl.

"To hell with what's right." But Bell shut the door.

"You ain't got to tell her about this girl or what you heard. Miz Allen don't deserve it. She knows who he is, but I don't think she understands just how bad he is."

Ella Ruth looked at the girl. "How old is she?"

"I figure thirteen, maybe even twelve. Hey girl. Can you hear me?" Lacy shook the girl.

She didn't move or speak.

"I hate him," Ella Ruth hissed.

"Well that ain't a new feeling. Lots of women do. There ought to be a club or something."

"Put her on the bed, Buster, and get on out of here. Menfolks don't need to be here." Lacy directed him to the small room on the back of the tiny house. There must have been fifty of the small white boxes that looked the same on Settle Street.

The young girl opened her eyes and looked at Buster as he put her down. "You ain't him. Is he here? He's going to kill me."

Lacy cut a look at Ella Ruth.

"I'll go outside and wait. Ella Ruth and Mrs. Allen will need a ride home."

"You can't. The folks around here would be skittish if you're hanging around. Go somewhere and come back in a couple of hours. Lord knows this girl can't keep that baby in much longer."

Buster looked at Ella Ruth. "Okay."

Ella Ruth could tell he didn't want to leave. "Go on."

He smiled. "I'll be back."

"You girls get her undressed," Bell said. She was all business. "Lacy, get us some hot water." She looked at the girl. "How old are you?"

The girl's eyes fluttered open again, and she stared at Bell.

"You're just a baby yourself. How in the world are you going to take care of a baby?"

"I ain't going to live through this anyway." The words came out with pain looped around them.

Ella Ruth softly worked the girl's dress over her head. She didn't even have on undergarments. Blood was seeping out on Lacy's bed.

A bad pain hit the girl, and she screamed out. "Dear Lord in Heaven."

"Lacy," Bell yelled just as Lacy came through the door with water. "I ain't got no time for hot water, Miz Allen. It takes too long to heat."

Bell nodded. "Prop her up on some pillows." Bell looked at the blood on the sheet. "Little too much."

Ella Ruth glanced away. She was useless at this, so she decided to talk to the girl, try to keep her calm. "What's your name?"

The girl looked at Ella Ruth. "Tarie. I live in Asheville with my mama. She don't know I'm here. I thought he might help me. It will kill my mama. She thought I was a good girl. I ain't."

Ella Ruth didn't look at Bell, only at Tarie. "You hush now. There's nothing bad about you. You must be awful scared. I would be and I'm older than you." She touched the girl's hand.

Lacy looked up at Ella Ruth. "It's getting close to time, Tarie. If you feel like pushing, then give it all you got."

A pain hit Tarie, and she grabbed Ella Ruth's hand, squeezing. "It hurts."

"You got to push, sweetie." Bell was at the foot of the bed.

Tarie pushed.

"I see the baby. You have to be strong."

Ella Ruth saw the sheets were solid red. There was no way she was ever going to have a child.

"We got to hurry, Lacy." Bell gave her a purposeful look. "Push, Tarie."

Tarie cried out but her voice was weaker. "I'm going to die. My mama don't even know where I am. I'm going to die."

"Hush up now," Lacy fussed. Tarie let go of Ella Ruth's hand.

"That baby is coming. Come here, Ella Ruth." Bell had a worried look on her face. "You get ready to take this baby from me. There's too much blood. I'm going to have my hands full."

Tarie screamed and pushed.

"The baby is upside down. We got to get it out. You got to push hard, Tarie."

Tarie looked gray. "I can't push no more."

"You got to, girl. You don't give up on me," Lacy yelled at Tarie as blood poured onto the sheet.

Tarie managed to push with a soft cry of pain.

Bell pulled on the baby's feet and eased it out without any more help from Tarie. It was like a little rag doll, so tiny. Bell popped it on the bottom, but nothing happened. She hit the baby again, this time a little harder. Blood pulsed from Tarie. All this took place so fast, in a blink, like a bad dream creeps into the night and leaves almost instantly.

69

Bell handed the baby to Ella Ruth. "Try clearing her mouth. Give her another pat. I've got to save this little girl here." She looked at Lacy. "We need Dr. White, but I don't think he'll come here. Rip those sheets. I'll pack her and see if that will stop all this bleeding. I've only seen this once when I was a young girl."

Tarie opened her eyes. "Did I have the baby? What was it?"

Ella Ruth ran her finger through the baby's mouth. The child was blue and not breathing. "Please live, little girl."

This child would be her sister. Damn Paul Allen. Why was he allowed to live?

"You got a girl, Tarie," Lacy whispered.

"Is she pretty?"

"Beautiful."

Bell ripped the sheets.

"Ah, I hear her crying." Lacy looked at Ella Ruth.

"That baby don't look like him, does she?" Tarie talked so quiet that Ella Ruth barely heard.

"No ma'am. She looks like you, Tarie." Lacy rubbed her head.

"I'm dying, ma'am," the girl said to Lacy.

"I know. Who is your mama so I can go tell her?"

"Mrs. Carleen Lord. You look her up in the phone book. You'll see her. She works real hard and got us a phone for our house. Me dying will kill her. But she'll take the baby. Tell her I want her named Marly after Grandma."

"I will."

Ella Ruth looked into the baby's face. Tiny Marly never even took a breath.

The truck pulled up to the porch outside, and soon Buster stood in the bedroom door.

"This ain't one place for a boy," Bell said.

"Ma'am, no disrespect, but I ain't been a boy since Daddy died. What can I do to help? I made Dr. White come out here. He's not real happy."

"No, son, I'm not." Dr. White stood behind Buster in the door. He took one look at Ella Ruth and then the baby. "Seems like things went the wrong way." He didn't sound mean at all, just settled into

70

the truth. "There are a lot of folks that would say I need to be run out of town for being here." He put his fingers on Tarie's neck. "She's barely got a pulse. You're doing right, Mrs. Allen, but I don't think it's going to help. She's bled way too much. By the time I get her to Asheville, I'm afraid she will have been dead a while. Hand me that baby, young lady."

Ella Ruth passed the baby into his large hands. "She never even took a breath, sir."

"She's too early. Way too early." He looked at Tarie again. "Sometimes when the mamas are so young like this one, that happens."

"Someone beat her." The words came out hard and cold.

Dr. White nodded. "I guess, Miss Ella Ruth, that a lot of people beat on this girl in her lifetime. Makes me sick to my stomach."

There were no words left inside of Ella Ruth.

"Buster, why don't you run these fine ladies home before they are missed." He gave Bell a knowing look. "Mrs. Allen, you might want to clean up in Lacy's kitchen first."

Bell had blood up to her elbows, staining her arms.

"I'm going to sit here with this child until she moves on." The doctor said, placing the baby on Tarie's chest. "Then me and Lacy will find her family. Do you mind helping me with that? I don't think her family will take to me knocking on their door." He kind of smiled.

"Yes sir, I will."

"Come on, Ella Ruth." Buster held out his hand.

She touched his fingers and pulled them away. Her fingertips were cover in dried blood.

He took her hand back. "We got to get you two home."

She nodded.

∝

No one spoke much on the short ride. As Buster neared the drive, Bell held up her hand. "Let us out at the bottom of the drive in case Paul's at home. We will see you this evening. Everything has to stay normal. Paul has done this terrible thing, Buster, and he will make

71

someone pay if he finds out we helped."

Buster stopped the truck. "I'll be back to get you around six, Ella Ruth." He searched her with a long, sorrowful stare.

"Okay. I don't blame you if you don't come." The words fell out of her.

"I'll be here. You can count on me." Buster reached over and opened the door for them.

Bell and Ella Ruth walked up the drive together. Bell looked at her watch. "It's not even lunch."

A lifetime had passed as far as Ella Ruth was concerned. "He's still not here," she noted, looking toward the empty drive.

Bell nodded. "God was looking after us."

Ella Ruth stopped walking. "Maybe, but he sure didn't look after Tarie and her baby."

Bell touched Ella Ruth's arm. "Sure he was. It just wasn't the way you wanted. He took both them girls home to live with him. Neither of their lives would have been worth a plug nickel while Paul was alive." She was quiet a minute. "I've learned a lot about him since that day we came to get you. He's not a decent man. But I won't leave you behind. I'm here as long as you're here."

In those words, Ella Ruth found her first motherly love. And there was no blood connecting them. Maybe blood didn't have a thing to do with any of it.

Chapter 9

Buster knocked on the door at six sharp as he had promised. The afternoon had shimmered around the edges, moving fast and normal as if two lives were never lost. Ella Ruth wore a pale pink dress, belted at the waist and buttoned up the front with small pearls trimmed in gold. Her dark curls threatened to release from the clip she wore. It was Mama's clip that Ella Ruth had found in the old trunk in her grandparents' barn.

Bell tapped on the bedroom door. "Your company's here." Ella Ruth couldn't look at Bell.

"Come on, child and wipe that look off your face or we're doomed."

Ella Ruth stepped into the hall, and Bell looked her up and down. "God help us. You're way too pretty. Now smile, act normal."

Normal. Was she kidding?

Buster stood in the living room surrounded by Bell's bric-a-brac covering the tabletops.

Paul Allen turned to Bell. "I meant to tell you that I fired that girl today. You got to start looking for some more help."

"Okay, Paul."

His face hardened as he looked at Ella Ruth. "We'll talk about my reasons when the young folks leave, but her and her husband have gotten too damn uppity." Paul Allen nodded at Buster. "Now Bell here has to tell you about her rules."

Ella Ruth looked at Bell. Rules. After all they had been through?

Bell picked up the old alarm clock—one of the wind-up kind with bells on top. "This clock is set to go off at ten o'clock. You'd better have our Ella Ruth home in one piece before it quits ringing."

Buster smiled. "That won't be a problem, Mrs. Allen. I'll have her home right after the cookout. It will end a long time before then."

 CR

Outside, Ella Ruth let out a long breath.

Buster opened the door to his truck and helped her into the seat as if she hadn't ridden with him only hours before. "My mama wants to meet you so bad." He closed the door and ran around to his side, jumping behind the wheel. "This is sure different from today and the first time we met. We just don't seem to be able to be around each other in normal situations." He gave her a smile. "If you don't mind me saying, Miss Allen, you are a welcome sight. I think our first child will be a girl and she will look just like you." He gunned the truck backwards.

"No, Mr. Wright, we will have only one child and it will be a boy with sky-blue eyes and dark hair like yours."

He turned left on the road.

"The Kelly's place is back that way."

"I know. I want to show you my secret place. Hell, Ella Ruth, we've been through a lot today. I want you to know something personal about me."

"We should probably go to the cookout. I bet Paul Allen will check."

"Don't worry. I'm on my best behavior. I wouldn't miss wearing you on my arm. I want to show Swannanoa Gap that Buster Wright can get a good girl just like Sam White."

"Sam White never had me, Mr. Wright, and neither do you. I'm not some blue ribbon you won at the county fair."

Buster stretched his arm over the back of the seat, driving with one hand. "Shoot, we're getting off to the wrong start again. I'm always sticking my big foot in my mouth when it comes to girls. I figured you and Sam had to be writing to each other. He's such a better guy than me. I'm sorry."

"He might have outbid you for my supper, but one supper doesn't make him my guy. We did like all the other couples—ate our supper on a blanket and talked. He may be in the Navy, but he isn't very interesting." Ella Ruth thought of what she said to Gert on her visit. "But I have thought he'd make a good husband, a way to leave Paul Allen. I am looking to do that." She stared out the window.

Buster swerved the truck to the side of the road. "You know I'm the family disappointment. I'm sure you've heard about how I almost went to jail. Shoot, you saw me with the bugle in the rafters of the church. And most people have figured out I pulled down the jail-house. I'm not decent husband material."

Ella Ruth opened her door. Dragonfly River rushed and churned. "That river starts on top of Black Mountain. Did you know that? I grew up on the mountain. I've seen the spirit of my mother. Outlaws don't impress me. I'm going down here to the water." She slid off her leather slippers and moved with the grace of a fine animal. "There's a story of a woman who can turn herself into a panther. Have you heard it?"

Buster followed her. "No."

She stepped into the water, which surrounded her feet with numbing cold, splashing her calves. Smooth rocks pressed into the bottoms of her feet. "The story is she takes children, teaches them all she knows. Some say she was colored. Others say she was Cherokee. Either way, she knew magic."

The mimosa trees hung over the water. Their pink feathery flowers fluttered in the breeze.

Buster stood close to the bank with his pants legs rolled up.

Ella Ruth stepped out further, her dress twisted around her thighs. If she had been alone, she would have taken off her dress and swam like when she was young. "I love the water. The sound it makes. I miss not living close to the river."

"I bet it's a different life on the mountain."

"Yes. It was. Did I tell you I draw? That I wanted to go to col-lege for my art?"

He entered the water now and leaned toward her, as if trying to hear her better over the sound of the current. "What do you draw?"

"Mostly places and things that speak to me. Crazy sounding. But hey, my father is crazy. You saw that today."

"I'm okay with that."

She turned and pressed her lips to his, not having any idea how to kiss a boy. He wrapped one arm around her and took over.

Her legs went soft.

He released the clip from her hair in the front. "You're the most beautiful girl I've ever liked, Ella Ruth."

Her cheeks warmed. That's when she lost her footing in the

rushing water, pulling Buster down with her. The shock of the cold took her breath away.

"Look what you've done." Buster laughed. "God, we can't go to a cookout now."

"The old gossips at church would enjoy wagging their tongues about this." Ella Ruth said, standing and wringing out her dress.

"Shoot, they would die and go to Heaven to have another thing against me." Buster got to his feet as well, wiping at his pants as if he could brush the water away. "We just have to ignore the old biddies." He held out his hand.

She took it, moving with him one careful step at a time. "At least you've never had to deal with the folks on Black Mountain," she said. "You think the Gap is bad. People on the mountain don't trust anyone who wasn't born and raised there. You would be called a town boy." She gave a sad smile. "They didn't help Mama, and she needed help real bad. She wasn't from the mountain. Shoot, they would help Paul Allen quicker than her."

They sat together on the flat rocks as the last of the sun stretched over them. "People judge here too, Ella Ruth. Never mistake that. I think Lee ran away because of them and all the talk."

"What talk?" Ella Ruth knew Buster had an older brother who had left town right after their father's death.

He gave her a curious look. "You really haven't heard? I would think you of all people would know."

"Why? I don't know anything." A cool breeze replaced the hot, muggy air. Buster's arm touched hers. Ella Ruth liked how normal it felt to be with him. They had kissed only minutes before, and yet she didn't feel awkward.

"Lee left because of Lacy." He allowed his words to soak the air.

Ella Ruth figured maybe that was why Lacy had watched every move Buster made earlier that day. Maybe she shouldn't even know Lacy's story. Again, it felt like she was spying on the girl.

"He was in love with her," Buster went on, "and that is downright dangerous in a place like this or anywhere in the country. It was stupid. Lacy had been around since we were kids. We played together all the time. No one thought things would turn out like they did. I don't know if Daddy knew the day he died, but I got a feeling he did. I got a feeling Lee told him. If I know my brother, he was planning on running away with Lacy until Daddy died. Then, he just ran. There's been times when I wished I could have just run too."

"I'm glad you didn't." She touched his fingers.

He took her hand and began to tell her about how his daddy fell off the quarry wall, not far from where Ella Ruth lived at the time. He died before he ever knew Buster had blown that fool bugle and stirred up the church Grandmother Allen loved so much. When the lightning bugs began to blink, Buster pulled her to her feet and kissed her again.

"I'm taking you to meet my mama. Okay?" He led her back toward the truck.

Ella Ruth slid her feet into her slippers. "I'm still damp."

"Oh, she'll love you." Buster jumped into the truck beside her. Darkness wove in and out of the trees like a black ribbon as they headed down the road.

ᑳ

The Wrights lived two miles south of town in the biggest house Ella Ruth had ever seen. The windows were lit as if watching them while Buster parked his truck. A white wicker swing moved in the wind. Lush green ferns hung here and there on the large wraparound porch. One day she wanted to live in a house like that.

When Buster helped her from the truck, Ella Ruth began to wonder if she had bit off more than she could chew.

He opened the leaded glass door and yelled at the top of his lungs. "Mama, I got someone you need to meet." He pulled Ella Ruth in the door, and she nearly gasped at the sight of the chandelier hanging in the front hall, its light splintering into a rainbow of colors against the walls.

Mrs. Wright appeared at the top of the polished staircase. Her hair was covered with a bright red scarf, and she wore a robe. As she floated down the steps, she held the banister with one hand. "Buster, what in the world?"

Ella Ruth looked at her shoes, run down, cheap, shabby.

"Come meet Ella Ruth Allen. This is the girl I told you about." His voice echoed through the house. A young teenage girl came to stand on the upstairs landing and gave Ella Ruth a warm smile.

"That's my kid sister, Billie."

"Hi," Billie yelled.

"Now, y'all don't wake up your grandmother." Mrs. Wright stopped squarely in front of Ella Ruth. Her elegance filled the space between them, leaving no extra room. "Nice to meet you, Ella Ruth." She looked back at her son. "Is the cookout over so soon? I thought it went on till nine."

"We stopped off at the river," Ella Ruth explained, the words coming out in a rush. "I've made a mess of my dress and Buster's clothes. I decided to get my feet wet. I lost my footing and, well, you can guess what happened." Finally she shut up.

"Buster probably threw her in, Mama." Billie made a sour face at Buster.

Mrs. Wright glanced up at her daughter. "Thank you, Billie." She looked at her son. "I'm sure he was a willing victim. If I know him, he's the one who went swimming first."

"You know me too good, Mama." Buster laughed, and Ella Ruth could see that Mrs. Wright just melted over it.

"Yes I do."

The hall door squeaked open. Light spilled into space. An old woman tittered her way down the hall. "What's all this commotion, Sue? It's late. Buster, are you in trouble again?"

Buster laughed. "I got someone you need to meet, Granny."

The old woman shuffled closer, wearing a housedress that buttoned up the front. A faded flannel gown hung out from under the dress. Buster took her hand, drawing her into the circle. "This here is Ella Ruth Allen."

Granny Wright took a sharp breath and peered at Ella Ruth, head cocked to the side. Her eyes were covered by a film that looked like cheesecloth. Once, they must have been blue like Buster's. "You any kin to Agnes Allen?" Her voice bounced off the walls.

For a minute, Ella Ruth couldn't get her footing. No one had spoken of her grandparents since she'd left them. "She's my grand-mother."

"That woman never had a lick of sense when it came to that boy of hers. Let him run all over everyone. He tried to run over Frank, but it didn't work. And her poor husband never did anything to stop the both of them. He was way too soft. The worst was when that boy went off somewhere and brought that Yankee girl home. That was nothing but trouble. You're their girl. The Yankee was your mama?" She paused a minute but kept talking before Ella Ruth could say anything. "Your mama was pretty, but you know what they say—pretty is as pretty does." The smell of peanuts hung in the air.

"Mother Wright, I think it's time to go back to your room." Mrs. Wright spoke the words as a mother would to her child.

"You never liked me, Sue. You just put up with me for Frank's sake."

Mrs. Wright shot a smile at Ella Ruth, as if they both under-stood old women and their ways. "Let me help Mother Wright to bed. I'll be right back."

☙

Later, Buster stopped the truck in front of Ella Ruth's house. "I want to see you again." Before she could answer, he jumped out and ran to open the truck door.

"Okay." She allowed him to hold her hand as they approached her front door.

"Sorry about Granny. She can be a bit of a pickle when she wants to be," he said quietly.

"I understand." But Ella Ruth wanted to know what the woman knew about her mama.

Bell sat near the single lamp in the living room, knitting some-thing pale yellow, her fingers working with a rhythm—needles flash-ing in and out of the thread, catching the light. "Cutting it close, aren't you?" The alarm clock ticked on the table. The hands showed nine fifty-five.

Ella Ruth thought of all the blood on Bell's arms. How could she act so normal? How could Ella Ruth have acted like today was any normal day? Was she supposed to forget the girl and her baby?

Paul Allen stirred in the rocker. It wasn't like him to be home on a Saturday night. "You two have a good time?"

"Yes sir," Buster answered. "My mother wants Ella Ruth to come for dinner tomorrow night." He looked at Bell. "I'm sure she will call you, Mrs. Allen."

"Of course she'll go." Paul Allen slapped his knee and stood.

Suddenly, the room filled with a clanging, throwing a panic on Bell's face. She tossed her creation on the table while Paul Allen frowned. Buster knocked over a little whatnot on the table, shattering the glass figure of a raccoon.

With one solid motion, Ella Ruth pushed the button on the clock. Silence replaced the horrible noise.

"See what that damn rule of yours caused, Bell." Paul Allen laughed.

Bell's face turned beet red. "No need to swear."

"You tell your mother Ella Ruth would love to come to dinner." Paul Allen crunched the remaining pieces of glass under his boots.

"You're stepping on my raccoon," Bell fussed.

"Damn thing is broken anyway."

"I'm so sorry, Mrs. Allen. I'll get you a new one."

Ella Ruth had to look away. Buster was like a rainbow on a stormy day. If nothing else, he made her smile. And after the day they'd had together, that was a marvelous feat.

Chapter 10

The next morning, Ella Ruth woke with the baby on her mind. The sad little girl with blue skin, limp in her arms, who wouldn't come to life. The little head, so fragile, pressed in the crook of her arm and weighing little more than a feather. This little girl had been part of her, with genes from a father neither baby or Ella Ruth wanted. There hadn't been one breath, not one. And Ella Ruth saw this as a murder committed by Paul Allen. The facts ached in her body with real pain, a disease eating up her clear thoughts.

The gray fall light seeped into her room. She thought about how Paul Allen never had to pay for what he did.

She tiptoed down the hall and tried to open the cupboard drawer without a squeak. Paul Allen was still home, his truck parked in the yard. She chose a long, thin knife. One she happened to know was sharper than the others. The knife was heavier in her hand than the baby had been. She tucked it between the folds of her nightgown.

Her footfalls were like a ghost gliding from room to room. The door opened with complete silence. Two forms were visible. Paul Allen slept on his back with his mouth open. As she moved to the bed, Buster slid through her mind like the smell of lilacs caught in the spring air. She almost turned around. Bell shifted. A board groaned under the pressure of Ella Ruth's foot.

Bell sat straight up. "What are you doing?" She spoke so soft Ella Ruth had to read her lips.

Ella Ruth began to shake.

Bell eased out of bed and met Ella Ruth in the middle of the room, turning her to face the door and leading her out. When they were safely in the kitchen, Bell looked at Ella Ruth's hand. "What have you got, child?"

Ella Ruth tried to put the knife behind her back.

"Did you think you could kill him and walk away, Ella Ruth?"

"The baby." She could think of no other answer.

Bell looked terribly sad as she placed the knife on the kitchen counter. "Ah Ella Ruth, there's no telling how many babies there are. Do you think this is his first time doing something like this?"

And of course Ella Ruth knew better. She had seen him force Lacy in the truck.

"No."

"Is he worth losing your own life? They would put you in the electric chair. Then me being here with him would have been for nothing."

Ella Ruth looked away. "I just keep seeing that poor baby. I think he did something bad to my mother."

Bell took a deep breath. "You may be right, but killing him makes him win, Ella Ruth."

"How? At least he couldn't hurt another person."

"Yes, but you couldn't go on and make something of yourself, be that artist you want to be."

Ella Ruth gave Bell a quick look.

"You left your drawing book on the bed one day. I couldn't help myself. You're good. Don't let that man take the one good thing your mama left behind."

That made a lot of sense. "My mother's sister is in the sanatorium with tuberculous. When I worked there, I met her. She told me Paul Allen took the baby boy my mama had when she died and gave it away. I have a brother somewhere."

"All the more reason to do something with your life, Ella Ruth. Don't be like him. He's the one who would kill to answer a problem."

"You're right."

Bell relaxed. "Yes ma'am. I am right. You think about what you can do to get away from here. What about the aunt?"

"She wants me to live with her when she gets out. But I don't know when she will be well enough."

Bell nodded. "What else can we do?"

"I want to go to Black Mountain College. It's for artists and not too far from here. That's what I've wanted to do for a long time."

"Well of course you do, but Paul will not allow it. A girl in college. Ella Ruth, you know better. And don't start thinking about killing him again. What about that Buster? He's a nice boy, not at all like others have gossiped."

"Buster is kind and I like him a lot, but why does a boy have to be my answer? I don't want to get married. Look what happened to Mama and, no offense, Bell, but look what happened to you."

Bell smiled. "I don't take no offense, sweetie, but you're going to learn that a woman has to have a man. She can't get on in this world without one."

"That's not fair."

"No it isn't, but it's the truth." Bell walked to the refrigerator. "Time to cook breakfast." She looked at Ella Ruth. "Give Buster a chance. I can't believe I'm saying that, but he's a good boy."

Ella Ruth liked Buster a lot, but there had to be more to life.

☙

Two days later, along with the first cold spell, word came that Lacy had her baby, a fine boy.

"He be a little early but still just as healthy looking," Sarah said. She had come to take Lacy's place with helping Bell. She was a quiet spirit, even to a fault. Bell said she was perfect and might not draw as much attention from Paul Allen as Lacy had.

Ella Ruth missed Lacy. This surprised her, but in a lot of ways it made perfect sense. They were both around the same age, and it wasn't like Ella Ruth had any girls to hang out with. Here she was, seventeen years old with nothing to do. So that morning she set out, walking to the small house on Settle Road. Finding the house wasn't hard, seeing how she could never forget what happened there.

She tapped on the front door. In her hand she held a plate of chocolate chip cookies she had made the afternoon before. The house was silent. The street was empty. She knocked louder.

"Who is it?" Lacy's voice called.

"Me, Ella Ruth." Her cheeks heated. This was a stupid idea.

The door creaked open and Lacy stood holding a baby wrapped in a blanket. A boy of about two clung to her skirt. "What are you doing here?"

"I'm sorry. Sarah said you had your baby. I wanted to come check on you. I brought you cookies." Ella Ruth held the plate out.

"Girl, get in here off my front porch. You're going to start up some real talking." She pulled the door open wider. "Does Miz Allen know you're here?"

"Well, I am grown. I don't have to tell her everywhere I go."

Lacy shut the door behind Ella Ruth. "White folks don't come to colored folks' houses, Ella Ruth. Was you born in a barn or something? You could get in real trouble and cause me trouble."

"I'm sorry. I'll go." Ella Ruth turned to leave.

"You might as well sit for a while since you're here now. Take Tyler's chair." She nodded to a worn green velvet chair with a footstool.

Ella Ruth wanted to leave, but she sat down. "I wanted to check on you and that new baby. Sarah said you had it a few days ago."

"The day after the other baby was born."

Ella Ruth nodded and smiled at the toddler, silently wondering about his lighter skin. "Can he have a cookie?"

"This here is Tucker. He's my first boy." Lacy gave him a soft smile. "Yes, he can have one. Did you go out with Buster?"

Tucker took the offered cookie and grinned as he bit down.

"Yes. We went out. He took me to meet his mama. His grandmother is a piece of work."

Lacy adjusted the baby, still wrapped in the blanket, and hooted out loud. "You know it, girl. She used to make me want to cry, but I wouldn't give her the satisfaction. My mama still works for them. I've tried to get her to quit, but it's all she knows. Hell, I don't even have a job now." She stopped talking.

"The old woman started talking about how my grandmother let Paul Allen be who he was. And all that was true. I just don't want to hear about it."

"I can understand that."

Ella Ruth looked at the baby. "Can I see him?"

Lacy studied her for a minute. "Sure. His name is Mile." She brought the baby and placed him in Ella Ruth's arms.

"He's beautiful." And she told the truth. The baby had dark curls all over his head. His face was fat and peaceful. Ella Ruth prayed that this image would replace the other memory of the blue baby.

"This be pretty good." Lacy ate one of the cookies on the plate.

"Did you make them?"

"Yes."

"You're getting pretty good but you got to be thinking about leaving there, Ella Ruth."

"I know." She loved how warm the bundle of boy felt in her arms. "I tried to kill him this morning." She let the words settle in the room.

Lacy blew cookie crumbs out of her mouth. "Oh my God. What did you do?"

"I woke up thinking about that baby of Tarie's and I took one of the knives from the kitchen. Bell caught me near the bed. She made me leave the room. Told me he wasn't worth it." Ella Ruth looked at Lacy. "She knows all about him. Said she was going to leave when I did." She rubbed Mile's soft cheek with her fingertip. "Told me to get serious about Buster. Now she likes him."

"Buster is good, not like his stupid brother." Lacy spit out the last part of the sentence.

"I don't want to get married."

"Neither did I, but I ended up that way."

"Don't you love your husband?"

Lacy got another cookie, along with Tucker. "Love, girl. What the hell is love? I owe Tyler a lifetime. That's for sure. But love is for fools."

Ella Ruth shrugged.

"Oh I know you don't believe me but it's true. I was on my way to the river, the deep part, to put myself out of this world. All that happened right after Lee left. Stupid fool call himself loving me. Told me he'd be right here by my side and I wouldn't have to go through anything alone." She gave Ella Ruth a mean look. "He was some kind of a liar."

"What happened, Lacy? Were you going to kill yourself?"

Lacy looked out the one window in the small room. "Yes ma'am I was. Until Tyler came along and told me he wanted to marry me. He knew everything. I didn't have to make up no lies for him. I wouldn't have. He told me that boy there, Tucker, belonged on this earth even if his daddy ran off. Said he'd marry me and raise him as his own. Told me love was silly but friendship was the best. And he's right."

Ella Ruth took in all the information and looked at Tucker's face. "Friends are good, Lacy."

"You're smart for not wanting to get married, but it won't last. You'll need a man. Might as well be a good one. Buster is good."

"I know he is. I figured that out the first time I saw him in the rafters of that church playing a trick on the pastor. He was defending his best friend's father."

"Larry Mitchell? Now you put them two together and ain't nothing they won't do. Larry is younger too, but he's the influence, the boss, not Buster. Larry's got a streak of trouble down his back. Always has since he was little. It was like he was born with it. He's made his preacher daddy a patient man."

"I've only seen him around. I don't know him."

"Oh, you will if Buster's going to court you. Larry is sweet on Billie, Buster's sister. They're always sneaking around seeing each other. I don't think Buster or Mrs. Wright knows. Lord, what white kids won't do."

Ella Ruth wanted to point out maybe Lacy had done some of the same stuff with Buster's brother, but she kept her mouth shut. The baby started grunting and wiggling.

"Here, he's getting hungry." Lacy stood and held out her hands.

Ella Ruth handed him to her. "He's beautiful. Thank you for letting me hold him."

"Thank you for coming to visit me, Ella Ruth. I ain't never had a white woman care that much. But don't tell no one I said that."

"I won't." Ella Ruth laughed and stood. "Give some cookies to your husband if there are any left." She pointed toward Tucker, who pushed another cookie into his mouth. So this boy was Buster's nephew. She wondered if he knew.

"Here, I'll go get one of my plates to put them on." The baby began to wail.

"No, I'll come back and get the plate another day. Maybe I can visit these boys again." Ella Ruth smiled.

"Sure. Okay. Just don't let Paul Allen know. It would be hell for both of us."

Chapter 11

Buster Wright

1941

Buster was in love. He knew this when Ella Ruth pulled him down in the river that fall night the year befor. She wasn't only beautiful, she was smart. They saw each other as much as he could convince her. Paul Allen approved of him. Even Ella Ruth's stepmother had fallen for him, but Ella Ruth was another story. Half the time she acted like she didn't give a dern if Buster was around or not. But she never turned him down when he asked her out.

The truck idled in front of Paul Allen's house. Buster had taken a risk, did something personal, and if Ella Ruth didn't like it, he would give up and call it quits. He climbed out of the truck and went to the back door, giving it a tap.

Ella Ruth opened the door with a smile on her face. "Goodbye, Bell."

"Have fun, you two," Mrs. Allen called from inside the house.

"What have you got planned for this Saturday night?" Ella Ruth asked, nearly skipping to the truck.

"Why are you so happy?" He opened her door.

"Can't a girl feel good, Mr. Wright?" She gave him a wink.

"Yes." He closed the door and went around the truck. She was never that giddy. Something wasn't right. He got in, put the truck in gear, and turned it around.

Ella Ruth hummed.

"What is going on?" He gave her a quick look.

"I have a surprise," she said with a laugh.

"I have a surprise too." He smiled. But then he thought maybe it wasn't a good time to mention it. She was way too happy.

Ella Ruth tilted her head to the side. "What kind of a surprise?"

"You go first." He tried to keep the nervousness out of his voice.

"It's so great. I told you about Gert, my aunt—it's so strange calling her my aunt—anyway, she is getting out of the hospital, and I can live with her if I want. I don't have to live with Paul Allen anymore. Also, she's going to help me go to Black Mountain College. You know, because I love art. It's all too scary. Please don't breathe a word. Paul Allen would kill her. He may still try when I leave."

"Huh, you know he won't have it, Ella Ruth." Part of Buster didn't want anything to do with her moving in with her aunt. After all, the woman had been sick. And aside from that, what if Ella Ruth went to Black Mountain College and met someone else?

"I know, but I'm going to do this anyway, Buster. I have to learn more about my mama. Gert knows. And I could be with someone who loves me." Her voice kind of broke.

He swallowed. Didn't she understand how much he loved her? Maybe not. He was always trying to act like nothing bothered him, and it's possible he hadn't made his feelings clear enough. "Maybe it will work out. When does she get out?"

"Tomorrow." She looked at him. "I know. It was fast. I only heard late yesterday when I went to visit her. I could hardly sleep last night. I'm trying not to get too excited, but God, do I want out of there."

"I hope you get what you want."

"You don't sound happy for me." Ella Ruth studied him like she always did, as if she was looking for a reason not to like him anymore.

"I am. It's just a lot to find out at once. I mean, how will I see you at the college?"

"It's not that far, silly. Only up the road. And I haven't gotten in yet." She said this with such confidence that he knew she would get in, and so did she.

"Things always have a way of working out." Suddenly, he began to regret the whole evening. All his plans.

"So what are we doing?"

The sun was still above the trees. The air was crisp with the edge of winter creeping in. "I brought a picnic and thought we could have it before dark by the river. At our place." He didn't dare look at her for a reaction.

"How wonderful, Buster. I love it. Is there a special occasion?" Her voice sounded teasing and light, so unlike the Ella Ruth he was used to, the one with the cloud around her.

"You'll see." He turned down the road that ran beside the river.

"You said you had a surprise." She actually giggled.

"Only if I get a kiss."

She folded her arms over her chest and stuck out her lip. "That's not fair."

"It is to me." He laughed and pulled the truck onto the shoulder of the road. "Where do you want to eat?"

"Let's take the blanket and food down to the rocks. Don't you think?" She smiled at him.

He would do anything she wanted, but he couldn't say that. He had to be the man. "That is what I was thinking."

"Don't forget my surprise." She jumped out of the truck.

"Don't forget my kiss," he shot back, laughing.

"I won't."

The bag with the art kit and paper was hidden behind the seat. He pulled it out. "The supper was made by Billie. God help us. But she promised she knew what she was doing. I couldn't do any cooking."

"What about the cook, Lacy's mama?" Ella Ruth grabbed the picnic basket from the back of the truck.

"Lacy's little boy is sick and she needed help getting him to Asheville."

Ella Ruth stopped and looked worried. "Which one? Mile or Tucker? Is he okay?"

Buster watched her a minute. "You've been seeing a lot of Lacy. Your daddy wouldn't like that."

Her cheeks turned red. "I don't give a damn. She's my friend. You're friends with Tyler."

"Yep, but my daddy ain't the biggest colored hater this side of the Mississippi. You got to think about Lacy. If he found out, it would be worse on her than you."

She hung her head. "I know. But I'm really careful. And she likes me coming."

"Well, come on, then. We aren't going to ruin our date with that talk. And Tucker's the sick one, but he's going to be fine. Lacy's protective of both her boys. She can take care of them."

Her face lit up. "Thank you, Buster. You're too good to me."

"I know." He grabbed the blanket out of the back and slung it over his arm to hide the bag of art supplies.

They sat on a big flat rock where the evening sun warmed them.

"These chicken salad sandwiches are divine, Buster."

"Don't tell me. Billie made them. They are better than I thought, but a little sissy if you ask me. Men don't eat chicken salad sandwiches."

Ella Ruth blew a mouthful of lemonade into the air. "Tell me, Buster Wright, what do men eat on a picnic with their girlfriends?"

He thought of the manliest food he could think of. "Barbecue with lots of sauce. Corn on the cob."

She laughed. "I guess that is more manly. I'm not sure why." She nodded at the bag hanging out from under the blanket. "Is that my surprise?"

"Do you have my kiss?"

"You have sissy chicken salad breath." She wrinkled her nose.

He pulled her to him. "Give your man a kiss."

And she did. Her kisses erased his thoughts. She, as usual, was the first to pull away. "I want my surprise."

"Here." He handed her the bag.

"What's in here, Buster Wright? It can't be some silly necklace or earrings. It's too big."

He started to wonder if he'd bought the wrong thing.

"Oh no." She pulled the art kit and paper out on her lap. "Oh my."

"I can get a necklace."

"Buster Wright, are you crazy? This is beautiful." She pulled on the gold latch of the art box. "The wood is so nice. This was expensive."

"Yes," he admitted.

"Look at the charcoal and graphite pencils and watercolors. Oh Buster, this is the best gift I've ever received in my life. It really is."

"I know how much you love drawing." He looked away from those brown eyes.

She touched his arm. "I love you for this."

He looked back at her, drinking her in. "I love you, Ella Ruth Allen." And there were the words he had promised he would never say first.

Her cheeks turned red. "I love you too, Buster Wright. And that scares me to death." She laughed.

He laughed and kissed her again.

On the way home, all he could think about was Ella Ruth moving in with her aunt and going to college. As much as he loved her, he didn't want anything to mess up their relationship. But if he said something, she would think he was trying to keep her from going to art school. Maybe he was. Would that make him horrible? He wanted her to be in love with only him. But she loved art too. And at this point, he wasn't sure which one she loved more.

ʒʆ

The problem of Ella Ruth moving out to her aunt's house fixed itself. Her aunt had a setback, and the doctors ordered her to stay in the hospital at least through the holidays. And little did Buster know that by then life would swing in a whole new direction.

Chapter 12

Thanksgiving night, right after Buster dropped Ella Ruth at home, the biggest ice storm ever to hit Swannanoa Gap came barreling over the mountains and froze everything.

Restlessness took over Buster, making the ice that coated the trees and roads seem like nothing. Folks had problems. One of the big oaks came crashing through the middle of Widow Porter's house. Thank goodness she was in her bedroom on the other side. Buster and all the able-bodied men went to help remove the tree. That's what folks did in a small town, helped each other. Widow Porter was invited to stay in the extra bedroom near Granny Wright. And Lord, she didn't like that one bit. Granny and Widow Porter had an ax to grind, but no one seemed to know what the problem was.

All Buster could think about was Ella Ruth just out of town, frozen in solid. He wanted to touch her, make sure she was okay. He didn't dare voice any of this, especially to Larry, even though lately his friend spent more time with Billie than with Buster. Damn, how had all this love stuff happened? Somehow he and Larry were turning into their dads. They should go out and raise some roofs. But when the ice thawed some and Buster made the suggestion, Larry told him he had a date with Billie. That was the first time he outright admitted to liking Buster's own sister.

"Are you kidding me, Larry?"

"Don't act like you didn't know. Hell, you've had your ass with that Allen girl every minute since the first time you guys went out. You might as well marry her."

Those words hit him as hard as any rock. "I ain't the marrying type." But he knew he was. "I don't commit." Sure he would—to Ella Ruth.

Larry laughed. "You're a fool. Everyone knows you love her. Hell, even she knows you love her. I can love who I want, too."

"God, that hurts my ears." Buster covered his ears with his hands.

"Get used to it. When Billie and me are old enough, I'm marrying her. That is the way it is. I turned seventeen last week."

"God."

"Shut up."

"Gladly." Buster got in his truck and drove to Tyler Kurt's gas station over at the end of Settle Road.

"You look like a homesick dog, Buster. What's wrong with you? Is Ella mad at you?" Tyler frowned, then put his head back under the hood of someone's car. He was damn good at fixing cars. Without giving it a lot of thought, Buster had suggested that Tyler could repair Paul Allen's truck when the transmission went out. Later, he realized that when Mr. Allen asked him if he knew anyone, it was a trick question. Paul Allen had only given Buster a mean grin when he told him about Tyler.

"Why's everything got to be about a girl?" Buster's words came out tough.

Tyler stepped back from the car. "Excuse me, but it's always about girls. Believe me, I know." He laughed.

"It's this damn ice. I hate it. I feel like a caged animal. But there's something in the air too. Can't you feel it?"

Tyler shrugged and picked up another tool. "I feel the cold-ass temperatures."

"I guess. Listen, you need to know that I told Paul Allen he ought to bring his truck over here to you. He didn't like it one little bit. So watch out. He's a hard one to figure."

Tyler straightened again. "If you're colored, he ain't hard to figure at all. We know what he's about. He's bad news in a scary way. Lacy had a run-in with him. Lost her job because she threatened to tell Mrs. Allen what he was doing with colored girls when that girl turned up here having a baby. And Lord knows what he's done to hurt Ella Ruth. She's pure good. I can tell you that, Buster. You need to keep her."

"She don't love Paul Allen at all. He's messed with her mind, that's for sure. She swears he killed her mama, and I believe she might be right. She's a hard one to figure too. I never know what's going on in that head of hers."

Tyler hooted. "You ain't never going to know any of that, Buster. Women are hard to know. Us men, we keep things simple, but them girls mix up all the feelings on the planet and throw them in a big old pot for us to search through. It ain't no fun, and we always lose if we try to pick one of them out."

"Are you glad you married Lacy?"

Tyler smiled. "I never question that. She's the best thing that happened to me. Look at all this. It's all for her and Tucker, and now little Mile. She gives me a reason to work."

Buster nodded. "I always thought I'd leave the Gap. But since Ella Ruth came along, I ain't itching to go so much. And the thing is, that girl would go somewhere else in a heartbeat. She's got wandering blood, and she don't even know it. She's quiet and broods a lot. Most of the time she doesn't need a soul."

"She might need you more than you reckon. And you need a woman to walk through your life with. They all brood like the rest of us. They just pretend they don't. Some of them act happy all the time, but me, I'd rather have the truth. Most people aren't happy that much. Men complain and find so much fault at times, why would women want us to know their true feelings? We might just use it against them."

"I ain't like Lee, Tyler."

He looked at Buster. "Where did that come from? I'm glad you're not, though. See, I figure you're smart, Buster, and you've put two and two together. You know all about Tucker, who he belongs to. But as a friend, I'm asking you to keep that to yourself. Me and my family are right happy. Marry Ella Ruth and don't look back. That's my advice. You'll be a hell of a lot happier than Lee is right now. He'll always wonder what happened back here. You, well, you lived it, Buster."

95

Chapter 13

The dining room was decked out like they were having Thanksgiving all over again. Even the tablecloth and candles were on the table. It was Granny Wright's eighty-fifth birthday. Ella Ruth looked pretty next to the lace on the tablecloth, like she was meant to wear some. Of course, if Buster were to tell her this, she would frown. Maybe he'd give her lace on Christmas.

Larry was sitting next to Billie, who tried to act mature like Ella Ruth. One chair sat empty. Part of Buster wanted to pull it away from the table, but Granny Wright would have a fit.

As if the old woman could read his thoughts, she looked at the chair. "I wish I could see that boy one more time before I die."

Ella Ruth folded her hands in her lap and watched them all. She didn't care for Granny Wright, and Buster couldn't blame her much. It was like Granny Wright knew just the right things to say to get under Ella Ruth's skin.

"I don't even remember what Lee looks like anymore." Billie glanced at Mama.

"I don't think that's a face nobody could forget," Larry said with a laugh. "Lord, he gave us so much trouble."

Mama frowned. "If you boys behaved, no one would have given you trouble."

"He'll come back one day. I feel it in these old bones." Granny Wright wiped at her eyes with a napkin.

"I wonder where he is right now." Billie looked over at Larry.

"You never know. Maybe he's eating dinner just like we are. Having a good time with some family that has taken him in."

"Nobody made him leave." Buster almost yelled it.

Mama gave Buster one of her "shut your mouth" looks. "Close your eyes, all of you," she said, but her stare was still on Buster. "Now picture Lee the last time you saw him. Think good thoughts and send them to him."

Buster couldn't manage to bring Lee into his mind. He didn't want to. Instead, he thought of Ella Ruth.

No one at the table spoke for the longest time. Finally, Granny

Wright started talking about Mrs. BoBo as if she hadn't mentioned Lee.

When it was time to take Ella Ruth home, Buster stood. Granny Wright took Ella Ruth's hand and pulled her close, whispering.

"Granny Wright, we got to go. Ella Ruth needs to get home." Buster patted her shoulder and smiled at Ella Ruth, who was doing her best to keep from laughing. He waited until they were in the truck before he asked her what Granny Wright had said.

"She told me I would have been a good match for Lee. She said I was perfect for him. That he would appreciate a girl who could speak her mind. You, on the other hand, need a girl who stands in the background. That doesn't sound like me, Buster."

Her face was lit up by the dashboard, and Buster made a quick decision. "I'm taking you somewhere."

"Don't forget I have to be home soon."

"Don't worry." He drove to the old quarry and shut off the engine. The cold filtered in through the cracks. Night surrounded the truck. It was so dark he thought he might be in another world. He pulled Ella Ruth to him. Her kisses were magic, stopping time. He tried something new, running his hand down into her blouse, touching the warm, smooth flesh. A warning bell went off somewhere in the back of his mind, but he'd never been too much on warnings. A current shot through him. He worked at Ella Ruth's buttons one at a time, kissing her neck. She seemed to be enjoying herself too, so he moved his kisses over her body.

"Wait, Buster, we shouldn't be doing this."

In one smooth movement, he was on top of her. A wave roared through his head and he found the movement like a familiar dance. At some point, she kissed him hard on the mouth as he pushed into her. The tide went out, leaving him limp. He had to hold on tight to keep from drowning.

"I love you, Ella Ruth."

She only breathed.

"You're mine." He kissed her again. "I didn't hurt you too bad, did I?"

He couldn't see her face, but she was arranging her clothes. "I need to go home, Buster."

Buster buckled his belt and straightened up. "I love you, Ella Ruth. This was a good thing."

Still, she didn't speak.

They rode home in silence. When he pulled up to her house, he touched her shoulder. "I'll see you in the morning at church. And Ella Ruth, we're going to have a great future together."

"We'll see." She got out of the truck and ran in the door. He told himself she was just being shy.

God, he loved her.

ᘒ

Buster was stunned when she never showed up for church the next morning. What was going on? Mrs. Allen never missed church. He was so stupid. After what happened last night, he should have made the effort to pick her up. They were a real couple now. He had plans. But what if she didn't feel the same way?

Preacher Mitchell went to stand in front of the pulpit.

Buster looked around one more time to see if Ella Ruth had made it.

Preacher Mitchell looked pale and stammered as he began to speak. What he said put the congregation on their feet, crying. Buster left the church without explaining anything to Mama.

When he pulled the truck in front of Ella Ruth's house, Paul Allen walked toward him from the barn. "What's got into you, boy? You came up the drive on two wheels."

Buster didn't answer; instead, he knocked on the door.

Mrs. Allen opened it. "Ella Ruth is sick this morning, Buster."

"Excuse me, Mrs. Allen." Buster pushed past her.

"Buster." Mrs. Allen sounded put out.

Ella Ruth sat in a chair at the table. She frowned at him. "You're here, so I guess we need to talk."

"Have you heard?" He yelled past her words.

"Heard what?" Mrs. Allen sounded angry.

"What's wrong with that boy?" Paul Allen complained from the doorway.

"Buster," Ella Ruth said, "let me get dressed and we can go somewhere and talk."

He hadn't noticed she was wearing a flannel nightgown. He wanted to take her by the shoulders and shake her. "The Japs bombed Pearl Harbor! We're at war, Ella Ruth. There are so many people dead, and not all of them are soldiers."

Mrs. Allen clutched her heart. "Oh my sweet, sweet Lord."

Paul Allen stood in the room with nothing to say.

"They're calling for all able-bodied men to sign up. I want to marry you, Ella Ruth. You're the only girl for me. I want to know you're my wife while I'm at war." He dropped to his knees. "I don't have a ring, but I'll get one. Will you marry me?" He took her hand.

"Yes." But there was no smile on her face. It was as if she felt obliged to do what was right.

Buster stood. "Let's go tell Mama. We have to get married as soon as we can. We could get Preacher Mitchell to marry us tomorrow. I don't know when I'll ship out."

Ella Ruth followed him to the truck. Mrs. Allen stood in the door and watched them leave.

***

Mama, Billie, Larry, and Mrs. Allen stood together in the church. Paul Allen didn't bother to show up at his own daughter's wedding. This didn't surprise anyone there. Buster fidgeted. Preacher Mitchell stood before Buster and Ella Ruth.

Mrs. Allen stepped over to the piano and began to play the wedding march softly.

"Do you, James Franklin Wright, take Ella Ruth Allen to be your lawfully wedded wife?" Preacher Mitchell used Buster's legal name, Daddy's name. He smiled nervously.

Did he know why he was doing this?

"I do."

CR

Mama insisted on making a big celebration dinner before Ella Ruth and Buster left for a night in Asheville. While they sat around the table, even Mrs. Allen, someone pounded on the kitchen door.

"Goodness, who could that be at supper time?" Mrs. Wright stood. "Excuse me."

Ella Ruth had been quiet through most of the afternoon, but she gave Buster a smile when he looked at her. Weddings were supposed to be more fun. Happy.

"Buster, could you come here?"

It was dark outside, and Buster knew that if he and Ella Ruth were going to make it to Asheville, they needed to leave. With a sigh, he went to the door to see what was going on.

Carter Sims, Tyler's right hand-man at the station, stood there on the stoop. "Buster, there's trouble. I didn't know who to come get but you."

"What's wrong?"

"Come in," Mama said.

But Carter didn't budge. "They come and got Tyler a few minutes ago. Lacy is beside herself."

"What do you mean?" Mama asked.

"Let's go." Buster didn't even have to think. "Mama, get Larry. Tell Ella Ruth there's an emergency at Tyler's house. If I tell her, she's going to try and come. Her and Lacy are friends."

Mama frowned. "Buster."

"Don't, Mama. This is what Daddy would do."

Her shoulders dropped. "Yes, I know."

Larry followed Mama back to the door. "What's wrong?"

"The Klan has Tyler. Came to his house, burned a cross in his yard and everything," Carter said in a rush.

"Let's go." Buster turned back to Mama. "Tell Ella Ruth I'm sorry."

"She won't be happy. No matter the good excuse, a woman doesn't want to be set aside on her wedding day." Mama gave Buster a look.

"She'll understand." But he knew she wouldn't. She'd want to be right there with him helping. This was starting things off on the wrong foot.

Lacy held Mile in her arms as she paced her front room. Tucker made every step with her, like a little soldier.

"You got to tell me exactly what happened. I don't know what to do." Buster felt pretty helpless.

She stopped. "They busted down the kitchen door, wearing their white sheets. One of them knocked me on the floor and put his boot on my throat. I'd know his voice anywhere. This has been coming for months. He warned me that he was going to punish Tyler for taking white customers." She looked at Buster. Her bottomed lip trembled. "He took me to the quarry and had his way with me. Last year, I was pregnant with Mile. He told me that arrangement would work for a while."

"Who?" Buster's mind was racing.

"Paul Allen." But it wasn't Lacy's voice.

Buster turned and Ella Ruth stood in the front room.

"Did you think you could just leave me at your mother's when my friend was in trouble?" She pushed past Buster and wrapped her arms around Lacy and Mile. "I wished I had killed him, Lacy. I should have killed him."

"Yes." Lacy sobbed.

"Tell me where Tyler is, Lacy." In the corner was a large, dark puddle. Buster's stomach turned sick. "We got to get you and the kids out of here."

Ella Ruth took Mile from Lacy and grabbed Tucker's hand. "Where to, Buster?" Her tone was mean. She was angry but not because he came to help. Why? Maybe at this moment she was angry at all men.

"They took Tyler. They shot him in the stomach but he was still alive. They took him. God help me, they took my Tyler." Lacy was beside herself.

Lacy's mama pushed in the door. "I just heard, Lacy Renea. What has happen here? What's that cross burning in your yard for?"

"Mama." Lacy crossed the distance between them.

"What are you doing here, Mr. Buster? You just got yourself married. Why you here at my Lacy's house?"

"I want to find Tyler. The Klan took him."

"Shot him, Mama," Lacy sobbed.

"Mr. Buster, you go on back home. You know and I know you ain't one to go Klan hunting. He's gone and there ain't nothing any of us can do." She looked into the face of her daughter. "You know he's dead. Can't you feel it? I can."

"Don't say such things to her," Ella Ruth cried, holding the children closer. "There might be a chance."

The older woman looked at Ella Ruth. "You must be Mr. Buster's new wife. I know you been coming and visiting my girl, but we both know that ain't proper no more. You be a Wright now. Can't be friends. And child, in our lives we can't make wishes and dreams come true. We got to face what is right in front of us. If they shot Tyler and pulled him out of here, what do you think? You think they took him to the hospital to save his life or did they take him so they'd be certain he would die?" She stepped away from Lacy and took Mile from Ella Ruth. "You two go on and celebrate your wedding. That's a fine thing for the Wright family. I'll take care of what's mine." She took Tucker's hand too as if to make her point.

Buster gave Ella Ruth a defeated shrug. "I don't know what to do."

Larry spoke for the first time. "Can't see there is anything to do. Paul Allen owns Sheriff Cooper. Tyler will turn up. The only other thing we could do is hunt Paul Allen down and kill him."

"I think my wife would join you," Buster said. "In a heartbeat."

"But here's the thing. If we kill him, a jury would convict us of murder no matter how many he's killed. I'm not dying for that man. Are you?" Larry asked Ella Ruth.

"I guess not. But I hate him. I hate this whole place. I hate that I can't be friends with Lacy. I hate everything." Tears filled her eyes.

Lacy's mama's eyes turned to steel. "Y'all get on out of here, now. You ain't going to be any part of this. Get on."

Buster wrapped his arm around Ella Ruth. "Come on. Let's go to

Asheville. Larry here will let us know if they find Tyler. Won't you?"

"Yes, I will."

൪

The next day, a local farmer's hunting dogs found Tyler hanging from a tree as the road curved up Black Mountain. Some say it was on Paul Allen's farm property that his parents had deeded to him.

Buster thought of going to the funeral but Mama insisted that he give Lacy her privacy. Ella Ruth wasn't happy with his decision to stay away, but she didn't fight him for it.

Buster joined the Army two days after President Roosevelt declared war on Japan, sooner than he could imagine. He had gone from a boy to a man and now a soldier.

Chapter 14

Lee Wright

Lee knew Sam White the minute he came on deck.

"Lee Wright," Sam called. "You're alive. Lots of people at home think you're dead. And here you are."

Lee only stared at him.

Sam wore a foolish grin. Still a kid. "I came in last night. Damn, I never thought I'd find someone I knew on the *Oklahoma*."

Lee remained quiet.

"Does your family know you're here?"

Bingo.

Lee grabbed him by the collar. "If you want your ass beat. keep that hometown talk going. I'll beat it within an inch of your sorry life."

The grin faded. "Okay."

Lee let him go. "I'll only say this once. This is my new life. I left that place behind. I don't want any strolls down memory lane." He looked Sam dead in the eyes. Swannanoa Gap stared back at him.

Sam straightened his shirt. "Sorry. What's a sailor do around here for fun?" His voice was a little shaky.

Lee walked away. "We fish."

"Shit. That ain't no fun. I could do that at home just as easy."

CR

Late that evening Lee found Sam in his bunk. "You want to fish?"

Sam gave him a long look. "I guess, as long as you ain't going to beat my ass."

"Come on and bring your money."

They walked through the narrow passages of the ship, down to the belly.

Sam looked around. "How the hell are we going to fish down here?"

"We got us a hole cut in the bottom of the ship. We plug it when we're finished. Best fishing around."

"You're bullshitting me," Sam said, struggling to keep up with Lee.

"Naw." Lee took a sharp right through a door into a closet-sized room. Four sailors sat at a crate in the middle of the floor with cards in one hand and a beer in the other. The latter warranted a court marshal if they were caught.

One of Lee's buddies, Parker, flexed his arm at Sam. There was a large tattoo of the *Oklahoma*, and the rippling muscle made it look like the smoke was billowing from the stacks. "Fresh bait, Wright. We've been holding up this game just for you assholes."

Lee squeezed in next to Parker, motioning Sam to another place. "This here is Parker and that scruffy looking fellow is Allen Gibbs." He gestured toward the other two sailors, who looked even younger than Sam. "The rest I don't keep up with."

The sailors laughed.

"Sam wanted some fun. He brought money."

Allen cocked his head. "This here is five card stud. Can you play?"

Sam shrugged. "I guess."

"Sam here comes from a good Bible-thumping town. I'm not sure he ever learned to gamble. Did you, Sam?"

"Not really."

"We're going to have to teach him, boys." Lee winked at Sam.

Parker hooted. "So you got money, Sam, my boy. We're going to be good friends."

"Okay."

Sam won the second pot, which pissed off Parker. Sam picked up his third bottle of beer.

"Son, you better slow down," Lee warned. "Captain doesn't take kindly to drunks."

Parker gave a mean laugh. "Don't pay Father Wright any mind. You just get settled in. We got some more cards to play. See, I think you're a liar, winning like you did. I'm going to win my money back." He looked over at Lee. "There's something un-American about a sailor who doesn't drink."

"You like being in the brig, don't you, Parker? I don't."

"Yep, Wright here is going to be our next admiral."

"Better than scrubbing the head."

Parker pushed up from his sitting position and lost his balance. "You act like you're some kind of damn perfect ass, but you ain't nothing but a sweetheart." His words slurred.

"I don't mind being a sweetheart." Lee threw down his hand and raked in the pot. The others threw down their cards, mumbling.

"You cheat," Parker roared.

"Shut up, Parker." Allen said, nudging him.

"You guys might be scared of this asshole, but not me." Parker leaned over, placing his face close to Lee's. The beer breath turned Lee's stomach. "Show me just how tough you are, sweetie." He grabbed Lee's collar.

Lee punched Parker in the face. Parker fell backwards.

"Damn idiot makes me do that each time he gets drunk." Lee turned to Sam. "You ready?"

Sam nodded and followed Lee into the corridor. "Toughen up, Sam, or these guys will eat you alive. They smell fear a mile away. You were going to throw the game so Allen could win."

"How'd you know?" Sam said from behind him.

"Some things are just easy to see." He walked faster, leaving Sam to find his own way back.

ʒ

Lee took Sam to town on a two-day pass. Allen tagged along as always.

"You ever screw a woman?" Allen asked Sam, whose face turned a deep shade of red, telling the truth for him.

As much as Allen could be an ass, he knew how to walk the walk and talk the talk. If it came to combat, Lee wanted Allen with him.

"I think he'll like Millie's place," Allen said, laughing. "I need me a woman. How about you, Wright?"

The way Lee saw it, Sam had two choices. He could get broke in with Lee's help or without.

"Sure."

"What about little boy, here?" Allen poked his elbow in Sam's side.

"Oh, yes. He knows all about women." Lee nodded at Sam. The boy had to wise up.

Millie ran her establishment on the waterfront in a converted warehouse. She catered to sailors, knowing how much money they liked to spend. But her house was clean, free of disease, theft, and especially fights. If a sailor got too rowdy, she'd throw him out. Allen had used up his warnings.

"You'd better be on your best behavior tonight," Lee told him.

Allen grew solemn. "Millie didn't give me a chance to explain what happened. I don't like guys manhandling Joy."

"Just keep your nose clean."

"What, now you're my daddy?" Allen frowned.

"Is this a whorehouse we're going to?" Sam asked.

"I wouldn't be talking like that if I were you," Allen warned. "Someone will kick your ass, and it might be me."

"I see them as business women. They're making money. They don't look for all that love stuff." Lee grinned at Allen, who he knew had it bad for Joy.

"Hell, ain't no one making money off of you. What do you see in Millie? She's got to be old enough to be your mama." Allen punched Sam's shoulder. "Now, White here, he needs him a young thing, one to show him the ropes on his first time out."

Sam looked like a caged animal as they approached Millie's, where the crowd spilled into the street, waiting for the doors to open.

"We ain't never going to get in tonight." Sam's face showed relief.

"Lee, work your magic on the doorman."

Lee looked over at Sam—he knew it was wrong but he had to do it anyway—and pushed his way through to the front of the crowd. Millie stood at the door, talking to the bodyguard. She was beautiful with her dark hair wound tight on her head. Lee tried not to look at her dress slit up the side, but she still caught him at it.

"Well, hello, Mr. Wright." Her voice was smooth as silk. As always, he reminded himself that he didn't need any complications in his life. "Have you brought your friends?"

He cursed the blush spreading across his face. "I have two with me who might just die if they don't get in."

Her green eyes never failed to stir him. "And, how about you, Mr. Wright. Do you feel the same?" She laughed.

"You know how I feel," he said in almost a whisper.

She waved her hand to part the rest of the crowd like Moses parted the Red Sea. "Come, boys." As Allen walked past, she pointed a long slender finger in his face. "No funny business, mister."

Allen shuffled his feet, looking at the floor. "Yes ma'am."

When Lee walked past, she touched his arm. "Give me an hour or so. I'll be with you." Lee nodded. Then she looked at Sam. "Lee, are you corrupting a baby?" She touched Sam's shoulder.

Sam stammered, "I can leave."

Millie looked at Lee. "Fresh from the farm?"

Lee nodded. "He needs the special treatment."

Millie smiled with her straight white teeth, paid for by an old lover, an American businessman from the mainland who she lived with for five years. He still sent her little presents from New York with notes begging her to follow him. The very idea of him set Lee's teeth on edge. He wished he had something of value to give her.

"I'll take care of him," Millie assured Lee, breaking him out of his thoughts.

"Drink and loosen up," Lee told Sam as they sat around a table a few minutes later, Joy's sultry tones entertaining them with a song in the background. "It's Friday night. We're out on pass. This is the stuff life is made of."

Sam drank the beer, gulping like the world might end before he finished. "Lee, I think I might slip out of here," he whispered.

Lee placed his hand on Sam's shoulder. "You can't do that unless you want all the guys, your buddies, to rag your ass forever. Is that the life you want to lead for the next four years? Trust me on this, Sam."

Sam looked as if Lee had lost his mind.

Joy finished her song and strutted down to their table. She sidled up to Allen. "Where have you been, baby?"

Allen pulled her down on his lap. "Your boss threw me out for whooping that guy's ass."

She looked into his face. "It's just business, Allen. You got to remember that."

Allen hugged her. "You know I do, baby. I learned my lesson." He buried his face in her long red hair. "Let's go. We got a lot to catch up on."

As he stood, Allen clapped Sam on the back. "This here is Sam. Do you have a friend for him?"

"He's spoken for," Lee said. "Millie has hand-picked his date to-night." Lee grinned at the pure panic on Sam's face. "Sam, you look green around the edges. Don't go and puke all over her."

Joy smiled. "Don't worry, hon. It's like riding a bike. Once you get the hang of it, Lord, there's nothing to it. It comes real natural." She giggled as she walked off with Allen's hand on her butt.

"I don't know about all this shit, Lee." Sam tried to sound tough. "I don't want to catch some disease."

"First, don't talk that shit about disease around here unless you want your ass beat, and second, you can walk out of here right now and let the rest ride you like an old mare for the rest of your time. I don't give a damn. But if you're smart you'll trust me on this." Lee swigged his ginger ale.

Patty strolled up to the table, flowers in her hair, looking sexier than any woman there. "Hey Lee, is this your friend?" She sat beside Sam.

Sam blushed and held out his hand. "I'm Sam White from Swannanoa Gap, North Carolina. In the Gap we treat ladies with respect."

Patty smiled, taking his hand and looking at Lee. "I'm glad to know some men still have manners. It's nice to meet you, Sam White." Patty wore her age well. A guy had to really look at her to realize her age.

Sam looked as if he were on his way to the firing squad.

"Well, Mr. White, how about we go upstairs and get to know each other?" Patty pulled Sam to his feet. "I promise not to bite."

He followed her reluctantly, like a dog with his tail between his legs.

Lee laughed to himself. He knew that once they got to Patty's room, she'd pull out a pack of cards, and that's all they would do the rest of the evening.

"Are you plotting against someone?" Millie sat down at the table, touching his hand. "You go on up. I'll see you in a minute. I have a bath with lots of bubbles and a big steak." She pulled his hand to her mouth and kissed each finger.

Damn her for knowing every button to push.

ɷ

Not long after the visit to Millie's, Sam went home on a leave and came back complaining about Buster trying to steal his date at the ice cream social. He'd bought some girl's box supper, but Buster seemed to have his sights on her.

Lee pretended not to care, but deep inside he couldn't help wondering what his family was like since Daddy's death. Did they wake sometimes in the morning like he did, forgetting where they were for a minute, forgetting life had changed in a matter of moments? Probably not. They were at home, living the loss up close every day.

More and more, the SS *Oklahoma* went out on maneuvers along with the other ships. Lee began to think the other shoe would drop soon. It had to. War was right around the corner.

Thanksgiving in Hawaii was different to say the least. Millie tried to make it traditional for him, but her efforts failed to produce the picture in his mind. He saw the dining room at home decked out with lace and silver, even candles. Mama always went big for the show part. He saw Buster, Mama, and even Billie. All their faces were beginning to fade from his new life. At the beginning of December, he dreamed that Granny was sitting on the edge of his bunk.

Boy, I've been waiting for you to come home. Please don't wait too long.

Lee woke to Granny's honeysuckle fragrance.

Meanwhile, Sam had grown into a man. Lee wasn't surprised when he finally stood up to Allen's ragging—it was bound to happen. Allen met Lee and Sam on deck one morning; all were headed for town on a weekend pass.

"I'm going to see Joy tonight, and that bitch Millie will not stop me. My money's just like anybody's." Allen stared Lee down. "Hell, you don't even pay for your ass, Wright. I guess old ass is free."

A surge of hate flashed through Lee, but he controlled himself. It wasn't worth it.

"And you, little boy, you ain't fooling nobody. You're paying just to go sit in a room and pretend you're a man." Allen laughed.

Sam knocked Allen flat on his back. He jumped on him and began beating the shit out of him. "I'm sick of you, asshole."

"Attention."

Allen struggled beneath Sam, who kept throwing punches.

"White, to your feet now, sailor." The captain looked at Allen. "On your feet, sailor."

Sam jumped to attention. Allen struggled to his feet, bleeding. "Yes sir," they both chimed together.

"Do you sailors know what happens to those that fight?" The captain waited. "They go to the brig. Be forewarned. If I catch you fighting again, that's where you'll go. For now you can go to your bunks. You will not be using your passes."

"Yes sir."

The captain turned to Lee. "Wright, I suggest you leave before I decide to keep you here too."

"Yes sir," Lee rang out and saluted. A cold chill crawled up his spine and caused him to shiver. Granny would say someone just walked over his grave.

℆

Millie met him at the door to her apartment. "You're late. I thought you weren't coming." She clung to his arm. The arrangement they had was taking a different turn, and this drove Lee crazy. He didn't trust himself to start caring about a woman. It never paid off.

He gently pulled his arm away. "A fight between Sam and Allen."

"Who won?" she asked, relaxing.

"Sam, but both of them lost their passes."

She nodded. "Allen is a troublemaker."

"He's just in love, Millie. You got to cut him some slack." The words came out sharper than he intended.

She looked at him. "I have supper for you. Spend the night with me."

He always left before dawn. Somehow that made their relationship not as solid in his mind.

He sat at the table without looking her in the eyes. "This looks good. I could eat the whole cow."

She laughed. All the unspoken expectations left the room.

Later in bed, they cuddled together, content to just be quiet. But the longer they lay there, the more Lee wanted to explain to Millie his feelings about having a relationship, being boxed in. "I want to say I'll always remember you no matter what," he began, then stopped.

Why did the words come out like a goodbye?

She pulled away, looking at his face. A streetlight lit the corners of the room, turning them gray. "You're leaving me?"

"No, not now, but we both know this can't go on forever, this peace we are living. I may get orders at any time. When that happens, you may not know. One day I just won't show."

She shook her head, reminding him of a child. "No. You'll find a way to let me know. You're a good man. I'll always wait on you, Lee."

"Don't make promises, Millie."

She hugged him to her. "I love you."

"I love you too." The words slipped out, and he slept through the night.

At daybreak the room shook so hard he sat upright in the bed. Millie sat up too, more slowly. A screeching whistle filled the room, and then a loud explosion rocked them. Somewhere above the noise, Lee heard a siren, the warning for an air raid. It had to be a joke. This was the United States, the strongest country in the world.

He jumped from the bed. "Get dressed and go to the basement

now."

Millie slipped on her robe and shoes. The next hit shattered the glass, and Lee pulled Millie to the living room. The window overlooking the harbor revealed nothing but black smoke.

"Go to the basement with me," Millie screamed.

"You go. I've got to get to the ship." He pushed out the door.

"Lee, you can't. You might die."

"I'm a soldier. Go." He untangled himself. "Damn it, Millie, I have to go. Do what I said. Go to the basement." Doors to the other rooms began to swing open.

One sailor pulling on his pants looked at Lee. "What the hell is going on?"

"War. Fucking war." He turned to Millie, pulling her to him, kissing her. "Go. I'll find you when it's all over." He pushed her away and began to run behind the others.

The street was full of smoke choking the air. Planes screeched in low like metal against metal, mowing down the roads with bullets pinging off objects and downing people. He ran through what had become a battlefield. Fires burned everywhere. The mess hall at Hickam was gone, nothing. The *Arizona* was missing. He ran, surrounded by fire and the suffocating smoke. Planes screeched overhead, and the smoke parted long enough to show him a Japanese symbol on the bottom of one of them. The air raid siren continued to wail like a sobbing woman. His heart hammered in his chest. People ran as if they could save their own lives. Through the smoke he saw his nightmare come to life. The *Oklahoma*, beautiful, graceful, had capsized, propellers jutting out of the water. The world around him burned, and he fell to the ground, hunched over, his head in his hands. Somehow in the thick black smoke, he found the nerve to pray. God wouldn't even remember him.

"Save us. Save us."

"Sir." Someone tapped him on the shoulder. "Sir."

Lee looked into the face of a native man.

"Excuse me, sir. Could you help me? There are people alive in that ship." The man pointed to the *Oklahoma*. "I can hear them tapping on the hull. We must save them."

Lee jumped to his feet. "You heard tapping?"

"Listen."

The clinking began deep within the water, beating, begging. "We've got to get them out of there." Lee grabbed the man's arm.

"Yes, yes." The man pulled away. "We have to cut through."

"A torch? We can cut through the hull with a torch. I'll go find one. You stay here. Tell others to help."

"Hurry." But Lee knew this rescue could not be rushed.

Lee jumped into the water and climbed onto the exposed hull. He could hear the rat-tat-tat from a nearby machine gun. He took out his pocketknife, his only weapon, and began to beat on the hull. An answer came back like a glorious call from on high.

"I have a torch and sailors," yelled the man who'd heard the tapping. He held the torch high above his head like a comical Statue of Liberty.

The group came over to the hull. Someone lit the torch. More and more sailors and civilians gathered around the fallen ship, wet, with cuts, bruises, torn clothes, and pure expressions of determination.

The man looked at Lee through the blue-yellow flame of the torch. "My name is Julio."

"Petty Officer Wright."

The battle had arrived and departed without Lee. But he would make up for that. He watched the slow progress of the torch on the metal of the hull. "My buddies are in there," he said to Julio. This was his one chance to make up for being away from the ship when the enemy bombed.

&

Faces came and went. Hours turned into eternity. Lee held the torch, then passed it to the next sailor and used a fresh one. The tapping continued off and on. Always someone, sometimes Lee, answered by tapping back.

Finally, they had several torches working on the spot. "Almost there." Lee could feel it.

"How many are alive?" one sailor asked, lighting a cigarette.

"I don't know."

"Cap says you're sucking the life right out of the hull," another one said. "When you open it the pressure is going to blow water right through." A greasy strand of hair fell on the sailor's forehead.

"Well, you got anything better to do? I fucking don't know." Lee could hear the craziness in his words. "I wish I could just fucking go back to Millie's."

"Yeah, it's a damn shame, ain't it?"

"What's a shame?" Lee didn't want the answer.

"How long have you been out here?" The sailor watched him.

"Since the bombing. How long has that been? This is my ship. I have to help these guys. I should have been in there with them."

"Millie's place is gone."

"Gone!" The *Oklahoma* rocked. Lee thought of Christ walking on water. Where was his faith? Where was God?

"They're saying no one came out of there alive."

Blood beat through the vessels in his head, pounding red, orange, a pure white rage. He searched the air for a familiar word. *Millie!*

A cry surfaced from the hull, splitting the air like lightning. "Pull him up. Hurry. It's filling with water." Men scrambled from the hole like rats saving their lives.

A man, grease all over his face, gripped Lee's shoulder. "Wright."

Lee saw Allen through the cuts and bruises. He opened his mouth to ask the question.

Allen shook his head. "Lost that group twelve hours ago. That part of the boat started flooding. Sam kept putting men with families in front of him. He made us proud."

Lee turned away.

"I want to find Joy," Allen said, desperation edging his voice.

Scenes like a moving picture rushed in front of Lee's eyes. "Millie's place is gone. No one lived.

He looked out at the ocean. It was his home, his queen. He would fight this war with everything he had in him. Who cared if he lived or died?

Part Three

The War Years

1944–1945

Chapter 15

Buster

May 25, 1944
Dear Buster:

I guess I was living in a dream, praying you wouldn't go to war. I really started to think you were in the clear. You spent a long time in training. Then we got to stay in North Carolina. I thought for once in my life, my prayers had been answered. I let my guard down just like when I believed Gert was getting out of the hospital that time, and I planned to go to college. Dreaming. You'd think I would learn. By the way, Gert got out of the hospital finally. She's frail and pale, but I think she's going to stay in Swannanoa Gap. Who knows? I can't trust anything.

Are you in Europe? I made it back to the Gap all on my own. I have to tell you the truth, I almost kept on driving right to Atlanta. The last thing I wanted to do was end up here with Paul Allen again. I'm a married woman.

Your mama was kind enough to offer me to live with her, but let's face it, I don't think that would work out well.

Each day, Buster, the trains go by. I know that's no different than when you were here. The whistle makes me cry. See, these trains are full of soldiers, and they throw their letters out the windows to me for posting. Sometimes it looks like snow is covering the ground. I run and pick them up, so many it takes me a few minutes to gather them all. Each one could be a letter from you, depending on some girl to mail it. I haven't heard from you Buster.

Enough of that. Here's the big surprise. I sure didn't want to tell you like this, but I hope it will cheer you up. In four months I will be a mama and you will be a daddy. There. The Red Cross ladies said to always write cheerful things. I'm sorry I whined. This is cheerful. A baby, Buster. What will we name him? I just know it's going to be a boy.

I hope to hear from you soon. I love you.

Ella Ruth (your devoted and lonely wife)

PS. You know Larry was in training. He shipped out two weeks ago. Billie got a letter from him. We don't know where he's headed. His daddy was beside himself. I feel so bad for him, seeing how that's his only child. Larry didn't have to go but he did. I know. He saw it as his duty. But he's a kid. Not a man like you.

June 3, 1944
 Dear Ella Ruth:
  We move out tomorrow. I can't say where I am, but I miss you more than you'll ever know. You are what keeps me going here. Letters are slow getting out of here and finding us. I sure wish I would get one from you. I know you've written. I hope you get this one so you won't worry. I know how you are. Keep writing to me anyway. Maybe I'll get one soon.
  I love you.
  Buster

CR

Buster folded the letter he had written and stuffed it in the special envelope the Army had given them. Swannanoa Gap would be cool and breezy right now. Black Mountain's shadow always made the early summer the best time of year. But he couldn't think on that mountain, Swannanoa Gap, or his wife. It was just too much. He knew from the day he signed up that he'd go to war. Shoot, he had hoped to see some action. But that was a boy's foolishness. The more time he spent training, and especially when he remembered the time he spent with Ella Ruth, the more he realized what a fool he was for wanting fight. And where was he going now?

Right there in France on the front lines. He couldn't cry 'cause crying was for babies. And he was a man—no, a soldier.

"Mail call." A soldier stood on the crate, yelling from the middle of a clearing.

Tents of every size were scattered here and there. This would be the last mail call before battle.

"Andrews." Andrews grabbed the letter and waved it in the air.

"Baily." A soldier hooted as he snatched the letter.

"Taylor." Taylor grinned so big he looked like a goofy little boy. Buster's stomach twisted.

"Peabody."

Well, at least there seemed to be a lot of mail today.

"Wright."

He thought of Ella Ruth, all those red curls.

"Wright!"

Randal punched him in the arm, pointing to the letter the guy held in the air.

"Last call for Wright!"

Buster jumped to his feet. "I'm here. By God I'm here."

Everyone laughed.

Thank you, God. He tore it open. Her beautiful loopy handwriting made him feel that she was right there. He could smell her on the paper, or was that just his imagination? He read the words slow. A baby! A baby!

Randal—he was from Virginia, richer than sin—came to stand next to Buster. Every day now, he wore that gosh-awful tie with red polka dots that his mama sent him. It flapped in the wind. No one spoke up and said he couldn't wear it. That's how Buster knew they were in trouble, that they were headed into heavy fighting. Randal insisted that if Buster stuck with him and the tie, he'd be back in Swannanoa Gap just because of its good luck.

"What kind of news you got there, Wright? You look like you're about to bust."

Buster laughed and pulled on the tie. "I'm going to have a baby!"

Randal slapped him on the back. "You don't say? Damn! You're fast. I think we ought to find us a beer."

"No beer today. We got to have our wits."

"I'm finding me one anyway, Daddy." He elbowed Buster in the ribs and walked away.

Buster folded the letter and tucked it in his pocket. He could do anything to keep his country safe. He was going to be a daddy.

CR

Randal showered in the stall next to Buster's. "Damn, what I'd give to have a hot shower. The kind that burns your skin." He passed the soap over the wall. "Did I ever tell you I could have stayed back in Virginia and spent my evenings watching the sun go down, sipping one of Daddy's gin and tonics? Daddy wanted to get me off the hook. He could have because I'm his only child and, well hell, the old man has more money than anyone. But I was pretty sure girls would swoon over me if I became a soldier. Got to have pretty girls."

Buster listened to the same story again. God help Randal. He thought mostly about girls, drinking, and fast cars.

Benny from the Bronx stepped into the stall next to Randal. To hear him tell it, he fought wars on his street every day. "We're finally going to see some action. I'm ready." He turned on the water, lowering the pressure of both Buster and Randal's showers.

"I ain't in a bit of hurry," Buster said, thinking of Ella Ruth and the baby growing inside her.

"You don't know shit, Wright. Fighting is why we're here, buddy. We can't be sissies like Virginia there." Benny pointed towards Randal.

Randal rolled his eyes. "You'll have to teach me a thing or two. I can tell you I ain't going to look for a fight. I like the finer things in life like sitting on the front porch with a beautiful girl, watching life pass me by."

"Damn!" Benny cried out.

"What's wrong?" Buster turned off his water.

"I got something wrong with my balls, some kind of rash. Maybe bug bites."

Randal winked at Buster as he left his stall, water still running. "That ain't bugs. It's jungle rot. Didn't you listen during training? It's easy to catch in combat situations, even if you ain't in a jungle." He reached inside his bag and pulled out a little blue glass bottle, passing it to Benny. "Lucky for you my mom made sure I had the medicine for it. Rub it on when you get out of the shower."

Benny grabbed the bottle. "Thanks, buddy."

Buster pulled on his pants, and Randal motioned him to follow as he buckled his belt. "Don't forget to give it back to me." He called over his shoulder, nearly pushing Buster down to get out of the door.

"What the hell is that about?" Buster watched Randal place his necktie over his head.

"Mama made me pack that shit. It came in handy after all."

"What did you give him?"

A yelp came from the latrine that sounded like a dying dog.

"Vick's VapoRub!" Randal laughed so hard he stopped and doubled over.

"Damn. He's going to kill your ass."

"Naw, he'll have to catch up with me first. Right now he's got to figure out how to walk because that blast of menthol has frozen his balls."

⊗

Lucky for Randal, Benny shipped out on the first carrier without a chance to return Randal's medicine. Buster and Randal were all that remained of the 299th Combat Engineer Battalion. The two of them shipped out later that evening. Somewhere in the channel waited a LCPV (landing craft vehicles personnel) just for them. This would be the last leg of the journey. As the ship scooted across the glassy water, Buster caught the sound of a guitar, skimming the surface, a life preserver in the deep twilight on his last peaceful night of freedom. A big moon hung on the horizon, pushing up into the black sky. He tried not to think of home. He had to stay focused.

"Solider, no hands on deck."

Buster jumped.

"You can't be up on deck. This is serious business."

Buster looked at the captain bars on the fellow's uniform. Shit, he was in for it now.

"Name, soldier."

"Private First Class Wright, sir." Buster saluted.

"I have one question for you, soldier."

"Yes sir." Buster was at full attention.

"Where in the hell did you take my bugle that Sunday?" The

123

captain pushed his cap back on his head.

"What the hell?"

"Is that any way to speak to an officer?" The captain balled his fingers into a fist and socked Buster right in the nose.

Light flashed in front of his eyes. "Kiss my ass, Lee." Buster wiped blood from his upper lip.

"Baby brother." Lee laughed, offering his hand. Buster took it and stood.

"So you fight now?"

"There's more where that came from if you don't answer my question. I've been waiting a few years to find out."

"Well, the last I heard, the good preacher from that holy-roller church has it. A souvenir of his visit from the angel Gabriel."

Lee lit a cigarette. "You never brought it back home that day?"

"Lee smokes."

"I do a lot of things." He looked hard at Buster. "I hated you for a damn long time, Buster. I'm not sure I'm through hating you."

"You were always a self-righteous asshole." Buster braced for another punch. He couldn't believe he was standing there talking to his brother, who he had thought was surely a ghost by then.

Lee stared at the sky. He was bigger, broader than Buster remembered. "You were always causing Daddy trouble, getting his attention. He liked you more. You didn't have those big shoes to fill." He looked down at the cigarette burning in his hand. "I picked up this habit during my stay in Pearl Harbor."

"Pearl Harbor?" Buster watched his brother and realized they had been away from each other a whole lifetime.

"I made it out by a fucking piece of luck." He inhaled on the cigarette. "Your first combat?"

"Yeah."

Lee nodded. "Off the record, you're going into the worst hellhole you can imagine. They're already calling it D-Day. Most of the men on this ship will die. Does that tell you something?"

"I have to live."

"And what makes you so damn special?"

"I got a baby coming. I have to go home." Buster watched Lee's face.

"Who the hell would marry you?"

"Ella Ruth Allen."

"You're going to be a father." Lee shook his head, grinding out his cigarette. "How's Mom?"

"She's okay." Buster couldn't look at Lee.

"How about Granny?" The words were colder. Lee had a history with Granny. He'd never forgiven her for firing Lacy when she put two and two together.

"She's not well but still alive, or was when I left. She drew up a will, Lee, that leaves the whole farm to you when she dies. I think she's trying to make up for everything. Mama said she's just causing more trouble."

"Damn!"

"Yeah."

"That farm's got to be Mama's, not mine. You can tell Granny that. I'm not ever going back to the Gap."

"You'll have to tell her yourself. I won't even tell them I saw you. Write her a letter or something." Buster balled up his fist. "Nothing has changed. You're a selfish asshole like always."

Lee looked at Buster. "Well, you finally grew a backbone." He took off his cap. "I could have you court marshaled for speaking to an officer like that."

"Go ahead. At least I'll stay alive for my kid."

"What about Lacy?"

And there was the question. "She married Tyler Kurt. They had two sons, Tucker and Mile. Funny thing is Tucker has real light skin and was two months early. The Klan came bursting in one night and shot Tyler. He had him a real nice gas station. I guess he was doing too good. Lacy's back working for Mama. Mile looks just like Tyler."

Lee stared at him. "Are you saying her first boy is mine?"

"I ain't saying much of nothing, Lee. You have to figure that one out on your own. Write Lacy. Explain why you left her holding the bag."

"I didn't know."

"There's lots you didn't know because you left." Buster realized that he'd wanted to say those words for a long time.

Lee looked him in the eye. "You land tomorrow, and it's going to be a tough day. When you do, run. Just run your ass off for Swannanoa Gap, brother. Don't worry about defending your fellow soldiers. Go. Ain't no heroes going to make it on Omaha Beach."

Buster could see from the expression on Lee's face that he knew more about the upcoming battle. "I will. I ain't looking to be noticed. I got to live for my kid."

"You better go rest."

"Lee, I want you to do one thing."

Lee shuffled his feet. "I'm not good at keeping promises."

"Just find me after the war. Let me know you made it out."

"Don't worry about me. It's me that needs to be worried about you. I made it out of Pearl Harbor. I'm going to live."

"Come on, Lee, just commit this one time."

"Shit, if you make it through this damn battle, look for me. I'll find you somewhere."

"Okay."

"Get out of here."

"Stay safe." Buster held out his hand.

Lee gripped it and then pulled Buster into a half hug. "Go."

Buster let go and turned.

"Hey."

Buster looked back. "What?"

"I'll find you the first Christmas after the war. I figure you'll be in the Gap."

"You know I will."

"I said I wasn't going back there again."

"So you did, brother, but sometimes you have to face your devils." Buster didn't dare look at his brother again for fear he wouldn't be able to walk away.

⟡

The early morning dark hung over the men as they waited for the cargo net to drop to the LCPV. The choppy water made it impossible to

126

predict where the soldiers had landed once the net wrapped around them.

"Jump and roll. Watch yourselves," a sailor yelled as each soldier prepared to go over.

Buster searched the deck and saw Randal grinning.

"What will be, will be."

"I can't believe you're wearing that damn tie. If the Nazis don't see you with that thing on, no one will." Buster watched more men disappearing over the rail.

Randal clapped him on the shoulder as it came his turn to jump. "It's been a privilege." And he was gone over the rail.

Buster stepped up to follow.

"You got to wait for the next," the sailor barked at him. "Don't worry, it's right there. You won't miss a ride."

Buster stood back, thinking of Randal. He was alone. Maybe that was best.

"Okay!" the sailor yelled at Buster after what seemed a long time. He turned to have one last look at the upper deck.

There was Lee, standing above the others on a platform. Buster raised his hand in a salute. Lee saluted back.

"Come on. You were ready a little while ago." The sailor pushed.

Buster threw himself over the rail into the net, rolling out of control, flopping like a rag doll. He landed on the deck of the craft with a hard whack, jarring his head inside his helmet. Soldiers sat hunched around a raft that looked to be full of explosives. Great. They could just blow themselves up—all the fighting men—before they ever touched land. He didn't believe one person really knew what they were getting into or how to use the explosives. Shoot, training didn't prepare a man for the real thing. Buster crawled to his feet just in time to miss several men come rolling into the boat. He found a seat next to a young boy. More and more men dropped from the net until all the bare spots on deck were filled. The sky lit up like the Fourth of July.

"Men." A sergeant not much older than Buster stood at one end of the deck. "You are on the way to the biggest ass-busting you have ever had. In just a little while you'll arrive on Omaha Beach. This day will go down in history as the time when the United States turned the war around. That's what you got to be proud of. If you live through it, you can tell your great-grandkids the story."

The sergeant paused before continuing. "The captain of this craft will get you as close to the beach as possible. This will depend on the boats ahead of us. They will make you or break you. When they let down the ramp, move! Don't candy ass around! Other lives depend on your damn movements, so use your training, but most of all use your gut. Don't think. Don't sneeze. Don't cry. Move your asses down that ramp and haul them to the beach. The Nazis sit on the cliffs watching like foxes eyeing sweet little hens. Move your asses down that beach to the weak spot. You'll see it. It's the only way up."

They were going to die.

As if affirming Buster's thoughts, the sergeant added, "I will not lie to you, men. Chances are most of you will die today. You will die for your country. That is just a fact. The country, oh hell, the whole world depends on your sweet asses, and if just a handful of guys makes it, that is a handful to bust their Nazis asses. It's our chance to win this war. May God be with you today." He turned his back on them and waited in silence.

The boy beside Buster sniffled. Other men reflected his own terror back at him. Explosions filled the air. Smoke settled around them, blocking out any view, stinging his eyes and scratching his throat raw.

"Not long now, men," the sergeant shouted.

The boy made a small noise like a sob. No one looked at him. What sounded like hard rain began to pour around them, hitting the deck. It wasn't rain at all. God help them. The ramp slowly began to let down. Buster gripped his rifle, imagining how fast he'd move across the beach. Run! That's what Lee said. Run! The beach was further away than he planned. Beached ships littered the shore and spread into the shallow water, changing the plans for a closer drop point. What looked to be sandbags were slung here and there. Buster was caught in the wave of motion that moved him forward down the ramp without choice. Water touched his waist. The boy managed to keep up, hurrying along beside Buster. Suddenly he screamed, grabbing his arm that sprayed blood. Buster pulled him off the ramp into the deeper water. Water filled Buster's lungs. He held on to the boy's hair and kicked like a madman. A door of half-light opened above him. Paddling, he moved toward it.

The smoke stung his lungs. He pulled the boy above the water, both of them kicking and gasping. At least the boy was alive, but his arm hung limp beside him. Buster pulled the kid's collar and swam. His pack weighed him down. To his left, a soldier's face tore away from his skull.

Buster kicked, pulling the kid, who fought him. If he broke away, Buster would let him go. The soldier in front of him took a hit in the neck.

Still Buster moved forward, shoving bodies away. The closer he got to the beach, the calmer the kid became. The sandbags on the beach turned out to be bodies, hundreds of bodies, washing back and forth in the bloody surf. The music of bullets zinging on the metal snowflakes almost defeated his movement. The world slowed, became silent, only the lapping of water. He grabbed one of the snowflakes and looked back at the kid. He was turned facedown in the water. His arm was missing. Buster let him go, allowing his body to float, a raft on stormy waters.

Buster ran, tripping over a body, and an arm reached up and grabbed his leg. An eye was missing from the soldier's face. He pried the fingers away. Bullets zipped by, striking the sand and soldiers who had already died. The scene turned silent like an old movie. He dropped the waterlogged pack and ran into oblivion. Ships burned on the water as men ran in every direction. The dunes beneath the rock cliffs offered a chance, and Buster jumped behind one. A single soldier walked down the beach as if he were strolling in the evening after dinner. Around his neck waved a red polka dot tie, a good luck charm. The man turned and looked right at Buster. Half of his face had been ripped off. Yet Randal kept walking. Bullets struck him so many times he dropped to his knees.

Buster held his hands to the sky and an ungodly sound erupted from him. "Run, run, run! Damn it."

A soldier touched Buster's shoulder. "Come with us. We're going to get as many of those bastards as we can and die trying if we have to. Are you with us?"

Energy surged through Buster. He stood and took a rifle from a dead soldier. "I'm ready." The two set off across the beach. Men exploded into pieces. Buster moved to his purpose. Randal was dead.

They met others, and the gathering of soldiers pushed up the ridge, killing as many of the enemy as they could. They ran hunched to the ground, dividing into silent groups of ten, attacking three bunkers on top of the ridge. Pure gut guided the grenade out of Buster's belt.

He pulled the pin, wanting damage. He pitched it across the sandbag wall. The explosion rocked the ground under his feet. Two bodies flew out of the bunker into the air. One soldier was sprawled across the ground, his open eyes staring upward. "That's for you, Randal!" But it was a boy, nothing but a young boy.

A soldier stood beside Buster. "Part of Hitler's youth group," he said. "Fifteen, maybe? Hell, he could be my baby brother."

In the distance, a man pleaded in German. Buster made out the words "family" and "kids" before shots rang. He turned and looked at the beach. If not for the clutter, the smoke that filled sky, and the dead, the view would be beautiful.

A soldier clapped him on the shoulder. "Come on, let's get the hell out of this shit hole!"

CR

Somewhere in France

November 5, 1944

October 17, 1944
Dear Buster:
 I've only received one letter from you. I know you would write if you could. I keep writing. Who knows, you may not be receiving my letters. This war is crazy, and I so want it to end. I know you're doing what you should, but Buster we need to be together. I feel so young and stupid. And I'm about to be a mother. It's almost like some kind of joke. I wish I could be braver, like you are.
 You know what I'm thinking about right now? I'm thinking about that night in Fayetteville when we were walking on the beach and you decided it was time for me to learn to dance. Do you remember dancing to the sound of the wind under the moon and stars? The tide was coming in and covered our feet. At first I stepped on your toes. I couldn't hear your directions. The wind was loud, so I just followed. We moved together, and I knew all my fears of being married were stupid. I think, Buster, I fell in love with you that night. We made our baby that night. I'm sure of it.
 I'm fatter than you could even imagine. This baby will be a boy. I know it in my bones. He kicks all the time. He will be born sometime after Christmas. I'm so alone. I know I'm not supposed to write stuff like this, but Buster I need you. Part of me is missing. Am I in love with you or that night on the beach? Are they one in the same?
 I pray you are safe. I want you home. I love you,
Ella Ruth

ରେ

 "Wright." The voice summoned Buster from a long-needed sleep.

 "Yes sir." His dog tags jangled as he jumped to his feet, hitting his shoulder on the dirt wall of the foxhole.

 "Letter from home." The sergeant placed the beaten envelope, stained with water and God knows what else, in Buster's hand.

Buster looked at it for a moment. "Thank you, sir!" He saluted.

"You're damn lucky, soldier. Not many letters make it this far in."

"Yes sir. I know, sir."

When the sergeant walked away, Buster tore into the envelope. He had to fight tears, a luxury he couldn't afford. God, he loved that girl. He slapped the soldier beside him. "Baxter, you got some paper and a pencil?"

Baxter looked at him with sleepy eyes. "You're crazy as hell, Wright." But he began to dig in his pack.

"Crazy or not, I got a wife to write to." He held out the letter.

Baxter grabbed it and opened it. "You damn lucky dog."

Buster didn't bother to take the letter back. Other soldiers would share it. Words from home were a soothing tonic, no matter who wrote them.

Baxter looked at Buster. "Sounds like another world."

Buster had expected him to poke fun, but they were past that. Their days were so brutal and empty. "Yep." He began to scribble on the paper.

"She'll never get it from way out here," Baxter said, pushing his helmet back.

"I don't give a damn. I got to write to her."

Bombs and the tat-tat-tat of a machine gun provided background music as he folded the paper and pushed it inside his shirt. A movement from the corner of his eye caught his attention. Buster was on his feet, moving slow, cautious, into the woods. His gun was his best friend. *Movement by the trees. Careful. Don't shoot until you know it's time.*

A burst of branches, a soldier, a German uniform. Buster aimed and shot. The soldier fell against one of the large trees. He waved a pistol and fired two rounds, so Buster shot again. The German collapsed against the tree. Somewhere behind him, Baxter yelled. His brain was on auto. Kill or be killed.

Ella Ruth appeared in the field at the edge of the woods. She was standing in the dry brittle grass as pretty as he remembered. She watched him with sad, sad eyes. He saw her kill the soldier. His head

throbbed but he moved into the open field to hold her. His shoulder
ached and something warm ran down his arm. Maybe he had finally
lost his mind in that hellhole. Bullets whizzed by his helmet. Ella Ruth
smiled, and just as he reached her, she disappeared.

He began to fire his gun like a crazy man. The impact of a bullet
threw him off balance. Then his foot felt like it blew up. He fell to
the ground, but his presence of mind told him he was hurt bad, maybe too bad, maybe he would die.

Chapter 16

Ella Ruth

On the cold morning of November 5, Ella Ruth woke with a scream stuck in her throat. Her heart beat in her chest so hard she was sure it could be heard in the next room. For a few seconds she thought she was in Fayetteville, North Carolina, and Buster slept beside her, but she was in Paul Allen's house. God only knew where Buster was. The feeling that washed over her was leftover from a watery dream. It was the feeling that something was wrong—dread was the best word she could come up with.

She sat up. Her pencils and sketchbook were scattered on the side of the bed where Buster should have been sleeping. She gripped the charcoal pencil in her fingers, comfortable, familiar. Gert worried she would stop drawing, but Ella Ruth loved it too much. The tree she was sketching had taken on a life more real than her own as she worked, large and old with gnarled limbs for arms, thick exposed roots sunk deep into the ground. A heart was carved into the trunk: Ella Ruth loves Buster. As she shaded in the back, she hid the word "peace" within the bark's layers. Peace. The baby kicked.

Giving her drawing one last look, she threw her legs over the high bed and went to her cupboard for a dress. Another day without hearing from Buster loomed in front of her.

◌ଷ

December 17, 1944
Ella Ruth sat in the rocker close to the potbelly stove. Paul Allen hadn't been home since early November. Ella Ruth hoped he had died somewhere. Bell worried. She was too good for her own self, thinking she could change a man who was the devil. Ella Ruth's thick black pencil worked to form Bell's hands as Bell formed dough into balls for Christmas cookies. Veins popped out from the wrinkled skin that was soft as tissue paper, the kind of paper a person might

use to wrap a treasured gift. Bell came to stand over Ella Ruth's shoulder.

"Oh my. Those are my hands, Ella Ruth."

"Yes."

"Lordy girl, you're gifted." She clicked her tongue.

Ella Ruth smiled at the drawing. The baby's heel pushed at a place under her ribcage, stabbing at the home that grew smaller each day. She worked the pencil and hid the word "love" among Bell's many wrinkles. Her sketchbook was nearly full. Gert had a new one for her, but she'd been too tired to walk into town and get it. With Paul Allen gone off, they had no transportation.

A car rolled across the gravel in the driveway. The mail was early. Ella Ruth struggled to her feet. Why? Each day she believed the carrier would hand her a letter from Buster, and each day she was disappointed. A black car, official looking, sat in place of the mail truck. Maybe it was the state police, come to inform them that Paul Allen was dead or in prison. But then she saw the government seal and knew. She braced herself against the door.

"What's wrong?" Bell looked up from her cookies.

Two men, one dressed in an army uniform, the other in a black suit, came up the steps.

Bell wiped her hands on her apron and crossed the room, looking out the window over Ella Ruth's shoulder. "You got to be strong," she whispered. "For the baby."

The man in the uniform knocked on the door. Ella Ruth didn't even pause before she opened it.

They took her in for a moment. Her condition was evident. The one in the uniform spoke. "We're looking for Mrs. Wright, Mrs. Ella Ruth Wright."

The sound of the name swirled in her mind. Two of her fingers were stained with black charcoal. She rubbed them together. "I'm her."

The baby kicked.

"Please, come in." Bell pulled Ella Ruth back.

"Is he dead?" Ella Ruth made herself say the horrible word, the worst of her worries.

"No." The officer glanced at the man in black. "Can we sit down?"

Ella Ruth led the way to the round oak table.

The man in black picked up her sketchbook and studied it as the officer settled into the chair across from Ella Ruth. "You're quite good."

This man had to be a preacher. If Buster wasn't dead, why was he here? What use did she have for a preacher?

She looked at him. "Thank you."

"I'm the base chaplain in Fayetteville. I understand you lived there with your husband."

"Yes, I did."

He held out the sketchbook, and she took it. "You've hidden the word 'love' in the wrinkles of these beautiful hands."

She gave him a quick look. Maybe he was some kind of good luck. "You're the first to notice one of my words."

"Really? I'm honored. You do quite a good job of hiding the letters."

"I enjoy that part of drawing the most."

The chaplain held out his hand again. "I'm Chaplain Brown. Mostly everyone on base calls me Carl."

Ella Ruth took his hand. How had he put her at ease so quickly?

"What has happened to Buster?" Bell spoke over the handshake. Ella Ruth shivered and looked at her.

"Sergeant Wright has been wounded," the officer said. "It is serious. He received a dangerous head injury, but the doctors are confident that he will recover."

"Where is he now?" The baby became quite still inside of Ella Ruth, as if he were listening too.

The officer continued as if he had a prepared speech. "We're proud of your husband." He extended his hand to Ella Ruth.

She had to force herself to take it.

"I'm Commander Hart. Your husband saved his whole platoon. He walked right into a field, flushed the enemy out." He released her hand.

The two men looked at each other. Here came the bad part.

Bell squeezed Ella Ruth's arm. "Did you hear that, Ella Ruth? Our Buster is a hero."

"When he's well enough, he'll be presented with the Purple Heart." The commander smiled.

"Where is he? You didn't answer me." The tension grew thick in the room.

"He's been moved to England. He's going to be there for an undetermined length of time. He has to become stable before they send him home. The seas are not the safest right now. He'll come home on a marked Red Cross ship, but sometimes the Germans ignore such marking." Commander Hart looked her in the eye.

"How long?"

"That can't be predicted at this point."

The chaplain pulled out a paper from inside his jacket. "When he is moved, he'll go to New York for treatment and recovery."

"Exactly what is wrong with him?"

"He lost most of his right foot," Commander Hart explained. "He has a little of the heel left, and that will enable him to walk with less of a limp. And then there is the head injury. That is most worrisome at the moment."

The words hung in the air, but Ella Ruth felt a surge of relief. A foot seemed a small price to pay to get Buster home alive. The head injury, on the other hand, could keep him from being the Buster she knew.

The chaplain handed her a paper. "They found this on him."

Ella Ruth took it. Did she smell Buster there in the soft folds? When she saw his tight scrawled words, a pain spread across her back into her stomach. "When can I talk to him?"

"Maybe when he gets to New York." Commander Hart passed her another sheet of paper. "Here is the address of the hospital in England." He scooted back his chair. "I pray for Sergeant Wright's fast recovery. This is a slow process, but rest assured he is in the best hands possible." Both men stood as if on cue.

Ella Ruth stood too.

The chaplain took her hand again. "Trust in God."

A laugh almost escaped her. "Thank you."

Bell stood and wiped her hands on her apron. "That is where we stand strong."

"A good place." The commander nodded.

Ella Ruth watched the car disappear. "I'm going over to Mrs. Wright's." She pulled on her old coat from the hook.

"I don't think it's good to walk that far."

"What else can I do? I've got to get over there. You know how this town is. Someone will phone her, telling her a government car was here." A pain grabbed her stomach and held on like a toothache.

"What's wrong?" Bell took a step toward her.

"The baby is kicking the breath out of me." She continued out the door and down the drive. The letter grew soft in her hand. A few stubborn leaves clung to the bare trees. Patches of blue between heavy gray clouds turned the sky into an ever-changing painting. The baby twisted inside her. When the pain passed, Ella Ruth moved at a faster pace.

℞

Billie saw her coming and met her before she reached the porch. "Lord, Ella Ruth, why are you out walking on a day like this?" Billie's blue eyes looked so much like Buster's that Ella Ruth felt tears threatening to spill over.

"I came to see your mother." Ella Ruth often thought how nice it would be to have Billie as a real sister, something she'd never had. She rubbed her stomach. This baby wouldn't worry about family. She would be everything he needed.

"You don't look so good." Billie watched Ella Ruth.

"Would you look good if you were this fat?"

Billie's expression relaxed. "I was afraid you had some kind of bad news."

"Have you heard from Larry?"

"Yes, finally. The letter was a month old. He's cold, tired, and wishes that he had stayed home like his mother had begged him."

Ella Ruth squeezed her hand. "He'll be home safe before long."

"Of course he will."

Lacy came to stand on the porch.

"How are you and the boys?" Ella Ruth asked, but it was hard to look her in the eye. She reminded herself she had done nothing wrong. It was her father, Paul Allen, who had killed Tyler.

"How's Mr. Buster?" Lacy pushed the words at her, ignoring Ella Ruth's question. The look she gave was hard, harsh. Their friendship gone in one horrible night.

"All right," Ella Ruth said. Another pain worked across her stomach, and she looked at Billie. "Could I see your mother?"

"She's upstairs in the sewing room."

Ella Ruth climbed the stairs with Billie following. Lacy stood watching from the front hall.

"I bet you want to talk baby stuff." Billie smiled. "You know where she is."

ત્ર

Mrs. Wright sat bent over her Singer sewing machine, glasses pushed down on her nose, wisps of dark hair escaping the ball on the back of her head. When she looked at Ella Ruth, it was as if they spoke without words. Mothers in silence.

"Sit and tell me. I can take it." She motioned to the empty straight-back chair.

"He's alive but hurt badly. He's lost most of his right foot and has a head injury. They found this letter on him. I wanted to read it with you." She pushed it at Mrs. Wright. "You read it."

Mrs. Wright looked at the words and began. "Dear Ella Ruth: I am alive if you call this living, dear one. I miss you. It's hard here. I have one thing you must do. You must tell Mama that I came across Lee here in this hellhole of a world." Mrs. Wright stopped and swallowed before continuing in her calm voice. "He is alive and has come out on top as usual. He is an officer on a carrier. This is how I saw him. It's important that she knows this in case the worst happens to me. Take care of that baby and yourself. I love you more than anything in this whole world. I must go. Buster." A sigh escaped Mrs. Wright.

Then a strong pain grabbed Ella Ruth.

Mrs. Wright dropped the letter, and it floated to the floor. "What's wrong?"

The baby pushed and water rushed from Ella Ruth onto the floor, spreading toward the letter.

Mrs. Wright stood. "Billie! Call Dr. White."

Ella Ruth allowed a long moan to escape from her.

"Do not push here." Mrs. Wright pulled her to her feet. "Lacy."

Lacy was in the door far too quick. "Yes ma'am."

"Miss Ella Ruth's water has broken. I'm taking her down to the sick room. Could you gather the items we'll need?"

"I'm supposed to go to the hospital in Asheville," Ella Ruth protested. She watched Lacy pick up the wet letter. Would she read it? Of course she would.

"We've got a baby coming, honey." Mrs. Wright pulled her along as the urge to push came over her.

CR

Timothy James Wright came into the world in the same room where his father was born. He had all his fingers and toes. Ella Ruth held him close to her chest and allowed him to latch onto her breast. The pull was both painful and satisfying. She looked up and caught Granny Wright watching her.

"Now, I can be at peace. A boy to carry on the name. Amen." Granny died that night in her sleep, never seeing Lee again.

Chapter 17

Buster

Voices bled through a thick fog. Hands moved at him, rough, jerking. Hands with no faces, no bodies.

"You got a ticket home, soldier, if you'll just stay with us. You got it! Don't you damn leave us now. We risked our asses for you." The voice filtered into his mind, where he danced with Ella Ruth on the beach.

"That foot is bad. But I've seen worse. You're going to make it!" This was a different voice. "You saved your whole fucking platoon, soldier. You're a hero."

Buster struggled to tell him he was no hero, never would be.

"See, now you're going to talk to me. Good. Don't worry. I know you want to say you ain't a hero, but you are and we need folks like you out here. So you stay with us."

☙

December 19, 1944
Buster smelled smoke. He was limping through his mother's house and the smoke was so strong he was sure the flames would leap out at him. He kicked at a door and his foot exploded. Ella Ruth sat at the kitchen table, holding a bundle of blankets. "He won't live long without your help."

He jerked his head up from a pillow and the world twirled.

A man in the bed next to him grinned. "Damn, I'd given up on you." The man sat up, a sheet—flat where one of his legs should have been—spread over the lower half of his body. "They said you stepped on a landmine. I guess we got a lot in common. Everyone going around calling us heroes and we'd just as soon have a whole body instead." The grin was a mask, a clown's smile.

A nurse walked by.

"Hey, look here." The man pointed toward Buster.

Confusion worked in his head, rocking and floating, twirling.

"Sergeant Wright, it's good to see you're awake." The nurse had a British accent. She smelled sweet, like one of the gardenias on Mama's bushes. His stomach turned over. "The doctor will be glad for this news."

He wiggled his toes and pain shot through him, a welcome pain that proved he had both of his legs and feet.

"Rest."

He chose that moment to lose his insides all over the bed. The room spun like a merry-go-round.

"Whoa." The soldier next to him laughed. "That ought to make you feel better. "

◌⃝

He woke to bright sunshine and strong hands turning him on his side. "You need to wake up, Sergeant, sir. You've got some news." The man—no, he was a boy—tied his hospital gown in the back. "Here come the old biddies, sir."

"What news?"

The boy only winked as a woman with a gosh-awful hat with a blood red flower walked up to the bed.

"Sergeant Wright?" The woman wore pure white gloves. And why did everyone keep calling him sergeant?

Buster trained his attention on this woman's face. "Yes."

"My name is Elizabeth Young. I am with the Red Cross. I have some important news from home." She unfolded what looked to be a telegram.

Home. What a wonderful word.

"You became a father on December 17. You have a healthy son. He weighed 9 pounds even."

Buster pushed up on his elbows. "Ella Ruth?" The bile came into his mouth.

"She is fine. I can send a telegram on your behalf."

"Tell her she's the hero of this family, and that she is the love of my life."

The woman smiled. "It is my pleasure." Her short, practical heels clomped as she left his bedside.

CR

Buster opened his eyes to fog outside the window. Each time he woke up it was a little easier on him. The room had stopped twirling.

A nurse stood at the foot of his bed. "This one cannot be moved. I don't care what any of you say." The building rocked.

Bombs.

A soldier about Buster's age held a clipboard. "I have my orders to move out all American wounded. It's orders. They're going home. This area is too dangerous."

Buster pushed into a sitting position. "I want to go home."

The soldier looked at him. "See?"

The nurse crossed her arms. "He's not up to a trip across the ocean."

"I'm ready. It can't be worse than stepping on a landmine." Buster tried for a grin.

The nurse glared at him. "I hate this damn war. It takes apart everything we try to repair."

Buster glanced at his feet for the first time. Part of his foot was missing. No one had told him this. It could have been his whole leg. Hell, it should have been his leg. Fuck it all.

Chapter 18

Ella Ruth

Ella Ruth fed Timothy as Billie decorated a large fir tree in the front room. Mile, Lacy's youngest, sat at her feet while Lacy held the ladder for Billie, who was hanging ornaments on the upper part of the tree. Mrs. Wright was in town taking care of personal business concerning Granny Wright's death. It suited the rest of them to be at the house, trying to bring some cheer into days that were often dark and worried.

"I have to go change Timothy's diaper." Ella Ruth stood.

"Hurry back. You have to be here when I put on the star," Billie sang out.

Lacy frowned. "Mile, you stay put. Understand."

"He can come if he wants." Ella Ruth smiled at Lacy.

"That's okay. He will sit right here."

Mile was a handsome little guy who acted like he was an old man half the time. Sometimes Ella Ruth wanted to remind Lacy that he was only three, but she knew how well she would be received.

She heard someone humming as she entered the upstairs hall. She peeked in Lee's old bedroom and saw Tucker sitting on the floor. In his hands he held an open book. He kept humming, not noticing Ella Ruth.

"What are you reading?" Ella Ruth asked, holding Timothy on her shoulder and patting his tiny back.

Tucker looked at her. "This is a book about pirates. You know, pirates are like the ghosts that came in the night and took my daddy away."

The very mention of that night made Ella Ruth ache. "It's nice you can read so well."

"Miz Wright said I could read any of these books I wanted. She told me I could take them home, but I knew Mama wouldn't have it, so I read them up here." At nearly six, Tucker was a bright boy.

"No," said a voice from the door. Lacy had followed them up,

Mile at her heels. "Them books have no place in our house, Tucker. Now get back down here." Lacy's words held roughness that Ella Ruth had never heard her use with the kids.

Tucker closed the book and looked at his mama. "I wrote a letter to Santa. The kids at school said Santa is white and he don't come visit coloreds."

Lacy sucked in her breath.

"Well, those kids don't know a thing." Ella Ruth rushed ahead. "That's just being mean. Of course Santa comes to all children's homes." She knew right after the words came out that she had made a mistake.

"I asked Santa to bring Daddy back, but I know he can't. Don't worry, Mama."

Lacy looked away from her son.

"So I asked Santa for a complete set of encyclopedias." His face was bright with excitement. "In them books, Mama, ever secret is revealed. I seen a picture of them books back in the summer when that salesman was going door to door. He told me I could look up anything at all and find out all about stuff in those books."

"Tucker, that is one big wish. How much would they even cost?" She gave Ella Ruth a look.

"We don't need to know, Mama. Santa will make them in his workshop and you know he'll bring me books. Shoot, it ain't like I'm asking for toys and candy." He looked at the cover of the book in his lap.

"How much did that man tell you the books cost?" Lacy asked.

"Sixty-two dollars."

Lacy opened her mouth and closed it.

"Where did the salesman get the books, Tucker?" Ella Ruth asked.

"He lived in Asheville, ma'am. He gave me his card in case Mama wanted to buy them. I didn't say anything, seeing how hard it is for Mama to get money for food."

"Tucker, I don't have *that* hard of a time." She rolled her eyes toward Ella Ruth. "Things have just been tight since Mama had her stroke."

"I understand." Ella Ruth smiled.

"I really doubt that," Lacy hissed at her.

"Do you hate for me to read, Mama?"

Lacy dropped to her knees beside her oldest son. "No, darling. I want you to be smart. You just have to watch out. Some folks don't take to coloreds being smart."

"Like Daddy was smart?"

"Yes."

There was no chance of Lacy buying those books. Ella Ruth knew this. If she had the extra money, she would have given it to Tucker right then.

CR

"Miss Ella Ruth." Lacy stood in the door of the front room the next day.

Timothy had finished eating, and Ella Ruth was so sleepy she could cry. "Yes, Lacy."

"I need some help."

Ella Ruth sat up straight. "What do you need?"

"I got to get me a way to Asheville tomorrow. That man who sells the books ain't going to sell them to a colored woman without jacking up the price and you know it."

"Yes, I'm sure you're right. I'll get Buster's truck and go buy them for you."

Lacy nodded. "Okay. But first I got to get the money."

Ella Ruth knew better than to offer her any help.

She was about to check Timothy's diaper when the mail truck pulled in front of the house. Ella Ruth held her breath. Maybe she would hear that Buster was on his way home. The mailman knocked, and Ella Ruth stood.

"I'll get it," Lacy said.

"No. I want to." Ella Ruth rushed ahead.

"Hello, Miss Ella Ruth. Is Lacy Kurt here?"

"Yes." Ella Ruth tried not to show her disappointment.

Lacy looked at the mailman with surprise. "Yes sir."

"I got this letter for you but addressed for here." He gave her a look. Lacy took the envelope.

Ella Ruth didn't recognize the writing, and there was no return address.

"Thank you sir." She shut the door after the mailman turned.

Ella Ruth wanted to tear the letter open herself.

Lacy opened the envelope and out fluttered money, swirling to the ground.

"That's a lot, Lacy."

She raised her eyebrows at Ella Ruth. "Three twenties. Who would send me money here?"

Ella Ruth shrugged, and Timothy stirred in her arms. "I don't know but it's enough, Lacy."

Lacy smiled. "Yes ma'am, it is. Let's go. I got me some books to pick up. And don't tell me I can't ride."

"Let me get some things for Timothy. We will slip out of here before anyone notices we're gone."

And they were off on a Christmas mission. Books for a boy who wanted to read so bad he sent Santa a letter.

Later, when the books were hidden safely at Lacy's little house, Ella Ruth decided to take Timothy by Gert's. She answered the door before Ella Ruth could knock.

"You brought me a baby? What a glorious Christmas gift." She ushered Ella Ruth and Timothy into the warm kitchen.

Gert's face almost glowed. Only the slightest shadow was visible under her eyes. She was truly well.

"You look good, Gert."

"And you my dear look fabulous for a woman who just had a baby." She smiled warmly.

"I wanted to stop and see you before Christmas. I'm probably in trouble for taking Buster's truck, but Lacy, Mrs. Wright's maid, had a gift we needed to pick up. It was worth the risk."

"I would think, dear, that if the truck belongs to your husband, it is yours now as well." Gert narrowed her intense gray eyes.

"Mrs. Wright can be kind of funny. I think I will have to go back to Paul Allen's soon. He's been gone since early November. I love

Bell, but I don't want to risk taking Timothy there to live. Paul Allen could come back any time. My baby doesn't need to be around him."

"My dear, there is no reason to go there. Come here to my house. I so want both of you." She took Timothy from Ella Ruth. "He needs his great-aunt."

"We both know we would be taking way too big of a risk. Paul Allen would love a reason to hurt you."

Gert threw her head back in a mean laugh. "I'd like to see him try, Ella Ruth. I would love to shoot him when he does."

And she was serious.

◌

December 27, 1944

Buster's bedroom always took Ella Ruth back in time. On the windowsill was a collection of treasures that only a boy would love: a shiny blue rock, a crumbling bird's nest, the fragile wings of a Monarch butterfly, a June bug, and a rusted pocketknife.

She rocked Timothy as he nursed. Outside the window, snowflakes floated here and there. She was glad to be free of Paul Allen's house for a while, but really, this house wasn't any better. It was a different kind of jail. Mrs. Wright was kind, too kind. She delivered her advice with a syrupy smile. Ella Ruth should have been grateful that her mother-in-law cared, but she wasn't, because the caring didn't seem real.

She looked at the telegram in her hand for the hundredth time. What a beautiful Christmas gift. Buster was on his way home to New York. Home.

Mrs. Wright appeared in the door. "Up already?" She stepped in. Ella Ruth longed to shut the door, but it wasn't her home or even her room.

"I'm leaving as soon as I can to meet Buster's ship." Mrs. Wright ran her fingers over the top of Timothy's head.

"I'm going too. I just need to get a few things for Timothy." Her heart skipped a beat. Finally, she would hold Buster close again.

Mrs. Wright looked at her. A little frown replaced the big smile.

148

"Honey, you can't drag this baby all the way to New York City, especially in the winter. He could get very sick. He's just too young."

"But Buster is my husband. Of course I'm going to welcome him home." Who did this woman think she was?

"I understand, dear, but dragging your baby on that train trip is just not right. It's not being a good mother."

The words cut through Ella Ruth.

"I'll go alone. It's the only sensible thing. You wait here for news. Buster's not out of the woods yet. He needs time and his mother."

"I'm going," Ella Ruth insisted, fighting the tears building in her throat. "He needs his wife. He needs to see his son."

"You can't. I won't permit it. You have to act like a mother, Ella Ruth."

"I am acting like a mother! A mother would go to her husband and bring the child he has not seen. We need each other. We need to be a family." She stroked Timothy's soft bald head. "Who are you to tell me I can't come?" The words were sharp.

"A real mother would accept her role here. It's part of growing up, putting your children first. And how will you go, Ella Ruth? Will your father pay your way?"

Ella Ruth only looked at her. This was the true side of her mother-in-law. But the woman had won. No doubt. She had won. Who was Ella Ruth fooling? She would never be a real part of the Wright family. They only liked each other, not outsiders like herself.

"I'll call with news each day, and as soon as Buster can speak on the phone, I'll have him call you."

The snowflakes floated, swirled thicker.

"I'll let you know when I'm leaving." Mrs. Wright touched Timothy's hand. "It'll be fine, Ella Ruth."

"Fine with who, Mrs. Wright?"

She frowned and left the room.

Ella Ruth put Timothy in the cradle—the same cradle Buster had used as a baby—and went to the desk, pulling a writing tablet and pencil from the drawer.

Dear Buster:
  I cannot live here anymore with your mother. I cannot live with Paul Allen. I am without a home. So I'm going to the only real family I have. You will be able to find me at Gert's. I will wait however long it takes. I would be there to welcome you home if I could, but your mother refuses to allow us to go.
  Love Ella Ruth

She placed the note in a sealed envelope with Buster's name on the bed. Lacy was the only person she met when she left the house with her two bags and Timothy.

"Where you going?"

Did that girl always have to speak so mean? "I'm going to my aunt's."

"The snow is getting bad." Lacy put her hand on her hip.

"Really, Lacy, I don't need you accusing me of being a bad mother too. I'm leaving this place. You should be happy because you've done nothing but blame me for Tyler's death." Ella Ruth stormed out of the house, but not before she saw Lacy's mouth fall open.

ભ

Gert threw open the door as if she hadn't seen Ella Ruth in ages. "What are you doing out in the snow? Let me hold that baby and warm him up." She gathered Timothy into her arms and looked at Ella Ruth's bags. Her expression turned sober when her eyes met Ella Ruth's. "Bad news about Buster?"

Ella Ruth followed Gert into the front room. "No."

"You've come to stay here." It wasn't a question. "Good. We'll cross any problems we have when they appear."

Ella Ruth sat the bags on the floor. Warmth, light, and peace filled every corner of the room. This was a place to hide from the world. White plaster walls, long windows covered with beautiful lace, and space added to the perfection. A deep green sofa with curved arms and large wooden feet sat in the center. A beautiful rug with pink roses covered much of the polished honey-colored wooden floors.

What if she sprawled on the rug, the magic carpet, waiting for its passenger? A cherry wood table stood in the one of the corners. A pot of blooming tulip bulbs sat in the center. The fireplace mantle held several different-sized frames, all bearing photographs. Ella Ruth sighed contentedly. She could *breathe* here.

Gert stared into Timothy's face. "He looks like your mother. I have baby pictures to prove it. But we have plenty of time for all that. Sit down and rest."

"This feels more like home than Mrs. Wright's house."

"I'm glad, dear." A put-out look crossed Aunt Gert's face. "Your husband's family is viewed as the best in town. That's all they know. How did we all end up here in this place? With our assigned seats?" She sat in a rocker and chuckled. "We'll take a drawer from one of the dressers upstairs and make a bed for this one," she said, and then she looked up at Ella Ruth. "There's so much for you to learn about your family. And when you do, my job will be finished."

"What job?"

Gert smiled. "I have to give you your missing past, of course. That is how I honor your mother, because I can never find out what really happened to her. Are you ready for the truth?"

"I'm not a girl anymore." Ella Ruth met her gaze. "I need to know what you know."

Gert gave a firm nod and stood. "You take our boy, and I'll get us a drawer."

Ella relaxed on the sofa, drifting off into a sense of well-being, Timothy held close to her.

When Gert returned, they settled sleeping Timothy on a pillow in the drawer. He looked so cute. Gert motioned Ella Ruth into the kitchen. "You sit here and I'll make some tea." She pushed the cream pitcher and sugar bowl toward her. "Tomorrow I am taking you to Asheville, so we have much ground to cover."

Asheville. Two trips in one week. Ella Ruth felt free at last, the world at her fingertips.

Gert placed a thick mug in front of her. "Drink your tea. I'll be right back."

Ella Ruth took in her environment. Green feathery plants in

small clay pots lined the windowsill. Warm pine cabinets made the room cozy. The woodstove range burned coal, heating the kitchen to a toasty temperature. Several paintings, delicate, detailed flowers, soft blurry lines, a fuzzy vision between sleep and waking, hung on the wall. All were by the same artist, signed "EP."

Aunt Gert squeaked the door open, carrying a large picnic basket that she placed on the table. Then she sat across from Ella Ruth with her own mug of tea. "Go through this basket. When you finish, we'll talk. Why don't you take it into the front room so you can be close to our boy?"

Ella Ruth settled into the sofa, the basket beside her, and pulled out a lavender envelope covered with tiny pink flowers. It was addressed to Rochester, New York. The return address read, "The Nature Camp From Hell." This made Ella Ruth laugh aloud.

"Ah, you must have found a camp letter," Gert called from the kitchen. "Read on."

June 25, 1914
Dearest Sister:

I am so bored with this stupid camp. Whose idea was this? Mother's if I remember right. All we do is hike around the woods that have every living thing imaginable roaming in the shadows. If I'm not hiking, I am rowing a canoe around the roped area of the lake. We are forbidden to escape and venture further out, even though most of us are quite capable swimmers. A good day is rain. Then, I stay in my bunk and read my favorite books. Thank God I brought my books. You know Mother wanted me to leave them behind. I, like you, am not meeting Mother's expectations. You're so lucky! They've left you alone. I long to be grown. Camp is for babies. I want to be a painter, travel to Europe. Who knows, maybe I'll be a writer too. It can be done.

The rain is letting up. And we have a stupid dance to attend. Tell me, what fun is a dance with only fourteen-year-old girls in attendance?

Your Sister Always, Ella

Ella Ruth's hand shook as she placed the letter to the side. She reached into the basket again, and her fingers closed on a book cov-

ered in leather with gold-embossed letters, again, the initials "EP."
She opened the book and a faded picture of a young girl with dark
hair pulled high on her head fell into her lap. Ella Ruth stared into
the haint's eyes, the eyes of her mother.

December 12, 1917
> *Today I am seventeen years old, practically a woman, so unlike all
the impractical schoolgirls working so hard to become good wife material. Mother hates me for my lack of interest. But for some queer reason, I
think Daddy understands.*
>
> *I love to paint. Was it not Mother who introduced me to these
"skills" in the first place? I have my sights set on college. Mother will
not have it! I have to make Daddy see things my way.*
> *EP*

February 19, 1918
> *This is the coldest winter Upstate New York has experienced in
fifty years. The maids can't keep the stoves burning hot enough. I went
to bed tonight with a hot water bottle that cools before I can get comfortable. There is an art college I want to attend in New York City.
Mother refuses to discuss the notion, even when I pointed out that Gert
received an education. Mother says "Gertrude" is a special case since
Robert died. I say hogwash! Daddy says my dreams are too big for a girl,
but I can hear the pride he takes in me. He is my ticket out of here unmarried. Today, I will finish a painting that I started just before
Christmas. It is a painting just for Daddy, a likeness of his birthplace.
Daddy will return from business in Georgia. I will leave it in his study
for him.*
>
> *Gert is so happy at the teaching college. I told her that her talents
were wasting away, but she only writes smiles into her letters. I see her
teaching as an old lady, unmarried, alone. At least I will have my art.
That's all the company I will need.*
> *EP*

May 6, 1918
> *Halleluiah! I am going to Savannah, Georgia to study with Miss
Emma Cheves Wilkins, an outstanding artist who studied in Paris. It
is a rare opportunity and my stomach is full of butterfly wings. Daddy
does a lot of business in the city and feels it will be a much safer place for*

me. I will live in the house with a family called Owens. Daddy says that house is the best example of English Regency architecture in America. He says the Owens family is well established and will teach me something about culture. Of course this was for Mother's benefit. I'm in love with the place sight unseen. I have been allotted a set of rooms for painting and living. It will be Heaven on earth.

EP

Ella Ruth closed the journal and put it to the side. The smell of honeysuckles filled the room. She looked around to see where it came from. It was late December. A cold chill walked across her scalp. She sipped her tea, now lukewarm but still good, and took another letter from the basket. The journal made her mama real—like she sat in the room with Ella Ruth—and as much as she wanted this, it frightened her. There was so much to take in. Her mother, Ella, was a painter. She had struggled so she could study art. It turned out that Ella Ruth was very much like her.

May 6, 1919
Dear Gert:

I hope this letter finds you well. How is the weather? It is hot here. All I have to do is walk across the room and sweat breaks out on me like on one of Mother's work-hands. Mrs. Owens allowed me to setup a studio in an upper bedroom. It has wonderful southern exposure. I have painted six canvases since the beginning of the school year. Emma—yes, can you believe I'm on first-name basis with the most famous woman artist in the South—agrees I should show in the art show next month. Of course, this means I must stay the summer. Emma is off for Paris and promises next summer she will take me. Imagine, Gert. Paris. All my dreams are coming true. Mrs. Owens loves the idea of me staying on here full time and promised to help me sell Daddy on its advantages. I am a great asset to her. We are planning themes for her upcoming party. Whatever I have to do to remain near Emma I will do. Mrs. Owens is such a southern belle or maybe a matriarch would be a better term. She really doesn't care for girls looking for an education in art. She is much like Mother with a more tolerant side, but we have one thing in common: the love of this city, the river meandering close by, the stately old buildings, and the churches alone are worth a few days of looking. I want to paint when I walk the streets. When you stand in one of the squares and look at the massive old-world stained glass, the beauty of this southern oasis comes through. The cemetery tells stories of the city. Some of the headstones have complete events written on them. This place holds souls. Ghosts are everywhere. I've become accustomed to seeing an apparition gliding down the stairs of this massive house or across a yard. Pirates once came to these banks with their treasure. Blackbeard visited regularly. They've named an island for him close by.

Daddy will listen to you, Gert. You must convince him to allow me to remain in Savannah until I have finished my training. I've grown close to Emma. I do not want to lose my place with her. You asked after friends my own age. Who has the time? The girls are giggly and useless. The boys on the other hand are much more to my liking. They live, breathe, and eat their art. Many lively discussions take place on River Street in a small pub where we meet on some evenings. What a scandal. I argue as well as the boys and they have encouraged me to attend. They respect me and my paintings. If I ever marry—and I say if—it will be to a man like this, who loves his art and debates. It will be important to him to have a wife with talent. But artists are selfish and possessed when it comes to their work. Because of these traits, how can I ever marry?

Mrs. Owens works hard at finding me people my own age. Last night she had this uncouth lout, Paul Allen, over to dinner. He is some kind of official with the railroad, or so he told Mrs. Owen. He's from somewhere in North Carolina, some little village at the foot of Black Mountain. I think I offended him by laughing. He is five years my senior and a pig, Gert, just a true pig. This is the kind of man Mother would hunt out for me. He turned his nose up at my paintings, accusing them of being too watery, too girly. He likes solid scenes. What the hell is a solid scene? He probably decorates his home with dime store prints. Mrs. Owens is much taken with him, and this means I haven't seen the last of him.

Please speak with Daddy. Tell him about Paul Allen. Maybe Mother will believe I'll find a perfect husband here.

Your Loving Sister, Ella

Ella Ruth put the letter away and went to the kitchen to look at the paintings. Her mother's paintings. They were beautiful. Her mother had been an artist, a good one. A small canvas near the window featured a pair of high heels. One was flipped over on its side as if pulled off as soon as the woman walked in the door. After looking her fill, Ella Ruth went back to the letters, pulling one at random. Mama had found Paul Allen and disliked him. How had they ended up married?

December 19, 1921
Dear Gert:

How is teaching? I don't see how you stay in the same place all the time. I want to travel! I want to see everything there is to be seen. Don't you want more? You could be a writer. I hope one day you come to your senses and do something more. Move from that fortress of a college, where you're teaching, and experience the world.

I love my job at the Atlanta Constitution. My ideas are used often in the ad layouts. I know what you're thinking, but this is different. I am gaining exposure, not selling out to allow the males to get ahead of me. I have many friends. Tommy is my best friend. He is a reporter. I compete with him. He loves Dickens and quotes him too much. He has given me some great stories. For this I thank him, but I am quite capable of finding them on my own. It's just that the South is horrible to women, much worse than New York. They expect them just to look pretty, be gentle.

My hair is gone. It curls like crazy around my face like a crown. Short hair suits me. It makes the guys take me more serious. My studio apartment is a wonderful place to paint. Yes, I'm still painting. I'll never quit. The evening light in my apartment washes across the wooden floors in just the right angle. I'm working on a children's book about a little girl whose parents go off on a great adventure, dragging the girl along. I'm sketching the small pictures depicting the scenes. I am happy with life just as it is. If I'm still too long, I remember Daddy is gone. How could this have happened so quickly? The hole in our family cannot be repaired. But I don't allow myself to be still. That's the trick.

Sometimes I think I will write Mother a letter, but what would I say? We're both much happier without each other. She'll never like me until I find the right man. And I can't like her because I don't want a man.

Christmas will be upon us soon. I may go to a friend's house. It will be a nice trip. His name is Paul Allen. He is the man I wrote you about in my earlier letters, down in Savannah. Yes, the one I couldn't stand. He's working in Atlanta now. He's actually very charming. I do explain to him I'm not interested in love and such things. But Christmas is a social time and it gets lonely without family.

Do take care of yourself, Gert. I'll be thinking about you.

Your Loving Sister,

Ella

February 26, 1922

Dear Gert:

I write to you with the happiest of news. I hope you will feel the same and share in my joy. I know your reservations when it comes to Paul Allen. You've voiced them and have some good points; to say he hates women when you've never met him is a bit of a stretch. I am in love with him. I didn't plan it this way. It just happens, as I'm sure these kinds of things do. I plan to marry him May 9th. I wish you would come to the wedding. We will have it here in Atlanta and then move to his little farm on Black Mountain. It is beautiful country where I can paint, Gert. Yes, he knows I will still be an artist. It is time to move on from Atlanta and grow up. Don't you think? I can't stay here the rest of my life, writing articles for women in the Sunday paper and doing ad layout. I need to do something with my art, and having a family will be good.

I've sent a letter to Mother, but she has not written me since Daddy's passing, so I don't look to hear from her. I do wish you would come. Let me know if you can.

Your Loving Sister,

Ella

Another letter was folded within this letter and fell into Ella Ruth's lap.

March 25, 1922 Dear Gert:

Thank you for saying you will come. It means the world to me! I understand your concerns, but you must trust me. I think when you meet Paul you will understand why I love him so much. He is excited to finally meet a part of my family. He is in love with me and wants us to have a beautiful life.

Yes, I did finish the children's book. An agent in New York has agreed to review it. He seems to like the idea. I have not told Paul. I feel guilty, but I don't want to fail. I will tell him if the deal actually happens.

We have decided to have the wedding in Swannanoa Gap. You will not believe this town. It is so cute. You will just die when you get here. There's no streetcars or big department stores, but we're not too far from Asheville where all those things can be found on a smaller scale than Atlanta. And you will see my little house on Black Mountain. It is perfect for an artist. I keep in touch with Emma, you know, the artist. She says this quiet place might be just what I need for painting. I can't wait to see you dear sister.

Love, Ella

Ella Ruth marveled at how Mama seemed to fall head over heels for a man she despised earlier. There had to be a reason. According to the letters, Paul Allen was taking everything away from Mama, and she was helping him. Did love really make her that stupid? Grandmother Allen must have hated Mama the first time she met her. After all, she was an independent young woman who had her own life. Ella Ruth reached into the basket and brought out a large packet of letters held together with a faded blue ribbon and covered with dust. The hairs on her arm stood on end.

May 28, 1922

I am sorry to have waited so long to write you back. Paul and I are settling into our new home. We enjoyed ourselves immensely on the beach, but our honeymoon was cut short because Mother Allen sliced her hand with a butcher knife. She sent a telegram to our hotel. I never saw the injury, but the bandage covered her whole hand and a good portion of her arm. The details were too gruesome to hear. Mother Allen is lucky she didn't lose the use of her hand. Of course she was very sorry for spoiling our time, but what could be done?

Upon our return, I found a forwarded letter from both the paper and the agent. The paper wants me to write weekly stories from home and mail them in each week, a week ahead of time. The agent wants to come and see me. He is very interested in my book. I have agreed to meet him in Asheville a week from today. So, this presents the problem of going to Asheville without Paul knowing. Of course this is what I get for lying. It so happens he has business in Atlanta and will be gone for a week. I will have the truck. Simple. He doesn't like the idea of me working for the paper. He reminded me of my art. He's right, you know. I will keep you posted on how things go.

I hope your leg heals soon. A broken leg, sister. You missed the best wedding ever, but I do understand. You must be more careful. If I didn't know better, I'd say you were faking this to keep from watching me marry. I will be fine. I've made the right choice.

Your Loving "Married" Sister,
Ella

June 18, 1922
Dear Gert:

It was so good to hear from you. I love the picture of you in your cast. I was only kidding. A broken leg must be painful. I've decided not to work for the paper. I'm not sure how I'll handle the agent or the book. Right now I think it is best to begin a family. I'm not getting any younger. I am married. It is kind of expected.

Paul bought me a beautiful paint set with a leather portfolio from Atlanta. I have turned the extra bedroom into a studio for the time. When I become with child, this room will be the nursery.

You know Gert, people around here laugh when I talk about writing for the paper or painting. Mother Allen always points out that my place is supporting my husband, not outshining him. She has a point, but I can't be held back. I am so different from them it sometimes scares me. I fear I'll never fit in unless I become like them. Paul says it's only natural for a woman to put her family first. Women are considered second class all over this country but never so much as here on Black Mountain in the Allen Family. I know I'm on my soapbox.

Write to me soon,
Ella

October 3, 1922
Dear Gert:

What a beautiful autumn. The colors inspire me to paint. I do believe it is some of my best work. I no longer seek approval of my art. I am just painting like a mad woman, and it has gained me a reputation. I am thankful when Paul is out of town on business. It gives me day after day just to be myself.

The agent from New York has pushed again for a decision. You will be ashamed of my dishonesty, but I have accepted his offer to find a publisher for my book under the pen name John Barnes. Under the circumstances it seemed the best thing to do. He has begged me to come to New York and live, to leave Paul, so that I can write and draw in peace. He says the advance on the book would cover the expenses.

Paul can never know about the book. He would not understand or tolerate my dishonesty. I will not run away from my problems by moving to New York. It pains me to admit that you were right. I am not happy. I am compromising my values and passions every day that I remain in this union.

Pray for me. I am doing everything in my power to remain child-free. A baby would make this life too hard. I want to be a mother, but with someone I really love.

Write me your thoughts,
Ella

The letter shook in Ella Ruth's hand. The John Barnes book had been with her since she could remember. Grandmother Allen did not approve of it, but she never took it away. Ella Ruth would crawl under her bed when she was nine and read the book about a mother and daughter taking great adventures together around the world. The mother was a writer and the daughter wanted to be an artist. The father was never mentioned. This did not bother Ella Ruth. As a matter of fact, she liked the book for this very reason. Under her bed, she would sketch scenes of the mother and daughter team in Paris and London. They didn't look as good as the illustrations in the book, but she learned from trying.

And now this letter proved that her mother was John Barnes. All those nights of yearning for Mama, and really she was right there by her bed. The book was a love letter to her daughter. Ella Ruth wasn't sure how to combine that with the fact that her own mama had not wanted to be pregnant, at least not by Paul Allen.

January 10, 1923 Dear Gert:
Thank you for the offer to come and visit, but it is impossible. Paul will not allow me to go so far away. I think he knows if I leave I will never return. He has forced me to rid the house of my paintings. I took them to a small art gallery in Asheville. I spoke with the owner of the

gallery last week. He reported that a group of four paintings I called four seasons have sold for one thousand dollars. Enclosed is the check. Please deposit it in your account for safekeeping.

Things are not all bad. I am planning a flower garden for this spring. Paul thoroughly approves of this. He is so stupid. He doesn't get that I can create art in all kind of forms. I will not give up, Gert. I miss you so.

Love,
EP
PS. I have shed his name. I will not use it unless I'm forced.

April 29, 1923
Dear Gert:

Spring is here. I am planting my flower seeds. The fresh dirt takes me back to our childhood days with Daddy in his garden. Oh, how I wish things were different and that I somehow had made better choices. This marriage is bondage. I'm only alive outside in the fresh air. Enclosed is a check for two thousand dollars. Someone has bought the remaining paintings I had at the gallery. Keep it safe. I think I will need it soon.

Love,
EP

June 15, 1923
Dear Gert:

I suspect Paul is onto me. I fear he may be hiding your letters. I have not heard from you since April. If you get this letter, place an ad in the Asheville Tribune: "One baby cradle for sale to the right mother." I will know.

Paul has succeeded in his plan to have a family. This will not change my plans. If anything, it makes me more determined to get out of here. I have to save my child.

Love,
EP

August 28, 1923
Dear Gert:

I saw the ad! Thank God. I miss your letters. I am in prison here, but being with child has its good points. Paul refuses to sleep with me or to touch me since my belly is so fat.

I have a secret. I have a friend who bought my paintings from the art gallery. I meet him in Asheville when I can sneak away. We have lunch at the drugstore and take long walks around the town. I love being with him. We have done nothing to make me ashamed. We only talk of art and writing. I must escape my life.

Love,
EP

October 4, 1923
Dear Gert:

I love your idea of sending your letters to my friend John so he can get them to me. It was absolute Heaven to receive your words of encouragement. You mustn't come here. You know how strong Paul is, much stronger than you can imagine. He is capable of doing anything. My friend wants me to leave Paul, but I fear what he will do to both of us if I do. Yes, I am in love with this man. No, I cannot leave. Paul is capable of many things and killing someone is nothing to him. I know this. Pray for an answer.

Love,
EP

December 19, 1923
Dear Gert:

Christmas is upon us. I hate it. I hate a lot these days. I really hate my life. I'm lonely for you. I go through the motions only for this child I carry. I know it is a girl. I feel it in my bones. Paul will hate that. He wants a boy. I will write when the baby comes. When she is here, I know I will have to make my move.

Love,
EP

February 26, 1924
Dear Gert:

I named her Ella Ruth. This baby girl is the most beautiful child in the world. She was born at home yesterday morning. Paul has insisted that you be notified of the birth even if you will not write me. Why won't you write? Paul is quite happy with fatherhood and a loving husband.

Your Sister,
Ella Allen

March 24, 1924
Dear Gert:

    This is the first chance I have had to get into Asheville to mail a letter. Ella Ruth is a shining light. My friend gave me the pile of letters you've written. I miss you so. I can't take these letters home for fear Paul will find them. I will read them and allow my friend to keep them for me. He keeps all your letters. I have to do something. It is becoming too hard to sneak away to Asheville. I have to get out of there.

Love,
EP

May 26, 1924
Dear Gert:

    This is serious. I am with child again. This time I do not know who the father is. I know it is a mess. Paul has forced himself on me twice, even as little Ella Ruth cried in her cradle.

    My friend and I have made love once. He wants it to be his child. He threatens to come and get me and Ella Ruth. He has influence in the south. I think he can keep me safe. I have to try.

Love,
EP

June 13, 1924
Dear Gert:

    I leave today while Paul is gone away on business. He will find a note when he returns, but I'm sure Mother Allen will be here snooping before then. I pray God takes pity on the mess I've made.

Love,
EP

August 1, 1924
Dear Gert:

    Every day that passes I become more comfortable with Paul not finding us. I keep hidden. My friend pointed out I can't live my whole life inside his house without leaving, but right now I feel safer. As this child grows in me, kicking, I think of the freedom I've provided him.

Yes, I believe it is a boy. Ella Ruth will know a true life. I am enjoying your letters.

Love,

EP

September 12, 1924

Dear Gert:

Life glows for me. Ella Ruth is thriving. The baby is growing. I pray this life will continue. I do jump when I hear a squeak on the floorboards or a knock at the door, but maybe one day this too will pass. John says to feel safe with him. He has promised to protect us all. He loves Ella Ruth as his own. He takes us out to eat. But I find myself watching for Paul. He won't give up. I know him too well. I've hurt his pride. He will look for us.

Love,

EP

October 21, 1924

Dear Gert:

I believe just maybe Paul has given up. My life with John grows safer. His home is beautiful. The sun porch overlooking the back garden is my studio. I am painting and it is beautiful. Ella Ruth sits at my feet and the baby inside me kicks. It is a newfound music written just for us. I will feel safer when the baby is born this January. I will then file for divorce. God help us all.

God Bless,

EP

December 15, 1924

Dear Gert:

I look forward to your upcoming visit. This will be the best Christmas ever. Ella Ruth will meet her aunt. John laughs as he helps me decorate. You will love him. He is so good to us.

John has approached Paul. He wants our baby to be born with his name. Paul will have no part of a divorce. John has explained to him that he could make it very hard on Paul's business. John is an attorney and has found many criminal links to Paul. I am worried. I know Paul is stirred up now. He does not like to be threatened. I'm scared for us, but I can't back down. I have to be finished with him. That's it. I have

to provide this baby and Ella Ruth with a better life.
I love you, Gert. When I see you, we will catch up on a lifetime.
We've had oceans of time stolen from us. I love you, sister.
Love,
EP

Ella Ruth stared at the final letter. She was more convinced than ever that Paul Allen had killed her mother. He would never pay for what he did, and this thought made her stand up and stomp across the room.

Gert walked in from the kitchen, looking grim. "All finished?"

The tears bottled inside Ella Ruth since she could remember chose that moment to come pouring out, and Aunt Gert held her like a mother would until she grew quiet again.

CR

The fragrance of coffee floated up the stairs to the room where Ella Ruth dressed. *Her* room. In *her* house. For the first time in her life she was home. She checked on Timothy, sleeping peacefully in his drawer, and decided to explore the property while he napped. A glance out the window revealed a blanket of snow.

Downstairs in the kitchen, she found Gert stirring something in a pot.

"I thought I'd go outside for a while," Ella Ruth said.

"Aren't you hungry?"

"Oh, I'll eat when I get back. Will you listen for Timothy?"

Gert smiled. "Of course, honey. Use my old boots." She nodded at the man's boots sitting next to the back door.

Ella Ruth slid her feet into them. "These are a little big."

Gert laughed. "They don't make them for women. Be careful. I'm not sure what your father will do if he finds out you're here. How did your mother-in-law feel about it?"

"I don't know. I never waited long enough to find out." Ella Ruth opened the back door. "It's my life." In the barn she found empty stalls and a room that looked like it was once used for something more than barn life. It had a wooden floor and a big window facing

Black Mountain. A small coal stove stood in the corner. All she needed was an easel and a chair. She closed her eyes. Yes, this was the place where she would paint.

Gert smiled when Ella Ruth came back inside. She was cuddling Timothy on her lap. "Did you like what you saw?"

Ella Ruth returned the smile. "Yes. I love this place. And I love these paintings of Mama's." She walked over to the wall covered in framed canvases.

"I love them too."

"She was good."

"Yes, very good."

"I found a place in the barn where I could paint."

Gert's face lit up. "Oh, I'm glad!"

"You'll have to look at my sketchbook."

"I'd love to." Gert placed Timothy on a blanket and poured big mugs of coffee. "I'm almost out of my ration of real coffee, but that's okay. This is a special occasion."

"I agree. I've come home, Gert. I haven't ever felt like this before."

"You know, if he finds out, he will not allow you to leave your husband's home and come to me."

"He has no power over me." Ella Ruth knew Gert was right, but she was resolved to stand up against Paul Allen.

"Don't be a fool, Ella Ruth. Your mother believed the same thing. You read it for yourself. You have to understand what power he has to beat him." Gert touched Ella Ruth's hand. "Sit and eat."

Ella Ruth sat. "I won't let him treat me the way he did Mama."

Gert was silent for a few moments. Then she said, "Your mother-in-law came by while you were outside." She allowed the information to sink in. "She seems sincere about her love for you and Timothy, but I understand your feelings. You are a grown woman and should make your own decision about going to New York. Buster is your husband. But you must remember that she is his mother. You've only been a mother for a couple of weeks, but somehow I know you can understand her feelings. She must see her son. I'm sure she's terrified of losing him. She's lost so much already."

"I know, but I should be there too. It's only right."

Gert sipped her coffee. "If it means that much to you, I'll pay for your train ticket, but is this best for Timothy? Does he need to be pulled away from home in the winter on a train filled with germs? I can watch him, of course."

The point Gert made was the same as Mrs. Wright's concern, but it was softer, full of choices.

"I'm torn. I should be there, but I know Timothy needs to be here. I don't like choosing between my child and my husband."

"Welcome to this adult world." Gert held her mug in the air as if toasting.

Ella Ruth touched her aunt's mug with her own. "I guess I will stay here." She paused long enough to think about it one more minute. "Anyway, I can paint and get to know you so much better. I want to be here. Mrs. Wright leaves today, right?"

"Yes."

Ella Ruth nodded. "So, tell me how you found out about Mama's death."

"Your father sent me a telegram. Don't you know he enjoyed every minute of that?"

"Did he mention my brother?" Ella Ruth took a bite of oatmeal with brown sugar sprinkled across the top.

"The baby was born right before your mother died, or so he said. He gave me no answer when I asked about his whereabouts."

"So Mama's lover knew the baby boy had been born? Where was Mama when she had him? Where was I?"

Gert stirred her own oatmeal absently. "I was living in Chicago at the time, teaching at a girls' school. Of course, I bought a train ticket out as soon as possible. But by the time I got here, Paul Allen had buried your mother in the church cemetery up on that godforsaken mountain. The church donated a plot."

"But how did Mama die?" Ella Ruth pressed.

"I went to the sheriff, your father-in-law, and told him I suspected Paul Allen of murdering my sister because she'd left him for someone else. I could tell by the look on his face that this was not news to him. Later, Paul Allen denied that he knew of an affair. He said Ella came back, crying about how she missed him. That she had died in childbirth when the baby came too early. Since there was not a doctor present, no one could dispute this. And your father always gets the benefit of the doubt. I tried to get you. We had no idea where your brother was, and Paul Allen refused to tell. I thought that the sheriff would give in and allow me to take you. It seemed that way, but the next morning he refused and that was that."

Ella Ruth stared at Timothy stirring in his sleep. He'd be waking up anytime. What kind of childhood would she have led if Gert raised her? It was a silent question that would remain with her.

"I'm taking you to your mother's grave," Gert said suddenly.

"Then let me feed Timothy and we can go." Ella Ruth spoke with slow, measured words. She had long dreamed for answers, but now that the dream was reality, fear shook her bones.

ʒ

The road up Black Mountain was covered in snow. Ella Ruth had not been on the mountain since she had left her grandparents—before Buster, before marriage, before war and Timothy. Grandmother and Grandpa Allen, both dead for a while, would be buried in the same cemetery. She hadn't seen their graves either. The snow hung in the trees, fresh and beautiful, and a bright red cardinal sat on a low-hanging limb. What did Grandmother Allen say about red birds? A cardinal meant you would see someone unexpected. Who would she see on the mountain?

Mama was buried in the far corner of the cemetery under a dogwood tree. A small marker bore her name, birth date, and death date. A pile of snow covered the earth above her remains. Ella Ruth handed Timothy to Gert and knelt in the snow. She'd never been there. All her childhood, she had never seen her mama's grave. That was a sin.

"Hello, ladies."

Ella Ruth recognized the voice before she looked up. Preacher Mitchell had been a good friend of her father-in-law. She wondered how much he knew about her mother and Paul Allen.

"Good morning, Preacher Mitchell. What are you doing here on Black Mountain?"

"How's that new baby?" He leaned in to give Timothy a good look. "I was here on church business. Black Mountain Church has a temporary pastor. They're searching for a more permanent replacement. It's hard to say how long a pastor will stay at a church. God moves them around. Then I was coming to see you, Mrs. Philips." He smiled at Gert.

Ella Ruth stood. Mrs.? Who was "Philips"?

"You have a family member from Chicago trying to reach you. They called my house because they remembered you speaking of me." His face was smooth of any expression. "You don't have a phone."

"It must be Parker," Gert whispered, instantly white as a sheet.

"We could go use the pastor's phone if you don't want to wait. You could reverse the charges." He smiled.

"What's wrong, Gert?" Ella Ruth took Timothy into her arms.

"I'll explain after I make the phone call. You can sit in the car. I left the keys there."

"No sense in that. You can come with us, Ella Ruth," Preacher Mitchell offered. "Get that baby out of the cold."

"That's okay. I'll spend a little more time in the cemetery and then I'll wait in the car. Timothy's fine."

Gert walked ahead with Preacher Mitchell, and Ella Ruth listened. "Why don't I take you home in my car? That way Ella Ruth can drive back to your house when she is ready."

"It sounds like you want to talk with me, Preacher Mitchell." Gert gave Ella Ruth a reassuring smile. "Don't worry. I'll be home. Go back on your own. If you need to pick up anything from Mrs. Wright's house, feel free to use the car."

Ella Ruth was left on her own, but she didn't stay long at the cemetery and soon returned to Gert's house.

ᘓ

Her aunt was home within the hour. She took off her coat and motioned for Ella Ruth to sit on the sofa in the front room. "Well, Ella

Ruth, I haven't told you a lot about myself and I should have. You see, I am married. I left him early on because he just couldn't be a husband. We've kept in touch. He didn't want a divorce, and after your mother, I knew I would never marry again. Anyway, the man I married is in the hospital in Chicago. They don't expect him to live. He has asked that I come to him."

She stopped talking and stared out the front window for a few moments. Ella Ruth kept quiet, waiting. "You see, when I came here to find out what happened to my sister, I had another reason to stay. It was easier than going back and facing all pain between Parker and me. But I need to go to him now, Ella Ruth. Do you think you can manage on your own? Of course, this house is as much yours as mine. I will catch the train tomorrow and return as soon as possible."

"I don't know if I can do anything without you." Ella Ruth fought tears and anger. Once again she was being abandoned.

Gert placed a hand on each of her shoulders. "Ella Ruth, you're stronger than you know. I can take Timothy and you with me if you like, but you might want to be here for Buster's return in case I'm delayed. I will leave you plenty of money. But you must promise me you will be careful of your father. He's been away a long time. He's like that. There's always a chance he'll come rolling in again. Keep your guard up."

A cold chill walked across Ella Ruth's arms.

ʘ

That night, a pounding noise bled into Ella Ruth's sleep. She opened her eyes and the haint, her mother's spirit, stood beside the bed.

"He's here, Ella Ruth. You must protect your child and my sister." She looked as real as she had on the mountain.

As Ella Ruth's feet hit the floor, Mama disappeared, and the bedroom door flew open. Gert, hair standing on end, stood there with a rifle. "He came just like I said he would. You stay here with Timothy." She disappeared down the stairs.

Ella Ruth scooped her sleeping son into her arms. "Like hell I will."

The front door was open, spilling light from the bright half-moon into the front room; in the yard was a familiar figure also holding a shotgun.

Ella Ruth pushed past Gert, who grabbed at her shoulder as if to stop her.

"I want my grandson and that stupid daughter of mine," Paul Allen said. "You come on out here now, Ella Ruth. I'm taking you back where you belong."

"Kidnapping me like you did my mother?" The hairs on the back of her neck stood up, but a rush of pure pleasure pushed through her. "I'm not like her. I won't let you hurt me. I'll never give you the chance." She saw the shadows of more men behind him. "You come in the middle of the night because you're a coward. You're no man."

Careful, Ella Ruth. The voice was in her ear, and it didn't belong to Gert. "Go away and leave me alone. I won't be your daughter. You lost that right when you gave my brother away. Yes, I know all about it." She had been taking little steps to the edge of the porch. "I'll never let you near me again. Do you understand?"

Don't get within arm's length.

"You quit your mouthing and get yourself out here to this truck!" Paul Allen shouted, still sounding sure of himself.

"No. I'm a Wright now. Times are different. You can't just come in and get me against my will. There's people who will stand up against you." She could taste her tears.

He took a step forward and a shot rang out from behind Ella Ruth. "You take another step forward and I'll kill you, Paul Allen," Gert said. "I've been waiting for that opportunity for many years."

Paul Allen stared them both down. "Get your ass out here!" He moved out of the shadows into the glow of the porch light.

"We need to call the sheriff, Gert," Ella Ruth said, her voice still steady in spite of her fear.

"I did better than that. I called the state police. He doesn't own them," said another voice. Preacher Mitchell came from behind the house and stood at the corner of the porch. As if on cue, lights swung down the road. The crowd began to break up and get in their trucks.

Paul Allen stepped forward. "I will get you one way or another."

"I'm afraid no one is getting anyone." A policeman walked up behind Paul Allen.

Paul Allen stepped forward. "This is my daughter. She is to come home with me. Now."

"It seems to me your daughter is married. You have no rights over her. Preacher Mitchell has explained everything. I've known The Wrights for years. It's a pleasure to see that Buster has settled down. I also know the Wrights won't let you have their daughter-in-law. You lose this time, Allen."

"This is hogwash," Paul Allen bellowed.

The policeman moved closer to him, tense and ready. "I think you had better get out of here before I decide to take you in. I know you, Mr. Allen. We've been looking for a reason to arrest you since the Kurt death."

Paul Allen stepped back from the officer until he had reached the edge of the porch beside Ella Ruth. She looked straight into his stare as she tightened her hold on sleeping Timothy.

He came close and spat in her face. "You go to hell, girl." Then he turned around and marched back to his truck.

The spit marked her face, sliding down her cheek.

"Are you okay, Mrs. Wright?" The policeman came up the steps. Timothy opened his eyes and watched her.

"You stood up to him, Ella Ruth. That's more than I've seen most do." Preacher Mitchell touched Timothy's head. "Paul Allen's days are almost over."

Ella Ruth found some comfort in the words. She felt strong, stronger than she ever had.

Chapter 19

Buster

January 1945

Lady Liberty stood in the distance, her torch held high, welcoming those who were lost or looking for a home. The light of freedom. All the things Buster protected when he fought. Where was the spark of excitement inside of him? Wasn't the constant hope of coming home what got him through all the death? It was finally happening, so why did he feel this way?

Of course, he knew. He was an outsider now. No one he saw would understand what he had seen and endured. His stump of a foot took front attention, demanded notice. It floated through his thoughts at different times of the day and night, reminding him that he was a cripple, half a man at most. He'd murdered too many soldiers. The Army said it wasn't murder but a job to be done, a people to be protected. They gave him a medal. His world was the color of red like his hands, dipped into a bucket up to his elbows. His brain burned with a mixture of fear and pain. Where was Ella Ruth and his son? Mama's telegram never mentioned her or the baby, only that Mama would meet him at the dock. It seemed Ella Ruth didn't want a man with a missing foot.

Don't fool yourself. She doesn't want a man with blood on his hands.

The thought shot through his body, a flaming arrow hitting its target. One minute his body burned as if he were in hell, and the next it shook as if it were winter and he'd broken through thin ice on the lake. Someone said they had drained the lake at the quarry. A company was planning to put the quarry back into business. If only Daddy could see that.

The Lady of Hope stood tall, slender, still. She never tired of watching the ships coming in and leaving. This was her duty. It was fools like him that made her laugh.

Death flirted with him, but he never managed to grasp it be-

173

tween his fingers. He was a cat with nine lives, a black cat with yellow eyes. His blood boiled and roiled, hot, rushing.

"We're docking."

A chill shook Buster.

"Put this blanket around your shoulders, soldier." Randal stood beside him, that silly tie flapping in the wind.

"Sergeant Wright, did you hear me?"

Randal melted away and a pretty nurse stood in his place.

"He'd like you," Buster noted.

"What?" The nurse looked concerned.

"Nothing." He shook his head.

"Do you have someone meeting you?"

His head turned into a balloon, a lead balloon. "My mother is coming from North Carolina."

"Then let's go look for her," the nurse chirped.

"Yes, let's." The words coiled like a snake about to strike. "Sorry," he added. "I have a wife but she can't make it." The missing part of his foot ached and throbbed. The heat spread up his leg, burning under his skin. A million ants crawled on him. He brushed at them.

"I'm sure she'd be here if she could." The nurse didn't meet his eyes; instead, she scanned the city with a dreamy look. Her heart was already out there in New York. That was plain.

The people looked like bugs crawling on the dock. Then one figure formed into a solid person. It wore a long black cape with a hood. The fabric blew in the wind.

Thoughts moved through Buster's head like sparks. Heat waves wafted across the dock. "Happy New Year," he yelled. The figure turned.

"Do you see your mother?" The nurse patted his shoulder again. The bones snapped, broke.

The figure pushed away the hood. Larry. His old buddy Larry stared at him as black fog ate Buster's eyes.

CR

Buster's world turned white, full of needles and tubes.

Mama floated in and out of his fog. Mostly it was her talking that kept bringing him back into the hospital room.

"How is he, Dr. Marshal?"

"The infection is bad. I'm not sure if we can save the portion of foot that remains. There's a possibility that he could lose his leg to the knee."

"That will not happen."

Who the hell did the doctor think he was, talking about cutting off his leg? Mama wouldn't let that happen.

The fog wrapped around him, pulling him into a delicious oblivion.

CR

"Buster, can you hear me? It's Mama."

He forced his eyes to open. Mama stood above him in a blur.

"Ella Ruth is so worried, darling. You have to fight this infection. Fight it with everything you have. You want to go home whole, don't you?"

Whole. Couldn't she see he wasn't whole, would never be whole again?

"You have a son. Don't you want to see your son?"

A son, yes, he had a son. Every boy needed his father, even a gimp father. His leg was still there. Fight. When had he stopped fighting?

CR

Two days later Buster opened his eyes and looked straight at his mother. She was clear as a bell. "Mama."

She jumped up from the wooden chair. "Do you want another pillow?"

Laughing hurt his chest.

"Are you laughing, Buster Wright? Don't you laugh at me." Tears spilled down her cheeks.

175

He wiggled his fingers, thinking he might touch her face. She placed her hand over his.

"Do I still have my leg?"

"You have everything you came home with."

The pressure of her hand soothed him. He had his leg.

❦

When he woke again, his mouth was so dry he couldn't swallow. "I'm thirsty." His words cracked the silence.

A nurse looked up from her clipboard. "I'll give you some water." She moved to him, floating like an angel.

"Where are your wings?" A half-smile formed on his face.

She lifted his head and held the cup to his lips. "You won't think I'm an angel when I give you this shot in a minute."

Buster sputtered.

"See." She pulled the cup away. "I have to give it to you in the area near the wound."

So that's what they called his stump of a foot, a wound. "Shit."

"Shit indeed." The nurse pulled the sheet back.

The door to the room opened. Mama walked in wearing her Sunday best. He tried to whistle.

Her face smoothed. "Are you whistling at me?"

His head pounded. "Yep."

The nurse unwound the bandage from his foot. He pushed up on his elbows.

"You might not want to watch this."

"I've seen a lot worse."

"Buster." Mama stepped in front of him.

"Move, Mama. I have to see this sometime. I want to get it over with."

She frowned and stepped aside.

What remained of his foot was not the raw bloody stump he had prepared for. Instead, the skin was gray like a dead fish he had found once on the bank of Dragonfly River. He would have preferred the raw meat.

"An infection set in while you were in England and killed part of the skin cells. It will look better."

Better.

"You almost died," Mama whispered.

"I almost died a bunch of times."

The nurse blocked his view with her body. "You're not going to like this at all."

A pain ripped through him and he fell into the pillow. The tears pushed through his chest and into his throat, but he remained quiet.

ର

A week later, Buster looked at his foot again, the half foot.

Poor, poor Buster.

You know he's a hero. He lost his foot in the war. He's never been the same.

The skin around the stump had turned a sickening yellow, like the sky over the battlefield where he was wounded and lost his life as he knew it.

"Today you're going to walk down to the phone and talk to your wife." The nurse smiled, but he knew she would haul him out of bed if he didn't follow directions. "First you try using the crutches on your own. If that doesn't work, I'll be back to show you how." She marched from the room.

He eased off the bed. Pain shot up his leg into his head. He gripped the crutches and placed them under his arms. Here went nothing. One slow hop at a time he moved down the hall. Mama stood behind the nurses' desk and held out the receiver. "Ella Ruth is on the line."

Buster thought he'd never reach the phone. He placed the receiver to his ear and listened.

"Are you there?" Her voice was music.

"Yes." This was not the way his homecoming was supposed to go. Too many times he had imagined her jumping into his arms, wrapping her legs around his waist. She was no bigger than a minute.

"Are you going to talk to me?"

Then he heard the cries of a baby. "Is that him?" he managed to say.

"Yes, that's our Timothy. He's hungry. He stays hungry. He's like you." There was a smile in her voice.

"Let him cry. I want to hear him. Put the phone to his ear."

His son filled the line with complete anger. "Now, now, you settle down," Buster said. The baby's cries slowed. "Your daddy loves you." His boy became quiet.

"You got him settled, Buster." Ella Ruth's laugh wrapped the words like a package. "I need you to come home." Now she was crying. "I'm living in Aunt Gert's house now. She gave it to me. We have our own home. Come home, Buster."

"I'm a cripple," he whispered the words.

"No, you're not."

"I am. What will I do? Who will I be now?"

"My husband and Timothy's father. That's enough to start. We'll figure it out as we go. You're alive, Buster. That means everything to me."

"Yes, I should be thankful."

"Yes. We have to live our life as if it might end tomorrow, Buster."

☙

"I thought I'd stop by and introduce myself." A young priest held out his hand.

The whole collar thing made it hard for Buster to look him in the eyes. "Did my mom send you?"

"Mothers are good at that. They really worry after their sons. Can I sit?"

Buster nodded.

The priest took the chair and moved it close to the bed. "Your mother did not call me. I saw you talking on the phone and something told me to come introduce myself. I've learned to listen to that voice."

"I don't need God. He didn't bother to show up when my bud-

178

dies were being blown to bits. Why would I want him now?"

"My name is Rob."

Buster had to give this guy credit. "I'm Buster."

"I wish I could tell you something to make you feel good, but I can't. I know you saw some terrible things."

"How would you know? That's the problem. Everyone treats me like I might break, thinking they know something about what I've seen. You can't know anything about what I saw." Buster hoped that would send him out the door.

"I was on the front two years ago." The silence in the room was thin and easy to see through. Rob looked at him. "I don't know. There are no answers to why these things happen, but then, if you look at it, there are too many answers, just not the ones we want."

Rob continued talking and Buster listened. Somewhere in all the words, Buster found peace. Rob called it grace.

Rob came back every day and they talked. Buster told him all his stories, even the one about Randal. And then it was time to go home. Buster could walk, or limp, on his own.

"So it is time." Rob held out his hand.

Buster pulled him into a hug instead. "Yep."

"I'm glad. How is Ella Ruth? I bet she's excited."

"I haven't told her." He laughed. "I had to threaten Mama's life to keep her quiet. I really want it to be a surprise."

Rob clapped his shoulder. "All will go well, Buster. You'll find a way."

"Can I ask you something?"

"Shoot."

"How did you know that, well, that you wanted to be a priest?"

Rob smiled. "It wasn't a bolt of lightning moment. The decision came to me slow. It was a feeling that grew a little each day. I wanted something larger in my life. Finally I gave in to the whole priest idea."

"And God didn't care that you killed all those soldiers in the war?"

"God took me just as I am. Why all the questions?"

"I think something big is coming."

"Watch out. Your life is about to change for the better. Keep me up to date." He handed Buster his address. "I'd better let you get ready. You're going home."

Home. He'd be home in less than twenty-four hours. It hardly seemed possible.

Chapter 20

Ella Ruth

February 1945

Ella Ruth spread the old crazy quilt in a sunny spot behind Mrs. Wright's house. Timothy rolled from his back to his tummy, and she plopped down beside him. Gert had left in early January, and the deed to her house had arrived in the mail just that morning. Ella Ruth now owned a home.

Parker was no better or worse, Gert wrote. She had settled in his apartment and run into some of the professors she taught with so many years earlier.

They want me to teach again. Imagine, Ella Ruth, teaching after all these years. I must admit the idea appeals to me. Hope all is well with you. I hope you've had no trouble with Paul Allen.

Paul Allen had not bothered Ella Ruth, but she still jumped every time the old house creaked.

Gert deserved to teach. She deserved the best of lives after being so sick and giving up so much to find out what happened to Mama. Timothy rolled onto his back again and stared at the crystal blue of the sky. A breeze moved over Ella Ruth's arms, sending a shiver through her body. She turned on her back and looked at the sky while Timothy rolled around.

"He's a mess just like his daddy." Lacy had come out and was standing near the edge of the quilt.

Ella Ruth didn't bother to sit up. "Yes."

Lacy went to hang the wash. "How's things for you?"

It wasn't like Lacy to be so chummy. "Fine." The word stood in the air.

Lacy looked at her. "I heard what you did with that daddy of yours."

"I did what any decent person would do."

"I don't think so." Lacy pinned a shirt to the line, her back to Ella Ruth.

"It's good of you to stay here with Billie." Ella Ruth held her breath because history had proven that being nice to Lacy never came out good.

"I get paid."

Ah, there was the old Lacy.

"How are your boys?"

"Into anything and everything." Lacy's voice was lighter. "Wonder why that Larry hasn't written another word to Miz Billie? She just worries herself sick over the mailman coming."

"It probably means nothing." A white fluffy cloud built higher in the corner of the sky. "I hardly heard from Buster when he was overseas."

"He's better, I hear." Lacy looked over her shoulder, giving Ella Ruth a tiny half-smile.

"Yes." But she thought of his spirit. "I worry about him."

"I know you do."

"He's never been so serious. I hear Lee was like that all the time."

Lacy's shoulders became a straight line. "Lee was a brooder." She pinned a pillowcase on the line. The wind whipped her skirt, revealing her brown legs. Lacy was pretty. Ella Ruth had never noticed this before, but she was a real beauty. Her skin was almost the color of copper, and her hair was not as curly as most coloreds'. "I don't imagine Lee's changed," she said stiffly, picking up the empty basket. "You and that boy enjoy this weather. We're in for a snowstorm soon."

Ella Ruth closed her eyes and listened to the silence but found the songs of birds instead.

"Now that's a smart baby." The deep voice made Ella Ruth jump up. A man stood under a tree several feet away. He wore a uniform. For a second her heart skipped. Buster had come home. But the man was taller than Buster, thinner. A branch shadowed his face. "Buster will be mighty proud of him when he gets home." Ella Ruth stood with her hands on her hips.

"I never did like you much," the man continued. "I didn't know why. But you're a brave one. You're as brave as that husband of yours."

Had Lee come home?

The man stepped out of the shadow and the sun showed down on him, bright, almost like a spotlight. "I hate I can't stay long, but I had to see you. I had to tell you I know it all now. You will too before long. Just remember you're not alone, Ella Ruth, no matter how lonely you get."

Ella Ruth tried to believe her eyes. Maybe it was Larry. Billie would be so happy. Timothy let out a loud cry, and she looked down at him. "Billie will be so glad you're home," she said. But when she looked back up, Larry was gone. The soft ground where he had stood wasn't bothered a bit by footprints.

"Ella Ruth, do you want to eat some lunch?" Billie called from the backdoor.

Ella Ruth needed something to hold on to. She was losing her mind. "Did you see a man out here?" Maybe it hadn't been Larry. But whoever it was, he knew her.

"What?"

"I said did you hear from Larry today?" Ella Ruth searched Billie's face.

"No."

Something hard in her pocket dug into the side of her leg as she scooped Timothy into her arms. She pulled it out; a ring with a green stone and two small diamonds set on each side of it caught the sun. Where did she get this? Gert must have slid it into her pocket the day she left, but that didn't seem possible. The dress had been washed in the ringer washing machine since then.

"What have you got?" Billie took a step toward Ella Ruth.

"Nothing." She shoved the ring back into her pocket. "You'll hear from Larry soon. I'm sure of it."

It was a dream. She had fallen asleep on the quilt.

Billie took Timothy. "I hope you're right." They went inside to have lunch. All day, Ella Ruth fought a feeling of dread. She thought the ring probably belonged to Mama, but she had no idea how she knew this. Buster kept coming into her mind. That night as she put Timothy to bed, she saw a man in the yard again. The full moon washed the place with a spooky half-light. Her first thought was Paul Allen, but a calm "no" sounded inside her head and denied this thought. A cloud moved over the moon. The man was gone if he was ever there.

◖◗

Two weeks later, Ell Ruth heard from Gert that Parker had died peacefully with her by his side. His lawyer explained that Parker had left Gert the apartment in the city, where they first lived as newlyweds. She did not take the teaching job offered by her old friends. Even though her health had improved dramatically with the new medications, she knew that people would worry about her being contagious. She told Ella Ruth that being back in Chicago was best for her, that she was home. Ella Ruth worried after Gert, but there was no changing her mind. This stubbornness reminded Ella Ruth that her aunt had never viewed Swannanoa Gap as home.

Ella Ruth didn't see the man in the yard anymore, and she was glad. Some days felt warm, and others were bitter cold. She began to work on turning the room in the old barn into a studio. In one corner was an old desk that she cleaned and shined. It served as a place to draw. She pulled the heavy piece of furniture under the big window that faced Black Mountain. One of the six wooden kitchen table chairs served as a desk chair, and a soft pink ottoman and chair from one of the bedrooms looked cozy in the barn corner. The Sears and Roebuck catalog proved a wonderful place to order paints and canvases, even an easel. Gert had left her a generous account. It seemed that Gert's father—Ella Ruth's maternal grandfather—had left her enough money to live off of when he had died years before. Ella Ruth transformed one wall into a library by moving some bookcases from the house. In another corner, she placed a refinished cradle for Timothy. Later, when he was older, a warm rug would go there for playing. She hung some of her drawings on the free walls. One night, just as the sun was setting over the mountain, Ella Ruth sat in the pink chair. Timothy slept in his cradle, and a soft tune floated on the air, almost a hum. She wasn't afraid. She knew it was her mama. Something in her bones told her this. She decided that when her canvases and paints arrived, Mama would be the subject of her first painting.

184

The telephone shrilled from the house. Because it was new, she nearly jumped out of her skin. She tucked the sleeping baby into the crook of her arm and ran, out of breath when she answered.

"Ella Ruth, this is Carl Mitchell...your preacher."

"Yes?" Something in her stomach flipped over.

"Billie said I could reach you on your new phone. Could you bring your sister-in-law and come over to my house as soon as possible?"

Was it about Buster? Hadn't he been doing well? He didn't talk much, but he was getting better. That's what she was told.

"What's wrong?"

"Please just come as soon as you can."

"Okay."

"Thank you, Ella Ruth. I'll look for you." The line went dead.

The whole world slowed down. She ran out the door with only a few diapers for Timothy. Thankfully, the car started on the first try. *Slow, Ella Ruth.* A whispery voice sounded in her head. Finally she was at the backdoor of the Wrights' house.

Billie came out on the porch and smiled. "Wow, will you teach me to drive your car? Did Pastor Mitchell call you? He called here looking for you."

Lacy stood behind her. One look at Ella Ruth and her face turned hard. "What you come for, Miz Ella Ruth?"

"Billie, Preacher Mitchell has asked us to come to his house." Her voice broke.

"It ain't Mr. Buster, is it?" Lacy stepped in front of Billie.

Billie hurried down the steps. "I'll be back." She looked worriedly at Ella Ruth. "It can't be Buster. He's fine. If not, Mama would call." She jumped into the passenger side and pulled Timothy into her lap.

"You call me now, you hear?" Lacy stood on the porch with her hands on her hips.

"We will," Ella Ruth said.

"Oh God, I hope it's not Buster. It just can't be." Billie cried.

Ella Ruth looked into the face of her son. *Not now. Please not now. I need him.*

It looked like the whole town had shown up at Preacher Mitchell's.

"What's going on here?" Ella Ruth looked at Billie.

"Let's find out." But her words were quiet. Something bad had happened.

The kitchen was filled with women from the church. Pies, cakes, and other dishes of food were scattered all over the counters, spilling onto the table.

Ella Ruth's heart pounded. This couldn't be about Buster. She took Timothy from Billie before the group of women descended on him.

Sure enough, Miss BoBo, a widow known for her love of babies, grabbed Timothy away from Ella Ruth, but she looked at Billie. "It's all so sad," she said, hugging the baby against her big breasts. "This little boy is part of our future." Timothy gave her his sweet, toothless grin.

"Where can we find Pastor Mitchell?" Ella Ruth asked.

At that moment he walked into the room. His eyes gave away his heart. "Could you girls come into my study?" He touched Timothy's cheek. "What a big boy you are." Tears wrapped around the words. "Every time I see this boy, I think of how proud Frank would be."

Pictures of Larry hung on the wall in the hallway. It was the toothless, wide-eyed innocent ones that sent a shiver up Ella Ruth's back.

Pastor Mitchell walked around the desk and touched a picture of Larry in his Army uniform. "We received word this morning that Larry was killed in battle right outside a small German village. My son is dead." The words sat there in the room, waiting for one of them to speak out loud. Call them liars.

A long hollow sob escaped in the room and Billie's face collapsed.

Buster was still alive. Buster would come home. And this should have made Ella Ruth feel guilty, but she sent her love to him instead, thankful he had survived.

"I have no real words right now," the pastor said. "I'm sure God will give me some, but right now I'm empty." He walked over to Billie. "Will you go to Maureen? She wants you nearby. Could you do that for her? You're our family, Billie."

Billie looked at him, her eyes full.

Ella Ruth touched her shoulder. "You can stay with me if you need to."

Larry, her beloved, was dead. Ella Ruth felt that it was only right that she should live into that fact before becoming some substitute child for the grieving family.

"No, I'll go to Mrs. Mitchell," Billie said as if steeling herself.

Ella Ruth stood with her.

"Could you stay, Ella Ruth? I need to speak to you." Pastor Mitchell returned to his chair. Ella Ruth looked at Billie, a question in her eyes.

"I'll go. It's okay. I'll see you in a few minutes."

The pastor leaned back in his chair. "When you are desperate, Ella Ruth, you sometimes agree to do stupid things." He looked at her with a cool expression. "We all have secrets." He took a deep breath and picked up a glass paperweight. "I was young and loved my wife more than anyone can ever know. We had a baby, but she died before her time to be born. I thought I'd lose Maureen to madness. And then one night a man beat on my door full of rage, no pity, no remorse. He was one of the worst men I have ever known. He shoved a bundle into my hands. He threatened to kill me if I ever told where I got this bundle. The baby boy was no bigger than a puppy and in real trouble. The man told me I could throw the baby in the creek for all he cared, and then he was gone. Maureen doesn't even know about how I came to have the baby. I left for Asheville before she could know. I took that baby to the hospital. It was two days before we found out whether he'd live or not. I called Maureen and told her to come to the hospital."

He stopped here and looked out the window. "She was on cloud nine. I lied to the church and told them that we adopted the baby from Maureen's sister. Maureen didn't have a sister. No one questioned us. I told that same story so much I started believing it." He stood. "I wish I could say I'd do things different, but Larry has meant too much to me." He looked straight into Ella Ruth's eyes. "The man that brought me Larry was Paul Allen. The baby was the son he didn't want. Your brother."

The room swirled. "My brother?"

"I never told you because it would have only caused more trouble." He wiped his eyes with a handkerchief.

"Let's be honest. You didn't tell because you were afraid of Paul Allen. So Larry and me never knew each other as brother and sister." Her words sliced the air.

"I've always been haunted by my actions. I didn't learn until a few days later that your mother died in childbirth. I had a feeling there was a lot more to that story than the town would know. I knew Paul Allen was gone and your grandparents were too old. I did what I thought was right."

"Well, it wasn't right." Tears slid down Ella Ruth's face. "You hurt me. You hurt my aunt. Now he's gone." She turned and left the room.

In the kitchen, she took Timothy from Mrs. BoBo and held him close. Larry was her brother and he never knew it. Or maybe he had appeared to her because he did know. She walked home, leaving the car behind. She walked because she might start screaming and never stop. One long scream filling all the space left behind by Larry's unfinished life. A scream for all the wrongs this town allowed.

That night she painted her first canvas. It wasn't her mother. Instead, it was a ghost of a man standing in a rainstorm. The word "brother" was hidden in part of a black cloud.

ભ

Timothy howled in his cradle as Ella Ruth worked on cooking her breakfast. "Let Mama eat, Timothy." She poured her oatmeal into a bowl on the table and took the baby into her arms. "You silly little boy. You had your breakfast. Mama has to have hers." Timothy laughed now and bobbed his head. "You spoiled little boy." Ella Ruth laughed along with him.

"What has your mama been feeding you, son?" The voice filled the kitchen. The voice she had yearned to hear in person for such a long time.

Ella Ruth turned around and looked at the screen door. The morning air floated into the kitchen. A man, his face lined from sickness, stared at her. She ran to the door, pushed it open, and threw herself into his arms, knocking him slightly off balance.

He grabbed the doorframe. "Whoa, I'm not steady, you know." He leaned into her body, and they pressed Timothy between them. "I love you, Ella Ruth. I'm a broken man, but I'm home."

"I love you, Buster Wright. There is nothing broken about you. Do you understand?" In that moment, she kissed him. His smell, the one he had left so many months before on his pillow, overtook her.

"I'm a different man, Ella Ruth." He spoke this into her hair. "I have some plans. I have a new way to live my life."

Tears ran down her face. "Buster, I'm your wife and I trust and love you."

"Will you love me even if I become a pastor?" He waited. "Don't look so surprised. I'm going to be a preacher. God spoke to me in all this mess, Ella Ruth. I'm going to make this part of my life count for something besides death. Now please, let's sit down. I just want to hold this beautiful boy and look at my wife. I have a lot to tell you. A lifetime of stuff."

She nodded and they sat close together, the three of them, as she listened.

After hearing some of his hard stories, she looped her arm through his and said, "You're home, Buster, and that's all that matters to me." And she continued to believe that for a long time.

November 1946

Buster helped his mother and sister into the car. He was taking them Christmas shopping in Asheville and wanted to get going so they could be home before dark.

Much had changed since his return from war. His congregation had accepted him as pastor, even if they still remembered him as the boy who climbed the water tower. He limped to the car. Some days the limp was only slight. Ella Ruth hardly noticed it anymore.

"Are you sure you don't want to ride with us?" He wanted her to go. He worked hard at helping her become a better pastor's wife, allowing the church to see their closeness.

"No, I'm working on a painting."

"We're going to stop by Preacher Mitchell's house."

The pastor had retired to Asheville, but Ella Ruth didn't want to see him. Though she had never told Buster about Larry being her brother, the sting of his absence had only grown stronger over time.

"Not today."

Buster limped back to her side and kissed her hard on the lips. "You paint, my love."

"Now, is that any way for a preacher to act?" she whispered with a smile.

"Yes, when I have a wife like you." He released her. Billie waved. It was so good to see her smile. Timothy, secure on Ella Ruth's hip, grabbed his mother's hair.

Buster squeezed his little hand and said, "Now that he's toddling all over the place, we need to give him a brother or sister."

"One thing at a time, Buster." Ella Ruth laughed.

Buster blew them a kiss as he pulled out of the driveway.

Ella Ruth went into the kitchen to feed Timothy before carrying him back home so she could paint. As she dampened a rag to wipe the baby's face, she looked out the window over the sink and noticed a man walking on the edge of her mother-in-law's property.

Timothy laughed on her back as they crossed the field. "Sir, are you looking for someone?"

The man walked a few steps in her direction. His face was smooth but brooding. "I knew this family a long time ago."

"The Wright family?"

"Yes."

"Well, I'm married to Buster." She pointed to the Wright house. "There's no one there today but me and this little guy. Everyone else has taken off to Asheville. Did you know Buster?" His eyes were easy to look into, but Ella Ruth thought he would look much better without his beard.

He laughed and the sound echoed through the field. "Yes, I knew him."

"Would you like to stay until they return? I was feeding our son. You could relax in the kitchen. I have to get home, though. I have a painting to finish."

His eyebrows shot up. "I'll have to take you up on that some other time." He rubbed his hairy chin. "So Buster married an artist."

"I guess. He's a preacher now too."

This time the man howled. "War does change men."

"What's your name?"

"Just tell him I kept my promise. I showed up. Would you do that?" At this, the man walked away.

Ella Ruth wanted to run after him, but that seemed senseless.

She had every intention of passing the message on to Buster, but the day caught her up in busyness. Buster was much later coming in from the trip than expected. The car had problems and needed to be repaired. After dinner, he locked the door to his study and worked on his sermon for the next day. The man pushed back into Ella Ruth's memory and rode the fringes of sleep. She made a tired promise to tell Buster the next day, but again life got ahead of her. Days turned into months, months into years, and the message went the way of other memories.

Part Four

Beautiful Wreck

1955

Chapter 21

Timothy Wright

Barney Wilson stood his big lard ass right in front of Timothy. His breath smelled like some leftover puke. "That colored can't play on the team no more." He got closer to Timothy's face. "You got it, Wright?"

"That colored boy has a name, Mile, and he's been playing with us since first grade. What's your damn problem?"

Barney jabbed a finger in Timothy's chest. None of the other guys moved. They were just a bunch of chickens.

"It's either the team or your colored boy."

Timothy balled up his fist. Barney was eleven too but way bigger. Dad said fighting only begot fighting. Leave it to Dad to say something that dumb. He sounded real good, but a kid couldn't work with that advice.

Pop! Barney rocked back on his heels.

Timothy shook out his hand. "Go to hell, lard ass." He took a step back.

"You going to let him hit you like that, Barney!" Carl was Barney's best buddy.

Barney took a step toward Timothy, but the look on his face told Timothy there wasn't anything to worry about. "Take your colored boy and get on out of here, preacher boy. We ain't got no use for your kind around here."

Mile's face clouded, and Timothy worried he might cause more trouble. "Come on, Mile. These guys can go to hell." He grabbed his mitt and the only ball the team owned.

"Oh, now look what you guys done! You done gave away our only ball," said Freddy, the doctor's son and the town clown. "You dumbasses! Ah, don't go, Wright. We don't think like Barney does."

"Too late. I'm out of here." Timothy grabbed his bat and left.

"Barney, you got to buy us a ball now!"

Dad would have told Timothy to talk out the problem. He

couldn't remember that some things just couldn't be talked out.

"Get your tail on out of here, preacher boy," Barney called from the field, still trying to have the last word.

Timothy held up his middle finger but never looked back.

The two boys walked a good ways down the road before Mile spoke. "You ain't got to give up the team because of me."

"Shut up." Before Timothy could finish talking, a loud roar came over the treetops. "Here he comes, Mile. We got to catch him this time." His words disappeared into the sound. He ran as fast as he could.

Mile followed and tapped his shoulder. "You can't catch him this way. Cut across this field." Mile took a sharp right.

"Mom says..." But Timothy was right behind.

"You a mama's boy, Wright?" Mile said as they jogged together. "I ain't afraid of Old Man Allen. Tucker says he's just a bunch of talk." Mile was only a half-inch taller, but he could outrun any of the boys in town. "Anyway, you're younger. You got to do what I say." He seemed to crank up his speed.

For once, Timothy wanted to see that crop duster up close. And what he wanted most was to fly in that damn plane himself.

"What you boys doing in my field?" Old Man Allen stood by his truck, drinking from a flat bottle.

"Go on, Mile. I'll take care of him."

Figuring Timothy must have lost his mind, Mile didn't even look back.

"Get your ass over here, boy!" Old Man Allen was covering the ground between them fast. "You hold up!"

Timothy stopped partly because he wanted to see his grandfather up close. This was the man that folks feared. Mama had stood up to him, and the whole town still talked about it. They also talked about how he had killed Mama's mother. Timothy stood his ground.

"Where'd that boy go?"

"I don't know what you're talking about. I was crossing your field to get a look at the crop duster."

"Don't play me for a dumbass, son. I seen that other boy. I ain't that drunk yet." He gave a mean laugh.

Timothy looked his grandfather in the eyes.

"You're her boy, ain't you?"

"Yep."

"That's yes sir to you."

Timothy didn't say a word.

"You got one of those streaks in you, I can tell." Old Man Allen took another drink from his bottle. "Get your ass off my property and tell your mama I'll whip your ass the next time I see you. Go on now."

Timothy ran in the direction of the crop duster that seemed to be moving away. Damn! He'd missed it again. He looked back over his shoulder. Old Man Allen stood there watching him. The spooky thing was that he had the same eyes as Mama, only cruel. Still, he didn't look like the monster everybody said he was.

∞

Timothy rode his bike in ninety-five-degree heat, pumping the pedals as if his life depended on it. He took the field road just as the crop duster, the brightest yellow he'd ever seen, came roaring overhead. On each side of him were fields of corn. The sun hung above him in the hazy blue sky. Pedaling with all his strength, jumping a bump here, dodging a rock there, he pushed toward the plane. Sweat worked down his back. He wanted to take off his shirt, but he kept pedaling.

The plane made a loop. Heat waves rippled over the field, and a rabbit ran across the road. Timothy slowed as the plane came in low. What luck! He jumped off his bike and ran to the edge of the field, waving his hands in the air. That's when he saw the writing on the side of the plane: *Grover's Crop Dusting, Asheville.* He swiped the sweat burning his eyes. Asheville might as well be a million miles away. The plane made a loop and came in real close, so close he saw the shadow of the pilot.

Timothy threw up his hand. The pilot waved back.

He was going to fly in that plane. Somehow, he would figure out a way. One day he was going to be a pilot.

But for now, his new Timex Boy Scout watch showed that he was late. He jumped on his bike, still watching the plane make one more swoop before it began to spray.

෬

Grandma Sue sat on the front porch swing, pushing it with her foot. She looked up from her book over the top of her glasses and frowned as Timothy whipped his bike close, spraying dirt and rocks against the white lattice.

"Sorry I'm late."

"What if you fell, Timothy?"

He shrugged. "It wouldn't hurt none."

Grandma Sue sat straight up and ran fingers through her curly hair that was more gray than brown. "You've been keeping too much company with Mile."

He looked at the ground. "Sorry."

"You need to be an example to him, Timothy. You can't expect him to speak proper English. He learns from you, not you from him."

"Sorry. I'll do better." What if they decided he couldn't be friends with Mile? Mama would never do that, but Daddy might because of Grandma Sue. He did whatever she wanted. And as much as she acted like Mile, his brother, and his mother were the same as her family, she didn't really think that. In Timothy's opinion, she said stupid things.

Like about Mile not talking right.

"Now come here and sit with me before we get started. I want time with my grandson." She pointed to the empty space on the swing. "Your spot is cold."

He looked around to make sure no one was watching. Mile would give him the business if he saw.

"I'm reading a wonderful book," Grandma said. "I've read it twice. Once when I was a child and once right before I had your Uncle Lee."

"What is it?"

"*Tom Sawyer*."

198

"That book is as old as the hills."

She winked at him. "Just like me."

"I read it last year."

That was the wrong thing to say, because right away Grandma Sue struck up a conversation about Tom and Huck and Becky Thatcher that seemed never ending.

CR

Peanut butter sandwiches coated with homemade apple jelly—globs of it dripping onto his checkered napkin—and slices of lemon floating in a yellow ocean made Timothy smile. This was the life: a picnic in the woods. He took a sloppy bite of his sandwich and thought of the stories Grandma Sue told about the past. Most of them involved Dad and Lee, the uncle Timothy knew only from photos. Dad wouldn't talk about his older brother. He said some things were better left in the past.

Dad knew most everything. That's probably how he got his job as preacher. Sometimes Timothy wished he had a dad like other kids. The kind of dad who played baseball and went hunting, not that Timothy wanted to go hunting. The problem was that his dad just studied the Bible. He was smart but duller than the bark on a tree.

Dad believed Uncle Lee had died in the war. He didn't say this out loud, but Timothy knew from the look that came over his face, a sad and lost expression. Grandma Sue, on the other hand, believed Uncle Lee would come walking back into their lives just like he walked out.

"What are you so quiet about today, Timothy? You're a million miles away." Grandma Sue sat across from him, eating real dainty like a lady.

"You never told me why Uncle Lee left home."

Most of the time when Timothy asked about Uncle Lee's leaving, Grandma Sue skated around the subject like a butterfly jumping from one flower to another. Today she paused and looked at him. "The first time I looked into Lee's face, I knew he was in for more than he could ever live up to. Lord, he had a daddy ready to pin a sheriff badge on his tiny chest. He was soft around the edges, though, a sweet song. He was so much bigger than this town, Timothy. He had big thoughts. Have you ever seen lightning that streaks across the sky on a hot night, brilliant but without noise?"

Timothy could only nod.

"Heat lightning." She swiped at a tear. "Lee was born way before his time. There will come a time in the years ahead when his ideas fit. You'll see these changes, Timothy. I won't. I just want to see my Lee one more time."

"You got Dad." Timothy said this to fill the air between them.

Grandma Sue smiled. "Yes I do. I've always had Buster. I can count on him." She touched his arm. "I know you have big dreams about flying."

He looked away. What he wanted to tell her was how much he loved flying, how one day he was going to do it himself. He had the name of the crop dusting company. Now he just had to hunt down the pilot.

"Don't you try to hide it from me. I know my grandson. Your daddy had big dreams too."

Timothy grunted. "Serving God." The words cut through the hot air.

"Timothy, your dad is someone to be proud of." She sipped her lemonade.

"He's a preacher, Grandma Sue. He can't even play baseball. Mama is the one who plays catch with me. He keeps his nose in the Bible."

"There are worse things, you know." She raised one of her eyebrows. He hated that look.

"I love him." His cheeks burned with the confession.

"But you have to like him too."

"What's there to like, Grandma Sue? He doesn't like to do anything. He sure doesn't like me."

She took a breath. "What kind of talk is that? Maybe I should tell you the whole story about Lee leaving. Maybe then you'll understand who your daddy is. Maybe I'll just tell you a story about Larry too. You think you know so much about your father."

Timothy tried to speak, but she cut him off.

"This story has a lesson worth listening to, Mr. Big Pants." She stood and limped to the edge of the blanket. Her skirt had leaves stuck to them. "It all started a long time ago. Your daddy hated Lee, and Lee hated your daddy. I wouldn't allow myself to see it, but that hate rode the air in a room, sucking the life out of it. Anyone who knew them knew that one day things would come to a head, but I never thought it would end the way it did."

Grandma Sue looked at him. Her face wrinkled, and at first Timothy thought she was playing a joke on him. But then her features became a scary mask. One eye drooped and her mouth twisted sideways like a monster in a movie. The air turned hotter and the leaves stopped moving on the trees. The birds quit singing. Grandma Sue dropped to one of her knees, allowing her lemonade to spill. Her right hand curled like an animal claw. The light drained out of her face as she hit the ground.

"Grandma Sue."

But she only remained still.

Horrible sissy gulps escaped his chest. "Mrs. Kurt!" He screamed as he ran out of the woods into Grandma Sue's yard.

Tucker stood on the back porch. "What's wrong with you?" His normal sour look didn't put Timothy off this time.

"Grandma Sue." He pointed at the woods.

Mile came out of the kitchen door followed by Mrs. Kurt.

"Help me!" Timothy cried. "Call my daddy."

Mile watched him, looking scared.

"I'll go get him at the church," Tucker offered.

"Wait." Mrs. Kurt held up her hand. Something about her always settled Timothy. "What is wrong, Timothy?" Her black eyes reflected control.

"Grandma Sue is dead. She's in the woods and she died."

Mrs. Kurt's control rolled away. "Come on, Tucker. I need you." She started running.

Tucker pointed at Mile. "You go get Timothy's daddy." Timothy ran after Mrs. Kurt and Tucker.

"Show me, Timothy." Mrs. Kurt was crying. Timothy had

watched his mama cry before, but Mrs. Kurt was different. She was like a man. She never let on that anything bothered her. Why was she crying now?

Grandma Sue was turned on her side. Mrs. Kurt knelt down beside her. "Oh, thank the Lord. She's still alive. It's a stroke. We got to get her to the doctor."

Timothy looked into Grandma Sue's face. Her eyes were blank.

"We can carry her out of here, Mama." Tucker took Grandma's feet.

"Good boy." Mrs. Kurt grabbed her arms and looked at Timothy. Her face softened. "You help."

"I don't need any help," Tucker barked.

"Now you let Timothy help. He needs to help, Tucker."

Something in Tucker's face changed, turned kind. "Get this leg."

They hauled Grandma Sue out of the woods like a sack of potatoes. Daddy was nowhere to be seen. Tucker looked at the truck. "We got to take her, Mama. I can drive that old truck." He had been itching to drive. Timothy and Mile talked about this all the time.

"Let's get her in the front seat."

"No, we can't fit her up there. Let's put her in the back. Get a blanket." Now Tucker sounded like a man.

Mrs. Kurt nodded. They lifted Grandma Sue's dead weight into the back of the truck.

"This ain't right. This whole thing ain't right." Timothy tried not to cry as Tucker jumped into the driver's seat.

"You sit down so you don't fall out of the truck, Timothy." Mrs. Kurt leaned against the cab and cradled Grandma Sue's head in her lap. "You listen to me, old woman. We been together too long. You can't leave now." Her words were soft and sweet. She looked at Timothy. "I said sit down. I don't need you in trouble too."

Doc White's wife walked out on her porch as Tucker grinded the truck to a stop. A crease dug across her forehead. "You just get on out of here, boy. You go on and see your doctor. If you people would just stop fighting, you wouldn't have to see a doctor. My husband is going to have the Klan on him if he keeps treating you people. You go on now. You understand?"

"Mrs. White, I'm Tucker Kurt." He held his head high, looking her in the eyes. "We got—"

"I don't want to hear it! You get your uppity self out of here. Folks are saying you're going to die just like your daddy did." She pointed a finger at Tucker.

"I could only hope to be as brave as him," Tucker said.

Timothy knew that Tucker and Mile's dad was dead, but he never knew how it happened. Mile never wanted to talk about it.

Mrs. Kurt stood up. "But, Mrs. White? We need help. Time is wasting."

"Don't you 'but' me, Lacy. I won't have that tone!" Mrs. White stepped forward, waving her hand. "Shoo! Get on out of here."

Timothy stood. "My daddy is not going to be happy with you, Mrs. White."

Tucker looked like he might punch Timothy for talking.

Doc White stepped onto the front porch. "What is all the ruckus?" He looked at Timothy. "What you folks doing here? What's happened?"

Mrs. Kurt's face smoothed into a calm mask. "I was trying to tell your wife that I have Mrs. Wright back here. It looks like she's had a bad stroke."

The words sat in the air like a bad storm cloud. Life stopped for a minute, shifted. Timothy saw a change form in the expression on Doc White's face.

He jumped off the porch. "My God."

"My grandmother is dying." Timothy knew he told the truth. He knew that everyone else knew this.

"Call Pastor Wright."

"My brother went for him," Tucker said. His face showed the hate he held for the whole situation.

"How long ago?" Doc White hoisted Grandma Sue into his arms as if she were a child.

"At least twenty minutes." Mrs. Kurt touched the curls on Grandma's head. Tucker glared at her.

"Call an ambulance!" Doc White yelled at his wife. Then he gestured toward Tucker. "Boy, help me with her." He handed Grandma Sue to Tucker and jumped off the truck.

"Stop." Timothy stepped forward. Everyone looked at him. "You can't just take her." A shiver started in his stomach and worked through his body.

"You hush now." Mrs. Kurt touched his hand.

"Let him say how he feels," Tucker said.

"Timothy, let the grownups handle this." Doc White took Grandma Sue from Tucker again and ran into the house with her.

"Stupid asshole." Tucker looked at the sky.

Dad arrived at that moment in a spurt of gravel. Mile got out of the passenger's side, and Mrs. Kurt's face softened again. She met them at the car. "It's a stroke, Buster."

Buster looked at her for a minute. Unspoken words that Timothy couldn't guess passed in the air between them. "Does Ella Ruth know?"

Mrs. Kurt stepped back. "I don't think so."

He looked at Tucker. "Will you go get her? I think she's in her studio painting. She won't hear the phone." Dad shook his head. "Take Timothy with you."

Tucker nodded.

"I don't want to leave," Timothy said.

Mrs. Kurt put her hand on Timothy's shoulder. "You listen to your daddy."

Timothy shrugged her hand away. "You ain't my mama."

"Don't you speak to Mrs. Kurt that way, Timothy. Do what I say." Dad never even looked at Timothy.

"You don't even care." But this came out a whisper and only Tucker heard.

"Come on," Tucker barked.

Mile slid into the middle, and Timothy hugged the door.

When they told her the news, Mama hurried to her car, but not before she hugged Timothy hard. "It's not your fault. You got it?"

He could only nod.

She touched Tucker's arm. "Thank you for helping. Would you boys stay here and keep Timothy company?"

Tucker nodded, but Timothy could see he didn't want to be there.

"That's how I wanted to spend my afternoon, looking after two dummies," Tucker said to Timothy and Mile as Mama drove away.

◌

Dad and Mama spoke in calm voices at all times, but Timothy could still tell when they were upset. He wasn't a baby. Most of the time their disagreements were over silly stuff like Daddy not closing a door he opened. But the morning after Grandma Sue had her stroke was different. The air in the kitchen was tight like when a tornado was coming.

They were going to let Grandma Sue come home from the hospital in Asheville. She wasn't a bit better, but the doctors couldn't do anything else for her. Dad got it in his head to move the family to Grandma Sue's house. That was fine by Timothy because that put him closer to Mile, who spent most of his time there anyway.

But Mama had her say loud and clear. She stood in the middle of the kitchen with her hands on her hips and her mouth in a straight line. Her staring at Dad was louder than any words she could say.

Dad wasn't the smartest when it came to Mama. "What would the church think, Ella Ruth, if we didn't take care of Mama ourselves?"

Mama's eyes turned to a hard flint color. "Buster, I don't give a damn what the church thinks." She glanced over at Timothy, who did his darnedest to blend into the wall.

"Billie can't come home. You know that. So what do you suggest?"

Mama puffed. Timothy knew that puff, but Dad didn't. "How about if Lacy looks after her like she's getting paid to do, and we stop in throughout the day and evening? I'm not walking away from my home, Buster. Don't you get that this is our home? I don't think you understand at all."

Dad threw his hands over his head. "So now I don't understand." He shook his head and poured a cup of coffee from the percolator. "Mama comes home tomorrow, Ella Ruth. You need to decide if you're going with me or not. She's done so much for us."

Mama balled up her fist. "I won't stay over there at night. I'm living in my own home." And the case was closed.

ଓ

Dad and Mama went together, and Dad rode in the ambulance to bring Grandma Sue home. Timothy pedaled his bike to meet them. Grandma Sue was on a gurney, and the man driving the ambulance unloaded her. Her eyes were open, but she didn't seem to give a damn that she was home or care who would be living with her. What magic could make her better? This wasn't his grandma. He was glad Mama decided not to stay. He would stay where she did, not with this strange woman who looked like Grandma Sue.

"Grandma, look at me." But she lay there like he hadn't said a word.

Mama touched his shoulder. "She's not the same."

And the tears he'd cried out each day since Grandma Sue had a stroke came back, but he hid them by pretending to watch a big hawk circling the house.

"Is Mrs. Wright home?" Mrs. Kurt came out with a happy smile. "I have her some of that chicken soup she loves so much."

The ambulance driver pushed Grandma Sue over humps of grass. Timothy realized he should have mowed the yard.

"Are there fresh sheets on the bed in the sickroom?" Mama was looking for something to say.

"I thought we agreed to put her in her own bedroom." Dad glared at Mama, who took a long, deep breath.

But it was Mrs. Kurt who spoke. "Now, Buster, you know and I know that we can't put her up on the second floor all alone. That would be mean." She swiped at the sweat on her face.

"I just thought she might get better faster..." Dad's face turned pink and his head dropped. He limped behind the women.

☙

Mama stuck to her word. She stayed at home each night, and Timothy was right there beside her. As far as he could see, Grandma Sue had already left her body and been replaced by someone who didn't even know she was alive.

It was around this time that Mile got the idea to build a fort. Timothy thought only about planes and flying, but Mile said they had to do something besides chasing crop dusting planes around the fields. So Timothy helped him build a fort, even though it seemed kind of stupid to him.

Once it was complete, though, he had to admit it was nice having a secret place all to themselves. If only they could have kept it that way. "Mile. Timothy."

"Shit." Mile slid out of the fort window.

"Mile?"

"Damn." Timothy stood up. "He's going to see the fort."

They desperately wanted to keep the thing a secret.

"Yeah, and he'll be telling Mama."

Tucker stood at the foot of the tree looking right at them. "You got to come back to the house, Timothy. Now."

The look in Tucker's eyes made Timothy's stomach clench. Just then, the familiar roar of the crop duster sounded overhead. It was oddly comforting, and he strained to look through the tree. The bright yellow of the plane bled into the blue summer sky.

"Come on, now. Mama's going to whip you, Mile."

"What did I do?"

"You ain't supposed to disappear into the woods. This ain't even the Wrights' land."

Timothy started down the ladder. "This here is my fort. Ain't no one going to tell me I can't be here."

Tucker turned around. "Yeah, that's 'cause you're white. Mile is colored. He could get in big trouble for being here."

207

"Is that why you come to get us?" Timothy watched the sky.

"Just get home. Your mama and daddy want you." Tucker turned to Mile. "You're getting older. Things are going to change. You got to be more careful."

ʘʀ

They stood beside Grandma Sue's bed, her eyes finally closed in the peaceful sleep of death.

"She was too sick, Timothy." New lines had formed on Dad's face in the weeks since Grandma Sue had her stroke.

Timothy knew he should try to look sad, but the truth was that he was past it now. He hurt for Grandma Sue the day she had her stroke and left them all for good. He cried until the day she came home from the hospital as another person. After that, his grieving was done.

"Timothy, it's okay to cry." Mama touched his hair.

Timothy just saw himself flying that crop duster, cutting it close to the treetops. And Grandma Sue never flinched. She was sitting in the front seat watching him cut through the blue sky. She laughed and turned into herself again at last. He didn't watch for angels because they couldn't fly as fast as him. He worked hard to look sad and not let the grin spread across his face. No one would understand his thoughts like Grandma Sue did. He would miss her deeply, but at least she was herself now.

Chapter 22

Ella Ruth

Each morning when Ella Ruth got out of bed, all she could think about was working on a painting. Her fourth painting of Main Street, to be exact. She especially loved Saturdays because many of the families came down off Black Mountain and turned the perfect street upside down, chaos. Ella Ruth sat perched above these lives, painting. G.B. was good to let her use the top floor of his grill, even though it was plain he thought she was a little crazy. In the silent space, littered with pasteboard boxes, she watched the folks come and go from a large window. There she captured them on her canvas, or at least did her best. Her paintings were never what she saw in her head.

If she wasn't at G.B.'s, she was in her studio at home. Buster didn't approve. Ella Ruth was supposed to be a good preacher's wife. She wasn't good at pretending to like the fine ladies of Open Grove Church while they rolled their eyes and clicked their tongues at her.

From her perch above Main Street, Swannanoa Gap was exposed as a gossipy little town. Of course, she was no different from any of these people because her art was eavesdropping. She saw a lot as she sketched and painted. Mrs. BoBo made at least five trips a day to the post office. One had to assume her sudden interest in mail had to do with Mr. Clark, the new clerk from Asheville. And Meg Claxton went into the drugstore every morning and bought a large Coke float complete with whipped cream. Ella Ruth watched her sitting in the booth that faced the street. Her hips were beginning to show her love for sweets. Then there was Paul Allen, who walked to the jail each afternoon. His back straight, his hair combed back. His face would be turned away from her as if he knew she watched him, studied him, trying so hard to figure out how this man could be her father. In the painting she worked on, he stood in the middle of Main Street, hands on his hips like a gunfighter about to have a shootout. Yes, her Saturdays were near perfect because they belonged only to her.

Then, three weeks after Mrs. Wright died, on a Saturday a door opened and allowed fresh air into her life. Only it didn't feel like it at breakfast. Instead of her trousers, Ella Ruth wore what she called her funeral dress. Her curls were gathered on her head, and the seams in her nylons were straight. Each morning before she went to paint, she headed to Mrs. Wright's house to make breakfast for Buster. The tension between them was thick. They agreed on nothing since the death of Buster's mother. He had remained in his childhood home, and Ella Ruth refused to leave her house.

Lacy still worked at Mrs. Wright's house. Ella Ruth couldn't quite understand why. Lacy watched over Buster so that he didn't need Ella Ruth to cook breakfast or supper, but Ella Ruth braved her accusing looks anyway. She had decided that if Lacy gave her one more frown, she would invite her to be the preacher's wife instead. She was perfect material for the job, the one problem being that she was colored. Buster and Lacy were two peas in a pod since Mrs. Wright had died. Their heads always leaned into each other as they talked about one memory or another.

Buster could wallow in self-pity all he wanted. Ella Ruth had no use for any of it. There was a fine line between grief and chronic melancholy. Sometimes she worried that Buster had stepped over the line. Had he taken the time to ask how she felt about their life together, he would have found out that she hated it. She should have felt shame because she refused to be the envisioned preacher's wife. She was twenty-eight, a grown woman, very capable of acting the part, fulfilling the role. But she couldn't bring herself to do it.

That Saturday morning, Timothy sulked at the round table in Mrs. Wright's kitchen.

"This is an honor for me," Buster said as Ella Ruth piled scrambled eggs onto his plate.

The family planned to head for Birmingham, where Buster would preach at a revival.

"It sure is, Mr. Buster." Lacy had never put "mister" in front of Buster until he came home from the war.

"Can't we let Timothy slide by this time, Buster?" Ella Ruth ignored Lacy's hard look, resolving to speak with her in private as soon as she could.

"No." His face flattened. "I want my whole family there." In his tone rode the bullets of guilt. His wife was abandoning him once again.

"You got to be there for your daddy. Mile has work to do today so he can't play." Lacy patted Timothy's shoulder.

Ella Ruth tightened her fingers into a fist and shrugged at Timothy. "I tried, but this mom's plea doesn't seem to count." It was a crummy thing to say, but she took complete glee in it anyway. This is where Buster and Ella Ruth had arrived. What their relationship had become.

Buster shot her a look. "No one said you didn't matter, Ella Ruth." His deep blue eyes still made her stomach turn upside down. Would she ever quit loving this man who she didn't even know anymore? She sat at the table without speaking.

No painting. She would go be the perfect preacher's wife, embrace the lie Buster was telling himself and the church every Sunday.

The air, thick with a storm, hung heavy in the car. Rain had been scarce, and Ella Ruth hoped for a downpour. Sweat worked down the back of her dress before she even settled in the front seat.

Timothy stared out his window in the back.

"We're going to pass the airport on the way," Ella Ruth said, turning so she could see Timothy's reaction.

Buster flashed a rare smile at Timothy. "What's this about the airport?"

Timothy remained broody.

"We were talking about planes."

"What about planes?"

Ella Ruth turned back to the front and let a long breath escape. "Timothy is going to be a pilot. He can do anything he puts his mind to. He doesn't have to stay in Swannanoa Gap." She looked at her beautiful son in the side mirror.

"What's wrong with the Gap?" The edge in Buster's voice filled the car, but it was left unanswered.

Buster chose the route that ran through the middle of Swannanoa Gap. The people on Main Street moved through their errands, unaware Ella Ruth was among them today.

"Here he comes, Mom." Timothy sat on the edge of the back seat, straining to look at the sky. "It's his Saturday morning run." The crop duster rumbled over the tops of the trees.

"I love the color of his plane." Ella Ruth watched the bright yellow plane cross the sky and understood why her son wanted to fly.

"I saw enough planes in the war," Buster said.

She looked at him and then stared out the rolled-down window. Unspoken feelings surrounded them.

The wind whipped at her hair, freeing it from the confines of her preacher's wife hairdo. Had Buster glanced at her in that moment, the whole mess that approached them in the future might have been avoided. He would have seen the girl he married and transformed into the boy he once was, if not for a long time then at least for as long as it took to see his recent choices in a new light.

The peace of silence was delicious, and Ella Ruth almost missed seeing the man on the side of the road with a broken-down car. But not Buster. The do-gooder part of him made him slow.

The man wore a tailored pair of gray trousers and a dress shirt in a lighter shade. His hair was dark curls. A satchel hung in his hand.

As they began to pass him, Ella Ruth's stomach fluttered at the same moment the man made eye contact and nodded.

Buster pulled the Buick to the shoulder and got out.

The man turned around and watched Buster's lopsided walk and then trot.

"What's wrong?" Timothy hung his head out the window.

"It's probably someone Dad knows." She couldn't imagine him running.

To her surprise Buster put his arm around the man's shoulders. The man took a minute too long to return the hug.

"He's hugging him," Timothy reported.

Buster guided the man back to the car. "Look here, Ella Ruth. Do you know who this is?"

Dread rippled across her scalp. "No." But something about him was familiar. The man's cocky smile turned on her.

"You're my Uncle Lee," Timothy shouted.

"Yes, I'm the long-lost brother." He winked.

Ella Ruth knew him, but not because of old photos. He was the stranger who had come looking for Buster that Christmas years before. The visit she forgot to tell Buster about.

"Ah, the prodigal son has come home." A current exploded in the air. Thunder rumbled through the sky. Ella Ruth tried not to smile at Lee.

"Get in, brother. We'll send a tow truck for your car. I've got to stop and make a phone call. It looks like the First Baptist Church of Birmingham will have one less preacher for revival." Lee got in beside Timothy, and Buster slid back into the driver's seat, running his fingers along Ella Ruth's neck. The skin tingled from never feeling his touch. "We're going back home."

Well, at least one person could make Buster give up preaching for a day.

ᏅᎡ

Lee brought much-needed rain to Swannanoa Gap. It washed away the layers of dust brought on by the drought. Lacy had taken the weekend off, so Ella Ruth was left to cook a meal in Mrs. Wright's kitchen. Buster took Lee for a walk. How did a person fill in a gap of twenty years?

Ella Ruth decided on stew. It was the kind of supper a mother would cook on such an occasion. Lacy's garden was beautiful. It yielded enough vegetables for a salad too. While Ella Ruth picked tomatoes, wearing Timothy's jeans, Buster's old shirt, rubber boots, and her curls in a ponytail, she noticed Lee standing on the back porch. Was he finished with Buster so soon? His looking out at the surrounding yard brought a smile to her face, but thank goodness he couldn't see it. It wouldn't do her a bit of good to have him thinking she liked him. He was gone by the time she came back to the house. She dumped the vegetables on the counter.

"I like the way you look now."

She jumped. "Excuse me?"

Lee wasn't gone after all. It seemed he had been waiting for her.

He laughed. "You look like a little boy instead of a girl dressing up as a woman."

Ella Ruth frowned. "I'm not sure either is flattering."

"You don't strike me as a woman who cares for flattery."

"How would you know?"

"Truce." He held up his hands. "What can I do to help with supper?"

"You could chop vegetables for a salad. I have to wash and peel potatoes for our stew. Lacy took the weekend off or she'd fix the meal for you. I'm not much of a cook."

He took a knife from a drawer as if he had never left home. "I've been living on my own for a long time." He laughed again. "I'm not used to anyone cooking for me."

She gave him a small smile and placed some tomatoes and carrots in front of him. Then she gathered the potatoes from a basket in the corner. Wind ruffled the curtains at the window. Its crispness touched her arms. Long shadows stretched across the grass as big fluffy clouds pushed across the sky. Black Mountain stood guard over the scene.

Soon the trees would turn to fiery red, orange, and yellow. "I smell fall in the air," she said.

Lee looked up from chopping carrots. "That mountain is the best sight when the leaves turn. It's one of the only good memories I have of this place."

"What are the other memories?" The question slid out before she could stop herself.

He paused, the knife resting on the cutting board. "Well, I remember walking Lacy home on warm days. Helping her with the extra laundry she did for Granny."

Ella Ruth looked at him. "You know she got married and has two sons."

"Yes, Buster told me."

"Tyler Kurt was shot in the middle of the night. Right in his own bed. He owned a gas station that was doing too good for the some of the folks around here. When they finally found the body, he was hanging in a tree just as the road starts up the mountain."

Lee shook his head.

"Mile, her youngest son, was just a little thing. Tucker was two. I'm not sure what he remembers. But he's headed for trouble if he doesn't change his attitude." She looked at Lee. "Why did you come back here?"

"Do you always shoot straight?"

Heat moved across her face. "I don't play the social games. I guess that's why I'm not a very good preacher's wife. The church would love to trade me in. Lacy would be perfect for the job, but that wouldn't be proper either." The words had a bitter edge to them.

"Lacy must have changed a lot. I never saw her as a preacher's wife. But then I never saw Buster as a preacher either."

Ella Ruth poured the potatoes into the sink. The rumble sounded like thunder. "Me neither."

"I would imagine it was a shock for you."

The water ran over her hands, turning warm. "So how does it feel to be home?"

"This isn't home." The answer came fast without thought or pause. "I don't have a real home. I was on my way to Atlanta to work for the paper there. I didn't plan on stopping off in Swannanoa Gap. It was out of my way. I didn't want to come here."

At least he told the truth. She liked that.

"This place is like a fog bank. I know all the curves and dips, but I can't see a foot in front of me. So when I'm here, life comes down to survival. I bet you know what I'm talking about. So now what am I supposed to do?"

"Stay here or burn the house down. It doesn't much matter to me." Ella Ruth turned back to the potatoes.

"If I burned it down, I would get the pleasure of watching my childhood go up in smoke. If I stay, maybe I can learn what I didn't learn the first time around. You make a good case, Ella Ruth."

"I'm not making a case for you!" She glared at him.

Lee chuckled. "I really doubt my brother has any idea what a spitfire he married. The Gap needs someone like you. Hell, they need someone like me to balance out the feelings you stir up." He sliced a tomato.

A part of her was relieved. "Do what you want."

"Lacy could stay on. I mean, her job must be coming to an end with Mama dying. Who does she cook for now? You and Buster and Timothy? She could use another mouth to feed, keep herself employed. Yep, I'm needed around here."

Timothy burst into the room. "I want to go to Asheville, please. I can get a good look at the planes."

Lee looked at Ella Ruth. "Billie is coming in on the train tomorrow to see her long-lost brother, and she'll need to be picked up in Asheville."

He winked. "I can't believe they closed Swannanoa Gap stop. Guess it just wasn't big enough."

"The airfield's got to be around there," Timothy insisted.

Ella Ruth couldn't help smiling. "Timothy is taken with the crop duster that comes here."

"Please, can I go?"

"Why not?" Lee grinned at him.

"Be careful. Buster may not like you encouraging Timothy to be a pilot." Ella Ruth tried to sound stern.

"Yes, but what do you think of the little trip, Mrs. Wright?"

She looked at her son. "I think Timothy should go."

Lee nodded. "I knew we saw things the same."

❧

The next morning, Lee and Timothy went to meet Billie's train. Ella Ruth and Buster went to church. The congregation wasn't expecting them and Ella Ruth had lobbied for them to stay home, but Buster wouldn't have it. He stood in the pulpit and announced Lee's homecoming to silence and then a chorus of amens.

When they returned home after the service, the old truck was parked in the yard. They were back. Envy washed over Ella Ruth. She would have loved to gone on the trip to Asheville.

After hugs and kisses to Billie, Ella Ruth sent the brothers and their sister off for a talk while she pulled out leftovers from dinner the night before.

Timothy came in the kitchen raving about the airfield and the three different crop dusters he had seen. "One day I'm going to ride in one. Uncle Lee found one of the pilots and he said I could, Mama."

"We'll see one day, Timothy." The kitchen smelled good.

When Buster came back, he saw the table and smiled. "Thank you, Ella Ruth, for going to the trouble last night and today."

She did her best not to think about the thank-you too long. It wasn't like she was a stranger helping out. But then, she was just being spiteful. "You're welcome," she managed to say.

"If I can get Lee to stay here, I will be going home with you and Timothy tonight." Buster flushed like a kid. So much had passed between them.

"Well, of course you will." Ella Ruth looked at the salad to avoid Buster's happy expression. "That's where you're supposed to be. Your grandmother left the house to Lee to do with as he chose. She must have known he'd come home one day."

Buster frowned. "Maybe she could see the future."

Ella Ruth shrugged. "Who knows? But he may sell the place, you know. You have to be ready for that."

Buster gave her a stern look. "Not if I can help it. This was my home too. It's not just up to him."

Lee agreed to stay until they could sort out the details, and Buster came back to Ella Ruth's house for good.

Ella Ruth couldn't help but wonder if Lacy was one of the details.

A week later, Ella Ruth found a vase of roses in her studio, brightening the desk in front of the big window. "We're two of a kind," the note read.

Ella Ruth ripped the card in half. That evening when Buster came to the studio, he didn't even notice. He was too intent on her hosting a tea for the ladies at church.

Chapter 23

Lee Wright

The first night in his old bed, Lee woke in a cold sweat. Millie sometimes came to him in his dreams. She was always just as beautiful as she had been the night before the attack. Most soldiers dreamed about the horror of battles. Not him. He dreamed about those he couldn't save on that morning in December 1941. He got up and went downstairs to see if Ella—she was just "Ella" to him—had taken the leftovers with her.

Billie sat at the table with a large piece of chocolate cake Ella had baked. Well, he assumed she had made it. Maybe not. She did say she wasn't much of a cook.

"Hello, brother. I guess you woke up hungry too." Billie smiled and resembled the young girl he had known.

"Yes, I'm looking for that stew." He opened the refrigerator.

"On the top shelf. Ella Ruth can cook." Billie took a large bite.

"Yes, she can." He pulled out the bowl of stew and the salad.

"You're eating supper again?" She laughed.

"Looks like it." He found a pot and dumped the stew in, lighting the stove eye with the nearby match.

"So if your car hadn't broken down, and Buster hadn't come along, you wouldn't have even come home?"

The question sat in the air.

"No. I don't have a lot of good memories from here, Billie. I know you do."

She gave a mean laugh. "What do you know about me, Lee?"

He stirred the stew. "Not much, I guess."

"Exactly. Did you know I left here after I found out my true love, Larry Mitchell, died in the war? I became a doctor. I live in New York City because I wanted to be as far away from this place as I could get. So I just might know how you feel." She took another bite.

Lee emptied his stew into a clean bowl. "Where are those rolls?"

"In the breadbox." Billie gave him a long look. "Lee, be careful coming back here. I didn't know how bad it was, how the small-town life controlled everyone, until I left. I'm so glad I did. I look at Ella Ruth and ache."

"Why? She seems happy enough."

"Ha, to you maybe. The girl is miserable. Did you know she's a fine artist? Her mother was one too. There was a big scandal having to do with her father. She's dying here in the Gap. And Buster is killing her with one book of the Bible at a time."

"I don't know much about her. I do know Granny left me this house. I can't just walk away. I have to help settle things before I go. But I won't stay here for good. I can't."

She gave him a sly smile. "I know. You see, Buster and Ella Ruth don't get big newspapers down here, but I make it a habit of reading the *New York Times* each morning with my breakfast. When I get to eat it. But let's say I've read it enough lately to know you are a reporter for them. That business about Atlanta is hogwash and we both know it."

"Is hogwash one of those doctor terms you use at the hospital?" He sat down across from her.

"Don't try to get out of this. I know you're writing about the Klan. I've known all along that you have stayed only a few blocks from me when you're in the city."

Lee studied his baby sister. "Why didn't you contact me?"

"I figured you didn't want to know me. You never came home, Lee." She took another bite of cake. "Buster is the good one in the family. He has always been, even when he was getting in trouble. I don't have to chase you around to ease some guilt like he thought he had to do." Her words were hard to hear but true. "And I know you didn't just leave because of Lacy. You had to know that wasn't going to work out. Did you really think you could change a whole town, no wait, a whole region's way of thinking?"

He was quiet. What did she know about him? Of course he had left because of Lacy.

What other reason would have made him leave?

She turned her head to the side.

He thought about it a minute. ". I loved Lacy and would have married her. That was my plan, but Daddy died. Not only did he die, but he died right after I told him about Lacy and me. He was angry and scared. He told me I couldn't marry her unless I wanted her dead and me too. When he fell, I thought it was me that pushed him. Everything I was trying to fight for seemed silly. It's only been recently that I understand my ideals weren't so bad after all."

"What about Lacy?"

He shrugged. "We were kids, little sister. We moved on."

A serious expression settled on her face, and she looked more like their father than she ever had. "Be careful. Lacy's from the Gap, after all. She may not have moved on as far as you think. None of the folks here do, you know."

CR

Lee was standing at the sink, washing his breakfast dishes, when the back door creaked open. He waited for someone to speak, thinking Ella Ruth or Buster had come over.

"Are you a ghost?" Her voice sounded the same.

He turned to take in her image. Now she was a woman, and she was more beautiful. "No. I'm not a ghost."

Her shoulders remained straight. "I came by to see for myself. They said you were back." She waited a minute, never looking away from him. There wasn't much softness left in her face.

"It's me." Part of him wanted her to leave.

"Is Billie here yet?" Her tone reflected her love for his sister.

"Yes, Timothy and I picked her up at the train station in Asheville yesterday."

"Timothy? Aren't they gone to Mr. Buster's revival?"

"Since when do you call Buster 'mister,' Lacy?" The words just popped out of him. "Things sure have changed here."

"You wouldn't know because you ran off and left everyone hurting. I work for Mr. Buster Wright now." The look on her face told him she had a lot more to say.

"Well, that might be changing." The old defense came bubbling up inside of him.

Billie was right. He couldn't stay in this place for long. It was too backwards.

Lacy put her hand on her hip. "We both know you ain't here to stay. If you did, you'd have to commit to something, and you ain't got that in you."

He looked away. "My car broke down yesterday. Buster happened to be riding by on the way to his revival. He spotted me. That's how I got here. I'm staying for now. Everything was fine without me knowing, but now that I'm here, I have responsibilities. Granny left the house to me." Now he turned and looked her in the eye. "Once I know something, I have to follow through on it. I can't leave this house here for Buster to worry with. Billie is finished with Swannanoa Gap. She made that clear last night. I don't know how long I'll stay. I'm a reporter so I travel quite a bit, but maybe I need a home base."

Lacy frowned. "So you're telling me I don't have a job? Mr. Buster's not staying here anymore?"

Lee wasn't sure he could get past Lacy's prickly edges. "Buster is at his home. Was he staying here?"

"Ha, you bet he was. That foolish little wife of his has her own house. Her aunt gave it to her before she went back north. Miz Ella Ruth refused to move in here and help look after Miz Wright when she got sick. Not Mr. Buster, he stayed right here the whole time. He's been grieving so, he never went back to that girl's house. Least not until now, it seems."

"This is all news to me. I didn't know. But I have to say I agree with Ella for staying in her home. It sounds like you took good care of Mama. Why would someone give up their home for no reason? And as for Buster, he never let on when he left here last night. I assume both husband and wife were happy with the situation." He studied her reaction.

She folded her arms across the chest. "I need to know if I have a job or not."

She had changed so much from the girl he loved. He knew it was probably his fault. "You still have a job, Lacy, if you don't have a problem taking care of my house."

She flinched.

"Given our past, I worry if this is the best decision for you, but I also know if you had another option, you wouldn't be concerned about keeping the job. So let's leave things as they are, but Lacy, don't bring my brother into the business of this house. I can't tolerate that."

"I'm not some charity case, Lee Wright." She spit his name.

"I'm sorry if I made it sound that way. Let's begin again. Let's pretend we never knew each other and go forward in this strictly business relationship."

"Okay."

He nodded. "Good. Now, how much are you paid a week?"

"I get four dollars a day."

Lee had to keep the anger out of his voice. "How many hours do you work each week?"

"I reckon I'm here around ten hours a day, sometimes longer when Miz Wright was alive."

Lee took a deep breath. "This is all going to change, Lacy. You will work eight hours a day, no more. You decide what hours work best for you. I will pay you a one dollar an hour."

Lacy puffed up like she might explode.

"This isn't charity, Lacy," Lee insisted. "It's only fair you work for minimum wage. It's the law. I'm not breaking the law."

Her face went blank. "I guess."

"Yes, my family was paying you unfairly."

"I made more than any of the other maids in town," Lacy said.

"Maybe, but it's still not a fair wage." He looked around the kitchen. "You can let me know your days."

She stood tall again. "I guess any you want."

"It's Sunday, Lacy. You don't work on Sundays, and I'm capable of cooking breakfast, so come in when you want. Get the boys to school. I will be fine. I've been living on my own for some time now."

"You're not the same person, Lee." Lacy's words weren't mean, just truthful.

"Neither are you." Lee went back to the stove. He'd had enough of the talk. There was too much for him to think about. Like Lacy's oldest son. "I'd like to meet your sons soon." He kept his back turned so he couldn't read her face.

"Oh, you will. Mile is around here all the time because him and Timothy are thick as thieves. Tucker is sixteen and all boy. I have to keep a close eye on him." She was bumping around in a cupboard.

"Good. I look forward to it."

"When is Billie going back?" Lacy asked.

"I think at the end of the week." He chose a glass bowl from a cabinet.

"I'm glad she'll stay a while. I love that child."

He turned and smiled at Lacy. "We have that in common. She's turned into a fine woman."

"Amen to that."

"Yes."

"I don't have much use for church, so I won't be attending Buster's services." He said this casually but realized he was breaking a law in Swannanoa Gap with such words.

"Maybe we got more in common than you know, Mr. Lee."

Lee frowned. "Lacy, you are not to call me 'mister.' Do you understand?"

"Whatever you say."

ဆ

A week later Billie said her goodbyes and again warned Lee.

"Don't get caught up attempting to right some wrong from the past. If you have to, give the house to Buster and leave. You're too good of a writer to be stuck in this place." She kissed him on the cheek. "I'm off. Come see me when you're in New York. I'll be back for Christmas, but you should be gone by then." She winked at him.

Lee gave her a hug. "I'll miss you, baby sister."

Buster sounded the horn outside.

"Write to me. Keep me posted on the drama around here. And, Lee, there will be drama. Leave."

He laughed. "I will."

After a fine breakfast of pancakes cooked by Lacy, Lee sat at his desk in what his mother once called the front room. He had gotten

Timothy and Mile to help him pull Daddy's desk from the shed out back. They cleaned and shined the oak together.

Since he had placed it in front of the long windows, he found himself sure that Daddy stood looking over his shoulder. Lee wasn't crazy, and he sure as hell didn't believe in ghosts. But the presence was there. He figured it was guilt, pure and simple. He stared at his Underwood, hoping a column would spring to life. It had to be in the mail by tomorrow to make it to the news desk by the end of the week. He had pitched the column on the South to his editor and received a reluctant nod before he left to make his mark on journalism. Truth be told, though, he wasn't sure where to start.

Timothy ran onto the front porch and burst through the door without knocking. "You got to come quick, Uncle Lee!" The boy was all arms and legs. He was nothing like Buster.

"Why are you talking so low?"

"Tucker is in big trouble. You got to come. They'll beat the hell out of him if they find him."

Lee stood. "Who are they?"

"Paul Allen and his buddies."

Paul Allen was Ella's father. He knew that much. "What has Tucker done?" Lee reached for his dress coat, thinking it might say something to the group of men. He'd only met Tucker once, long enough for the boy to frown and leave.

"Just come on. Mile's hiding with him." Timothy looked over his shoulder. "We can't let Mrs. Kurt know either."

"Take a breath, son. I need to know what I'm getting into." Lee guided the boy out of the house.

Lacy walked into the front hall just as Timothy stepped out the door. "Did I hear one of the boys?"

Lee pushed the door closed. "No, but I'm leaving. I've got to find something to write about."

"Swannanoa Gap is too slow for a big New York reporter like you." Her words curled around the room.

"I guess you're right. I'll be back by lunch." He slid out the door, holding his finger to his lips.

Timothy got in on Lee's side of the car. "Mrs. Kurt don't like you much, does she?"

Lee laughed. "Not many people do, Timothy. That's one thing you're going to realize. I'm not popular here in the Gap."

"Mom likes you. I can tell."

"Yeah?" His face heated.

Timothy nodded. "But not much of the Gap likes her either." He pointed out the windshield. "Go to the cemetery as fast as you can."

"You want to tell me what Tucker did?"

"He drank from the white water fountain in the square."

This was an unforgivable infraction. The Jim Crow laws were alive and well. "Doesn't he know which water fountain is the white one?"

Timothy cut his eyes at Lee. "He knows plenty, Uncle Lee."

And then it was clear. The boy was making a statement. Lee liked the idea. Tucker just might have some gumption. "He's too young to be messing around with the likes of Paul Allen."

"Yes sir." Timothy nodded again, watching the road.

Lee wondered if Timothy had ever spent any time around his grandfather, Paul Allen. "Why didn't you go to your father about this?"

"Well, Tucker did something else too."

"What?"

"He spit on old Mr. Wilkins when he tried to stop him. Mr. Wilkins knocked him on the ground, decked him out. Tucker could have put him down, but he wouldn't pick on someone all crippled up like Mr. Wilkins. Tucker's got a shiner, though. And Mr. Wilkins left to get the sheriff. Everyone knows that Paul Allen owns him."

Lee shook his head. "Why didn't you tell your mama, then?"

Timothy looked at him. "'Cause she's a girl. She's strong and can do anything or more than Dad can do. But she's a girl. She'd come after Paul Allen. She's done it before, but I can't have a girl saving Tucker."

Lee almost laughed out loud. "Where in the cemetery?"

"Park over there." Timothy pointed to a little road going into some trees.

"I hid them in the old mausoleum. I just pushed the door hard. It's over by the crying statue."

Lee shut off the car. "Damn son, that's right in the middle of the world."

Timothy shrugged. "It was the closest place."

"Do they still tell the story about the crying statue?"

"Sure, but Tucker said it was bullshit."

Lee laughed.

"It ain't funny."

"I know." Lee led the way. "I'm well aware how serious this whole business is. I wonder if you know?" He cut a look at Timothy. His features reflected Ella's face. "Your mama will have a fit that I helped."

"Yes sir. But, right now she's painting and she never comes out of her studio this early."

"Okay. I want you to let me get in the front. You sneak and get your buddies. Put them in the car and don't be seen."

"How you going to distract them?"

"It won't take much. Unless things have changed, these men are like big kids."

Lee walked up the hill, glancing at the graves, taking his sweet time. The sheriff and several men stood further up the hill. It looked like the sheriff was listening to Mr. Wilkins. Boy, did Lee remember Mr. Wilkins. He didn't much care for anyone but himself. Lee strolled nearby, studying the gravestones.

The sheriff saw him. "Hey, what you doing roaming around? Don't you have better things to do?"

Parker Bass hadn't changed a bit from school. Lee guessed he still thought he was the star quarterback. "I'm actually working, Parker. As far as I know, it's still a free country and a man can visit his relatives in the cemetery."

"What you working on?"

"I write a column for the *New York Times* in New York City. I thought maybe the gravestones would give some ideas."

"Talking to the dead?" Parker laughed at his own joke.

Mr. Wilkins raised his cane above his head. "Let me give you something to write about, son. You're Frank Wright's oldest, right?"

"Yes sir."

"The one who ran out on the town. How about you write about that uppity colored boy that drank from the white water fountain this morning, right there in the square?" He pointed his cane across the street.

"I'm not sure there would be a story in a boy getting a drink of water."

Parker pushed his chest out. "Here in Swannanoa Gap, we know how to deal with our coloreds. This ain't up North. We don't put up with coloreds and whites mingling." He gave Lee a hard look.

Mr. Wilkins cut a look at Parker. "If you knew how to deal with them, we wouldn't have this problem."

"Who was it?" Lee looked around.

"They all look the same to me, but he was colored."

Lee laughed. "Well, it could be that he was just playing a prank."

"This is serious business, Wright. We don't put up with his kind in the Gap." Parker put his hands on his hips.

And there it was, his whole column. "Maybe you need to pick and choose your battles. I mean, how much harm can one colored boy do?"

Parker stepped closer to Lee. "You're one dumb son of a—"

"We found a colored boy down by the tracks," a deputy shouted from the bottom of the hill. "I think it's your boy, Sheriff."

Parker stepped back. "Let's go." But he gave Lee a mean look.

Lee watched them walk away, Mr. Wilkins trailing. He pitied the boy they caught.

Back at the car, he saw the boys hunched down in the backseat. He got in and looked straight ahead. "I'd say you're in a lot of damn trouble, Tucker."

"I ain't sorry for what I did." Tucker raised his head and glared at him in the rearview mirror.

"I would hope not. If you were, what would have been the purpose?" Lee backed the car up and looked right at Tucker. "I know your mama, and she won't stand for this. She'll put two and two together when the story gets out. Right now they are harassing some poor black kid down at the tracks. You have to be cleaner, Tucker, and brave enough to face the music your crime writes."

Tucker dropped his stare to his lap. "I didn't mean no one else to take my heat. And Mama thinks the old way."

Lee laughed. "I think if you knew anything at all about her, you'd know just how brave she is. And, understand, I'm not condoning what you did, but if you're going to do it be smarter and braver."

"Okay."

"What can I do with you guys?"

"Drop us near the woods. We can go to the fort." This came from the quiet one, Mile.

"So you're going to make me lie?" Lee looked at him.

"Timothy and Mile hadn't done nothing. Leave them out of this. You ain't got to lie for me. Tell Mama what I did." Tucker tried to sound tough.

The look on Tucker's face was familiar. It was a look Lee had seen in the mirror.

Had he been questioning whether Tucker was his or not, this would have convinced him. "I'm going to let you out, but I can't lie to your mama. If she asks, I'll have to tell her. We've been friends too long."

Tucker snorted. "How are you friends?"

"We just are. You don't know anything about me, or your mama for that matter."

ᘓᘔ

Lacy met him on the back porch. "I done heard the news and figured things out. You went after Tucker and them other two were right there with him. Where they at?"

Lee shouldn't have been surprised at how fast news spread. "I don't blame you one bit, Lacy. I felt like giving them all three a beating, but he believes in what he's doing. You can't fault him for that."

"That's easy for your white self to say, Lee." He saw just a glimmer of the old Lacy.

"I guess it is, but I just saw that belief in his face. Sorry."

"I won't have him die from being stupid." This was almost a scream. Lee took a step forward.

"Don't you even touch me. He's my boy. Not yours. He's mine."

"I know."

"He had a good daddy when you weren't around."

Lee studied the screen door. "I know."

"You ain't going to do nothing but hurt people more by being here."

"That's not my intentions."

"Something I know about you, Lee. You got the best of intention but no backbone." She turned and went into the house.

***

Later that night, Lee inserted a blank page into his typewriter. As an owl hooted in a tree, he wrote the truth.

> *Looking into the Negro boy's beaten face, swollen with a new hatred, a hatred passed on to him from generations of wrong, I saw my true self, ignorance at its worst, sleeping, traveling through life without any true concerns. I have taken basic human rights for granted. I enjoy them with a selfish stupidity. Complacency is a disease that gets under one's skin and convinces the person to risk nothing, to walk a fence one foot in front of the other, maintaining a fragile balance at all cost. It's within this balance we lose our self-respect and create a world that will allow someone to be hated for their differences. In our ignorance, we refuse the responsibility. And we will, fine readers, reap the consequences.*

Lee sat there looking at the column. His vision blurred. As he reread it he saw his son. He also saw his own poor choices, and he was afraid.

Chapter 24

Buster

"Buster, it's great to see you and this new office. You're looking good. It's been too long." Preacher Mitchell—Buster would always think of him this way—shook Buster's hand. "If my office had been this big, I might have stayed." When he grinned, age lines crinkled around his eyes. His hairline had moved back a couple of inches.

"If I had to work as hard as you did, I'd go crazy." Buster motioned Preacher Mitchell to sit.

"Well, I have to say I never saw you as a preacher, Buster, but you fooled me and everyone else. I always thought it would be..." The words hung in the air.

"So you're on your way back to Florida?" Buster asked.

"Yes. I hear Lee came home."

"He did. He's been home a while. I don't know how long he'll be around."

"That's good. Your mama and grandmother would have loved to seen him." He looked lost in thought.

"Yes. It makes me sad that he missed Mama by three weeks. But he's home, and that's good news for all of us."

Preacher Mitchell slapped his knee. "How is Lee, anyway?"

"Lee is Lee. He won't be anything else. He writes a column for the *New York Times*. His first column was about the Civil Rights Movement in small towns around the South. Of course anyone that knows Swannanoa Gap would recognize her in it. Thank goodness most of the folks here read *The Asheville Examiner*."

"I read the piece. He's got excellent points, you know. The movement isn't going away. If anything, it's going to get bigger. I say it's about time."

"But the Gap is a quiet town. Lee took on one little incident involving children. I can bet my bottom dollar who those children were."

"I think you're wrong. This little town has had its share of problems and unrest. Look at Lacy Kurt's husband, Tyler. Explain that, Buster. The problem is that none of us wanted to speak up."

Boy, Preacher Mitchell had changed.

"How's Ella Ruth?"

Buster moved to the edge of his chair. "Ella Ruth is wonderful."

Preacher Mitchell raised one eyebrow. "She's not happy being a preacher's wife?"

Buster sat back in the chair and his shoulders slumped. "I'm not sure what it is. She paints all the time."

The old preacher nodded. "She's an artist, and son, you did spring the preacher thing on her."

"That was years ago." He was sick and tired of feeling guilty about his choice.

"Well, she's still young and has ideas of her own. Her wounds are not healed. And I carry around the burden that I'm part of those wounds. She never leaves my mind. I've written, but she doesn't answer my letters. I don't blame her."

"What do you mean?" Buster asked.

"If I had talked to her earlier, she would have known Larry was her brother. But I was too worried about Maureen." Preacher Mitchell's forehead pinched into several wrinkles.

Buster's head pounded.

"You look like you've seen a ghost, Buster."

"I'm shocked."

Preacher Mitchell sat still. "Don't tell me she never told you? I asked her to keep it a secret, but I thought she'd tell you, her husband. I was mostly concerned about Maureen and Billie. Maureen knows now." He shook his head. "I've really made a mess of things."

Buster tipped his chair back. "I think Ella Ruth and I need to talk."

"I didn't mean any harm, but I've caused it anyway."

"Don't be so hard on yourself. I'll let her come to me."

"But will she? Maybe you should ask. Maybe that will free her."

"Maybe." Buster stood. "I want you to see the new sanctuary," Buster said, using his preacher voice.

"I can't wait." Preacher Mitchell got up as well.

Buster opened the door and there stood Timothy in the hall. How long had the boy been there? What had he heard? "Timothy, this is Preacher Mitchell. He was the pastor of this church the whole time I was a kid. I was best friends with his son, Larry. Do remember me talking about Larry?" His son always looked guilty about something.

"Yes sir." Timothy held out his hand. "Nice to meet you, sir." At least he had good manners.

Preacher Mitchell grinned as he took Timothy's hand. "You are nothing like your dad at your age."

Timothy smiled without looking at Buster.

"What can we do for you, Timothy? We were just going over to take a look at the sanctuary. Do you want to come?"

Timothy looked at his feet. "Mama said to remind you Uncle Lee wanted us to come to supper."

Buster's face turned warm. "Tell her I won't forget."

Both of them knew Buster had forgotten.

Timothy turned to leave.

"Son..."

Timothy looked back.

"Tell your mama that Preacher Mitchell is here for a couple of hours. She might want to come say hello."

A knowing look came into Timothy's eyes. "Yes sir." Timothy left through the side door.

"Show me these new cushioned pews. I can't wait to sit on them." Preacher Mitchell laughed uneasily, as if he were trying to diffuse the tension he had caused.

☙

Ella Ruth came to life when Lee asked questions about her painting. Buster sat there at the dinner table wondering why he had never asked his wife these things. He scooped a spoonful of mashed potatoes out of the bowl.

"Preacher Mitchell was here for a while today." He said, looking at Lee.

"You should have brought him to dinner." Lee cut into his steak and smiled at Ella Ruth. "This is the best steak I've had in a long time. You're a good cook."

That was news to Buster. He had assumed Lacy cooked the dinner before she left. He was worried about her because Lee always made her leave after eight hours. Didn't he understand that Lacy filled her lonely hours working? It was all she had.

"Why did Mitchell move away from town?" Lee asked.

Buster cringed. "I think the family needed something new after Larry died." He looked Ella Ruth in the eyes, but she turned away with a frown.

"I never saw him as that flexible." Lee sat back in his chair. "It's hard to think of Larry dying in Germany."

If Buster didn't know better, he'd think they were all some big happy family. But as far as he was concerned, nothing could be further from the truth.

"I'm going to Mississippi to cover the Emmett Till trial," Lee said.

"Who's Emmett Till?" Buster asked, taking a bite of salad. He loved salad with mayonnaise.

"He's a Negro boy who was beat to the point that when they found his body, he was unrecognizable. Tucker is doing some of the background research for me. He's insisting on going with me to Mississippi. I told him he'd have to go through Lacy first. I also told him it wouldn't be safe enough and he had no chance getting her to agree."

Buster wanted to ask his brother what it was like to have Lacy working for him. How did that fit in with all his new high and mighty beliefs of civil rights? It was much easier to talk about changing the world than to actually change it.

"I heard all Emmett Till did was talk to a white woman." Ella Ruth took dainty bites. How had she known about this story?

"You heard right, Ella. He just spoke to her. Now he is dead. But the mob that killed him weren't counting on someone attempting to make them pay." Lee never took his stare from Ella Ruth now. People will pay attention to what's happening in the South. This boy was from Chicago. The Klan can't slide his murder under the rug."

"I hope those men get what they have coming to them," Ella Ruth said.

"If the boy's mama has anything to do with it, they will. But it's not as easy as having a trial."

"Well, God is the judge here," Buster noted. "Wouldn't you say?" He looked at Ella Ruth. But his words sounded pompous, even to him. God didn't approve of killing anyone.

Ella Ruth took a deep breath. "Murder is murder. These are the kind of men who need to be punished." She met Buster's look with resolve. "Kind of like an eye for an eye."

"I don't think you have that right."

"I'm sure I don't. You're the Bible expert, Buster."

"The sad thing is these men won't go to jail because they killed a Negro child," Lee said. "It won't happen. Remember I said that, but this will start a wave."

"Be careful, brother." Buster chewed a bite of steak that turned to rubber. The light in Ella Ruth's eyes as she listened to Lee made him feel sick.

Ë

The cover of *Time* showed a crowd coming out of a courthouse somewhere in Mississippi. In bold red letters was his brother's name, crediting him with the article on the Emmett Till murder trial. As a result, a big can of worms was open and crawling all over Swannanoa Gap. Some boys in town had threatened Timothy. Ella Ruth wouldn't even talk to Buster about the article. Lee had become some kind of hero in her eyes. Once again, Lee was standing front and center in Buster's life. And yes, Buster was a preacher but he was a human. He was getting madder by the minute.

There was a hard knock on the door of his office. "Come in."

Sheriff Parker Bass walked in and removed his hat. "Preacher Wright."

"Parker." Buster slid the magazine under a pile of papers.

"Can I have a few words with you?"

The sigh deep in Buster's chest escaped. "I guess you can since you're here."

Parker ran a hand through his hair. "Your brother is stirring up a lot of hard feelings." He watched Buster with eyes so dark they looked black. His weasel features reminded Buster of a cartoon character.

"I'm not sure what you mean."

Parker threw a copy of *Time* on Buster's desk. "This. He ain't done nothing but run our town since he came back home. Now he's writing trash."

"Did you read the article, Parker?" Buster fingered the magazine. "It's not about Swannanoa Gap."

Parker straightened his shoulders. "I don't have to read it. I know what he wrote about the Gap."

Buster walked to the window and saw Paul Allen's truck. "So you decided my brother has written something bad without even reading it?"

"Well, uh, it's bad having someone like him here in town."

"Parker, who sent you to see me?"

Parker's face turned bright red. "No one sent me, Buster. I came by myself."

"Well, someone had to read the article and tell you how they felt about it."

Parker puffed out his chest. "Let's just say a few of the boys don't like your brother's kind. We think he ought to go back under the rock he crawled out from." He looked so cocky Buster thought of hitting him.

"Well, the boys should be getting pretty old by now, don't you think, Parker?" Buster used his stern voice. "You can tell your buddies if they want to talk to me, they have to come face to face with me. I see most of them every Sunday anyway. Tell them I know who they are. My brother has never been controlled one day in his life." Buster laughed. "Parker, try reading the article for yourself. Make up your own mind. Swannanoa Gap isn't mentioned in it. Tell your buddies that the Emmett Till trial proves things are changing. I bet they're scared something good."

Parker balled his fingers into two fists. "You tell your brother to be careful or all the Wrights will be sorry."

Buster lifted one eyebrow. "Tell him yourself, Parker, and tell Paul Allen to leave us alone. Ella Ruth wants nothing to do with him. I can't say I blame her."

"You've changed, Buster. I remember when you and Larry knocked down the jail."

Buster put his hand on Parker's shoulder and led him to the door. "Things turn around more often than not."

೧

Buster dialed Lee's number after Parker left. Lacy told him that Lee was busy doing research with Tucker.

"Is this about that article he wrote?" Lacy asked.

"Have some men been there?"

"Naw, but I know the group coming. I can feel it."

"Be careful, Lacy. They'll come after Tucker if they find out he's working with Lee."

She took a breath. "I've spent too many years being careful because of that group. I ain't going to be scared no more. The Klan can go to hell."

"Well, tell my brother I'm on my way over there. He can make the time to talk with me."

The breath Lacy let out traveled across the telephone wire and trembled in his ear. "This ain't about your brother. Don't get me wrong. He can make trouble and he's stirring it everywhere he goes."

"I know, but I'm still talking to him, Lacy. It's time to talk about what he's doing here in town and when he's leaving."

"I'll tell him you're on the way." The phone went dead.

೧

Looking at his parents' house shocked him sometimes. So much had changed.

They were gone, just like the old wicker swing that once hung on the porch. Lee had put two rockers in its place.

236

"What's up, Preacher?" Lee pushed out of the screen door, followed by Tucker. In spite of his caramel skin, the boy was so much like his Daddy that it hurt Buster to look at him.

Buster stopped in front of the steps. "Hi, Tucker. How are you doing?"

Tucker smiled. "I'm fine, Mr. Buster." He looked at Lee. "Me and Lee are looking for colleges."

"That's just the best news. I know your mama will be proud when you finish school and go off to learn even more."

A frown passed over his face. "Yeah, well she's just Mama."

Buster narrowed his eyes at Lee, knowing that Lacy stood somewhere in the shadows. "I got a visit from the sheriff today."

Lee rolled his eyes. "That doesn't surprise me."

"He talked for his friends. It seems they think I need to rein you in. Things have changed. You're not the good guy putting up with a wild brother. I am."

Lee laughed. "So I'm supposed to quit writing because some of the town doesn't like it?"

"I'm just letting you know what happened."

"Tell me, Preacher, how do you feel about my article?" The old competition rode in his eyes.

"My opinion doesn't matter." Buster knew it was a safe answer.

"Ella thought it was brave. That's what she told me."

Buster refused to give in to the anger he felt. "Ella Ruth speaks her mind. But I don't want her being hurt over this mess. I've received threats against my family."

"Somehow I just can't see your wife beside herself in fear."

The anger continued to wash through him, swelling with every word Lee spoke. "You don't know my wife."

"The preacher can still get mad. Good."

"Look, I know you're just as selfish as ever. But please think about my family if you don't care about yourself."

A flicker ran over Lee's face. "You better go back to your church and pray. I got a column to write."

Buster turned to leave.

"I'm nothing but careful, Buster. You'd better be careful too."

Ella Ruth worked on a canvas at the edge of the field. Black Mountain was shrouded in dark clouds. His heart moved in his throat to see the muscles in her bare arms. How long had it been since he'd kissed her and made love to her?

"What's wrong? It's the middle of the day." She never even turned to look at him.

"I got a visit from your father's cronies today."

"Lee's article, right?" She loaded her brush with the perfect shade of gray.

"Yes. We may get trouble from this." He noticed the tiny gold bracelet on her wrist. "Where did you get that bracelet? It's perfect for you."

She looked at it as if for the first time, as if she had worn it so long that it resembled her wedding band. "I bought it with some of the money I made off the painting I sold."

He nodded. "So, you're not worried about your father?"

Her shoulders turned into a mountain ridge of strength. "I'm not afraid of him." Then she finally turned to look at him. "How about you, Buster? Are you afraid of Paul Allen? Are you afraid of the change that is coming?"

"I have beliefs to stand up for, Ella Ruth." Why was he defending himself? "I believe in family. I believe in family before anything else."

She laughed at him. "That sounds so noble. I'm sure your congregation would love that belief, but sorry, I'm not buying one thing about it."

"Why do you say that?" He controlled his voice.

"Your family is the church, not me and Timothy."

"That's not fair."

"Fair! Let me tell you about fair, Buster Wright! How about the fact that the man I married went off to war and died? In his place came a man I didn't know. I didn't much like him either." She looked across the field. "I do what you need me to do, Buster. But we're not together like a husband and wife should be. You left that behind over-seas. I lost you."

"I never had you. I don't even know who you are. You're not there for me and never have been! You've lied to me. You didn't even tell me about Larry. Preacher Mitchell had to tell me. You never came to New York when I was wounded! Who left who, Ella Ruth?"

The slap stung his cheek.

"I hate you." She walked toward the mountain with the paint-brush still in her hand.

He didn't move until he couldn't see her anymore.

☙

Lee's column ran in the Asheville paper and the Atlanta *Journal*—subscription rates had soared in Swannanoa Gap. He bashed the Jim Crow laws and accused small-town citizens of turning their heads the other way, of being what others portrayed small Southern towns to be. Bigots of the worse kind. He named the Gap as an example and opened the wound even bigger.

The phone rang. Buster threw the paper on his desk. "Hello."

"This can't happen, Preacher. You can't handle your brother. He's breaking the law."

"What law, Parker?" Buster held in a laugh. "I have to say my brother has a point about the Jim Crow laws. They were born of ig-norance. Are you telling me you stand up for ignorance?"

"This is bad business."

"Yes, Parker, you're right. This is bad business. I'll tell you what. Come to church on Sunday. You'll understand where I am with this whole mess. Invite your friends."

"Be careful, Preacher."

Buster slammed the phone into its cradle and looked up. Tucker Kurt stood in the door with a grin on his face.

"Is this a service coloreds can come to?"

Buster couldn't help smiling. The boy looked just like Lee but acted like Tyler. "By all means, Tucker, by all means."

Tucker pushed a box in Buster's direction. "Lee told me to bring these to you. He said you might want them. They're Sheriff Wright's old case files. I found them in the basement closet."

He was reaching for the box when glass exploded in the room. Buster ducked at the same time as Tucker. "What was that?"

Tucker pointed at a rock. "There you go, Preacher."

"You in one piece, Tucker?" Buster came around his desk. Jagged pieces of glass were scattered across the floor.

Tucker gave a small smile. "I don't guess you ever get used to this kind of thing." He stood up, towering over Buster.

"You sure don't get your height from your daddy." With that comment, Buster was thinking of Tyler, the man who helped bring Tucker into the world and stood by him as long as he was able.

"Which one?" Tucker brushed off his pants.

Buster did a double take. He knew his face was an open book. "Well, I was talking about Tyler, your daddy. What are you talking about?"

Tucker shook his head. "I know, Preacher. I figured it out the minute I saw Lee. I always felt like something wasn't right. When I saw him, I knew I wasn't Tyler Kurt's son."

"Tyler was your daddy. That's something that can never change, no matter what you think you know."

"That's true, sir. He was a good one. I learned my beliefs from him, his strengths, the stories Mama told. I can't remember him good. But I know Lee's my father."

"It doesn't take much to father a child." Buster tried not to let his words turn hard. He bent down to pick up the box.

"I know that too. But he's trying now. He's trying, and he don't even know that I know. He's a deep man."

Buster laughed. "I never thought of him as deep."

Tucker smiled. "That's 'cause you're his little brother. I can tell you Mile don't look at me as deep or smart."

"Have you told your mother what you know?"

It was Tucker's turn to laugh. "You're kidding, right?"

Buster took a deep breath. "Yeah, she can be something else when she gets riled up."

"She sure likes you, Preacher. That's rare for Mama. She don't much like anyone, especially Lee."

"I like your mama, too." He handed Tucker the box of old files. "Carry this to the car. I don't want to forget to take it home this afternoon."

෨

Buster went to the hardware store after Tucker left. He gave Bob Simmons, the owner, measurements for a new window. Bob couldn't look him in the eye, which made it clear that the whole town knew about this.

Bob handed him the glass wrapped in paper.

"Thank you. You have a good day now." Buster walked out of the store. The old box of files caught his attention as he put the glass in the backseat. The folders were wrinkled and stained with Daddy's writing penciled on the tabs. One caught his eye: "Allen Death."

"You're treading on dangerous ground, son! Men have been killed for less. If you don't believe me, just check with your brother's colored maid."

Buster took a deep breath and turned around to face Paul Allen. "Are you admitting to Tyler Kurt's murder? Or the rock that came through my office window this morning?"

"I don't throw rocks," Paul said. "My work is clean and is never traced back to me."

"Don't you think your time has come and gone, Mr. Allen? The folks in this town are growing real tired of you and your buddies."

Instead of getting mad like Buster expected, Paul Allen laughed. "Who you think you are, son? You ain't nothing but a cripple come home from the war. You got no power here. Your wife runs all over town painting and following that brother of yours. Don't tell me you haven't noticed what was right in front of your eyes."

"My wife is your daughter. The daughter you haven't spoken to in over ten years. You don't even know your grandson. What kind of life do you have, Mr. Allen?" His voice broke out of the calm preacher tone.

Paul Allen took two steps toward Buster. "Don't mess with me,

241

boy. Something real bad is going to happen to you. I ain't worried one bit about that girl with my blood. You see, the apple doesn't fall far from the tree."

Buster punched Paul Allen as hard as he could in the nose, and damn it if it didn't feel good to do it. "That's my wife you're talking about, and I won't have it." His knuckles throbbed.

Several folks on the sidewalk stopped to gape. Who could blame them? The preacher had just socked his father in-law in the nose. Buster started laughing. He couldn't help it.

Paul Allen put his hand over his bleeding nose. "You'll pay, Wright. This ain't the last you heard out of me."

Buster looked at a group of ladies standing nearby, whispering to each other. "Sorry you had to see that. But it's been a long time coming." He turned and got into his car, heading to Dragonfly River. What the hell did Ella Ruth think she was doing? Lee wasn't nothing but trouble. Hell, Paul Allen was probably just making the whole thing up. But deep down, Buster knew better. He'd seen something different in her face. Maybe Lee had put the new look there because it sure wasn't him. But he wasn't going to lose her, especially not to Lee.

CR

Buster pulled into the drive. Ella Ruth stood on the back porch. On most days he had to go find her in the studio. "What's for dinner?"

"What's for dinner? Is that all you can say? The whole town is talking, Buster. I've had so many phone calls I lost count. Where have you been? Preachers don't punch people, even bad people, in the face. Not on Main Street."

Buster laughed. "Don't tell me you're worried about me losing my pulpit?" He tried to keep the words light.

"So you really punched him?"

"Yes, ma'am."

She shook her head. "I didn't know you still had it in you."

"I'm just human." He opened his hands before her.

"I had almost forgotten." She laughed.

The phone rang. Buster answered it even though Ella Ruth shook her head.

"Buster!" Lacy sounded so upset he almost didn't recognize her. "Help us."

"What is it?" But he knew. "Call the state police. I'm on my way over."

Buster slammed the phone down and looked at Ella Ruth. "Where is Timothy?"

"He's with Mile."

Buster grabbed Ella Ruth's hand and they ran for the car. "They've done something to Mama's house."

Her pulse quickened under his fingers.

A rusty pickup barreled by as Buster took the driveway on two wheels.

"That has to be them, Buster!" Ella Ruth screamed.

The house was quiet. Buster was out of the car fast, but not as fast as Ella Ruth.

"Timothy! Timothy Wright!"

Timothy threw opened the back door and ran out on the porch. "Mama."

Tucker followed. "Come look at my mama. She's hurt."

Buster took the steps two at a time and patted Timothy on the shoulder as he ran by.

Lacy was bent over the table, blood dripping from her nose. "It's not that bad. I'm alive."

"Lee is going to throw a fit." Tucker balled his fingers into a fist.

"I think you're giving him way too much credit, son." The resignation in Lacy's voice made Buster shiver, like a shadow walking over his grave. "He just stirs trouble and then leaves others to clean up." She looked Buster straight in the eye and then looked past him.

Ella Ruth stood in the door and stared back. When had they become such enemies?

"What happened, Lacy?" Buster turned away from Ella Ruth.

"I was hanging clothes out back and a man dressed in them fool sheets came out of nowhere. He ask me about Lee. I told him he was gone. Then he ask me if I was Tyler Kurt's wife. I told him if he

243

knew to ask such a thing, he knew the answer. He slapped me down and told me the family would be punished if Lee didn't leave. He ain't nothing but a coward. I'd know him anywhere. It was that stupid sheriff."

"Lee has to be reasoned with." Buster turned back to get a look at Ella Ruth. She only shook her head. "All of you come stay with us."

"I will not," Lacy puffed. "They won't run me off. I'm going home in a little while anyway. If they want me bad enough, they'll get me. We both know that. I won't live afraid."

◌

After Buster took his family home—along with Mile—they all sat down to eat. Buster saw plain as day what his Sunday sermon was supposed to be about. He'd lose his position, but he really didn't give a damn. God didn't make him to be some kind of doormat.

Jesus used parables as swords. Buster would use words too. When the boys went up to Timothy's room, Buster looked at Ella Ruth.

"When did you and Lacy start disliking each other?"

"When Tyler was killed by my father, things changed between us. She blames me. I don't dislike her, but she makes me very uncomfortable." She waited a minute. "That's not true. I don't like her. She's mean and has tried to cause trouble between you and me. I don't want to talk about it."

"Lee needs to be careful. If he gives one dern about Tucker."

She was quiet.

Damn, all the words she didn't say hurt worse. "Come with me." Ella Ruth followed him to the car. The pasteboard box still sat on the seat. "I think you might want to take a look at these files Tucker brought over this morning before the whole mess started. Lee sent them to me from Mama's basement."

"What I want to know is why Lacy is still working in that house for Lee. Wouldn't it be better for Tucker not to be around Lee all the time?" She looked at Buster in the dying light.

244

"Can we look at these files?"

"Yes." She looked away.

They walked up the stairs together. He put the box on the table.

"Let's go to bed," she whispered.

He followed her without a question. Maybe she was right. The files could wait.

They needed to mend their marriage.

CR

The Sunday morning sky was pink. Wasn't there some saying about pink in the morning, a sailor's warning of a storm to come? Buster tried to keep his mind on the task before him. It wasn't easy, considering all that had happened. At that moment, he wanted nothing more than to be back in Ella Ruth's arms, together the way they were last night, hungry for each other again after such a long time.

When he took the pulpit, his heart raced. He faced the crowd, and there was a crowd. It seemed the whole town sat in the pews of his church. In the middle of the sanctuary sat Paul Allen with his wife. Ella Ruth was in the second row. Timothy frowned next to her. He had wanted Mile to sit with him, but Mile chose to sit with Lacy and Tucker. Buster had begged Lacy to come and finally she agreed. The only person missing was Lee.

"It's good to see everyone here on such a fine Sunday morning."

People began to whisper louder. He was sure this had to do with Lacy and her boys.

"Thank you for coming to this service, Mrs. Kurt. I know your own church will miss you this week. Today I'm breaking with tradition. If at the end of the service you no longer want me as your preacher, I will understand." He looked out across the faces. "You see, I thought it was time we proved my brother's columns wrong. I know everyone here doesn't mind a bit that Mrs. Kurt and her boys have come to our service. I know this about you. I want to prove that we, as a town, are decent and caring."

Paul Allen stood. His face was beet red. "Wright! You've gone too far! You'll never stay in this town. We ain't putting up with the likes of you!" He looked around for support. The people just stared at their hands or feet or each other. "You mean you bunch of people believe in this man as your preacher? He's going to ruin our town. You believe in him?"

One lone clap began at the back of the church. Lee stood near the door. Tucker began to clap too, and then Lacy. Ella Ruth stood and clapped. Before Buster knew what had happened, the whole church was on their feet clapping.

Paul Allen walked up the aisle and stopped near Ella Ruth.

His wife stepped pulled on his arm. "Come on, Paul, you're finished here. Ain't no more bullying."

Paul Allen didn't move. "You go to hell, girl," he yelled at Ella Ruth. Then he left the church.

Buster turned to his head deacon, Bob Daniels. "You think I got a job tomorrow?"

Bob smiled. "You stood up to Paul Allen. You done become a hero again."

Buster looked to the back in order to smile at Lee, but he was gone.

After church, Buster went by his mama's house, but Lee wasn't there. It was just like him to do something to help and then hide out. But something told Buster that all was well. For a while there, he had begun to believe the nonsense of Ella Ruth and Lee being together. But it wasn't true. And this thought was enough.

⚬⚬

That night Buster pulled the files out of the pasteboard box. "Ella Ruth, come down here."

She entered the kitchen.

"These are my daddy's unsolved cases." He pointed to one. "See this one."

She looked at the file. "'Allen Death.' Oh my God."

"I thought you'd be interested."

She nodded and sat down to read.

December 20, 1924

Paul Allen showed up on my doorstep in the middle of the night. He was way too calm for a man whose wife had just died. But I guess everyone handles situations different.

Something about the whole thing felt fishy. Of course feeling ain't facts. When I got to his house, I seen that little room in the back had one bed and it was covered with blood. It was like a train wreck they had in Asheville one time. I've seen blood before, but this was the worst. I told Paul Allen we had to call George to come examine the body of his wife and find out what happened here. He just shook his head and told me it was the baby that came too soon. It killed her. That's when I seen a little girl sitting in the corner of the room sucking her thumb. Those big brown eyes will haunt me the rest of my life. I gathered the child in my arms and asked Paul who she was. He said it was his girl and not to worry over her.

I asked Paul what happened to the baby's body and he said it was alive and he gave it away because his wife had slept with another man.

I got to say I just wanted out of that place. Allen ain't nothing but trouble. But then Allen's sister-in-law came snooping around. She was from up north and wasn't one bit afraid of Paul. She just kept pushing and pushing. Paul Allen isn't a man you go and push, even if you're sheriff. I had no proof that he did anything to his wife. It wouldn't stand up in court.

December 23, 1924

Sue is not happy with me investigating this case at Christmas. I did find the mysterious lover of Allen's wife. He is an attorney in Asheville. He broke down like a husband should when he heard she'd died. God, what kind of creature is Paul Allen? It seems that Allen's wife had run away and was living with the attorney. They planned on marrying just as soon as her divorce was final. Now, I was getting somewhere. I warned Allen to expect an arrest warrant.

December 24, 1924

I am closing this case. It is a coward's way out. I have to let down Allen's sister-in-law. The Klan busted down my door last night and threatened to kill my children. This is where a man draws the line. They set fire to our front room and ripped open my wife's dress. I fired a pistol and that's all that saved us. But I can't be everywhere all the time protecting them. I'm closing the case. God please forgive me.

Ella Ruth looked at Buster and then closed the folder. She went out to her studio without a word.

Chapter 25

Timothy

School let out early after a swarm of termites took over the classroom. Mrs. Bishop tried to ignore the first small cluster that gathered in the back corner. Timothy watched them grow in numbers. Their movement was like a math project spreading out from the corner into the shape of a triangle and then a rectangle. They fell out of the electric outlets, squeezed between the molding and the floor.

Most of the time termites swarmed in the spring. Maybe it was the extra heat that wouldn't let loose; even the crop duster was still coming way past the fields needing dusting. There was a tingle in the air that Timothy breathed in each morning. Everything was different. He figured it might be the mountain at work. The old folks believe it was alive and magical, that souls were trapped there, wandering around. Sometimes they made it as far as the Gap.

He was eleven and didn't much believe in magic. Most of it was just lies, like Santa and that stupid Easter Bunny. He never believed in the Easter Bunny anyway. A giant bunny hopping around with a bunch of stinking boiled eggs? He wasn't a fool. But the termite invasion was a real event. They were taking over the whole room, crawling around, wiggling their wings.

Mrs. Bishop stood in front of the class trying to make the kids understand how to dissect a sentence as if it were a frog in science class. Timothy could see how taking a frog apart was useful, but not a sentence. He just wanted to fly. He paid attention to social studies because it had lots of maps. And of course he worked hard on math because it came in handy for a lot of stuff, like building a flying machine, a glider. That's how the Wright Brothers got started. Like them, Timothy was bound and determined to fly.

Bobby Stewart dropped a book on the floor and the swarm of termites took to the air. The girls were screaming and the boys were laughing. Mrs. Bishop started swinging her arms around like a bird. Timothy laughed so hard he grabbed his side.

"Class, form a line!" Mrs. Bishop was already out the door. "Follow me. I'm letting you go home early today."

"Yeah!" The chorus of voices burst into the hall.

"There will be double work tomorrow." Mrs. Bishop was still waving at her hair.

Timothy was free to do whatever he wanted. He headed straight for the fort to work on his gilder. He was making it look like a picture he had found in a book about flying and early machines. Mile thought it would never work, but Timothy was undaunted. He had to tell Mama he was out of school. She'd be painting.

He came up on the barn without a noise. It wasn't intentional. He was just the quiet sort. Mama said he was like a house cat slipping out an open door. The door to her studio stood open a little. There was a tangle of arms and legs. Neither person had on clothes. Now, he knew all about coupling. He'd seen cows and horses, but grownups were a whole other thing. Especially when the woman was his mama and the man was Uncle Lee.

His heart beat in his head. He turned and left the barn as quiet as he had entered, breaking into a run once he was in the yard. At the road he threw up his lunch. What a big damn baby he was. Then a mean thought hit him square in the chest. He stomped back into the yard and when he got to the barn, he yelled, "Mama! I'm out of school early because of a swarm of termites."

Mama rushed out of her studio door with her shirt turned inside out, but at least she had clothes on. "Goodness, Timothy, you scared me to death."

"What are you doing in there?" He could look innocent when he wanted.

She came toward him. "Let me make you some lunch."

He stepped back. "I already ate." The words came out mean.

"Are you okay?"

"Ain't nothing wrong with me. I'm going to the fort." He turned and walked away.

CR

He crossed through Grandma Sue's yard on his way to the fort. Mama was crazy and Uncle Lee was stupid.

"Timothy." Mrs. Kurt stood on the back porch.

Shit. "Yes ma'am?" He kicked at a rock.

"What you doing here so early?" Mrs. Kurt enjoyed playing mama over him.

"We had a termite swarm at school."

"Lord have mercy." She frowned. "Did you tell your mama you were home?"

"Yes ma'am. I'm going to my fort to work on something."

"What are you boys working on?"

"Just stuff."

She huffed. "Stuff can get you in trouble. You be careful out there. Did you see your uncle at your house?"

"Yes." There it was, the truth. At least he wasn't a liar.

Mrs. Kurt glared at him. "You go on now and mind your p's and q's."

Timothy marched off to the woods. The stupid glider wasn't going to work. He needed to fly. He had to fly. His life depended on it. About that time, the crop duster flew over. He was probably helping with the termites. Timothy broke into a run, leaving the fort behind. He was going to find that crop duster if it was the last thing he did.

CR

The yellow plane was sitting on the edge of Old Man Wharton's empty field. Timothy was out of breath and sweating like a pig. The pilot was smoking a cigarette near the wing of the plane.

Timothy stood there until the pilot looked up.

"What you staring at, kid?"

"Your plane."

The pilot moved to the body and ran his hand over it like someone might rub their dog. "She's a beaut, a PT-13 in the war. She saw a lot of action. She's a good one."

Timothy could only stare at his dream.

"Come on over here. She ain't going to bite." The pilot stomped out his cigarette.

Timothy had a hard time breathing as he came close to the yellow wonder. "Can I touch her?"

"Sure, she ain't a dog. Better, actually." The pilot had a big handlebar mustache and sharp blue eyes that reminded Timothy of his daddy's.

He touched the smooth yellow side. "I'm going to fly me a plane."

"Ain't nothing like it." The man looked at the sky.

"What are you doing out here today?" Timothy couldn't take his stare away from the plane.

"I just fly sometimes. I like this field 'cause Old Man Wharton appreciates my skills as a pilot. I can land here anytime. I even took him up a time or two."

Timothy could hear his heart beating.

"You want to get in and see what she's like?"

Timothy's insides were shaking so bad he couldn't speak, only nod.

"Here, use the wing and crawl back. That's where I fly her."

Timothy scrambled up the wing and back to the seat.

"Careful now, don't fall." The man came behind him.

He sat down and looked at all the dials. "What do they mean?"

"That's hard to explain. They tell you how not to crash." The man laughed and held out his hand. "I'm Carlson Baker. Everyone calls me Carl."

Timothy shook the hand of a real pilot and then gripped the steering wheel. There he was in the cockpit of a plane.

"That's called a yoke," Carl said. Timothy looked at him in disbelief.

"Yep, like in a egg."

There was so much to learn. Timothy glanced out over the field. "I bet it's something else to see from the sky."

The man leaned on the side of the plane, his feet on the wing. "There ain't nothing like it."

"Where'd you learn to fly?"

"Where most pilots learned—action in the war."

"Whoa."

"Ah, don't think it was great, 'cause it wasn't. But once in a while, when the enemy wasn't around and I could just fly, it was beautiful." The man looked like he was far off somewhere.

"I'm going to learn to fly."

The man looked at Timothy. "So you've said. Son, you can do anything you put your mind to doing." He slapped his leg, and Timothy knew it was time to leave. "I'll tell you what. You call me when you're good and ready, and I'll give you a couple of loops around. That is, if your mama and daddy don't care."

"Oh, they don't care. When you want to do it?"

"Let's say the day after Thanksgiving. Is school out then?"

"Yes sir."

"What's your name, kid?"

"Timothy Wright, sir."

"Well, Timothy, I'll see you after Thanksgiving." He helped Timothy jump to the ground. "Now don't go bringing a bunch of kids."

"I promise, sir."

"Good." The man jumped into the cockpit. "You want to get out of the way."

Timothy nodded and ran in the opposite direction of the plane. When the engines started, he whipped around and watched the pilot guide the plane across the field. He threw his hand in the air as he pulled goggles over his eyes. The plane wobbled a little but took to the air.

Timothy finally released his breath. He was going to fly.

Chapter 26

Ella Ruth

Ella Ruth stood in her studio. There were no words. There was no one to blame.

And really, who was she? She was a cross between her mother and Paul Allen, who wouldn't think twice about sleeping with his brother's wife. She had slept, on more than one occasion, with her husband's brother. On some days she thought she might just get in Gert's old car and drive as far as she could. On other days, she loved Buster with her whole heart. She ached for him, for what they almost had but never seemed to own. Then, she had her moments when all she wanted was Lee. With Lee, she was a grownup with no real past. The time had come to give Lee up before Buster found out or, worse, Timothy.

The new canvas sat in front of her.

"Hi."

She jumped. "I didn't hear you. Don't sneak up on me like that."

"I just came by with some news." Lee smiled.

Her stomach flipped. "What news is that?" She turned back to the empty canvas.

"I want you to bring the town paintings and come for a ride with me."

"I can't."

"Why?" He watched her. "You won't regret this trip, Ella Ruth."

"Timothy gets out of school in two hours. Will we be home by then?"

He shook his head. "But I'll tell Lacy that he'll come by there."

"Buster suspects something. I can feel it."

"I don't think so." Lee's face was serious.

"Okay, maybe I'm wrong."

"He'll figure it out sometime. It has to happen."

"Why?" Anger came into her word.

"Well, I guess if I just go away, he won't."

She shook her head and folded her arms. "Where are you taking me?"

"It's a surprise. Let's load up the paintings."

"No one around here likes them, Lee. I don't get what you're up to."

He stopped and looked her in the eye. "Just let me do something for you."

She nodded with a sigh.

"I promise we won't do anything you can't tell Buster about."

This made her laugh. "I'll believe that when I see it."

He pointed the car away from town. "Did you call Lacy?"

"Yes." She looked in the side mirror. "She hates me."

"I've noticed her smile tightens when you're in the room. What did you do to her?"

"Nothing. But Paul Allen did plenty. She blames me. Also, she suspects us." She turned and looked at the side of his face. He looked nothing like Buster. She couldn't stand it if he did. "You never have talked about Tucker being your son." She couldn't look him in the eye.

The line around his month twitched. "I didn't know we wanted to talk about our pasts. I thought you and I were starting new, a beginning."

"You're right."

"Buster told you?"

"I've always known. Lacy talked about it. But Buster knows."

"What do you want to do about Tucker being my son?"

Her heart beat harder. "Nothing now. I don't know. Maybe we should just stop all this, Lee. It's horrible for Buster, and for Lacy too."

Lee pulled the car to the side of the road and moved toward her. "Why? Why, Ella?"

He had a certain smell. "I don't know. It's wrong because I'm married."

He nodded. "I should never have left this town. If I'd known you were here, I wouldn't have."

Her head spun. "This is too much."

He moved back behind the wheel. "You're right. I'm taking you on a completely innocent trip."

Her laugh opened her heart to him. "I really doubt that, Lee."

"No." He grinned at her as he pulled the car back on the road. "I promise. When I'm finished with you today, you'll know where my heart is." He stepped on the gas. "I've spent too much of my life roaming, Ella Ruth. I don't want to roam anymore."

She put her hands under her legs so he wouldn't see them shake. "I love you, Lee." There, the words were in the air.

"I'm glad you said that before we get where we're going." He was quiet for a minute.

"Where are we going?" But she didn't care. All she wanted was that moment to last forever. She was in love with her brother-in-law.

"I want you to know, Ella Ruth, that I have been with a lot of women. I'm not a liar. I didn't come here to cause trouble." He looked over and grinned. "Honestly, I never forgot seeing you that day. I knew there was something different about you. I remember being jealous of Buster all over again."

"But we're wrong." She looked out the window at the mountain.

"Yeah? Who said so?"

She couldn't speak. The river was deeper from the rain, and the churning sound reached the car.

"I've only loved two women in my life."

She held her hand up. "I'm not sure I should hear this."

"Come on. You can say what you feel but I can't?"

The water churned as the car glided along the road.

"I loved Millie. I would have married her if she had lived."

A catch in her chest ached. "I'm sorry."

"She was beautiful and she knew me inside and out. I didn't have to hide myself from her."

"How did she die?"

"Pearl Harbor. I didn't take her out of the building with me. She begged me to come with her to the basement. I thought I was saving her life."

Ella Ruth wanted that kind of love. Had she ever loved Buster that much? Did she love Lee that much now? "What about Lacy?"

Lee smiled. "I was a kid. What do you know when you're a kid?"

"Yeah." What did she know?

"I thought I loved her, but Daddy was right. Who was I to think I could change history?"

"But you are changing history."

He laughed. "Naw, I just write about it. I haven't done one brave thing."

"You liar. You write columns that tell the truth whether your readers like it or not."

"Thanks for believing in me, but Buster standing in front of the church yesterday is one of the bravest acts I've seen, Ella Ruth."

"It was brave." She wouldn't lie. "He's a good man. But we stopped loving each other a long time ago."

"I think he still loves you, Ella Ruth."

"Really?" She hadn't thought Buster loved her since he signed up with God, but they had made love the other night. She couldn't let Lee know. Now she was cheating on Lee with her husband. How difficult had she made her life?

"Yes. Does that change anything?"

"No."

"Good."

CR

The art gallery in Atlanta was beautiful. She wouldn't return until way after Buster came home. There would be questions, but she refused to think of that. The owner wanted to show all her town paintings. They went for coffee to discuss the details, and the city worked magic on her. For a few minutes, she allowed herself to pretend that she was married to Lee. What a different life she would have had.

He reached over and squeezed her hand. "Her work is some of the best I've seen."

"I agree," the gallery owner said.

"Have you noticed the words she hides in the paintings?"

The owner was a man with a tiny pencil mustache, older than both of them. "No." He looked interested. "You must show me, Mrs.

Wright."

"Please call me Ella Ruth."

"Ella Ruth it is. I look forward to showing your work. They are small town, and people just love small town."

❧

On the drive back to the Gap, they watched the sun set behind the trees. Buster was at home wondering where she was. Was he scared? He might not even care.

"I can't wait to see the look on Buster's face when we tell him that your paintings are going to be shown in Atlanta."

"He won't like it." She looked at him. "Is that why you did all this?"

"What do you mean? I did it because I love you, Ella Ruth. I'm ready to tell my brother that I love you. I'm ready to take you to Atlanta to live. I can't stay in Swannanoa Gap. It's going to kill me, and you too, if we don't get out."

Her heart beat in her throat. "Wait. We have to think about Timothy."

"Timothy will come with us." He gave her a pleading look. "Buster loves you. He's a fool if he doesn't, but can he make you happy, Ella? Can he be there for you? All I've seen is you being there for him."

"I'm the bad one, Lee. Let's just get that clear. I won't blame Buster for my adultery."

He snorted. "So you're taking what we have down to something cheap and physical?"

"No. Don't put words in my mouth. Let's just take things slow."

"I can't stay here much longer. I can't play second to Buster. I'd rather leave."

"Just give me time to think and do things my way. I don't want to hurt him any worse than I have to, Lee."

His face softened. "I know."

❧

Buster came to the door before Ella Ruth could get out of the car.

Lee opened the door. "Here we go," he whispered.

And suddenly Buster was in Lee's face, grabbing his collar. "What the hell are you doing with my wife?"

Timothy stood in the door.

Ella Ruth moved toward him, but he turned and walked back inside.

"Brother, think hard before you start something." Lee was calm, too calm.

"You take my wife off and I'm supposed to ignore this?"

"What are you assuming?" Lee balled his fingers into fists. The porch light spilled into the yard.

"Stop," Ella Ruth managed. "Buster, you stop right now. You don't even know what we were doing."

Buster cut his look at her. "Ella Ruth, I know everything. I know you love him. I know he walked back in our lives and got his revenge on me."

"This isn't about you, Buster," she screamed. "For once this is about me. Lee helped me take my paintings to Atlanta. A gallery there is going to show them, Buster. Would you have done this for me? Would you?" Her voice trembled. "No, you wouldn't. Buster, I wasn't doing anything wrong today. But you're right. I'm in love with your brother. He notices me. With him, I'm more than a preacher's wife."

Buster stepped back from Lee. "Have you slept with him, Ella Ruth?" His voice was a little wild.

"She's coming with me. We're going to Atlanta."

Buster dove into him, all fists. Lee punched too.

"Stop! Stop!"

Timothy came running out of the house and flew into Lee.

"Timothy, get away from them," Ella Ruth said.

"You go on. Leave my mama alone. I hate you. Leave my mama alone."

Ella Ruth grabbed Timothy in all his fury and pulled him away from the fighting men, who didn't even notice them. This was not about her. It was their stupid childhood hatred. She had been a pawn.

She hugged Timothy to her as he cried. "Don't do this to Daddy, Mom. Don't do this to me."

His face was hot, sweaty. She kissed him. "I'm not going to do anything, sweetie. I'm staying right here with you. You're my life." She turned to her husband and her lover. "Stop. I want both of you gone. Now! I want you gone! You've used me. Both of you!" She took Timothy and went inside the house, locking the door behind her.

Chapter 27

Lee Wright

Lee turned into the drive of the house on two wheels, car tires spinning. The slam of the car door brought Lacy to the door, a plate in her hand. He'd left that morning with a cocky grin on his face. Now everything had fallen through.

"I'm going to Atlanta to stay for a while, Lacy."

"Running gets old, don't it?" She stared him down.

"I want to take Tucker. He needs to get out of this damn town before they kill him."

She flung the plate at him. "The only person causing him trouble is you! You leave my boy alone."

"I gave you more credit, Lacy."

"You ain't going to make me feel dumb, Lee. You're the one sleeping with your brother's wife. I got enough sense to act like a decent human."

He watched her. "Tucker will get chances with me he won't get with you."

She laughed. "Now you're looking down your nose at me, Lee. You done marked your territory like some old dog. Well, I won't have no part of it and neither will Tucker."

"He'll hate you for it."

She took in a small breath. "He ain't your son. He had a daddy. I messed up bad by trusting you, Lee. When I tangled with you I ruined my life. Do you understand? You quit stirring his hopes. He ain't going to no college. I don't care what I have to do." She picked up a clay flowerpot on the porch. "You go on and ruin your life and Ella Ruth's, but you ain't messing with mine."

"I'm talking to Tucker."

"You go ahead, but remember this: I ain't letting him go no matter what I have to do. Consider this your warning. You go on down to Atlanta and stay. We don't need you here."

"You'll get paid just like always. I'm not leaving for good. I'll be back for Ella Ruth when she comes to her senses. And she will."

The pot shook in her hand. "If she's got any sense, she'll kill you."

☙

Mile met Lee at the door of his house. "You better get away from here. Mama will kill you for coming after Tucker. She done told him to stay clear of you."

"You don't worry, Mile." Lee looked at Tucker standing in the front room. "Are you going with me?"

"Yes sir."

So Lee and Tucker left for Atlanta together.

Chapter 28

Timothy

Thanksgiving came to the Gap. Timothy's dad had moved back to Grandmother Sue's house, and it didn't look like he'd ever come home. Uncle Lee had cleared out like some kind of chicken. Boy, was Grandmother Sue wrong about him.

Timothy and Mama sat down to eat their Thanksgiving dinner, a little roasted chicken and some pineapple upside-down cake. Mama worked hard at smiling, but he could see that faraway look in her eye. A man in Atlanta had bought all her town paintings and one or two more. The money would take care of them for a long time, or so Mama said. But Dad's chair was empty and the house was empty without him. Couldn't Mama see that? Timothy had thought on this situation so hard that he almost forgot his date with Carlson Baker, the pilot, the next day. He'd kept it a secret from everyone, even Mile. And he really hated that because Mile was his best friend.

"Timothy," Mama said suddenly, interrupting his thoughts, "I'm going out to work on my painting." She took their plates and began rinsing them in the sink. "Do you want to walk over and see your dad?"

He knew this was not a choice. Dad was expecting him. "I'll walk over, but tomorrow I got some things to do."

Mama tilted her head to the side. He had to be careful. She could nail him in a lie. "What do you have to do?"

"I'm going out to Old Man Wharton's field and watch the crop duster."

She pulled her sweater over her head. It was one of Daddy's old sweaters and Timothy felt baby tears pushing at the back of his eyes. "Go on over and visit with your dad."

He lit out across the field. The roof of the old house was easy to see from far off.

Tomorrow he would fly, and nothing else mattered.

Mrs. Kurt smiled when he came in the kitchen door. He thought she'd be at her house having her own Thanksgiving dinner. "Mile's out at the barn. Your daddy is in the front room making a fire. I got the finest turkey you've ever seen and it'll be ready soon. I made peach pie and your grandmother's favorite dressing recipe."

For several days, Timothy had noticed something was off about Mrs. Kurt. Of course, Tucker had left with Uncle Lee. She tried to act all happy, but Mile said she cried each night. At least Mama wasn't crying, but it might make things a lot easier if she did.

"I'll go see Dad." This was expected of him.

"Good boy." Mrs. Kurt went back to stirring something in a bowl.

Dad sat in a chair close to the fire. There was no sign that Lee had ever come back home. The desk and his typewriter were gone.

"Hey, Dad."

Dad looked up from his book. "Timothy, I'm glad you came for dinner. I thought we'd invite Mrs. Kurt and Mile to eat with us."

Mile being there would be great, but it felt funny to have Mrs. Kurt sitting at the table. She normally hovered, waiting on them. "Okay."

"It's a chilly day. Finally that hot weather left." Dad closed his book.

Here Timothy was, talking about the weather with his dad. It was stupid. "I guess."

"How's your mother?" Dad looked out the window.

Anger swelled in his chest, but he pushed it down. Tomorrow he would make a dream come true. "She's fine." He was tired of being his parents' go between. "You could go over and see her for yourself."

Dad looked startled. "I guess you want to go see Mile."

Timothy's shoulders slumped. "Yes sir." He turned to leave the room.

"Son."

Timothy stopped in the doorway and looked back.

"It's not that easy."

"It seems pretty easy to me, Dad. You get in your car or you walk over there. That is what adults do. They go see each other."

Dad looked away. "One day you'll understand."

"I really doubt it, Dad. I don't mean any disrespect, but the way you and Mom act is stupid."

Dad actually laughed, but it was a mean laugh. "I guess you are exactly right, Timothy. Go on and find Mile. Thanks for coming. I know this is hard on you."

"Nope, not hard at all." This time Timothy couldn't hold back the anger. "You and Mom are the ones making everything so hard. I'm fine. Don't try to make me feel like you do. Mom doesn't feel like you. She smiles and paints. She's living, Dad."

Dad seemed like he might cry, and Timothy had to look away. "Your mom is the strong one."

"She's the smart one." He went down the hall and was out the door before Mrs. Kurt could fuss at him. She had ears that heard everything.

∞

Mile was sitting in the fort and stuck his head out the window when Timothy whistled. "I didn't think you'd come to the house on Thanksgiving. I wouldn't be here but Mama made me. I can't take all the sad looks. She tries to act like Tucker ain't gone."

"Dad's like that too. Mom just goes on about her work. I know she did wrong stuff, but she's easier to be around."

"So you think she really fell in love with your uncle? Mama says she's crazy."

The anger worked in Timothy's head. "She ain't no more crazy than your mama, who's pretending Tucker is coming home any day."

Mile looked like he might get mad, but it passed right off his face. "They all are crazy."

"Yep."

"We got to eat with them."

"Yep, but I got something to look forward to." He just let it slip right out.

"What?"

"I can't tell. I promised I wouldn't."

"We're friends until death. You got to tell me."

Mile had a point. "If I tell, will you promise not to breathe a word? 'Cause if you do, I'll kick your ass all the way down the road."

Mile straightened his shoulders. "You tell me and I'll tell you the biggest secret I got. It's a big one."

"Okay."

"You go first 'cause mine is so big it will spoil yours."

"You're full of it." But now Timothy was about to die to know Mile's secret. "Tomorrow, I'm going to meet Carlson Baker in Old Man Wharton's field."

"What kind of secret is that? I don't even know who Carlson Baker is." Mile looked like the wolf who had swallowed a sheep.

"Let me finish. Carlson Baker, Carl, owns the crop duster." Timothy allowed this news to sink in. "He's promised to take me flying."

Mile sat up straighter. "Does your mama know?"

"Hell no. What do you think?" Timothy stretched out on the floor.

Mile shook his head. "You're messing with fire."

Timothy pushed up on his elbows. "I don't give a damn."

Mile nodded. "Can I go too?"

"He said I couldn't take a bunch of kids."

"I ain't a bunch. I'm just one little colored boy. I don't even count."

Timothy laughed. "I'll tell you what. You tell me your secret. If it's as good as you say, I'll let you tag along." He doubted Mile could tell him anything surprising, but he was playing along anyway.

"Well, this is the honest to God truth."

"Just tell it, Mile."

"Mama told me in one of her fits of grief. Right after Tucker left with your uncle, Mama threw a big old fit. She went around the living room dumping stuff into the floor. I thought she might kill me. She took every one of our books and ripped as many pages from them as she could. I thought I was going to have to call your daddy. He's the only one that can do anything with her."

Timothy hated that. "Go on."

"Anyway, she looked at me and her eyes went real crazy like she

266

might kill me for letting Tucker go—except I couldn't stop him if I wanted. Then she took my shoulders and pinched them so hard I yelled at her. She looked me in the eye and said I was the only son my daddy had."

"That's 'cause she's mad at Tucker for leaving." What a letdown.

"Naw. I thought the same thing, but she shook me real hard and ask me if I knew what she was saying. I told her she was just mad at Tucker. And that's when I thought she'd kill me and her both. Her eyes got wild and she picked up a book and threw it through the glass window."

Timothy thought on this a minute. Mrs. Kurt never acted like that. "Are you sure?"

"Well I sure as hell ain't fibbing! Do you want to hear what she said next?"

"Yeah." He tried to sound like he didn't care.

"She said that Tucker was my half-brother. Now, I didn't even know what that meant and she laughed at me real hard. She told me that your Uncle Lee was Tucker's daddy." Mile got quiet.

Timothy couldn't look at his best friend. What kind of person was Uncle Lee?

"Did you hear me?"

"Yeah."

"My brother is your uncle's son."

"I heard it already." Timothy jumped up, shaking the treehouse and bumping his head on the roof.

"What the hell is wrong with you? You got a problem with Tucker being your uncle's son?"

"I got as much a problem as you do," he yelled back at Mile. "That man has hurt everybody."

Mile lost his mad face. "Yeah."

"He caused my mama and dad to break up."

"I know. Mama said that Lee and your mama was doing the bad thing together."

Timothy's stomach turned and he grabbed Mile's shirt collar. "You'd better shut up."

"I'm just telling you what she said. Hell, he done took my brother in more ways than one."

Timothy let go of his collar. "Sorry. I just hate him, Mile."

"Me too. I hate him enough to kill him."

And there it was, enough hate to put both of them in jail for the rest of their lives. "He ain't worth it."

Mile looked at Timothy. "Yeah he is, but I ain't going to ruin my life for no white man."

"You can come with me tomorrow."

Mile nodded. "But I ain't flying."

"I know."

ʒ

Mama was still in bed when Timothy left. He wrote her a note so she wouldn't forget where he was going. Mile was waiting on the road for him.

"Mama is driving me crazy. She won't hardly let me out of her sight. I could kick Tucker's ass for leaving. I want to tell her that my daddy is dead. She don't have nothing to worry about. I ain't got nowhere to go."

"That's tough. Come on. We're going to be late."

"It's cold. Can he fly when it's this cold?"

"Sure he can."

"I ain't going in that thing."

"There's only room for two." But Timothy sure wished his friend could go. His stomach flipped. "You could sit with me if he'd let you."

"No."

"What, are you scared?"

"I ain't scared. I just know God gave us feet, not wings."

"Your ass is scared." Timothy laughed a little too hard.

"Shut up or I'll whip you right here in front of the world."

"There ain't nobody around, Mile."

"I'll whip you anyway."

Timothy could tell he wasn't mad anymore. They were best friends. Mile was his only friend.

The yellow crop duster barreled over the trees and their heads.

"Run." Timothy ran across the field with all his might. He didn't want to miss his chance to fly.

"Slow down." Mile was behind him.

The crop duster rolled to a stop on the far end of the field. Timothy waved his arms and ran at the same time.

Carl jumped from the wing. "How did I know you'd be here?" He eyed Mile. "What you got here?"

"This is my best friend ever. You got to let him fly with me." Carl looked at Mile.

"I don't have to fly today. I can watch from here."

Carl laughed. "I'll tell you what. I ain't supposed to fly but one passenger, but if you don't tell, I won't tell." He bowed. "I suggest you boys take your seats."

Mile hung back.

"Come on, Mile. You got to go too. It's like a dream."

Mile frowned. "Your dream, not mine." But he followed Timothy into the seat.

"Now, you boys are scrawny enough to squeeze into the seat together and put that belt on. I don't want you falling out."

Mile took a deep breath, but Timothy poked him. "He's just joking."

Carl was right. They both fit into the seat and the belt snapped snug over them.

"This belt ain't going to hold shit if we fall out of the sky." Mile looked scared.

"Shut up. Don't let Carl know you're afraid."

Carl checked their belt and then jumped into his seat. "Let's go, boys. Let's go meet our maker." He started the engine.

When the plane began to move, Timothy took in one big breath. The faster they moved, the harder his heart beat. Mile just stared straight ahead. The wheels lifted from the ground and the plane titled to the right. Timothy was airborne. The treetops seemed to bow down and allow the crew to take complete flight into the blue sky. Timothy finally allowed his breath to seep from him. Carl grinned and held up his thumb when Timothy looked back at him. He was a bird. Life was so tiny and meaningless.

He pointed to the top of Mama's house, and Mile looked down and relaxed, even smiled. They looked down on Swannanoa Gap as Carl headed in the direction of Black Mountain. Below him were all the people Timothy knew. He was free, free from Mama and Dad, free from Uncle Lee. He took in a deep breath and relaxed. Whatever he had expected, this was much, much better. Mile hung his head over the side.

The plane climbed as Carl pointed it at the mountain. Timothy closed his eyes and just felt the wind. He never wanted to his feet to touch the earth again. A sputtering started and grew louder. Mile looked at him with wide eyes. The plane jerked and dipped.

Timothy turned around to look at Carl, who was studying the dials in front of him. The look on his face said a lot. The plane jerked again and sputtered louder.

"You boys hold on. We got to put her down." The words mixed with the wind, but Timothy understood.

"We're going to get killed," Mile yelled.

"Shut up. There ain't no way. We know how this plane flies. We watched it too many times." But Timothy's stomach flipped upside down.

The engine sputtered and produced one loud bang, and then all was quiet. The plane moved fast, faster.

"I'm going to try and land her in that clearing," Carl shouted.

Timothy could see what looked like a tiny square of grass on the side of Black Mountain. He thought of Mama and Dad finding out how he died. He looked at Mile, trying not to cry. Babies cry. Mile had tears sliding down his cheeks. The plane moved close to the treetops. They were going to make it. Timothy smiled at Mile and the wings fell apart. The whole plane began to fall apart and the world went black.

ଓ

It was nothing but black when Timothy opened his eyes. He'd died. But if he had died, then Heaven had wind, freezing cold wind. He felt dead grass poking his neck, but when he tried to move his right leg, he couldn't even feel it. A terrible pain grew in his left side. What had happened? Then he remembered flying. He was flying in the crop duster. What was his name? He heard rustling in the undergrowth, and then he heard the voices.

"Anyone there? Is anyone alive out there?"

Timothy opened his mouth, but the effort was too much.

"I know folks in that plane have to be around here somewhere." The man wasn't too far way.

"Here." But it was only a whisper, more like a whimper. Was this how it felt to die? Was he dying?

Timothy moved his hand and touched something cold. His whole world turned into a dense fog.

Chapter 29

Ella Ruth

The rumble shook her studio and rattled the door on the old cast-iron coal stove. At first she pushed the noise away, thinking of thunder. But it was thirty-two degrees outside, with snow threatening to fall. She continued working on a watercolor of City Hall with the mountain in the background.

"Mom."

She set her brush down. "Yes." Her voice sounded kind enough, though sometimes she showed her aggravation when interrupted during her work.

There was only silence. Outside her studio the air was brutally cold, colder than earlier when she had come out to paint. "Timothy?" she yelled and walked in the direction of the quiet house. A chill walked across her arms. On the mountain was a spiral of black smoke, quickly turning gray. Who would be burning on such a dry day? "Timothy." As she called his name, she heard in her voice a desperation that had not yet clicked in her mind. "Timothy." She trotted to the house and found the kitchen as she had left it. Timothy's note was still folded on the table. He had gone to see the crop duster.

Her heart skipped a beat. He wouldn't fly in that plane without telling her. She knew this. The pilot would never agree to take him. The phone was in her hand and she dialed Buster at his mother's house before she even gave it a thought.

"Wright's residence." Lacy sounded grouchy, but she always sounded grouchy.

"Lacy, are the boys back?" Ella Ruth attempted to keep her voice calm.

"I haven't seen Mile since he slipped out of here this morning." There was a pause. "There sure is a big cloud of smoke on Black Mountain." It wasn't like Lacy to make any kind of small talk.

"Did you hear the rumble? You know, like thunder?"

"I ain't heard no sound, but that smoke sure don't look too good.

Looks like the woods are on fire."

"Is Buster there?" Ella Ruth knew he wasn't, but she was talking to hide a growing fear in her stomach.

"He's at the church. You know that." The edge in Lacy's voice told Ella Ruth that all was back to normal.

"I'll call him there." She waited a second, trying to decide what she should say to Lacy without scaring her for no reason.

"I'll send Timothy home when they get back here. I hope they got their noses clean."

Ella Ruth should have told Lacy about the crop duster, but it seemed too little of a thing. Timothy would never fly in that plane without telling her. She was certain of that. He was a good boy.

Buster answered on the second ring.

"Hi."

He was quiet.

"Have you seen Timothy?"

Papers shuffled and he took a long breath. "Not this morning."

"Okay." He was useless.

"Wait. Is something wrong?"

She could hear his desk chair squeak. "No, I just got worried. I'm being silly."

"What? Where is Timothy supposed to be?"

"Well, he told me yesterday that he was going out to look at the crop duster plane in Mr. Wharton's field."

"You let him do that?"

"He was just going to look, Buster." Why in the world had she called him?

"I'm going over there."

"Wait, I'm sure it's okay. I just heard this rumble and saw some smoke on the mountain. I'm being completely silly." The mountain was hidden from her view when looking out the kitchen window. All of a sudden, she wanted to make sure the smoke wasn't worse.

"I don't see any smoke." Buster's office had a view of only part of the mountain.

"No, it was higher up. You'd have to go outside to see it. It's probably some fool up there burning and it got away from them.

Timothy is fine. I'll let you know when he gets home."

"It's lunch now."

"Well, it was a plane he went to see."

"Is Mile with him?"

"Yes. I talked to Lacy. She said she'd call if they showed up there first."

"I can go check." But she could tell he was already back into his church work.

"No. I'll get Timothy to call you."

"Okay."

"Bye."

"Ella Ruth."

"Yes." She didn't like the sound of his voice.

"We have to talk sometime."

"Not now. And actually, I don't see a reason to talk at all. You've made up your mind about everything. Your talking would just be preaching." Those words were downright cruel and she knew it. "I have to go." She hung up the phone before he could speak again.

Out in the frigid air her mind cleared. The smoke was gone from the mountain. "You're so silly." She spoke into the silence. Overprotecting Timothy would not help either one of them through this tough time. If he didn't come home in an hour, she'd go looking for him. She got caught up in her painting and didn't notice the time until she heard the crunch of tires outside in the drive.

Buster looked upset. "Lacy hasn't heard a word from the boys. She's been calling you for the past three hours."

The tone of his voice made her want to scream. She took two steps back. "I've been painting. I'm sure he's fine." But the truth was that once again she had been lost in her art and not present for her family. "Let's go to Mr. Wharton's field."

Buster looked disgusted. "I've beat you to it. Mr. Wharton said the plane took off around 10:15. He never saw Timothy or Mile."

Her mind twisted. "He said he was going to look at the plane." She headed toward her car, Gert's old car. "I know he wouldn't fly in that plane without asking first. He just wouldn't do that."

"Where are you going?"

Where was she going? She was going to the place on the mountain. The whole situation was turning into a sharp picture. "I'm going to where I saw the smoke on the mountain."

"That was this morning."

She whirled around and stared at Buster. "Just shut up, Buster." The words sat between them.

He opened his mouth and then closed it.

"You can come, but by God, you can't talk." The keys were in the ignition where she always left them. "Get in."

Buster slid into the front seat beside her. She gunned the car out of the driveway. Her head felt like it might blow up. Timothy was the only one in her life that she would die for.

As they hit Main Street, one of Buster's deacons flagged them down.

"We don't have time for this, Buster." She intended to fly by the man.

"Just pull over for a second, Ella Ruth." Buster rolled down his window. "Hi, Walter, I'm looking for Timothy. Have you seen him?"

Walter shook his head. "No preacher, but that crop duster has crashed up on Black Mountain."

A sob caught in Ella Ruth's throat. She threw the car into gear. "We have to go."

"Do you want me to drive?" Buster's voice shook.

"No. I just want to get there. Oh God!" The tears were running down her face.

"We need to get word to Lacy."

She looked at him, tears stinging her eyes. "First we have to find our son."

☙

The sheriff's car along with several state police vehicles were parked on the mountain road. Ella Ruth drove as if she were not in her body. She pulled the car to the side. Buster jumped out before it stopped good.

"Sheriff."

The sheriff turned and looked at Buster. "Yeah?"

"Have you found that plane?"

"It's way down the drop-off over there. We found the pilot's body. Why are you here, Preacher?"

Ella Ruth ran up to the sheriff and touched his arm. He pulled away. "I think my son and his friend were flying in that plane."

A state policeman had walked up to them. "We've been to the wreckage and no one was there. The pilot was found way up here. I don't think anyone could survive that accident."

She ran at the policeman and hit his chest with both fists. "Don't you tell me that. I know my son is still alive. I feel it. I'm going to look while you stand up here and talk."

Buster grabbed her arms and she pulled away. "Ella Ruth, we can't just take off down the side of the mountain. It's getting dark. We have to get flashlights."

"You do what you want. I'm finding my son." She ran to the edge and saw it wasn't impossible to climb down to the wreckage. "Timothy?" The first step was the scariest. She slid, caught herself, and slid some more. The plane still smoked. The ground was black all around. "Timothy?"

A man, dressed in old-fashioned clothes and wearing little round glasses, looked at her, through her, really. "You need to go down that way. Bodies could roll in the brush or on down the mountain." He looked at her and shook his head. "I'm not sure if you'll get there in time."

She opened her mouth to scream at him, but Buster yelled behind her. "Ella Ruth!"

He was clinging to a small tree.

"This man said the bodies could have rolled down the mountain."

"What man, Ella Ruth?"

Ella Ruth looked over her shoulder and saw the man had left. "I don't know where he went. He's dressed kind of odd, like someone would a long time ago."

"Was he wearing little round spectacles?" A man, wearing overalls, suddenly stood behind Buster with an old-fashioned lantern.

"Yes."

The man shook his head. "Let's have a look down there in the brush. It's getting dark and we won't be able to see. I'm sure some of the boys already looked here."

"Do you know the man she's talking about?" Buster asked.

The man looked at Ella Ruth. "We'd best start looking for your son, ma' am. What you saw wasn't a man. It was a haint."

"A spirit?"

Buster looked at her. "A ghost?"

"Merlin Hocket, to give the haint a name. He shows up anytime there's doom. He can be right helpful and he can be evil. Just depends on what he's thinking on that day."

Ella Ruth pushed her way past way down the mountain. "Timothy."

The woods were quiet, too quiet, as if all of nature had left. "I know you're here, sweetie."

A cold wind blew through the dead leaves. She walked further into the woods and the overgrowth.

"Don't get so far ahead, ma'am. There's lots of drop-offs."

Ella Ruth still pushed forward. "Timothy."

She made out a shadow standing ahead of her. It raised its hand. "Timothy?" But she knew it wasn't her son. He wasn't that tall. "Do you know where Timothy is?" Then, for some strange reason, she could see clearly that the shadow was Mile. "Mile, where is Timothy?"

Mile beckoned her to follow and disappeared into a bunch of thick brush. She moved fast, sliding down and getting back on her feet.

"Ella Ruth, wait. Who are you talking to?" Buster was too far behind.

The brush was so thick that it looked like dark night. A boy was on the ground.

His arm was folded up under his back in a horrible way. She rushed to his side. The first thing she noticed was how cold he was, too cold. A bright light spread into the brush. There was Buster, standing over them with a lantern.

"Look." She saw that the boy with the twisted arm was Mile, sweet little Mile. He was alone, and he was dead. Then she saw an arm under one of the bushes. "Timothy!" Silence. "Timothy?" She touched the hand. It was cold but not like Mile's. She squeezed the fingers. "Son!"

"Mom." The whisper came from under the thick branches. "Buster! He's alive. Our son is alive." Her head spun.

Buster touched her shoulder. "He's alive. Oh, God in Heaven, my son is alive." He dropped to his knees, breaking away the branches and shining the light on Timothy.

His face was covered with blood and his right leg was pushed at an odd angle. "Timothy?"

Timothy wiggled his fingers in Ella Ruth's hand.

Buster looked at Ella Ruth, past Ella Ruth. "God help us."

Ella Ruth looked behind her. Mile seemed to be asleep. Except for his arm twisted under his back, he looked perfect.

Buster looked back at Timothy. "We're going to get you out of here. You're going to be fine. I love you, son."

Those three words sent Ella Ruth into silent sobs. Her whole body shook. God forgive her, but she was so glad it wasn't her son that was dead. She was so, so glad.

☙

Ella Ruth sat on a bench outside the train station. The cold numbed her hands and feet. Timothy was in a hospital in Asheville. Buster had told Lacy the terrible news, and she turned stony in the face and walked out the door. Lee was bringing Tucker home. The train whistle sounded in the distance. Gert was on her way too. The train pulled into the station, but Ella Ruth remained on her bench. Lee and Tucker came off the train before Gert.

"Ella Ruth." Lee walked up to her. Surely he didn't think she'd come to meet him.

Tucker looked shrunk in on himself, and she touched his arm. "Tucker."

He looked at her. "Where's Mama?"

"She's locked herself in her house and won't let anyone in, not even Buster. Maybe you can help her."

Tucker hung his head. Ella Ruth put her arms around his neck and hugged him.

"She needs you now, Tucker," she whispered.

He nodded and moved apart from them, watching the people come off the train.

Lee stepped closer. "Ella."

If he touched her, she would fall down that deep, deep well. Fortunately, at that moment Gert worked her way down the stairs of the train.

Ella Ruth held up her hand. "Gert." She was still beautiful, even in her older age.

She stepped back from Lee. "I have to see to my aunt."

"Please, Ella Ruth, don't do this."

Anger over what had happened flashed through her. "Do what? This isn't about you."

"I've made a mess of everything."

"There's my aunt." Gert worked her way toward them. Ella Ruth moved as if to meet her, but Lee's voice stopped her.

"Ella, I love you."

Love, what was love? She refused to look at him and walked away. Gert wrapped her arms around Ella Ruth. "Child, child."

"I'm so glad you're here."

"Let's go to the hospital. You need to be there."

Ella Ruth nodded. They walked right by Lee without a word.

附

Mile was buried on a clear blue day. Lacy stood by the grave, with Lee close behind. Tucker held his mother's hand.

So much had changed. Mile was gone. Timothy was hurt. His leg would never be the same. He would have a limp for life, just like his father. The doctors had refused to let him come to the funeral. As she stood beside Buster, Ella Ruth realized that Timothy looked more like him since the accident. In the depth of Buster's eyes, she saw

279

guilt, years and years of guilt that being a preacher had never removed. She resolved to save her son from his father's fate.

A hawk glided over their heads, circling three times before flying to the mountain.

Chapter 30

Buster

Buster watched Lee as he stood by the window at the other end of the room. He could kill him. Here he was, a preacher, and he wanted to kill his brother. The only family left to him. Lee had no business coming back from Atlanta. It was clear that he thought he was still in love with Ella Ruth. Maybe he was really in love with someone besides himself, but Buster doubted he had that kind of emotion. Lacy sat at the rickety table in her kitchen. Ella Ruth stood close by while Gert spoke with Lacy. Tucker hovered, but Lacy paid him no mind.

Buster walked away from the kitchen door. The room was full of coloreds paying their respect. "Tell Ella Ruth I'm in the car."

"You don't have to leave your wife here alone because of me." Lee's voice was flat and he continued to stare out the window.

"Why did you come back?"

"I'm here because..." He finally turned to face Buster. "I love Ella." He said this loud enough for others in the room to hear, but they talked among themselves, ignoring the brothers. "You have no idea what she's about, what she's made of. You gathered her in your cocoon to change her into your wish, but..." He stepped closer to Buster. "Can't you see her for what she is? Are you a fool? She doesn't want me. If I could make her, I would, but she doesn't."

"All she wants is her art." The words were bitter and tasted that way in Buster's mouth.

"You stupid fool. I won't give up on her. I won't. But you have." Lee's nose cracked when Buster punched him.

A woman took in a deep breath. Ella Ruth was looking into the living room. "What are you doing?"

"I just have a nosebleed." Lee laughed with blood dripping out of his hand.

"Let me get you something for it." She turned away without speaking to Buster.

Timothy was discharged a few days later, and Buster drove them home from the hospital. Timothy was pale but fine except for his leg. Ella Ruth sat beside him on the backseat, holding his hand. "Is Lee still staying at your mother's?"

"Yes. And Lacy came back to work today. Your aunt convinced her that work was better than sitting around. Tucker doesn't want to go back to Atlanta, and Lee is trying to wait out his decision." He paused.

"Where have you been staying?"

"At the church."

"You can come to our house."

"I'd like to go by Mother's and check on Lacy first."

"I'm sure you would."

Did he detect some jealousy? But her face was straight and her attention was on Timothy.

He drove to the house where he'd grown up. Lacy came out on the porch as he pulled the car into the drive. When he walked up to her, she folded her arms over her midsection.

"Where have you been staying?"

It was a strange question. "At my office."

"I want him gone from here!"

"It's his house, Lacy."

She looked wild for a minute.

"It's your house and you darn well know it." The words were a hiss.

"This isn't the time."

"I'm waiting on you to come back." She looked at him. "I need you here so I won't go crazy."

Buster shifted his weight off his bad foot. There were still days when the missing part ached. "You're so strong, Lacy."

She looked out at the car. "Is Timothy in there?"

"Yes. He got out of the hospital today."

"It's not fair." Her voice broke. "Timothy's like her, Buster."

A cold chill walked up his back. "Lacy, you're not rested. You've got to rest. Maybe you shouldn't have come back to work yet."

"I got to be here. Okay?"

He nodded. "I'll talk to you later." He walked back to the car, hoping Ella Ruth hadn't been able to hear Lacy.

When he pulled the car out on the road, Ella Ruth spoke.

"You can take the bedroom. I'll stay in the room with Gert."

"No, I can go back to the church office."

There stood their house in the distance.

"That's silly, Buster."

"He's asleep. He didn't hear Lacy talking about him, about fairness. She can't be allowed to speak to him."

"I know." Buster turned into the driveway of the house where he and Ella Ruth had once lived together. Had they ever been happy?

Chapter 31

Ella Ruth

"Ella Ruth, you can't blame yourself for that child being hurt or the other's death. You simply can't. I know that's what you're doing, but Timothy is alive. You have every right to be happy and relieved." Gert sipped her tea.

"I don't know how I feel about anything. I have secrets. I spend too much time on my art. I'm not a preacher's wife."

Gert smiled. "Did you think that because you were a preacher's wife you couldn't spend too much time on your art? Who is he?"

Ella Ruth looked into her aunt's eyes. "Am I that easy to figure out?"

"Only to me, dear."

"He found a gallery in Atlanta to show my town pieces."

"You could have done that on your own. You owe him nothing."

"Don't you want to know who he is?"

Aunt Gert shrugged. "When you're ready, you'll tell me. I won't even have to ask."

"I don't think I love Buster anymore."

"That doesn't surprise me, Ella Ruth. You were a child when you married him. How could you know anything at all about him?"

"I think I might love the other man, but he's bad news. He will only hurt me in the long run. I know it."

"I've always said men are men, dear."

"Yes, you have, Gert."

Today, Ella Ruth didn't have to think about what to do next. Buster was at the church. Timothy was safe in bed. Lee was taking care of Lacy as much as she would allow. Tucker was there too.

"I've missed you, girl. You've turned into such a fine woman. And that brings me to my whole reason for this visit, besides seeing my beautiful niece again and helping with Timothy. I'm here to finish up this whole business of your mother's death, and then you will come back with me to Chicago. I have a beautiful apartment. I want you and

Timothy to stay with me for a long time. Get away from here. I've found a private school for Timothy, and I want you to work on your art."

Ella Ruth's head spun. Leave Swannanoa Gap for good, or a long time anyway? "Wow, Gert, let's take this one step at a time."

"We are. We'll begin with your mother." She looked at Ella Ruth. "Now, let's go see that boy and then make a big meal. If Buster shows up, so be it. If not, it will just be us."

CR

Timothy looked so sweet as he slept. His leg was elevated in a sling and pulley. Ella Ruth rubbed her fingers through his hair. His eyes fluttered and focused on her. "Hi."

"Hi you."

"What happened?"

The doctor had warned Ella Ruth that Timothy would probably forget what had happened and to take it slow.

"Well, you broke your leg pretty good." She stroked his hair.

"I went flying."

Ella Ruth fought the tears. "Yes."

"I hope you're not mad, Mom." His voice was so weak.

"No, Timothy. I couldn't be mad at you."

"We crashed."

Ella Ruth nodded.

"Where's Dad?"

Ella Ruth opened her mouth to answer, but Timothy answered for her.

"He's at the church."

"Yes."

"Did Mr. Carl die?"

Ella Ruth swallowed hard. "Yes, honey, he did."

"I'm sorry."

"So am I, son." She played with the edge of the sheet that covered him.

"I still want to fly."

The outrage worked in her mind, but what could she say? Flying for Timothy was like painting for her. "Maybe. A long, long, long time down the road."

He smiled for the first time. "I can't wait to tell Mile all about it."

Her mouth opened and then closed. "Gert is here to see you."

He smiled again and drifted off to sleep. What could she do? The doctor said to take it slow.

෨

Buster arrived in the middle of Ella Ruth and Gert's cooking session. The kitchen was full of laughter and late afternoon sunshine. Ella Ruth stopped talking mid-sentence and glanced at Buster. He looked so lonely.

"Where is Timothy?"

"He's resting. I thought I'd help him down for supper. Timothy talked to me. He remembers some, and some he doesn't." She tried to keep her tone natural.

Buster turned to face Gert. "Finally we meet."

"Yes, and me, an old woman, had to come here. I kept waiting for you to bring her to me." Gert cocked an eyebrow at him. "Are you afraid of leaving this place?"

Buster took a corn muffin from the basket.

"I'm here to convince your beautiful wife to come back with me. I want her to work on her art in Chicago. I have rented a loft for her studio." She smiled at Ella Ruth. "I know it's outrageous, a woman, a preacher's wife, moving to Chicago, but surely you want her to spread her wings?"

Ella Ruth had not seen fear on Buster's face until that moment. "I don't know what you want me to do."

"You will, my boy. You will."

෨

Ella Ruth woke in the night and for a minute couldn't place where she was. Then she remembered. Buster was staying in their old bedroom,

286

and she was in here with Gert. She went to the window and saw Buster standing in the yard.

Curious, she headed outside.

"There's a lunar eclipse tonight." He pointed at the full moon. A tiny thumbnail edged over the surface. As she stood beside him, the thumbnail grew into a half.

"I want to go behind the eclipse," Ella Ruth murmured.

Buster looked at her for one long moment before he took her hand.

His body felt the same, but instead of giving up and becoming part of him, she held her own. He kissed her.

"Will we ever work this out?" he whispered into her neck.

They made love in her studio as the moon disappeared into a full eclipse. There was no talking. Only Buster's question hung between them, full and bright.

¨

"I have an old acquaintance I want you to meet in Asheville. Do you think we can do that?" Gert asked somewhat secretively.

"Sure. Buster will come to sit with Timothy."

"Good." Gert clapped her hands.

"What do you have up your sleeve, dear aunt?"

¨

As Ella Ruth drove the highway to Asheville, she cut a look at Gert. Only a coward would drop a bombshell on someone while driving, able to avoid eye contact. "I know who my brother is."

Gert remained quiet for a beat longer than normal. "Who?"

"Larry Mitchell. He died in the war. He was Buster's best friend. The Mitchells adopted him right after he was born."

Gert seemed to be thinking. "Doesn't surprise me."

"Really, because I was knocked off my feet." The edge in Ella Ruth's voice stood out in the car.

"How long have you known?"

"Since he died. Preacher Mitchell decided to tell all then."

"Aren't you glad to know?"

"I'm not sure, Gert. I never got to know him. It's not fair."

She nodded. "A lot of things aren't fair, but we learn from them."

"I know some of what happened the night Mama died. I was there, Gert. I know Paul Allen had something to do with her death, but I don't know what. The medical examiner said childbirth killed her, but even Buster's father thought Paul Allen did something."

"You must face that you may never know for certain. Paul Allen is the only person who knows, and I don't think he'll tell you."

"No. He won't."

"But I'm going to give you the final piece of the puzzle. We're going to meet with Richard Kennedy, your mother's lover."

Ella Ruth nearly ran off the road.

"It's all I have left to give you." They were silent until Ella Ruth, with Gert's directions, pulled into the drive of a large brick house.

Ella Ruth sat in a beautiful sunroom that over looked a walled-in garden. Mr. Kennedy was covering the last of his rosebushes with a large plastic sheet. He smiled as he walked in their direction.

"Hello!" he said cheerfully. "Welcome. I want Joyce to meet you two." He looked at Ella Ruth with curiosity. "She's been my wife for nearly thirty years now and knows the whole story of Ella, your mother. She loves Ella's art. I have her pieces hanging all over the house. Maybe you would like a tour." His far-off look stirred Ella Ruth.

"That would be wonderful."

"I have one in particular you must see. But first, shall we have a nice long talk? Then I'll take you girls on a complete tour."

"Girls. I think you're stretching it a bit in my case, Mr. Kennedy." Gert laughed as if he were her oldest friend.

Mr. Kennedy's eyes shone, and in that instant Ella Ruth saw what Mama had searched out. "Ah, but my dear, you are a girl at heart. We must nurse our illusions." He turned his charm on Ella Ruth. "Now, young lady, I'm yours. What do you want to know? I'll tell you what I can."

Ella Ruth hadn't thought of this. She didn't have to plan a response. It had been sitting inside her for years. "I want to know about my mother's last day."

A cloud passed over the sun and the room turned darker. The aging lover's hand shook ever so lightly. "Ella woke early. She always did. It was cold and dark, but she lit up the kitchen as always." He looked at Ella Ruth. "You trailed along behind her. She waddled like a penguin with the baby she carried. We talked about our Christmas plans. Gert, here, was coming. Your mother told me she wanted to wrap some presents. I warned her that ice was predicted and made her promise to stay home. But I was more worried about Paul Allen than ice. She promised to stay in."

He looked at both women. "I wish I had not made her promise. I wished she had left and went on a shopping spree. She would have lived. I know she would." He stared through Ella Ruth. "I never thought I wouldn't see her again. The last time I saw her, she stood at that door with you by her side." Taking a deep breath, he closed his eyes. "I was afraid of Paul Allen. He was a bad man, but I never thought he'd have the nerve to come to my house and kidnap her."

"That sounds like the man I know." Ella Ruth knew Paul Allen was capable of anything. "She was having another man's baby. He wouldn't allow that no matter what."

Mr. Kennedy cleared his throat. "But see, I know the baby wasn't mine. I can't have children. A bad case of mumps saw to that. The baby was his as much as you are."

The information sat in the air, rocking like a boat on turbulent water. "If he had known that, he wouldn't have killed her. He gave away his own son. God, that would just kill him." Something like a thousand-piece puzzle came together in Ella Ruth's mind. She knew what she had to do.

Mr. Kennedy touched Ella Ruth's arm. "I told the sheriff that he killed her. I think the sheriff believed it too. I know your mother didn't leave here on her own. For one thing, she left behind all your clothes, toys, and books. I sent those to your grandparents' farm later. And I know Ella was happy with me. We were going to marry as soon as she could divorce Paul Allen." He took a long sip of tea. "But the real clue was her unwashed paintbrushes and the tubes of paint left open. The woman was a fanatic about her art supplies. There is also the canvas she was working on." He stood. "Come."

Joyce—who either wore her age extremely well or was twenty years younger than her husband—met them in the front room of the house. The soft grains of polished woods, fine carpets, and artwork of every kind showed the woman's influence. The couple kissed and ushered Ella Ruth and Gert into a study. The wall was almost covered by a huge canvas. Ella Ruth looked into the face of a small child, smiling, reaching for some unseen temptation. The foot of the child was only sketched in pencil, with wispy gray lines and a blob of blue paint smeared in the far right corner, as if dragged across the canvas. Ella Ruth could almost see Mama painting, large with child. Paul Allen must have slipped into the house through some window or door.

Mr. Kennedy touched her shoulder. "This painting is yours to take."

Joyce drew in a breath. "Are you sure? This is your favorite."

Tears brimmed in his crinkled eyes. "Ella would have wanted Ella Ruth to have this portrait of her."

Ella Ruth looked at the child on the canvas. It was her. Yes, she knew what she had to do.

ଔ

Ella Ruth parked the car by the side of the road. The drive was curvy and kept her from seeing the house. But she knew the way with her eyes closed. Deep ruts ran through the steeper places. With each step, her stomach came into her throat. He would probably kill her for this.

The windows in the house were eyes, watching her every move. The paint was peeling and the roof sagged. She knocked on the door. A board squeaked from inside.

"I know you're there, Bell. Open the door."

"She knows better than to open the door to you. She has her orders." His voice was the same as it had always been.

Ella Ruth turned around and looked her father straight in the eyes. "I want to talk about the day my mama died, and you're going to do it."

"I don't have to talk to no whore." He was older, tired.

"Oh, you will talk to me."

He laughed.

"I want to know what happened that night. I was there. I know that." She kept her voice strong.

"You ain't got the stomach for it."

"I've got more of a stomach than you think." She thought of Timothy's twisted body.

He huffed and turned to walk back to his barn.

"Wait. You're going to tell me or I'm not ever leaving."

He stopped suddenly. "I could kill you right here in this yard."

Her legs shook. "Yes, you could, but I'm not leaving." She followed him into the barn.

"I guess if I did what I did to your mama today, I'd be sitting in prison somewhere. But…" He stepped close to her. "I ain't no murderer like you think. I know that disappoints you, and I almost lied just to keep you thinking it. The truth is, she had her baby early. She had it early with a little help, mind you. I never thought that baby would live. He was supposed to die and she was supposed to live. I didn't want her to get off so easy."

"You tried to kill her baby and ended up killing her!" Ella Ruth heard her voice get louder and louder.

"You can scream about it if you want to, girlie, but I didn't murder your mama." He shook his head. "If I wanted to kill both of them, I would have shot her in the chest. It would have been easy. I just wanted that damn baby dead." He was so close to her face she could smell the whiskey on his breath.

"That baby was yours, you fool." The words came out as a hiss of poison.

He backed up. "You're crazy like your mama. That boy was his. He belonged to her lover."

"I visited Mr. Kennedy yesterday, and did you know he had a bad case of mumps when he was a teenager? Did you know he couldn't have children?"

A wave of uncertainty moved over Paul Allen's face.

"You tried to killed your only son." She allowed this to sit in the air. "You are a murderer. You killed my mama. I watched you. I was there. You killed her and you will go to hell for it."

He came right in her face again, but she didn't back down. "You some kind of fool, girlie."

"You killed my mama." She spit at him.

For a second he looked surprised, and then he pulled back his hand into a fist.

"Go ahead." She didn't move. "I want you to put a mark on me because I will press charges with the state police."

He watched her with pure hate in his eyes.

"Paul!" Bell called from the house. "Paul!"

"Get on out of here. You're trash." He let his fist drop.

Ella Ruth didn't move. "I'm just like you. We're a lot alike, you and me." Ella Ruth spun around and left him standing there.

A lifetime passed before she made it back to the road.

A car was stopped closed to hers. Lee got out. "What's wrong? What are you doing here?"

She couldn't speak. Her body shook, and he pulled her into his car. "Let's go somewhere and talk."

He drove the car toward the old quarry. "What happened?"

"I had a little talk with Paul Allen."

He parked and looked out the window. "Daddies are tough to figure out."

"I need to go home, Lee."

He touched her arm. "Ella, I love you."

She pulled her arm away. "No you don't. This has always been about you and Buster. It isn't about me. I don't have time for either of you anymore. I've done my share of bad things. Mile is dead because I didn't pay enough attention to Timothy."

"You know that's not true, Ella."

She looked at him. "You know it is true. I've been running from my life ever since Mama died. I'm tired of running. I want to go home."

"You know I love you. You're wrong."

"You don't know what love is, Lee, neither does Buster, and especially me. We're all in this mess. We're like some train barreling down the track that derails. We're a train wreck, a mess. Look at the people we've hurt. Look at Lacy. I don't want any more. Now take me to my car." She pointed at the road.

Chapter 32

Lacy Kurt

Lacy never went home in the middle of the day, but she thought she heard Mile calling her. He'd been calling her for a day or two, but she never could find him. Tucker told her that Mile was dead, but he was a liar. She had told him so. He just wanted to be with Lee, anyway. When the car turned out of the quarry road, she saw him first. Lee was driving that heifer around. Lacy knew what couples used the quarry for. Trash, they were both trash. Her knuckles turned white on the steering wheel. "You going to pay for stealing my boy. You going to pay. I want him back." She broke into tears as he passed. He hadn't even noticed her car. He didn't care.

She searched her house, but Mile was nowhere to be seen. "Mile." The house was quiet. "Mile."

"Mama." His voice was like a whisper on the wind. He wasn't dead. Lord no.

That boy wouldn't die on her like his daddy did. No way.

ॐ

"Mama."

She jumped, thinking Mile had walked into Lee's kitchen, but it was only Tucker.

"Lee says we should have some pound cake tonight." He grinned.

"He does, does he?" Her voice was steady. She was perfectly fine.

"Could we have pound cake?"

"I don't have a damn pound cake in me."

Tucker took a breath. "Mama, do you need to go home?"

"No."

"You ain't yourself."

She turned and looked at him. "Listen here. I know Mile is alive. He's been calling me. When I find him, I'm going to get the person that did all this. You understand?"

Tucker got big tears in his eyes and put his hands on each of her shoulders. "Mama, if Lee hears you talking like this, he'll send you off. You got to stop. Why don't you go home and rest?"

She pushed his hands away. "I need you to leave me alone, Tucker. Go on back to our house and get out of this place."

"I got to run some errands for Lee. I won't be back until dark. You got to promise me that you won't act crazy. Please."

Poor Tucker. "You go on, sweetie, and do what you have to do."

His face relaxed. "Do you promise not to do any crazy talking about Mile?"

"Don't you worry about me. I'm going to take care of all that."

"I'll be back. I'll see you at home." He walked toward the door. "Are you going to make Lee his pound cake?"

"Yes. I think I'll do that, but first I got to go see Mr. Buster."

"You want me to drop you over there?" Tucker smiled like he was feeling better.

She loved him. He couldn't help who his daddy was. "I think I do. I think I will like that."

○ℛ

Buster smiled his sad smile when she came into his office. "Lacy."

She so hoped he wouldn't get up to touch her. If he did, she would slap him. "I got something to tell you."

He looked concerned.

"I seen him with her today." She held her purse with both hands in front of her.

"Don't tell me these things, Lacy. I don't want to hear them from you."

"I saw them coming out of the old quarry road. I'm just telling you, Buster, 'cause I care. I don't want you to get to the place where I'm at."

He stepped around his desk. "You're not telling me because you care. You're telling me because you're angry with Lee and you don't like Ella Ruth."

His talking didn't faze her. She had come on a mission, and she had to finish what she had to say. "Lee's going to stir up the Klan again. He's here to cause trouble. Something has to be done."

"That talk is gone, and hopefully it won't come back. I think you need to take a rest, Lacy. Too much has gone on." He stepped closer.

"She's not worthy of your love. She slept with your brother. I know it."

"I know it too, Lacy." He spoke quiet.

He smelled good, like peppermint. She placed her hand on his shoulder. The heat was there. "I ain't trying to hurt you. I just think with us being friends I got to tell you the truth."

Buster took her hand off his shoulder and held it. "You can't live on hate, Lacy. I know bad things have happened, but hate will get you nowhere."

Lacy kissed his lips and he didn't pull back. The kiss felt good, true. For the first time in many years, she was at home.

Buster stepped back. "I'm going to think that happened because you are not in your right mind. You're hurting over Mile."

Lacy couldn't listen to all his mixed-up words. She kissed him again, but he pulled back quickly.

"You can't do this. Do you understand? I'm not going to be like my brother."

Heat filled her chest. "Or like your wife?"

He smiled. She had never been able to make him angry. "You're a beautiful woman, a good woman. You don't deserve the things that have happened."

She backed up from him. "Don't feel sorry for me. How can you be so stupid? Ella Ruth knows just what she's doing. She doesn't give a damn. She killed my boy!"

"No, Lacy. Ella Ruth didn't kill anyone."

In that moment, Lacy understood. Buster was right. Ella Ruth was just Ella Ruth. She didn't kill Mile. Her laughter filled the office, echoing. "Buster, you're exactly right. I had it wrong all the time. The whole damn time."

CR

Lee strolled into the kitchen. "Do I smell pound cake?"

Her hand trembled as she picked up the knife. "Yes sir, you do."

He smiled. "Are we back to sirs, Lacy?"

She cut through the cake. "I am who I am, Mr. Wright." The room moved a little.

Her heart beat hard in her chest as she moved toward him. He smelled like the day she first rolled in the leaves with him. Her feet were slow. She pressed her face into his shirt.

He stood still for a moment and then touched her shoulders. "I know you're hurting."

Stupid. He was just plain stupid. She looked up and kissed him. He kissed back. "Come with me." She pulled him to the sick room.

He took the knife from her hand and placed it on the table, frowning. "I keep catching a whiff of gasoline. Do you smell it?"

Her dress fell to the floor.

ଔ

The fire sprang to life upstairs, an explosion of orange and then oily black smoke. The tail of her dress caught fire. A laugh built in her chest. She turned and ran down the stairs as the flames licked at her every step. The fire was purifying. For the first time in her life, she had control. Black smoke filled the kitchen as the house began to burn with a fury.

She felt her way to Lee on the bed in the sickroom. Her hand closed around the handle of the knife sticking out of his chest. In that split second, she wondered if her choice, as if it had been a choice, was wrong. But she reminded herself that Lee shouldn't have hurt her. He shouldn't have taken her boy. She screamed as a crack spilt the air. The ceiling came down and there was Mile, standing in the air. He was waiting. God, she had finally found this sad little boy with no father. He held out his hand, but she couldn't get to him. The flames brought her to her knees. Screams soaked the air. But they weren't real. They were only last thoughts leaking out of her head.

Chapter 34

Buster

In his dream, Buster saw Lee, and just behind him stood Mile. Clouds of black oily smoke swallowed them. Buster opened his eyes to a red glow, bathing the bedroom with ocean-wave movements, rippling on the walls. He reached out next to him before he remembered Ella Ruth no longer slept in his bed. Orange lit up the sky outside the window. Sparks shot into the air.

"Fire!" he yelled like a terrified soldier, looking for his foxhole. The world was on fire.

The bedroom door burst open. He jumped from the bed. Ella Ruth ran toward him but caught herself and stopped. "It's your mother's house. It has to be!"

Buster grabbed his pants and hopped on one leg as he wrestled the piece of cloth. Ella Ruth turned to leave the room. "I'm going with you."

"What is going on?" Gert stood in the hall.

"The old homeplace is burning." Ella Ruth spoke with an urgent edge in her voice.

"Oh my." Gert grabbed her chest. "Is anyone there? Isn't that where the brother lives?"

"My brother for sure, and maybe Lacy's son." Buster spoke as he grabbed a shirt. The sirens sounded in the distance.

CR

The house was crumbled on the left side, the kitchen side. Red lights from the fire trucks circled the yard, like a lighthouse in a harbor, searching for the lost. Buster jumped from the car.

"Don't you dare, Buster. You can't go in there!" Ella Ruth wrapped her arms around his waist from behind and held on tight. "I won't have you in the hospital or dead. I can't take you getting hurt too. Please listen to me."

He almost believed her.

A window blew out, shooting glass near Ella Ruth.

Buster looked one long time at the house. Part of the roof over the front room gave. He allowed Ella Ruth to move him backwards away from his home. The old lilac bush burned. "He's in there. Lee..."

"I know." Ella Ruth held him, cradled him like a child. A fireman ran around the house with a hose. The flames leapt at the walls, eating everything in their path. Ella Ruth's eyes got bigger, and he followed her gaze. The little truck was parked in its normal spot.

"Lacy's in there too," he yelled, but his voice was soft in the roaring of the flames.

What about Tucker?

Lee's car sped into the driveway, and Tucker jumped from the driver's side. "Mama." The fireman with the hose turned to face Tucker as he closed in on the house.

"Get back. Get back. There's nothing you can do for anyone in that house."

"You got to get her out."

Buster felt Ella Ruth's grip on him loosen. She left him and pulled at Tucker, speaking to him as she stroked his arms.

Buster was frozen in place. He wanted to cross the space between his wife and him, but worse yet, he wanted to enter the burning house.

Tucker fell to his knees, and Ella Ruth watched Buster over his head. He searched her face for an answer to the whole mess. She reached out with her free hand.

The space between them was a valley, a deep valley. Finally, his legs worked. He touched her fingers.

"They're dead, Buster." Ella Ruth's tears tainted her voice. "How could this have happened?"

"I don't know." But something deep inside of him knew that this was no accident.

CR

The fire marshal shuffled around the steaming coals of the house. The trees were blackened on one side. Lacy's truck was dark with soot. The windshield had cracked up the middle. Buster should have driven on to the revival in Birmingham that day and never looked in his rearview mirror, never stopped on the side of the road. At least Lee would still be alive. But in that moment, Buster saw clear as day that Lee had been traveling his road since he was seventeen, headed to the same destination. What had come from it all? Tucker, Timothy, Miles? Timothy was home safe in the bed with Gert looking after him. Timothy would live. Tucker would live. Would they change the world their fathers had created?

Buster was stuck. For the first time in his life, he was so stuck that his faith seemed far away, out of touch, a dream, a joke.

Tucker stood looking at the rubble.

Buster walked over to the fire marshal. "What do you think?"

The man shook his head. "It's arson."

The answer sat in Buster's stomach. "My brother wasn't well liked."

Another man walked up. "Did you find them?" he asked the marshal.

"No. We're looking for two bodies, female and male." The fire marshal looked at Buster. "I'm aware of how well your brother was liked."

The other man held out his hand to Buster. "I'm John Mason. I'm the arson investigator from Raleigh."

"So you think it was set?" Buster's words sounded hollow, false, a lie.

"It sure looks that way. I didn't catch your name." He looked Buster over.

"I'm Buster Wright, Lee's brother."

John Mason nodded. "The preacher."

"Word travels."

"Yeah. I also know your brother wasn't too loved around here."

Buster laughed.

"Something funny?"

Buster looked at the smoking floorboards of the house, felt

Tucker look his way. "My brother made enemies as fast as I can pray."

Mason smiled.

"The Klan threw rocks through his windows, through mine, and burned a cross on his lawn. It had gotten so bad, he moved to Atlanta for a few months. He had just come back. They must have been waiting on him." Why not? The whole story could have been written like that.

Mason nodded and began to scribble in a notebook. "Want to tell me who these Klan members are?"

Buster rubbed his head. "Paul Allen. He lives a couple of roads over. He's always been the ringleader. No one around here is going to tell you that because they're afraid."

"You're not?"

"He's my wife's father. I'm sick of the threats, the misery he caused." Buster could have done this for Ella Ruth a long time ago. What was one more bigot? They'd never pin it on Paul Allen anyway. What was one more lie?

"What was Lacy Kurt's relationship to your brother?"

"She worked for him. She was like one of the family. I don't know why she was here so late. I'm sure it had to do with Lee coming back to town. Maybe she just wanted to be somewhere besides home. She just lost her youngest son." There was a truth.

"That's her older son?" Mason nodded toward Tucker.

"Yes." The anger filled him. He thought of Lacy seeing Lee and Ella Ruth at the quarry. He thought of Tucker all alone.

Mason shook his head. "Let me go talk with him a minute and then I'll suit up. I want to see if I can find the bodies."

"In all this? How?" Buster couldn't imagine what would be left.

"I'll find something. The human body doesn't burn as easy as some might think."

Buster thought it would take hours, but within thirty minutes Mason yelled over to Buster and Tucker.

"The fire started somewhere upstairs, above here. I would guess gasoline. What room was this?"

Buster walked over to the foundation. He recognized the melted metal bed frame. "It's the old sickroom."

Tucker came closer.

Mason kicked with his heavy rubber boots. "Shit." He looked at his foot. "You two might want to leave."

"What did you find?"

John Mason frowned. "I think we've found one of the bodies." He bent down to examine one place and then turned toward another place to the right. "I think we may have two bodies right here together. Close to the bed frame. I can't be sure until I get the medical examiner here."

Buster looked at Tucker. "How long will that take?"

"I'm not sure."

"It's Mama and Lee." Tucker spoke for the first time. "It's both of them together." His voice was bitter.

"There's a lot about this whole fire that makes no sense." Mason stared at Tucker. "I'm going to want to question both of you."

"We'll be available anytime, Mr. Mason." Buster touched Tucker's shoulder. It turned stiff. "Will you question Paul Allen?"

"Yes."

Buster's head banged with pain. "Tucker and I are going to get some distance. We'll be back."

Tucker didn't resist his lead.

In the car, Buster stared out the window. "No reason to involve people that don't deserve to be involved, Tucker."

He heard Tucker let out a sigh.

"We both know that some things are better left unsaid. And really, what do we know?" He put the car in gear.

"We don't know a thing, Preacher. We don't know a thing."

When Buster let Tucker out at Lacy's house, the boy bent back down and looked in the car window.

"Preacher..."

"Let's not ever speak of this again."

"Yes sir." And he walked away, his nephew, his blood, the best thing Lee ever did.

CR

Lee was buried beside Daddy, Mama, and Granny in the big town cemetery. No one came from town but Ella Ruth and Buster. Lacy was buried in the colored part of the cemetery right by Tyler and Mile. The whole street of Settle showed up. It was a right fine funeral, and she deserved it. Buster locked her secret in his heart.

As Buster stood by Lee's grave, his eyes on Lacy's burial across the cemetery, Ella Ruth looked as if she had already removed herself from the whole scene. He couldn't read her. Had he ever known her?

"We have to go check on Timothy," she said, touching his elbow.

"Okay." He wanted his son.

ʒ

Timothy was reading a novel and looked thoroughly bored. No one had told him what had happened, but of course he suspected something. Gert peeked in the door as Buster settled in the rocker.

"Timothy is doing very well today, so well he wants out of bed." Gert raised her eyebrows.

Timothy gave Buster a shy look. "So, Dad, are you mad at me for flying?"

Buster's chest felt as if it were crumbling in on itself. "No, son. You were following your dream. People have to try to make their dreams come true. I can't fault you for that."

"I'm like Mama."

"Yes, you are, and I'm proud for it."

"Really?"

"Of course." Buster wondered if Timothy had seen the fire last night. He was taking pain medicine that probably let him sleep right through it. He was lucky.

"Nobody will talk about Mile. Is he hurt bad? He hasn't been to see me. I know he would. He didn't want to go that day, Dad, but I talked him into flying."

Buster reached out and put his hand on Timothy's arm. "Son, I have to tell you something." He had thought Ella Ruth would have talked to Timothy by now. It had been a week. But why was it Ella Ruth's job? He was Timothy's father. It was time to act like it.

"What's wrong, Dad? Is something wrong with Mama?"

"No. She's fine. A lot has happened and, well, you need to know."

"Know what?" Timothy looked like he might cry.

"Mile died in the plane crash." Timothy's face turned pale. "It's not your fault or the pilot's fault or Mile's fault. The crash was a terrible accident."

"Why did God let this happen?" Tears ran down Timothy's face.

Buster moved to sit on the bed. "I don't have an answer for that question. I wish I did. But I do know that you're alive, and you have to make something good come from your life. Don't waste time trying to make up for things you think you've done wrong. Look into the future. Mile is part of you. He'll never leave."

Buster held out a handkerchief, and Timothy took it. "What about you and Mama? Do you still hate each other?"

Buster looked out the window. "Son, grownup love is very difficult to understand sometimes. I can tell you we don't hate each other. I can tell you I love your mother a lot."

"So, you're living here?"

Buster shrugged. "For now. I don't know what will happen. I have to tell you something else. Mrs. Kurt and your Uncle Lee were killed in a fire last night. Grandmother Sue's house burnt down."

Timothy looked out the window. "Nobody told me. You didn't wake me up?"

"We wanted to keep you safe, Timothy. You're our precious cargo, kind of like in that book *Treasure Island*." Buster pointed at the novel. "We have to protect you. We haven't always done a great job at this. Especially with your mother and me fighting. I'm sorry."

"Tucker doesn't have anyone, Dad. His father and mother and brother are dead."

Buster studied his son. "How did you know about your Uncle Lee being Tucker's father?"

"Mile told me. His mama told him. Just before we went to fly." Timothy gave a shiver.

"Tucker is going to need us in the future. He needs a family."

"Yep, Dad, he does." Timothy looked at the door. "Gert told me she has found a private school for me where she lives. I guess me and Mom are going to her house for a while."

Buster couldn't look into the face of his son. The thought of him leaving made his heart hurt. "If that is what your mother decides, but you'll be back, Timothy. You're my son. I can't ever let you go for good. No matter where you live."

Timothy touched Buster's hand. "Dad, you need to tell Mama that." He was such a wise boy.

Chapter 34

Ella Ruth

"I'm sorry. I'm just not moving fast today, dear." Gert shuffled toward the stove. "You know you could have gone without me."

"Don't be silly, Gert. I have all the time in the world."

Gert wore her all-knowing look. "You're still sleeping in my room."

"Do you ever dance around a subject?" Ella Ruth laughed, but truly she hated thinking about her and Buster. She was numb. The more she thought of having a talk with Buster, the sicker she felt.

"I never dance." Gert winked. "You know how much I want you to come to Chicago. I think you two could use the time apart."

Really, could she afford to walk away from Buster? A part of her knew that if she left, what little still existed between them would dissolve. Ella Ruth went to Gert and hugged her close. "I don't know what I would do without you. You've always been there for me."

Gert pulled away. "I really don't think that's true. Do you? You've always been there for yourself. That's all we can ask. And where is that lovely husband? Is he still with Timothy?"

"I think so."

"Maybe he's explaining what happened about his friend and last night."

Ella Ruth laughed. "I don't think so. Buster doesn't give the serious talks around here. He saves himself for the church." The bitterness in her own voice didn't surprise Ella Ruth.

"You're right. I haven't been the husband I should have been, much less the father." Buster stood in the kitchen door. "But that's changing. I know you don't believe me. Shoot, I don't even believe me. It's something I'm going to have to learn." He came closer to Ella Ruth.

Part of her wanted to run. Being angry at him was so much easier than this. "Buster."

"No, hear me out. I'm tired. So much has happened. I need to

307

say this as it is forming in my mind." He looked at Gert, who was attempting to sneak out of the room. "You should stay. I want you to hear this from me."

Gert sat down in a chair.

"Ella Ruth, I've never been the kind of husband I should have been. I came home from the war trying to make up for all the bad I had done. I thought I ran Lee off."

Ella Ruth gave a little jerk at the mention of Lee's name.

"I thought I killed Daddy. I thought I was personally responsible for all the men who died in that war. I never told you about my friend Randal. He was a hoot, and I lost him. I lost him right in front of my eyes. And now I've lost Lee and Lacy. And you, I'm losing you. I've lost everything."

Ella Ruth crossed the room and tried to wrap her arms around Buster's waist, but he held her off.

"No, listen. You have to hear me. I need to do this for Timothy, for you, and for me. I want you to go with Gert. You need to go after your dream. One of us needs to dream big, Ella Ruth. Take Timothy. Get him out of this place for now anyway. I will stay here until they find another preacher." He looked at Gert. "And then, if you will have me, I'll come to stay in Chicago. I'll find what I love, Ella Ruth. A dream that belongs to me."

Ella Ruth couldn't speak, her heart was so full.

"I think you might have a keeper here, dear niece." Gert smiled. "And you know how I don't care for men. I think you have a wonderful plan, but it's not me who has to agree to it." She looked at Ella Ruth.

"Come with me." Ella Ruth took Buster's hand and led him to her studio in the barn. "I have something you need to see."

She pointed at the one long wall that was once covered with her paintings. Now they were all sold. Against the wall leaned a large painting of a little girl, a cherished daughter.

Buster studied the painting as Ella Ruth watched him. "It's you."

How could he have known? Maybe a good guess.

"That's love, Buster. I don't know a lot about anything, but I know unconditional love." She looked at him. "We can't be everything to each other. We aren't capable of giving that kind of love. Our lives are tangled around the pureness of just loving. So it will never be perfect. There will always be fights. There will always be mistakes. There will always be hurt. That's what grownups do to each other. But somewhere in the midst of it all, if we're lucky, we get it. We find out it's about working at a relationship rather than allowing passion to rule the day. If we continue to work at our marriage, it has to be accepted that it will never be perfect. No illusions."

Buster pulled Ella Ruth to him. The scent of smoke hung on him. "I can try."

She pulled back. "And Buster, that's all any of us can ever do."

CR

It snowed a foot the day Buster arrived in Chicago to live with Ella Ruth. She met his plane at the airport with Timothy, who was full of questions about the flight. He stood on his crutches. The doctors had promised his leg would one day be normal. Yes, he could be a pilot if he chose. He stood taller than Buster, much taller than Lee. At that moment he looked more like Paul Allen than Ella Ruth wanted to see. How could that be?

Tucker stood nearby. He lived with them for now. Lee had left a will, giving everything to Tucker except the silver-framed photo of Lee and Buster as a teenagers, standing next to their father, the Wright men. That he left to Ella Ruth with a note.

May you find peaceful sleep above the chaos that these two brothers created.

She touched the note in her pocket, where it had stayed since Tucker brought it to her. There wasn't one wrong she could correct, not a thing she could do to erase her choices. Nothing. It was finished. And yet...

Buster gave her that goofy smile, and she stepped closer into the circle to welcome him home.

—The End—